Veronica LaRose

Valerie Rachel Martin

To My Grandmother

i

1. CRYSTAL BEAD

My life changed on a gray Saturday in October.

I woke up early and lingered in bed, watching the autumn leaves dance outside my bedroom window like yellow butterflies. The tip of my nose tingled from cold. Grandma hated heating the house at night. She always said, "Why waste the heat when you sleep, Veronica. Put wool socks on, and no complaining."

My ten-year-old self never complained about anything. I enjoyed solitude, and reading fairy tales in the gazebo built for my dead mother. I could spend an entire day looking for colorful pebbles on the bottom of the stream, and listening to fairies whisper from the mysterious shadows of my garden. My magical garden hid behind ivy covered grey granite walls that embraced the house where I was born, LaRose Gris. Not even the icy winds from the Atlantic could disturb me in my realm.

The birch tree by my window beckoned to come outside, flailing its graceful branches. But, this was not the day for solitary outings. I hated Saturdays because grandma wanted me to "make friends." It was the day for visiting her fat mean friend Mrs. Rochelle. We usually went to her dingy uninviting house where grandma warned me not to touch anything. Grandma and Mrs. Rochelle would have tea and gossip, while I had to visit with Adele, Mrs. Rochelle's granddaughter. Grandma told me to make friends with Adele and learn good manners from her. Adele went to a boarding school on the weekdays. She was not home schooled like me. Pudgy pink Adele whined a lot and carried on like such a little snob, so I nicknamed her Pigele. I tried to tell grandma on Pigele, but she ordered me to be grateful and play with her anyway. I had nothing in common with Pigele, just sat in her playroom, and watched her arrange ugly dolls and serve them 'tea' in tiny pink porcelain cups. She did not let me touch her toys, and we never spoke. I wanted to tell her a story once, and she only stared, munching on a piece of soft candy like a dumb cow. I called her that, and she told on me.

Ms. Rochelle called me "insolent like Lydia." It was my mother's name, Lydia LaRose. She died when I was born, and nobody ever mentioned my father. Every time I asked about him, grandma would glance at me above her half-moon glasses and say the same funny line: "Do not stick your long LaRose *nose* where it does not be*long*."

On that gray October Saturday, I was standing in front of the mirror in my grandmother's bedroom trying to invent poses that would make me pretty. No matter what pose, nothing could hide my spindly legs, bony wrists, sly green eyes, and especially the freckles all over my nose. I felt like a statue dressed in a stiff brown wool dress chosen by grandma. My head hurt from the tight black ribbons in my braids. Grandma always tried to tame my dark curls by braiding them, but it never worked, they always escaped. My shoes shined with floor wax. "Why waste good shoe polish on a child's shoes, they will be dirty in a second anyway, Veronica use this," said grandma when she gave me the stinky orange paste a day before. Black wool leggings itched, but seemed to be presentable, unlike my usual cotton pair with darned knees. I asked grandma why I did not have pink silky leggings like Pigele. "An urchin like you should not be allowed frivolity," she said with a not too gentle pat on my head.

In one of the old photos in the drawing room, my mother wore a pretty dress with a lace trim, her hair dark and curly like mine. I always asked grandma why my mother wore pretty clothes and not me, but never got any answers. I knew my mother went to school in France, because my grandfather was French. Sometimes people dropped bits of information about her or about my grandfather, and I saved those bits like little Gretel from the fairy tale, one precious crumb after another.

A ride to town in grandma's enormous car highlighted the boring day. She named the car Hermes after the messenger of the gods.

Hermes impressed everyone with its polished black body, mirror chrome, and shiny leather seats. It was grandma's pride and joy, a remnant of the days when my grandfather Etienne LaRose was alive, and we had a lot of money. "If you do not go out in style, do not go out at all," was another of grandma's favorite sayings. She looked very stylish in her long maroon velvet coat and a small black hat with a silver owl pinned to the brim.

The drive to Boston where Ms. Rochelle and Pigele lived usually took close to an hour, but to my surprise grandma decided to do some shopping before the visit. We were supposed to meet them by the music store in town.

I spotted Pigele dressed in a pink coat standing by the shop's window. Mrs. Rochelle towered next to her in an ugly green hat with a bird's nest on top. She greeted my grandma with her usual "Good to see you Cecilia. What's wrong with this child of yours, so skinny and pale. Don't you ever feed her?" To my surprise, she invited us for ice cream at the confectionery shop. Pigele wanted to try a new flavor she had spied. Grandma tried to decline, muttering something about a "Frivolity and indulgence not being helpful to a child's upbringing" but followed Mrs. Rochelle in anyway. I wanted ice cream so much I could taste it, sweet and cold, sending shivers down my back. I got ice cream once per year in May, on my birthday. Still, I did not beg. Begging never worked with grandma.

The confectionery shop smelled of chocolate, a touch of burned sugar, and something fruity. The glass displays tempted with colorful boxes, and rows of jars filled with every kind of candy imaginable. My eyes popped when I saw all the delicacies. Grandma slid a coin in my hand without saying a word. I squeezed her hand with gratitude and broke away to browse for a perfect treat.

I stood in front of the jars, imagining what the morsels inside would taste like. Should I get a chocolate cluster or a honey-glazed almond square, or a small chocolate beetle filled with caramel and wrapped in a shiny foil? It felt like being lost in a beautiful sweet dream. To me, imagining the taste of the treats was more fun than eating one, which I knew would disappear as quickly as a snowflake on my open hand.

While I was taking my time choosing the perfect piece of candy, Pigele ordered two pieces from each jar without even looking. Then she demanded the pink ice cream and stared licking her lips as the clerk packed two scoops into a sugar cone and presented it to her with a flourish. She grabbed the cone with both hands and plunged it in her mouth. I watched, holding my breath wishing it was myself eating it. All of a sudden, Pigele whined, her double chin quivering,

"I hate this ice cream. It tastes like cranberries. I hate cranberries."

Mrs. Rochelle glared, and without a word snatched the cone from Pigele's hands, dropped it into a garbage bin, and ordered another flavor.

I edged over to the garbage can and looked inside. There it was, the poor ice cream cone bleeding its cool sweetness on the bottom. I had a sudden urge to pick it up, run out, and eat it. However, my grandmother had been watching me. Her face turned scarlet, she grabbed my arm and dragged me outside.

She shook me hard. "Why were you looking in the garbage? Were you about to take that cone?"

"I hate Adele, she's a pig," I broke away from her grip, "and it's not fair!"

"Good lesson in that, child. Many things in life are not fair. Better to find out sooner than later, not like your poor misguided mother. And where are your manners?"

Stunned by the events in the candy shop, I curled up on the back seat, watching the icy raindrops make tiny rivers on the car windows as we drove. Nothing would make me happy, ever. Not even a hundred treats. I hated life's unfairness. Why did horrible people like Pigele get everything, and poor good ones like me did not? Shivering, I yearned to return to my garden, my books, fairies, and solitude. I wanted to run away, to disappear, not to be. Instead, I had to face a long afternoon with greedy Pigele and her untouchable dolls.

In the silence of Pigele's room, amusing myself by counting seconds and minutes, I slid off the hard ottoman, leaned against the wall, and stretched out my legs. Pigele, busy with serving her stupid dolls, had forgotten about me. I looked around and realized never seeing her room from the floor level before, both above and the below became visible. I was used to the dinginess of Mrs. Rochelle's house but had not expected to stumble upon such shocking amount of grime under Pigele's furniture. Cobwebs, dust balls, torn up stuff, and even dried grass - plain filthy. So unlike home, where grandma made everyone scrub, wash and sweep all nooks and corners. She always warned me that a muddled house caused disordered thoughts and bad behavior. Pigele's room was very muddled.

I craved to tell grandma about her darling Mrs. Rochelle's total lack of housekeeping. Helping with the chores made me happy. Someday, I thought, cleaning would help me to become a princess. Just like in a story about a handsome prince, who searched for a girl to be his bride. He sent a royal order for every young woman in the country to bring him dust from her home, to help him choose. When everyone showed up with sacks and barrels stuffed with dirt, he chose a poor orphan who was able to scrape up only a half of a thimbleful because her house was spotless. I imagined myself to be that princess.

My daydreams vanished when something caught my eye under the sofa, a blue gleam in the dust, a spark. I inched closer and saw the blue gleam again. I glanced in Pigele's direction. She had her back to me. I stretched my arm and grabbed at the spot in the dust. My hand closed on something round and hard. I rubbed my hands together. Sitting on my palm was a crystal bead, a most beautiful thing I had ever seen in my life. The bead was the size of my knuckle and had many crystal facets with a blue twinkle inside. Excited, I thought of the ways to keep the bead. My dress had no pockets, and someone will certainly see it clutched in my hand. To hide the bead in my mouth seemed like a good idea, just like Fagin's little orphans in *Oliver Twist* hid their stolen coins. I cleaned the bead with the hem of my dress, popped it behind my cheek, and crept out of Pigele's room in the direction of the parlor where Mrs. Rochelle and grandma were having tea.

At the door, I caught a snippet of their conversation.

"I would prefer to have a dead daughter like you, Cecilia, not a loose one like mine," said Mrs. Rochelle and sniffled.

"Stop thinking about Richard, he is gone. It's time to accept..." Grandma put the cup down and stopped mid-sentence when she noticed me.

I came closer and whispered about not feeling well. Grandma placed her cool dry hand on my forehead and agreed I was a bit warm. She apologized, and we left. Mrs. Rochelle's round face showed relief. Perhaps she thought I would infect her perfect Pigele, Queen of the Dirt. On the way home, I wondered who Richard was.

The few days following my amazing discovery were an absolute bliss. I pretended to be sick so grandma would let me stay in bed. Preparations for the winter kept her busy, and she did not mind me being under our housekeeper's care.

Grandma had converted my grandfather's distillery into a small cider-making plant. This business became our only source of income, aside from some of our land sold to maintain the huge seaside estate.

My grandfather Etienne LaRose earned the title "Finest Absinthe maker on this side of the Atlantic" according to the labels on the empty green bottles grandma kept in the cupboards. Once, I found a half full bottle on the sideboard in the dining room and got caught drinking the strong green liquid which made me feel funny. Grandma did not yell. Instead, she sent me to the kitchen to peel potatoes for the entire afternoon.

I thought it was a special fairy drink, because of a laughing green fairy sitting on a gray rose pictured on the label. Grandma said Absinthe LaRose became a rarity because my grandfather had taken the recipe to his grave. At night, when I could not sleep because of the stories in my head, I imagined creeping into the LaRose mausoleum, opening my grandfather's tomb, and prying the recipe from his dead hands. It would make grandma happy. She would stop worrying and order a pretty outfit for me, just like my mother's lace dress.

I considered hanging the crystal bead by a thread around my neck, but decided not to for the fear of it being noticed and taken away. No guilty thoughts crossed my mind for taking the bead from Pigele's room, because I was sure she did not even know about its existence. I hid my treasure in a sock by day and inside my pillowcase at night.

I loved to place it on the palm of my hand, cool to the touch and a little heavy with mysterious never-ending sparkles. The multitude of colors amazed me. I imagined holding a miniature rainbow rolled into a ball. I never had anything this pretty. Gazing through its facets I saw countless objects wrapped in a rainbow just like a dragonfly from my garden would probably see. The bead became my magical spyglass that turned regular things into something strange and exciting. In the morning sun, hundreds of tiny points of light shined on me, and when I rolled the bead between my fingers, the sunbeams danced around the room. Hours passed in marveling of its magical beauty. The books and the garden lay forgotten. At times, I heard the bead whisper to me.

"Where do you come from?" I asked

A crystal necklace, Veronica, help me find the rest of the beads

"Is it magical? How did it end up in the dust?"

You can find magic in the most unexpected places.

"How do I find them?"

Follow the sparkles, find the beads, for me, Veronica

I believed the crystal bead, dreaming that my mother was talking to me, and losing the count of days. Every time someone came to my room, I pretended to be asleep, or complained of not feeling well to make them leave.

Once, a knock on my bedroom door surprised me, because grandma always came in without knocking. This time she came in with Dr. Schuele, a family friend and my doctor. He visited often to check on us and sometimes took me to the hospital for tests. I did not like the smelly hospital, but he said my health was important.

Twinkling eyes sized me up from behind his silver framed glasses. He stroked his goatee,

"Our young lady is not well? Let's take a look, now."

He asked for my hand. I reached out, he checked my pulse, took the stethoscope out of his little bag. He inserted the buds in his ears and warned me about the cool touch of the instrument.

"Why the young lady is not eating? Why has she complained about being sick? Show me where it hurts, now."

I did not know how to respond, and just sat there clutching the crystal bead under the blanket, looking up at their questioning faces. How could I tell them I was fine, aside from the dancing butterflies in my stomach, because of the fear they would find my bead?

After an awkward silence, the doctor patted my head and left, with strangely silent grandma in tow. I strained my ears to hear them talking in the hallway, and heard grandma crying. Frightened, I covered my head with a blanket.

Grandma was not supposed to cry. This task belonged to Tilde, our housekeeper. She liked to cry and lament "the good old days". Tilde lived at LaRose Gris from the start, even before my grandparents' wedding. My grandfather gave the house its name, because of the grey granite used in its construction. I always begged Tilde to tell me stories about my family. About beautiful Cecilia, my grandmother, who came here as a young bride. I could not believe she had waist-long silvery blonde hair and appeared to be shy.

Tilde told me stories about Lydia, my mother. She was different from quiet Cecilia. Lydia always found silly adventures around the estate with her friend Marie Gordon, Mrs. Rochelle's daughter, and Pigele's mother. Gossip of disagreements my grandparents had about my mother's upbringing and education fascinated me. To my delight, I heard grandfather allowed my young mother anything she wanted, but Cecilia insisted on life without frivolities. Just like mine.

A little later, after the doctor had left, grandma came back. She sat on my bed and told me how my absence of appetite and paleness worried her.

"Lydia had similar symptoms at your age," she sighed and went on telling me about my mother's poor health, and the cold damp New England climate causing her illness. She had to spend months at the sanatorium in Europe. When she grew up, she moved to a warmer place, but had to come back home to have me. Dr. Schuele feared I might also get sick like Lydia, and suggested sending me to the same sanatorium to become stronger. His brother, also a doctor there would take good care of me.

"Where did my mother live? What warm place? Why?"

"She lived in Thailand for a couple of years. But, never mind that now. You need to think about going to a spa and getting healthier."

"Where is it? Will you come with me?"

"In Germany, Dr. Schuele will accompany you on the plane. He is originally from Baden, a beautiful little town. This is where your grandfather and I met him when he treated Lydia. He became our friend. I promise to come over once I finish with the cider-making at home."

"I don't want to go, I am happy here with..." I almost said, "my crystal bead."

"It's for your own good, Veronica. You will be leaving in a few days. Remember, the trip will cost me a pretty penny. So, better listen to what you are being told and stop being stubborn like your mother. Although I must tell you, she liked Baden a lot when she was a girl. This city is right by the Black Forest and full of many beautiful gardens."

"The Black Forest from my fairy tales?" I became excited and less afraid.

"Yes, the Black Forest from the fairy tales. Your grandfather and I," She said with a faraway look on her face, then caught herself, kissed me on the forehead, and left the room.

I waited until the door had closed behind her and threw myself on the pillows, surprised by the turn of events, but not concerned about being sick. I was sure I was not. My first thoughts went to the crystal bead, and my mother's voice. Grandma would not rest until she found the real cause of my 'illness' only if I hinted that I simply forgot to eat because of daydreaming.

I had no other choice but to go along with grandma's plans. Also, I realized grandma had talked about my mother for first time ever. I could not stop thinking about her. Did my mother believe in magic, maybe she even found a crystal necklace in the Black Forest? I took out the crystal bead and asked for guidance. It did not answer and I fell asleep worried.

I woke up earlier than usual. My suitcase stood all packed up at the foot of my bed. The house was quiet and shadowy in the early light with everyone still asleep. I got up, kissed the crystal bead, and approached the window.

The ground below appeared painted white. The first snow of the season covered my garden. The sun had just begun to show its first rays. Still in a nightgown, I ran outside to say a final goodbye. My bare feet left funny prints on the white path, and goose bumps appeared telling me to rush back. I ignored the cold, charged further, buried my face in the late yellow chrysanthemums, and inhaled the faint bitter scent of the dying flowers. Brilliant morning sunlight enveloped the garden. The snow sparkled in the sunshine just like my crystal bead, the brightness brought tears to my eyes. I started running again, following the sparkles as the bead's voice had said, and suddenly I fell.

Blinded by the sun I had forgotten about the stream under the ice and snow. The freezing water painfully washed over my head. I clutched my crystal bead tighter and tried to look up through the ice. In the bright light, someone called my name and a pair of strong arms grabbed me by the shoulders. I thought my mother had come for me at last. I stopped fighting the cold water and ice, the light became even brighter, and I knew no more.

2. SHADOW GIRL

I kept my eyes shut, even when I heard the whispering voices, the chair pulled close to my bed, someone's breathing, rustling of book pages. I could not help hearing, but did not want to look. Until one morning, I decided to open my eyes and see my room. The birch tree waved at me through the window as always. I tried to wave back, but my arm seemed too heavy. Voices came from behind the door and two people entered. I recognized Tilde and Dr. Schuele.

"Good morning young lady, good to have you back with us at last," said the doctor and felt my wrist for a pulse.

My throat hurt too much to answer, so I blinked instead. Loud sniffling startled me. Tilde had a handkerchief to her face, her eyes puffy. Dr. Schuele waved her out. I watched Tilde leave and turned to Dr. Schuele, raising my eyebrows in question. Even that hurt.

"Don't mind our Tilde, my dear," said the Doctor and I felt a tiny pin prick at my shoulder. I relaxed, tried not to think, and fell asleep.

I woke up a little hungry and my throat was better. I waved at the tree and saw my hand, thin like an old woman's, untrimmed fingernails, blue veins under the pale skin. I must have been sick for a while. A tall pole with a clear bag and dangling tubes stood in the corner of my room, a monster ghost of sickness. The door opened and someone came in again, Dr. Schuele and a silver haired stranger in a black suit. The doctor invited him to sit down on the chair by the bed. He complied, and looked at me with the most piercing gaze I had ever seen. I hid my hand under the covers fighting the urge to hide my head there as well. His grey eyes were clear as glass, as if he could read my thoughts. I shut my eyes instead.

"Now now Veronica, we know you are not asleep. I want you to meet someone," I heard a hint of annoyance in Doctor's voice.

I waited for them to go away, but they remained silent until I looked up again.

"This is Sebastian Van Stratten, an old friend of your family. He came all the way from Thailand to speak with you. You have been ill for a few weeks, very ill, my dear. We kept you at home under a constant care with all the latest treatments. Now you are much better, trust me. Well enough to listen to what Mr. Van Stratten has to tell you." The doctor turned to leave, his back straight and stiff.

The stranger waited until the door closed. He left his seat and walked over to the window.

"You must have a beautiful garden under all this snow, the gazebo looks like a small ice castle."

He sounded different from Doctor Schuele, his accent softer, the speech smoother.

"The Snow Queen's castle," I said warming up to his recognition of my favorite place, "I am a Snow Queen with a heart, not a piece of ice."

"Yes, I remember the story of the Snow Queen, even at my age I can learn from it. Devotion and kindness will melt the coldest of hearts." He took a seat beside my bed again. "I also have a story to tell, a sad story, but I am here to help."

I liked the way he spoke. He reminded me of someone from the books I read. His story turned out overwhelming. I did not remember the events he described.

On the morning when I had to leave with Dr. Schuele for Germany, I went out to the garden and fell through the ice on the creek. Grandmother saw me from the window, rushed down, and pulled me out of the water.

She saved me, but became ill with pneumonia and died days later from the complications, leaving me a complete orphan. I had pneumonia too. Dr. Schuele and nurses from the hospital tended to me around the clock.

The stranger also told me how my grandmother, Cecilia LaRose, left a will. She wrote that in the event of her demise Sebastian Van

Stratten had to become my full time guardian until I reached the age of sixteen.

I did not know how to react. Death seemed strange. I had not known anyone who died before, except grandfather and my mother. But they were always dead to me, and grandmother was always alive. Now she was gone.

In books, people cried when someone had died. My tears refused to come. The guilt raged in my heart instead, because I blamed myself for what happened. I had pretended to be sick, did not tell the truth on time, and lost everything including the crystal bead.

Sebastian Van Stratten waited for my reaction, the weight of his gaze made me uncomfortable. I swallowed hard and blurted out, "I'm glad grandma chose you to be my guardian, and not Ms. Rochelle. I'm thirsty."

Tilde came in with tea and soft butter rolls. She kept wiping her eyes with a wrinkled handkerchief tucked in her sleeve. Tears irritated me. They meant I had to cry too. For some reason I could not feel anything. *Maybe I am a Snow Queen after all* I thought consumed by guilt.

Next day Dr. Schuele took me to the Boston hospital in Hermes, my dead grandparents' old Rolls Royce. Mr. Van Stratten drove, and Tilde hovered over me in the back seat like an annoying mother hen. Uncomfortable tests and x-rays took a few hours. I did not complain and considered the procedures my punishment. My new guardian must have sensed my discomfort and whisked me out of the green hospital room despite the objections of the nurses.

"Later. You can tell us the results later," his voice was gruff and eyes cold.

I slept all the way home. When we arrived, someone carried me up to my room. Too tired to care I fell asleep again.

Mr. Van Stratten was sitting by my bed when I woke up. The time of day seemed unclear, simply grey. I tried to sit up, he tried to help and called Tilde. She rushed in to attend to my immediate needs while he waited outside. Later, Tilde spoon-fed me some oatmeal with honey. I had a few spoonfuls and coughed. The horror in Tilde's eyes scared me and I asked Mr. Van Stratten to lead her away.

"Dr. Schuele is here to talk to us about your final diagnosis. Are you ready?" asked my new guardian.

"As long as you stay, Mr. Van Stratten," I said remembering how he rescued me from the hospital.

"Just Sebastian will do from now on, please," he smiled went to get the door.

The doctor came in with Tilde. She pulled me into her soft embrace. I knew she was crying again. The doctor talked at length. I thought he was trying to impress Sebastian with the boring medical terms and description of my illness. Then he patted me on the head as he always did, and left.

I raised my eyes to Sebastian questioning the meaning of doctor's speech. He smiled, and told me we have nothing to worry about for now. My lungs were clearing up with no other complications, as the doctor had hoped. My heart was weak. I needed to be under the medical observation, follow a light exercise regimen, and gain some weight.

When Sebastian mentioned my weight, Tilde wailed about me being as thin as a little bird. She kept calling me a shadow of my former self. Yet I smiled, because my grandmother always said, "If you have bones, the meat will grow." I repeated grandma's saying to Tilde and she ran out sobbing. Sebastian gave me a long look and said,

"Your grandmother was a wise woman. Be kind to Tilde, she is grieving."

"Grandmother said my mother had weak health too, but she did not die of a sickness. She died because she found life was not fair."

Sebastian turned and left my room without a reply. *Why is everyone running away from me?* I wondered and fell asleep again.

Every passing day made me stronger. Tilde stuffed me with all my favorite food. I took little shaky strolls around the house enjoying its warmth, very different from the days of grandmother's rule when she did not allow the heat at night. Guilty thoughts squeezed my insides. One part of me missed her. The other part enjoyed my new life without her. Why did it seem better without my grandmother?

One morning, I was sitting by the window amusing myself by drawing pictures in the fog patch left by my breath. The fog iced over and I wondered if my nose would stick to the glass if I tried. Sebastian came in for his daily greeting. I found it difficult to understand his ways, because most of the time he was not quite present. His body was, but he himself was not. I wanted to ask him about the impression he made on me, but he answered first.

"Forgive me, Veronica, for being absent-minded at times. I will explain my thoughts to you later," said Sebastian, "I think you are growing tired of your pajamas. The time has come for you to dress up and participate in the household activities."

"You want me to be like a proper little lady, like Pigele?" I said dreading the 'activities', "you are just like grandmother, making me do things I don't like."

"Veronica, I never met the person you mentioned. I think a new routine would make you stronger and give you purpose. This week you will select recipes from the books I left in the kitchen and assist Tilde with food preparation as your introduction to a vegetarian diet."

"Vegetarian? What's that?"

"It means we won't be eating anything with eyes, except potatoes. This diet will make you healthier."

After he left, I smiled for first time in days. "I won't be eating anything with eyes," I kept repeating to myself and to bewildered Tilde whom I had found in the kitchen leafing through an array of cookbooks.

"I can't begin to imagine what Cecilia would say about all this. Not fitting for a child, I say. You need to eat three square meals with meat meant to stick to your ribs, make you grow. Not some silly 'toofooo', or 'chicken peas', said Tilde leafing through a colorful *The World of Curry* cookbook.

Despite Tilde's ominous mutterings, I must have grown in the past few weeks. My dresses became shorter, and sleeves stopped a few of inches above my wrists. My entire meager wardrobe seemed to have shrunk. Even my shoes fitted tighter. I suffered, but decided against asking Sebastian about a new dress and shoes. I did not wish a rebuttal or be accused of frivolity. I did not want to be disappointed in him.

In the afternoons, I kept busy by helping Tilde with dinner. Sebastian's suggestion to get involved worked out well for me. I enjoyed the warm cozy kitchen on the snowy days and listening to the Christmas tunes on the radio. The New Year was a few days away. Old sad '79 slipped out together with my old life.

One day Sebastian came in, and with a tilt of his head asked me to follow him to the central hall where I met two visitors. The young woman looked like a model from a magazine cover in the bookstore, and a man had a measuring tape in his hands. Behind them stood a clothing rack draped in black cloth.

"Mr. Gert and Ms. Lucille, this is Veronica - my ward. Please outfit her according to her wishes," said Sebastian and left me alone with them. The young woman called herself a stylist and the man a tailor. I thought they were joking. Once Mr. Gert unfolded the rack packed with outfits, I knew Sebastian read my mind again. Ms. Lucille told me how he insisted on clothing suitable for a young girl.

"When I asked him about your taste, he told me how you liked reading and fairy tales. You are a lucky little girl to have such a generous guardian," said Lucille helping me into yet another dress.

I had fun trying and selecting four long dresses, in the black soft wool, the black silk with stitched flowers, in the burgundy trimmed with lace, and one cream with a green sash. I did not care for the funny bell-bottom pants, and the platform shoes, shirts with the long collars or the mini dresses they showed me. I wanted to look like a girl from the fairy tales. I also selected two shawls, black and deep cherry red. For shoes, I picked a pair ankle boots, knee-high lace up boots and patent shoes with the shiny buckles as a Court Page would wear. And of course I went for the silky leggings which were never allowed before, by choosing five pairs of black, red and purple. Lucille laughed when I said 'leggings' and called me old fashioned and cute, because the real name was 'tights'.

"I guessed you would choose long dresses," said Sebastian when I presented a fashion show for him and Tilde. How did he guess? How did he know what I wished for, or thought, or liked? This was a mystery to me. The one I would very much enjoy solving. Only if I had the courage to overcome my shyness every time I felt his clear grey eyes on me.

In a few weeks, I became strong enough to go out for a walk. I broached the subject to Sebastian at dinner. He gave me one of his long stares and said the time has not come yet.

"I know that you wish to visit your garden, but the winds are too strong and chilly. You needed to gain more substance."

Tilde, at the other side of the table, sighed and called me a shadow of my former self again. Her lamentations irritated me, and I left the table without finishing my stew. Later, I regretted not taking the bowl with me when I caught myself thinking back to its delicious smell. On the other hand, I showed them my resolve.

In the morning, I laced up my new boots, bundled up in grandmother's long coat, tied on the shawl, and sneaked out by the back door.
The cold air singed, and my eyes watered from the wind gust. Massachusetts' winter ruled strong with icy chill and bloated stormy clouds.

I pulled the shawl over my nose and mouth and ventured into the garden, but had to turn back soon because the snow came up to my knees making it difficult to walk. I circled the main house and the carriage house, curious to find what was happening in the front. Near the garden wall, I spied a narrow path in the snow leading through the back gate towards the dunes and the pebble beach. I followed the path craving a fresh adventure, trying to ignore the gusty wind.

The footpath led me by the small copse of stunted evergreens, snaked around the boulders and ended up at the dunes. I climbed up and the dark open sea greeted me.

Ice had piled up in fantastical angled forms past the surf line. Magic lurked in the blue crevices. I looked forward to exploring them when something hard hit me in the back. I turned and saw a small rock flying in my direction, and did not have time to duck, it struck me on the shoulder. As I bent to pick it up, someone giggled behind the boulders. Curious, I went around and came face-to-face with three kids, about my age, their hands full of rocks, ready to throw more. When they realized I was staring at them they sprang, yelling "Shadow Girl, Shadow Girl."

They confused me, but when a new barrage of rocks hit again, I became angry. Hot in the face with the shawl flapping behind me like the wings of the chimera I picked up the first thing my fingers found in the icy sand and hurled it back with all the might I could muster. One of the kids, a boy with straight yellow hair screamed and clutched his forehead, a dark stream of blood appeared between his fingers. My assailants dropped their pebbles and started to grab the snow to apply to his face. In a few moments, the ground around them shined with bloody polka dots. I watched, ready to fight. With the last of my strength, I picked up another rock, just to show off.

The kids shrieked, "Evil Shadow Girl, run!"

On the way home, I decided not say anything to Sebastian. Tilde must have talked about my illness in the village, and the stupid kids made fun of me. I went straight to my room. Numb from the cold, but feeling victorious, I curled up and fell asleep wrapped in the floppy shawl.

Loud voices from below woke me up. I listened in the twilight, whoever did the talking sounded angry. I opened the bedroom door and walked to the top of the stairs to check who was making all that noise.

Sebastian stood with his arms crossed, and Tilde argued with a large man in a plaid jacket. A man in the uniform stood nearby, his hand on a shoulder of a straight haired boy I threw a rock at earlier. The boy had a bandage around his head. His golden hair bristled up like a porcupine. He looked funny to me.

Sebastian placed a finger over his lips and motioned to come down. I did as he asked and stood beside him. A few moments had passed until the boy noticed me and immediately turned bright red.

"That's her. She attacked me on the beach!"

The large angry man pointed, "You will pay for hurting my son. Officer, arrest her."

Sebastian moved to shield me.

"What is your name, young man?" asked Sebastian. His icy tone of voice brought an instant silence.

"Evan Wood," said the boy and wiped his nose with a scarf.

"Now, Master Wood, please tell us about what happened on the beach this afternoon, in a quiet dignified manner, and no lies," said Sebastian.

"My son doesn't lie, this wild child harmed him," said Evan's father in a loud booming voice.

A thin smile appeared on Sebastian's face as he stared him down. The silence descended with all eyes on the boy. Now, with an incredible blush, he resembled a wounded beardless Santa. I giggled into my hand. Evan's father charged at me, and with one flick of a hand Sebastian had him collapsed on the floor.

It happened very fast. Even Tilde did not have time to gather up her wits and lapse into her usual hysterics. The police officer helped the man up. During the tumble his shirt rode up and revealed a barrel of a pink belly covered with red fuzz, I giggled again.

"We'll do as this gentleman asked," said the police officer as he took hold of the man's arm to calm him down.

In a squeaky voice, Evan told everyone about how he and his friends decided to play hooky from school and found their way to the beach to spy on the LaRose Gris. Stories circulated in the village about the young girl who had died on the estate and came back as a shadow. They wanted to get the proof by searching for a fresh grave, but met me walking in the dunes instead. To convince them I was not a shadow they threw rocks.

"You admit throwing rocks at this girl?" asked the policeman and pulled a notebook from his pocket.

"Yeah, guess so, she sure acted alive," Evan glared at me with such resentment I had to sit down on the stairs.

"Evan shut up," said Mr. Wood and turned on the policeman.

"What about his bloody face? She cannot prove they stoned her, but we can. I demand compensation."

My head spun, watching this was better than reading. I also thought everything happened because of Tilde's gossiping. If she kept quiet, we would not have those awful people in our house.

Sebastian stepped forward, gave Mr. Wood a polite little bow, and asked, "You know where you are, Mr. Wood?"

"Well sure I do, at your posh estate."

"And you are aware how large this estate is?"

Mr. Wood did not answer.

"You should know the beach is part of it as well."

Mr. Wood opened his mouth to object, but nodded instead.

"Now, Officer, Veronica acted in self defense on her own property. Master Wood must apologize."

The policeman regarded Sebastian with respect.

"This sounds fair enough. Evan, you better do what the gentleman says, or face the unpleasant consequences."

Mr. Wood gave Evan a defeated pat on the shoulder. Evan mumbled an apology staring at his shoes. Sebastian took me by the hand to escort me out. I kept looking back. Evan watched, and when no one paid attention to him anymore, shook his fist at me. I guessed he hated to see his father humiliated. Not to be outdone, I stuck out my tongue back at him.

Sebastian left me alone in the drawing room and went back to settle the issue. The voices beyond the wall grew fainter and finally I heard the front door close with its usual thud.

When Sebastian returned, he found me watching the snowflakes dancing in the blue evening glow and thinking about my crystal bead somewhere beneath the ice and snow. I grieved about connection to magic and to my mother was lost forever.

Sebastian poured himself a drink from a glass decanter and sat down in front of the cold fireplace. Silent for a while in the semidarkness, calmed by the light from the lamppost outside the window we sat still until Sebastian spoke.

"Tilde deserves a break. She is quite old and needs to retire. Work at the mansion is too strenuous for her. I will make arrangements for a small house in Cider Village, it's close by and we can visit at any time. She would be welcome here as an honored guest, and not as a servant."

My earlier efforts to compose a meaningful speech went to waste. He was aware of my thoughts about Tilde's unfortunate love of gossip. He guessed the origins of the "Shadow Girl" incident. I had another pressing new question in mind.

"How are we going to get her a house? Grandmother always said we had no means. She did not buy me new leggings, or even ice cream. You got me the new dresses and now Tilde's house."

Sebastian switched on a stained glass lamp on the side table. The room glowed in its amber light. He smiled and shook his head.

"I am not familiar with your grandmother, Veronica. In her will, she left you a substantial amount of money. Don't worry about it for now. She must have learned how to save for the rainy day. The estate has plenty of land in case we would need more funds."

"Land, what land?" I asked.

"I see nobody educated you about your legacy, my dear. I will tell you some of the history now, and when you grow up you will discover the rest."

Sebastian told me about the documents The Law Firm sent him. Grandmother sold some of the estate land to finance the conversion of grandfather's famous absinthe distillery into a small cider factory. He suspected the fear of poverty must have taken a strong hold on her because the bank statements had shown she continued to live in a modest way.

"So Mrs. Rochelle was not richer and more important?"

"Who is this?" asked Sebastian.

"She was grandmother's friend. We used to go there every Saturday until, you know."

"A friend would come and visit in times of trouble. No one by this name came to Cecilia's funeral, except some ancient Boston friends of your grandfather and a few locals," he said with a dismissive wave, "don't dwell on the past, Veronica. It has gone forever, concentrate on the moment, and do not worry. Just be yourself and trust your heart, wonderful rewards will come to you soon enough."

"You say so many interesting things Sebastian. Can you tell me a story?"

"I will do better than telling stories. I will show you how to create a new story for your life. I imagine Cecilia did not consider your schooling of much importance."

"I had a tutor before. He came over every week and napped during our lessons. I liked to read the books he brought though."

"Tell me what kind of books?"

"Alice in Wonderland and Tales of Hoffman, and my favorite stories by Hans Christian Andersen, The Three Musketeers," I was excited to talk about books. No one had asked questions like this before.

"Oh yes, sad tales and wonderful adventures. I promise to read them with you again. Now go and say good night to Tilde, and get ready for bed. Tomorrow will take us to a new beginning, Miss Shadow Girl."

We both smiled.

3. SOUND OF ENLIGHTENMENT

The small Cider village came into existence when my grandmother Cecilia LaRose sold some of the LaRose Gris land. She converted grandfather's absinthe distillery into a cider factory and seasonal workers settled nearby. A few of them remained, and the settlement grew into a small fishing village with a dock and a few dozen buildings. Sebastian purchased a tiny salt box cottage for Tilde near the center of the village.

At first, she wept as I expected. After a while she warmed up to the idea of having her own place and found a new reason to cry, the amount of work she had to do before moving. Sebastian hired the village carpenter to repair the cozy cottage. People from Boston came with samples of wallpaper, carpeting, and drapery. I felt important when Sebastian asked me to help with the colors, just like decorating a big dollhouse. Tilde and I settled the walls to be lilac like flowers in the garden, the carpets dark blue as the ocean, and the curtains soft white as the clouds in the spring sky. I missed the spring; so much grief came in the winter. Now, the sadness was melting away with the deep snow. The winter had overstayed its welcome. I remembered grandma's saying "In Massachusetts one is born with certain notion about the good weather, it arrives not sooner, not later, but when the time is right."

Tilde moved out in early March, almost six months after my grandmother's death. I refused to visit the LaRose mausoleum where she found her final rest. Sebastian never mentioned I should, but Tilde kept nagging. Now Tilde was gone, no more nagging and no more guilt. Sometimes I missed Tilde's comforting embraces, and visited her on good dry days. I liked the small freedom of the walk over to the village. First, I walked the length our driveway with tall elm trees on both sides, and beyond the property gates the narrow road leading right to the center of the village, past the bakery, a general store, and the post office.

One early afternoon I came home from one of my morning visits. The shy sun peeked from behind the elephant clouds. The promise of spring in the gusty ocean wind lifted my spirits. Strong enough now, to take a few steps at a time I reached the front doors. They did not seem to be as heavy as before. I squeezed through, caught a strange scent drifting in the air, and followed my nose to the kitchen.

To my surprise, Sebastian and a peculiar looking man stood there enveloped by the wisps of flower-scented smoke. I smelled burning dried herbs and rose petals. They were both barefoot. The bold headed stranger wore an orange robe, which left one of his shoulders bare. He had dark tanned skin, and brown squinty eyes, like the Chinese people I saw in Boston Chinatown.

"Hello, excuse me, what are you doing?" I said trying not to stare.

Sebastian smiled and placed a hand on the man's shoulder to stop him from waving the smoke sticks.

"Veronica, I want you to meet an old friend of mine. His name is Winai and he is kind enough to came here and take Tilde's place as our housekeeper."

"Nice to meet you, I am Veronica LaRose," But the man bowed with palms pressed together instead of shaking my hand. I liked him right away for his gentle non-judging gaze and repeated the gesture to be polite.

"Winai is a Buddhist monk, from the retreat where I used to teach when I lived in Thailand. You can talk to him, he understands English. But I warn you, he won't reply."

"What is wrong with him?"

"Nothing, he has given a vow of silence. Our Venerable Teacher had passed on, and Winai is honoring him by not speaking for seven years."

I never heard such a strange story, but listened without interrupting Sebastian. He never proved me wrong, never berated or criticized. He respected me and I tried to do the same.

"What are the smoke sticks for?"

"They are called incense, and when lit, the smoke induces harmony and cleansing."

"Don't you use mops and buckets for that?"

"It's cleansing not cleaning, Veronica. The monks believe when people leave or die, their energy imprint remains. In our case, we need to clear the old energy in order to give way to the new beginning. Winai and I were performing this ritual of cleansing the mansion.

"Can you please show me how, I want to help."

With another bow, the monk invited me to join them and gave me a few long incense sticks.

"First," continued Sebastian, "we must burn the incense around the perimeter of the walls and corners, especially the corners. This purifies the energy and banishes the *narakas*, bad memories. I will chant prayers to invite light into this house."

"Will you teach me the chant?"

"Chanting may be a tough task for you. This is why we also use these," he said and showed me two brass cymbals joined by about ten inches of string with dragons etched on top. They made a clinking sound as he passed them to me. I touched them together, and the cymbals produced a soothing long tone.

"These are called Tingsha, used instead of the chant. The melodic sound cleanses energy and induces enlightenment." Sebastian turned one cymbal over. "Here are the engraved prayers, and every time you clink you evoke one."

We worked in unison for the rest of the afternoon. Sebastian chanted, Winai waived incense sticks, and I followed with the

Tingsha. I never had so much fun or imagined such soothing rituals existed, even in fairy tales.

When we completed the cleansing, Sebastian invited us to sit on the area rug in the middle of the central hall and share a meal of rice, dried fruit, and green tea supplied by our silent monk-house keeper. Grandmother would be livid if she found us sitting on the floor and her precious round walnut table with porcelain figurines of dancing girls pushed to the corner.

"We won't make a habit eating here, but today it seems suitable. Celebrate change by doing something different," said Sebastian raising his teacup. I never got used to him reading my thoughts.

"Tilde is going to blow up when she finds out about Winai," I said and smiled at the monk.

"Winai is here because he is kind enough to help us. We will be too busy to pay attention to the housekeeping."

"Why?"

"The time is right to pay serious attention to you. You are physically strong now. You have some knowledge. You have a good mind. We need to create a river bed for the flow of your thoughts. Now you have a collection of wild streams, they need unity and purpose. Life is an ocean."

"Yes, with sea monsters," I said giggling. Winai also laughed, without making any sound. Sebastian's complicated speeches did not daze me anymore.

"Did you arrive today Mr. Winai?"

The monk nodded, and flapped his arms like a bird.

"You flew?"

Winai laughed again. I liked his smiling and laughing much better than Tilde's frowning and crying.

"He means he came by an airplane. I picked him up from the airport late last night while you were asleep. The world is not as magical as you might think."

"Is too."

"Well, you are right. Magic lurks in some forgotten corners of our big round world. Right, Winai?"

I waited for a moment like this, but could not overcome my shyness. It seemed like a good chance to ask and I took a deep breath.

"Will you teach me how to read thoughts?"

His eyes turned icy, "Please explain, Veronica."

I looked at Winai for support, and described the feeling I always had about him knowing my thoughts.

"I noticed it before, and was too scared to ask, but I want to learn. The same way you told me about the energy. Please?"

Sebastian and Winai looked at each other and Winai nodded.

"The journey to knowledge is a long road with no horizon. We will start tomorrow. You need your rest, go now."

Later, lying in bed, I went over the day's events. It started out as an ordinary day and ended in the most unusual way. I had an odd sensation of lightness and wondered if this is what being happy felt like. Right when I was about to fall asleep a memory jolted me.

Thailand. My mother had lived in Thailand for some time according to my grandmother. Sebastian admitted today that once he was a teacher at a retreat in Thailand. Maybe they knew each other?

The next morning I had found Sebastian waiting for me in the library with my breakfast on the table. I heard a loud clunking and stuck my head through the door to see a much brighter and cleaner kitchen. Winai was hard at work sorting cooking pots and rearranging cabinets.

"We will do an inventory of our own as soon as you finish your breakfast," said Sebastian, without taking his eyes from the book in his hands.

Following my convalescence, I had developed quite an appetite. Even Tilde complained I did not eat a lot, just all the time. In a hurry, I gulped down my oatmeal wishing for more. While I ate, Sebastian took a set of keys from a small chest on the desk and told me we needed to find a special room in the house for our studies.

I was born and had grown up at LaRose Gris, but never even

been to some rooms. They were always off limits and locked up. I tried to wheedle the information about them from grandmother or Tilde, but they never answered. Sebastian's plan to explore was a gift.

"Here are the keys for the rooms on the main floor, second floor and also from a cellar in the basement. Cellar will not suit our purpose. We need a bright room with large windows. But we will start with the cellar anyway, for the exploration sake."

We took the stairs to the basement from the kitchen and found dry and cold storage rooms for food or furniture, a cedar room to protect wool and fur clothing from moth, a messy room filled with the discarded household stuff, a wine room that smelled funny and a trap door to the cellar.

I prodded the padlock with my foot while Sebastian tried several keys until it gave in with a loud click. Sebastian grabbed a metal ring and lifted the wooden trap door. It must have been heavy because Sebastian's neck muscles bulged and his pale face turned red, he resembled a boy on a quest. The door opened like a book and we were standing above a dark square void. A smell of stale damp air sprang from below. Sebastian got down to his knees with a flashlight.

"There must be a ladder. Ah, here it is," he said and stretched his body further into the cellar. Nervous he might fall I grabbed at his coat. After securing the ladder, he turned to face me, grinned, and began to descend. In a moment, his head disappeared and I plopped on my stomach to peer down. I heard nothing until a dim light went on below followed by Sebastian's muffled voice,

"Come down, Veronica. Do not be afraid. It is quite all right. I'll help you."

Excited not scared, I climbed the stairs as Sebastian did, my feet tangled up in a rush to reach the bottom. The ladder shifted and threatened to fall. Just as I was about to tumble down like an apple, Sebastian straightened the ladder and helped me."

"Thank you..." I said afraid of the dim surroundings illuminated by a single light bulb with a pull cord, the dusty tiles on the floor and the walls covered with spider webs. The light reflected off white dust on the shelving where rows upon rows, like a dark green army, stood my grandfather's absinthe bottles. Sebastian took one and wiped the grime off with his sleeve. I recognized the curvy sealed bottle with a small tussle on top, we had many empty ones upstairs in the cupboard, but these were intact, unopened, with a label of a laughing green fairy sitting on the gray rose, Absinthe LaRose. Hundreds of these bottles stood in rows on the cellar shelves.

"Veronica, I think that we had found a treasure," said Sebastian examining the bottles with the flashlight, "I have been doing some research and learned only a few intact unopened "Absinthe LaRose" remain in private collections. And none are available for sale, unless they are auctioned."

Not sure what to say I poked around. The dusty bottles did not excite me. I imagined entirely different type of treasure, the kind found in wooden chests under huge rusted padlocks, hidden by the pirates.

I spied a small suitcase on the top shelf and pointed it out to Sebastian. He used the ladder and pulled down the dusty case covered with cobwebs. Secured with a flimsy clasp and stuffed with yellow newsprint, not exciting at all. The cellar unsettled me. I felt like we were running out of air and asked to leave. Sebastian helped me up and passed several bottles to me together with the suitcase. In the brighter light, I noticed tarnished initials by the handle, ELR. It must have belonged to my grandfather.

Snacks were waiting for us on the kitchen table when we came up. Winai cleaned out most of the clutter and moved on to scrubbing the stove. Now I believed he was even a bigger cleaning fanatic than my grandmother ever was. Best of all, he did not berate me for not helping. He changed his orange robes to a gray set of cropped pants and white shirt, a black bandana tied around his head. I liked the way he dressed too.

"Are you ready Veronica?" Sebastian's voice came from the sitting room. I stuffed some cookies in my pocket for later and rushed to continue our exploration.

"Next on the agenda, the main floor, and the room hidden behind the library," said Sebastian jingling the keys.

I never even knew we had such a room. Someone concealed it by blocking the entrance with the bookshelves. Sebastian and I removed the books piling them on the floor and with Winai's help moved the shelf.

Sebastian took a few moments to locate the correct keys again. I watched, impatient for a new discovery. The door had two locks. They did not give in easily, but Sebastian won the match and went in first. I followed on his heels and bumped into his back, solid like a garden wall.

Shadows danced inside, very little light came through the heavy red curtains. Sebastian went over and drew them apart to shed light onto more bookshelves. Two interesting red chairs with carved lion's feet and a huge ornate desk faced the windows.

To make the room brighter Sebastian turned on a floor lamp shaped like a nude girl holding a shade. The lamp produced more light for us to notice paintings of wine, fruit, dead rabbits, and birds on the walls. Later, I learned the proper name was still life, or *nature morte* for this type of paintings. I did not like the dead animals on those paintings and looked away.

A few picture frames were laying face down on the desk, I turned one over. A beautiful young girl with long light hair smiled at me from the black and white photo, beside her stood a man with a grand mustache in a suit and a tall hat. The girl held a bouquet of roses overflowing in her arms. I examined the girl's face and my hands numbed as I read the inscription on the frame. It was a photo of my young grandmother, the man with her was my grandfather.

"Such a fragile beauty," said Sebastian looking over my shoulder.

"I only remember her with grey hair and tough. Is this what happens to people when they get old?"

Sebastian did not reply and reached for another picture and froze. I had to pull his sleeve and call his name twice to show it to me. He stared at another wedding photo of a man in a uniform and a young woman wearing a short wedding veil. Their heads touched and they looked straight at me. The inscription said *"Robert Gordon and Lydia LaRose Gordon, September, 1965"*

I recognized my mother right away.

"Do you think Robert Gordon is my father? Why then my name is LaRose? Where is he now?"

I turned to Sebastian for answers.

"You said that you lived in Thailand, so did my mother. Grandma told me. Maybe you met her there?"

Sebastian shook his head.

"This must have been your grandfather's study. Someone barred it for a reason might never know. Veronica, please bring the Tingsha and call Winai please. With proper dusting and cleansing, the windows facing the gardens and the library right next door, I believe we had found a perfect place for our lessons."

"You did not answer me," I said. Getting answers from him was like trying to catch air.

"On the other hand, a good walk on the beach would clear up your head. Go put on your coat and boots. We'll be back before dinner to explore the rest."

"Well, at least now I know she had freckles too," I said stomping out.

Sebastian either was hiding something or truly did not know.

I was inclined to believe the latter.

Veronica LaRose

4. THE LIBRARY

The conversion of grandfather's office happened right after its discovery. Sebastian and Winai removed all furniture and placed an area rug and several cushions on the floor. He also replaced the still life paintings with multicolored mandala images of vivid flowing patterns used for meditation. The low table with a thick candle in its center completed the new minimalistic decor.

For my first class, we sat on the floor at the opposite sides of the table with the lit candle between us. I understood Sebastian's lessons were not the usual kind.

"Remember when you wanted me to teach you to read minds?" asked Sebastian, "Well, it's not about reading minds, but about developing your intuition. A sixth sense is another name for this. Intuition helps to capture moods, emotions, and sometimes thoughts of others. Once you become attuned to your intuition, you might even be able to predict events."

"Just like magic. How do you capture thoughts?"

"In a way like magic. You will learn to be in tune with the world by practice and patience, imagine taking a dull rusty blade, and slowly turn it into a sharp Damask steel."

"Sounds hard. Can I read a book about it instead?"

"To master this skill one should practice an art of meditation every day. In time, you will be able to do it. I know."

"You mean if I learn meditation I would be able to read the thoughts of others using my intuition?"

"No, you will be able to recognize what you already know."

His explanation sounded complicated, but it captured my

35

imagination.

"Concentrate only on this small flame. Just observe, no thinking."

Flame watching did not seem difficult at first. I liked the little blue speck inside the yellow glow. So like my crystal bead. The memory saddened me. The flame wavered.

"Veronica concentrate, I know you are thinking of something else."

I tried repeatedly, but after a few moments, my thoughts shifted to the fireplace, or I wondered how hot the sun must be, and dozens of other fire thoughts invaded my mind. I had to start over until Sebastian extinguished the candle. To my surprise two hours had passed.

"When you're accessing your inner self, the energy flow alters and you stop living in the regular time. Your consciousness shifts, musicians, and artists experience it often," he said and gave me a book, *Mindfulness and Wisdom. Thoughts on Meditation.*

We practiced the candle meditation for weeks, until I learned to obliterate all thoughts. After that, Sebastian asked me to close my eyes and picture the flame in my mind, which proved to be harder. Once I learned to hold a constant image, Sebastian told me to think of any question and concentrate. An intuitive answer would replace the image of the flame.

I have begun to rely on my inner voice and sometimes caught myself in a moment of joy when I was able to predict or solve a situation by mere thinking. He taught me how to improve concentration by breathing and encourage the positive flow of energy through chakras, the energy centers in my body. At the end of our lessons, I felt hungry and refreshed. Winai's delicious vegetarian dishes were a happy reward.

Our household established a comfortable routine of meals, studying, and free time to read or help with the chores. The memories of my previous life when grandmother was alive slowly faded like a distant dream.

One afternoon, I received a permission to visit Tilde for lunch. Questions about my mother's wedding photo still nagged at me. Wrapped in my favorite shawl, I went through the garden first to check on the waking plants and to welcome spring. I inhaled the scent of moist soil liberated from the mounds of winter snow. To my delight, the warm sunny patches near the wall already showed signs of early growth. The stream freed from the ice bubbled along, oblivious to the sad events of the last fall. I remembered the crystal bead lost in the murky cold water, the memory sent shivers down my back, and I left.

On the way to the village, I enjoyed pleasant thoughts about planting and flowers, the gazebo where I would ask Sebastian to move our lessons for the summer. The wind increased, forcing me to pick up my pace. The brisk walk warmed me up, but the happy vigor evaporated when I spotted Evan Wood by the general store. I intended to ignore him as usual on my outings to the Cider Village.

"Freak," he said as I passed, "freaky vegetable, that's what you are."

"Excuse me. Are you talking to me?" I said turning around ready for the confrontation.

"I know how you threw the old lady out from your fancy house. I know all about the freak who lives there now and how you're all vegetables."

I thought about his absurdity for a moment, and understood.

"You're just a dumb pea-brain, Evan. We are VE-GE-TA-RI-AN. And, it's none of your business what's happening on my estate. "

I tried to stay cool, but embers of anger begun to glow inside, urging me to punch his mean face and kick him. But Sebastian's lessons took over. With a deep breath, I continued on my way trying not to care about the mean words he said. The unjust insults he aimed at my friend Winai wounded more than anything did.

I knocked hard on Tilde's front door and without waiting for an invitation stormed in. She was in her favorite chair, knitting.

"How could you talk about us again? Why do you keep

gossiping? Everything turns upside down by those people! Do you really think we threw you out?" I cried and felt hot angry tears singe my face.

She tried to stand up. The knitting fell on the floor by her feet.

"I am never coming here again!" I slammed the door in her face and ran home.

I do not remember getting home with hurt and anger burning up my heart and squeezing my throat, meditation lessons forgotten. Tilde had to protect us, not gossip about us. She was family. Now, she became as ignorant as the villagers.

Sebastian stood outside at the top of the stairs, warned by Tilde's phone call, his long silver hair whipping in the wind.

Later in the kitchen over a cup of warm milk, I told him everything. He listened tapping a finger over his mouth.

"You know what you have to do," he said at last.

I held the steaming cup between my hands and concentrated on his words until an answer appeared.

"I have to stop paying attention to the nasty twisted gossip, and to apologize to Tilde."

"Good. Do you understand why she talks about you to other people?"

"Yes, because she loves me."

"Now go and rest. Tomorrow we are going to the temple of knowledge, the Boston Library. I hoped it to be a surprise," he said and stroked my cheek with the back of his hand. I wanted to hug him but did not dare.

A beautiful castle in Copley Square turned out to be the Boston Public Library. The gray imposing building with a sloping red roof awed me. I had never been to a public library. Sebastian said not all libraries were as grand as this one. Boston Public Library halls awed everyone who entered. Two bronze statues flanked the sides of the entrance provided the first clues: *Art* holding a brush and a palette and *Science* with a sphere in her hand. *Art* held the names of famous artists written on a tablet, and *Science* the names of scholars. Sebastian explained all this as we read the inscriptions. I wanted Sebastian to tell me more.

"This is why we are here Veronica, to learn new things. Knowledge is power."

Pink polished marble shined in the vestibule. The magnificent vaulted ceilings of the central hall made me feel tiny like Thumbelina. I kept turning trying to grasp it all, the names on the ceiling and the symbols of the zodiac on the floor. I loved the splendid lions at the foot of the grand stairway and asked Sebastian if I could pet them. He pulled me further.

"Maybe the next time, we have a mission."

"Where are we going?"

I tried to catch a better view of the murals above us and stumbled, he gripped my hand tighter.

"We are taking a tour to learn more about this place. Stop or your head might fall off from all this turning. Please pay attention where you are going, Veronica."

We signed up for a morning tour and received our library cards at the information counter. Then we waited at the Bates Hall where people sat reading or writing at the tables under the green glow shaded brass table lamps. The silence reached the high vaulted ceiling. Sebastian whispered that the guide would take the visitors around the building to discuss its history and works of art.

A young woman invited us to join the group. The tour lasted for about an hour. Soon the guide's speech became too complicated and I stopped paying attention. Sebastian urged me to follow. I continued to daydream mesmerized by the artwork, until Sebastian laid a gentle hand on my shoulder.

"Do you have any questions for our guide? The tour is over."

"Do you really have one million books here?"

"Yes and maybe more. The library is growing. We had a new addition built."

"You have books about everything? Even magic?"

"Yes, even magic," she smiled.

"I would like to read them please."

"You have a beautiful daughter, Sir."

She wrote the name and location of the department on a card. Sebastian acknowledged her remark with a smile and we went in search of the magic books.

We found the Children's Place on the first floor. A librarian showed me a shelf with books she called *magic*. The covers displayed party trick books, colorful clowns, black top hats, rabbits, and playing cards.

"This is not what I wanted," I said a little annoyed, "I would like books about magic from the fairy tales, the supernatural kind."

It must have astonished the librarian and she questioned Sebastian.

"She knows what she wants," he said shrugging.

"All right. You may try The Rare Books and Manuscripts on the third floor."

At the Rare Books and Manuscripts department we encountered another librarian whom I also surprised by my question.

"Are you sure you want books like that? They are beyond the child's age and might frighten her."

I think that the subject infected Sebastian's curiosity and he confirmed my request.

"Well, we have a large selection in on astrology, divination, and also philosophers like Steiner, Jung, or Crowley. And you would have to sign in for temperature controlled vault to examine an old occult manuscript collection."

"Yes, I want to read manuscripts written by real wizards, please."

"Then you need to see Ms. Varley, an assistant to the professor in charge of the collection. It's in the basement, B-2. Good luck."

We took the long stairs down, and more stairs, the ceiling became lower with every flight below the ground floor. The signs on the painted white walls brought us down to a long sub-basement corridor and a door with a peephole.

Sebastian pressed the buzzer twice. A muffled voice demanded what we wanted. Sebastian asked for Ms. Varley. Nothing happened for a while until the door opened with a screechy protest. A person dressed in the black outfit stood hidden in the shadow.

"I am Anna Varley. What do you want?" she said in a loud whisper moving closer.

Anna Varley was paler than a porcelain plate, as if she had never been outside. Even her lips had no color. Her hair and part of her face stayed hidden under an odd hat with a red ostrich feather. I stared at her pale hands with long crimson nails.

"Now I know why the lady upstairs wished us luck," I said to Sebastian under my breath and hid behind him.

"We were informed by the librarian in non-fiction you would be able to show us manuscripts on the occult. May we come in?"

She opened the door wider with evident reluctance.

"Hurry, the draft is dreadful."

Inside, we stumbled on books and magazines scattered on the floor, and had to tiptoe around the large desk piled high enough to hide Anna Varley up to her hat feather. I gaped at the art posters pinned with total disregard for neatness or order.

"Rule number one, you have to sign in."
The red feather bobbed over the pileup.

"Rule number two, no pens or food, pencil and loose paper are okay. Rule number three, gloves must stay on."

She handed Sebastian a tray with a pencil, sheets of paper, a pair of white gloves and long tweezers.

"The child can wait outside."

Before Sebastian could contradict, I stepped forward.

"The tour guide told us this library was built for everyone who wants to read."

"Fine, it's your choice. Beware, some of those manuscripts are as creepy as hell."

I was not sure what she meant. Was she serious or making fun of me?

"Ms. Varley, I understand your reluctance to have Veronica in the vault, but frightening her is not appropriate. She will remain my responsibility," said Sebastian and signed the book.

The pale lady's remark unsettled me and I searched Sebastian's eyes for clues. He shrugged, and went ahead through the short tunnel. An automatic door opened with a hiss, we entered a cave-like room. A large reading table with mounted magnifying instruments stood in the middle. Stone shelves lined up in all directions, materials arranged by order in total contrast with Anna Varley's office. A thick catalogue sat on a separate pedestal. I came over to check it out.

The names of manuscripts were listed on the left followed by a short description, year of issue and their location. The lists consisted of topics on alchemy, astrology, conjuring, demons, elemental magic, and other unfamiliar subjects. I took a pencil and a piece of paper to copy the topics, which interested me most. Together, decked in white soft gloves, we carried some volumes over to the large reading table.

My hands trembled with excitement. In front of me, I had manuscripts with descriptions of the magical world of fairies and angels. Perhaps the answers about the angel's voice from my life-changing crystal bead rested within my reach.

Sebastian and I opened the large tomes. Some yellowed fragile pages contained beautiful and scary illustrations. As we turned the ancient paper, I admired pictures of a cute half-boy half-goat with a wine goblet in his pudgy hand, a crying vampire, a ghost chained to the gravestone covered with red roses, a dancing shaman with a rain stick, and a beautiful young girl in a coffin.   I tried to read the calligraphic text. The letters looked English, but not the words.

"Can you read it, Sebastian?"

"Well, this one looks like French, but I can't understand it. And this one is in Spanish, I think. Ha! This one is in Italian for sure, but in old Italian...."

We went through a dozen more books and manuscripts and found only one in English, but the writing confused us. Sebastian said it could be Welsh. I was on the brink of tears. My hopes of learning about fairies, angels, and illustrated magical beings seemed dashed.

"Don't be upset, I have a solution," said Sebastian.

"What is it?" I asked, fighting tears.

"You will have to learn all those languages if you wish to read these books."

Suddenly, a loud noise that sounded like a sneeze came from the back of the vaulted room and interrupted us. We came closer to see the source of the noise.

The strange-looking person, stranger than anyone I had seen, stranger than described in books, stepped out of the shadows. How did we miss this lanky man with a mop of red hair and bristling leprechaun sideburns?

"Eh, no need to do that! One. You have to learn only one and the world is yours."

The redheaded stranger smoothed his wrinkled Rolling Stones tee shirt, attempted to fix the polka dot tie, and pulled up his ripped bell-bottom jeans to reveal black canvas sneakers on his sockless feet.

"Gaspar Dix at your service," he bowed like an actor on stage and hiccupped, "A research Professor banished from NYU, dwindling my life away in this hole of holes, without a drop of ale to sweeten my mouth."

"Sebastian Van Stratten. This is my ward Veronica LaRose. I apologize for disturbing your sleep. We are in the midst of exploring this collection."

The men shook hands and Professor Dix held my hand in both of his for a moment. I glanced over his shoulder at the place where he appeared from, and saw a pile of newspapers, a wrinkled jacket, and a bottle on the floor. He must have been taking a nap when we came in. Sebastian, as always, was way ahead of me in his observations.

"And you were saying?" asked Sebastian.

"I heard you trying to read the manuscripts. You are damn right. They are written in French, Italian, Spanish, and Welsh." He said bending his long bony fingers one-by-one, "and in old style too. Those languages have not been uttered in hundreds of years. Call them dead, kaput, or whatever. By gods, there is no reason to learn all of them. One is enough. *Unum est et latine.* Latin, learn Latin and you will understand *omnes* little girl. I should know. I am an ancient languages Professor in charge of this caboodle."

This is how our friendship with odd and wonderful Gaspar Dix had begun. He was born in New York, the only son of a Professor of German literature and a pastry chef. His parents called him a Wunderkind, the wonder child. His doting mother stuffed him with food. His intellectual father stuffed him with knowledge. Gaspar started University of New York at the age of sixteen, and never left. A self-proclaimed eternal student, he completed two postgraduate degrees, Ancient Languages and Quantum Mechanics. He confessed his dream was to become a professional beer taster and because of this very ambition, they dispatched him to Boston to take over an obscure manuscript collection. The loneliest job one could imagine for a merry fellow like him, but a fascinating one.

"*Aeternus Discipulus,* eternal student that's what I am. I hope that somewhere in this vault, I may discover a cool incantation to turn water into beer, better yet to fill the empty pint with a snap of my fingers. Dig it?" He said winking at me and asked about my wish to learn wizard magic.

"Quite a heavy ambition for a young bunny, but looking at you I would swear you were a pixie yourself with those groovy green eyes."

I liked him a lot, and hoped Sebastian did too. Gaspar Dix guessed Sebastian's native language was Dutch, and he asked if Sebastian had ever been a sailor.

"Yes, how did you guess? I sailed for nearly two decades, must have been around the world fifty times on the cargo lines," said Sebastian, visibly delighted by Professor Dix. This revelation surprised me. He never mentioned any of it to me, but again, he never talked about himself. It was all about me.

"It's your posture, man. Legs apart, straight shoulders, hands clasped behind the back. And, the way you speak. I hear the influence of at least five different dialects in your speech, a smorgasbord of an adventurer. Now, Veronica my green-eyed pixie, tell me, how would you like to learn Latin? I have a doctorate in this language and it would be awesome to teach someone cute like you. Another *quaesitor magicae*, seeker of magic."

"Thank you Professor Dix. Can I Sebastian?"

"I learned languages by travelling and adventures. French, German, Italian, Thai, Sanskrit - are all in your power, Veronica. I suggest you concentrate on academics now and adventure later," said Sebastian.

"What about magic? I want to learn about magic too."

Professor Dix became serious.

"These manuscripts are beyond your capabilities for now. Let's begin with something else. How is your schooling?"

"Veronica is home schooled, Gaspar," said Sebastian and turned to me, "perhaps it's time for your tutor to start academic lessons again."

My tutor Mr. Prendergast used to be a high school teacher, before he retired. He would give me a book, then sit in a chair by our fireplace in the library and nap while I read fairy tales, adventure, and ghost stories. Reading became my second nature. Through books, I discovered geography and history, some science. Whenever I read something new and unfamiliar I would go to our library and look it up in an Encyclopedia. We had a hundred large tomes with golden edges full of information and illustrations.

"We have to include mathematics and science in your studies," said Mr. Dix.

"But why mathematics?" I never understood the need for boring numbers.

"Mathematics is just like Latin. It helps you dig things. Makes you analyze, memorize and prioritize. *Operor vos agnosco?* Do you dig?"

Everything was settled. We would meet at the library every Saturday morning with Professor Dix for Latin, math, and science lessons and Mr. Prendergast would help me with homework and English during the week.

"I must insist on paying you for your time," said Sebastian.

"Sure, I could use some bread," said Mr. Dix.

"Why does Professor Dix want to be paid with bread? And what do I need to dig?"

They glanced at each other trying to hide their smiles. Sebastian explained about the words with double meanings, in this instance 'bread' meant 'money', and 'dig' meant 'understand'.

"I want to learn more words like that. It's fun."

We slipped on the white gloves again and Professor Dix helped us to put the heavy manuscripts back on their shelves.

I remembered the pale Anna Varley in the front office, and it was impossible to leave without signing out. She made me a bit nervous.

"This lady librarian does not like anyone, does she?"

"Oh, never mind that Cheese Weasel, she is out to lunch," Mr. Dix pointed to his head and drew an imaginary circle above his ear.

Anna Varley was not out to lunch. She was in her messy office dancing to silence.

"I hope the music in my head is not too loud for you."

She sang a bizarre tune, which sounded like cats outside in the spring.

Sebastian and I quickly signed out. Gaspar Dix stayed behind, and a few moments later, he emerged with his arm wrapped around Anna's shoulders. She was quiet now with a pleased expression on her face. The hat disappeared, and jet-black hair fell to her waist in one shiny gorgeous wave. I realized she was beautiful and young, like my mother in the wedding photo.

"Until next Saturday, friends. Don't forget to get the textbooks I recommended. Now, therapy time." He gave us a wink and they sauntered in the opposite direction to the door at the end of the corridor with a *Private* sign.

Sebastian helped me with the coat.

"Let's go home Veronica."

"No, not right away. I would like to stop at Tilde's to apologize for yesterday. We'll get her some bread, I mean the real bread."

We arrived at the Cider Village in the late afternoon. Tilde behaved as if nothing had happened and offered to make tea. She busied herself setting up cups and the raisin bread we picked up at the bakery when I came over hugged her ample waist and rested my cheek on her soft bosom. The familiar scent of love and security enveloped me as she stroked my hair and kissed the top of my head.

"Stop worrying, pretty flower, no harm done, you little hothead. Now go ask Sebastian to help with the tray. My back is giving out as always, and it's too heavy for you."

My heart fluttered from knowing I was forgiven. All of a sudden, I have remembered not eating anything since morning aside from an apple Winai slipped into my coat pocket. I guess I carried the guilty weight in my stomach as well. Sebastian never paid much attention to meal times.

We made ourselves comfortable at the small round table in Tilde's pretty sitting room. Sebastian discussed a possibility of an early spring. Tilde told him no such thing ever happened in Massachusetts. The winter always came like a lion and left like a lion, we should expect another snowstorm by the end of April. In the meantime, I tried to figure out a proper approach for Tilde.

"We were clearing some rooms in the house and came by lots of interesting things," I said trying to be vague at first and catch her reaction.

"Oh yes, which rooms?" asked Tilde taking a dainty sip from her teacup.

I met Sebastian's eyes. He did not say anything. I was grateful for that.

"Just the cellar, we found a collection of grandfather's absinthe and an old suitcase stuffed with newspapers."

"I have counted over one thousand bottles. A treasure in its own right," said Sebastian.

"How odd," said Tilde, "Cecilia said she had none. Where did you say you found it? In the cellar? Well, I have not been down there for decades. My back," she patted her lower back, "Cecilia always took charge of that area."

"You mentioned about living at LaRose Gris prior to her," said Sebastian.

"Yes, I have worked as a cook since Mr. Etienne built the mansion. I remember the house with no front stairs or the stone walls around the garden. Young girl of twenty I was. Mr. Etienne brought Ms. Cecilia in a few years as a bride of eighteen. Soon Lydia was born, your mother." Tilde glanced at me and sighed.

"And my mother became a bride too. I found a picture in grandfather's old study."

When Tilde heard this, she put her cup down with such clatter it almost chipped.

"Was that man my father? Tilde, please tell me."

Tilde kept silent, her eyes downcast. We waited without forcing her to speak. A few moments passed until she said in a clear voice, "The man in that picture, the one in the uniform, is not your father. I hope Cecilia forgives me for saying this. But you need to know the truth."

"Then who is he?"

"His name was Major Robert Gordon He married your mother just before leaving for Asia with his marine unit. She went with him, the climate was good for her, and frankly, she was happy to escape her mother."

"Robert Gordon." The name sounded familiar to me. I concentrated as Sebastian taught me, erasing all thoughts. A snippet of the conversation between my grandmother and Mrs. Rochelle on the night when I found my crystal bead, floated from the depths of my mind. Her last name was Gordon, Rochelle Gordon. This meant Robert Gordon...

"...was Mrs. Rochelle's son! My mother married Mrs. Rochelle's son?"

"Yes, for five years Lydia lived abroad with her husband. She did not write a lot. Mr. Etienne always swore when the letters came. Blamed your grandmother because he thought she forced Lydia into marriage. I guess the news were not happy."

"Then what happened?"

"One day in the winter, she showed up without a warning. Said she left Robert for good. It started a huge row. She cried, and Cecilia cried."

Tilde started crying herself. I came up to her and hugged her again. She wrapped her plump arms around me.

"The biggest shock came when Lydia announced that she was expecting, and the baby was not Robert's."

"So who is my father then?"

"That, my child, I do not know. Lydia spent most of her time alone and refused to communicate with anyone. Dr. Schuele said she had depression and it would pass when the baby is born. But it did not happen, the birth was difficult, she was even more depressed after."

I found it disappointing. The handsome man in the picture was not my father. I had already dreamt of going to Thailand and finding him. I imagined running up to him in a new dress and saying, "I am your daughter Veronica!" He would grab and toss me in the air and tell me I was as beautiful as my mother. I turned to Sebastian and bit my lip to stop from crying. He gave me a napkin and excused himself.

"What happened to Robert Gordon?" I asked.

"He died in Vietnam. Rochelle took it hard. She also had a daughter, Adele's mother Marie. She ran away when at sixteen to join some crazy jazz band in New York. Rochelle was so disappointed by her..."

Tilde could go on forever with her memories. The events of the day caught up with me, I yawned. Sebastian came back, helped me with the coat, and wrapped his arm around my shoulders, an unexpected gesture.

"Take care of my flower," said Tilde wiping her tears with an apron.

"Always," promised Sebastian and drove me home, half-asleep beside him.

5. LAUGHING ANGEL

Veronica, please repeat these verbs."
Professor Dix pointed to the string of words on a small blackboard. We used yellow chalk for verbs, white for nouns, pink for adjectives.

"Olfactus, gustus, videre, tactus, cogitare, *if only Latin was as colorful*, I thought while repeating. Latin bored me, it removed mystery, and magic out of everything I ever hoped to read. So far, I studied verbs, structure, tenses, but no stories. I wanted to give up, and throw Professor's colored chalk at his jolly face.

Anna meandered into our classroom. It adjoined her office.

"Call for you, Gaspar, sounds important, something about canceling the happy hour at The Suds Palace."

"Such dorks. Veronica, use the verbs in five sentences each, while I sort out this grossness."

Anna rolled her eyes, and when Professor Dix disappeared behind the door, she grabbed my hand and pulled me out of the classroom.

"I scream, you scream, we all scream for ice cream, now that would sound hilarious in Latin," she said dragging me up the stairs and out the library to the café next door.

"Anna, you kidnapped me, what would Professor Dix say?"

"Chocolate, strawberry or vanilla? In Latin."

"Socolata, fragum, and I don't know 'vanilla' yet," I said stunned by her attention.

"Who cares, I was joking, let's get it all. For two months, I have been watching you torture Latin, and Latin torture you. Take a break, and I will let you in on a secret."

Surrounded by dishes full of ice cream sundaes and two banana splits, my hands and face sticky with strawberry sauce I listened to Anna recite the Latin verbs and use them in little funny sentences, which actually made sense.

"Use the language in real situations, that's the secret. Immerse yourself, apply it to your life, go crazy with it, and do not be afraid to make mistakes. *Vita est valebat*, life is an adventure. Why are you so gloomy?"

A lot sat on my mind lately, but not my studies. I had snooped in the suitcase we found in the cellar, and read the collection of newspaper clippings. Right away, I called Sebastian to show him the story. He looked remote, and his eyes filled with an unfamiliar emotion I never seen before. I did not know what to feel about it. I thought for a minute, and then decided to tell Anna everything. After all, she was the only girl I knew, she was nineteen, she might understand.

"I read the old newspapers from my grandfather's suitcase. My mother did not die like grandma said, she disappeared after I was born. She went out for a walk and never came back. They never found her body, and decided she drowned in the sea." This revelation poured out of me like a stream of water out of the open tap. Sebastian and Dr. Schuele believed it too, that she was dead. But I did not. I heard her voice coming from the crystal bead. She must be alive somewhere. I could not stop thinking about it.

Anna's dancing eyes became serious at once. She took my sticky hands in hers, "Believe in what makes you happy, it must be true. But give it some time."

"Give what time? We were looking all over for you," Sebastian's voice came from behind us. He did not sound amused.

"Oh, just two girls enjoying a little break from Dixie," said Anna and winked. I smiled at nickname she gave Professor Dix.

"I told Anna about the newspapers and my mother, and she was helping me with Latin."

Sebastian looked at both of us, his eyes warmed up. He understood my need to confide in someone, a girl.

"I would prefer if you did not dwell on things you can't change. Just live for today and concentrate on the future. If Miss Varley really wants to be a friend, she can help us plan your birthday party. Right, Miss Varley?"

"Sure, I will. Name the time and the place," said Anna and shot Sebastian a fiery gaze. He replied with a polite little bow. I toughed he did it to hide how startled he was by her. So was I, startled with the realization that I had a new friend.

From the seat at the head of a table, I watched flushed tipsy faces around me and realized it was a happiest day of my life. Silent waiter gave me a crisp linen napkin to protect the new dress while we dined. One year ago, I would never have dreamed about having friends or presents on my birthday. After the meal, two waiters carried in a tall cake decorated with chocolate roses and eleven candles. Rich vanilla crème and raspberry sauce dripped from the sides of this sweet work of art.

"Make a wish, Veronica. Make sure to blow out all of them," said Sebastian dressed in a black tuxedo jacket and a bow tie. His silver hair reached to his shoulders. I blew out the candles, the sparkling chandelier above tinkled from the clapping and loud singing of a birthday song. "Thank you, I already got my wish," I said and gestured at the smiling people at the table and at the pile of bright packages on the chair beside me, "may I open my presents now?"

I had never received so many presents before. Excitement gave way to impatience. Voices of encouragement rose from around the table as I reached for the first package.

"This one is from Professor Dix," I said reading the attached card. I removed the silver ribbon and unfolded the wrapping paper from a large volume of *The Complete History of Art*. Gaspar Dix never stopped teaching, even on my birthday. I could not wait to immerse myself in illustrations of Greek statues and frescoes from the

Renaissance. Professor gave me thumbs up and grinned. He looked very dapper with a long purple scarf wound around his neck reaching past his waist, which in my opinion went well with his tie-die shirt.

Anna Varley resembled a movie star with her shiny black hair, pale face, and blood red lipstick. She handed over her present. A small purple velvet pouch with a golden string held a small mirror in a filigree frame.

"This is a breath mirror," she said in her throaty voice, "to check if someone is alive or dead. Put it by the mouth like so. It can be handy one day, just saying."

She took the mirror, held it to her mouth for a second, and showed everyone a tiny spot of mist. Everything was such a joke to her. She took the oddest things, and made them amusing.

"Holy moly she's alive," said Gaspar Dix and kissed her on the scarlet lips.

I knew Anna tried to delight me in her own strange way, and said the small pocket mirror was what I always wanted. Sebastian glanced at me with approval.

"This one is from Winai." I put my hands together and gave our silent monk-housekeeper a little bow, unwrapped the cloth, and found a jar filled with green tea leaves. Winai had created it himself, with my initials embossed in the clay.

"You can also use this jar as a tea mug," said Sebastian.

Tilde gave me a cozy sweater, scarf, and mittens made of gray wool. She must have knitted all winter. I got up and hugged her, and as usual, she started crying. Winai reached out, touched her shoulder, and shook his head.

After came Dr. Schuele's present, a black lacquered box. Inside I found another box, and another smaller one after, ten altogether fitted into each other. He smiled watching me over his glasses and said every girl needs a special place to keep her secrets. Now I had to find more secrets, it was exciting.

My tutor Mr. Prendergast was unable to attend because he had a cold. He sent a calligraphy set with an instruction book. Later I planned to write a calligraphic 'Thank You' note for him.

Finally came Sebastian's present in a small package. Inside a silk pouch, I found my first brand new Tarot deck. I had been asking for one since I read about these fascinating divination cards in a library book. This deck turned out to be Waite Tarot, one of the many decks I would collect in the future, and my favorite. Anna promised to teach me. Professor Dix told me to get a Latin translation of each card. Anna and I glanced at each other and burst out laughing.

I thought about my first birthday party while watching Sebastian's sharp profile as we drove home in the mild spring rain. The entire day became one huge present. I thought it all happened because of him.

"Can I ask for a last present, Sebastian?"

He nodded without taking his eyes off the sleek road.

"I would like to move into my grandmother's suite. What do you think?"

"I don't see why not."

"Thank you. Can we stop by the cemetery on the way home?"

Sebastian nodded again. I appreciated his silent support.

The time has come to say a final goodbye to grandma. Although the tears refused to show, I had immense gratitude owed to her for saving me from the freezing stream last fall. I felt a little guilty, because my life had split in two parts. The solitary part before I found the crystal bead and the new life with Sebastian. I liked the second part much better. Even though I had lost the magic bead along with my grandmother, I found Sebastian and the good he brought with him instead.

I used to come to the LaRose mausoleum quite often with grandmother, to clean up and to prune surrounding rose bushes, but never noticed its resemblance to LaRose Gris. On my eleventh birthday, I realized it was a small-scale mansion of death. The black iron front gate had golden rose buds that ended with a sharp tip. A statue of an angel resembling an absinthe fairy sitting on a rose stood inside. The angel-fairy had a sly grin on her face, not at all sad. More like "See you here soon enough." I pointed it out to Sebastian. He chuckled and waived to Winai to come over with Tilde. She had fallen asleep with her head on Winai's shoulder during our ride. She was surprised to find herself at the LaRose Mausoleum.

To me, the cemetery looked like a sculpture garden with weeping willows, peaceful, full of quiet secrets, with clues written on gravestones. Now even more serene in the spring, with the new plants sprouting around, as if the buried encouraged life from beneath the damp earth. The gentle mounds of the graves appeared to be painted tender green with the fresh grass. They beckoned me to lie down and fall asleep. No sense of death, but peace walked the narrow path between the willows and the headstones. The peacefulness resonated in my soul as I arranged the flowers from my birthday table by the entrance and whispered, "Good bye grandma, I will always love you and wish you told me all your secrets before you died." I kissed the angel-fairy. The kiss left salt of the sea on my lips. Or, was it the taste of tears which finally had come and were running down my face like rivers from the heart? I felt Sebastian's arm around me and we left. The gates clanked behind us with the finality of death and for the first time the sight of Tilde's tears failed to irritate me.

I could not sleep for a long time lying in bed and listening to the rain's impatient fingers drumming on the roof. The spring decided not to wait. It awakened the slumbering nature, and my garden was calling.

Next morning Sebastian opened grandmother's rooms for the first time since her death.

6. THE LORE, THE CRAFT, AND THE GIFT

gathered enough courage, standing at the entrance of grandmother's bedroom, to face memories of my old life. As I stepped over the Ithreshold, nothing happened. The room appeared neat and indifferent with the furniture in its proper place. The wardrobe with a long mirror where I used to pose, the huge carved bed with *LR* carved in a chain of mahogany roses on the headboard, a dresser with an oval mirror, and a couple of stuffed chairs with curved legs. No memories remained, good or bad. They all drifted to the past.

Sebastian insisted on performing the incense and Tingsha ritual. We gave the room a good scrub after. Winai washed the windows and floors, I polished the furniture with lemon oil, and Sebastian checked and replaced the lights.

I favored a small alcove by the window with a chunky sofa and a shelf filled with books on gardening. I even had my own cute bathroom covered with a flowery wallpaper and resembled an inside of a gift box.

"Are you happy in your new castle, no sad thoughts?" asked Sebastian after we finished cleaning and moved my belongings.

"I feel grown up, and that I belong here."

I perched on a stool by the dresser and checked the drawers. They were all empty except the top one. Sebastian stood by the fireplace leaning his elbow on the mantle watching me. I could see his reflection in the mirror.

"Oh, look Sebastian. Face powder and lipsticks," I said pulling out a drawer, "and perfume, Chanel N°5, Chanel N°19 and N° 22."

I lined up the small bottles and opened them one by one to

spray all over myself. The bold fragrance enveloped me in the cloud of glamour and I sneezed. So did Sebastian.

"Very nice, Veronica. Only, please try to use just one. Chanel perfume is elegant a spray at a time. What are you doing now?" He asked as I unscrewed the bright red lipstick, and began to paint my lips.

"I want to look like a Queen of Hearts from Alice in Wonderland."

Sebastian came over, examined the collection of powder boxes, makeup tubes in the drawer, and whistled.

"Cecilia had quite a taste. Let me transform you. It's been ages since I played with face paints."

It astonished me to hear Sebastian would play with makeup like a little girl or a lady. Until he told me a story as he turned me away from the mirror and worked on my face.

The war in Europe left Sebastian an orphan and he had to live with the distant relatives in their inhospitable home. He left them at fifteen and joined the traveling theatre troupe. They entertained audiences throughout the central Europe after the liberation. For two years, he played either male or female roles and learned the art of acting in vaudeville, an old-fashioned comedy show with dancing, music and singing.

"Sometimes I had two or even three parts in a play, with a few minutes to change between the characters. We had so much fun, people loved us. The simple comedy gave them a happy escape from the grim after war reality."

A wistful note crept in Sebastian's voice as he was sharing his story. He became silent, and I had to pry out the rest, without much success.

"And then you became a sailor?"

"Yes, the theater company dissolved in a few seasons, and I got a job on one of the cargo ships from Rotterdam. That used to be the largest seaport in Europe. Perhaps still is."

"And you sailed for ten years and have been around the world many times?"

"Yes. Now close your eyes and do not peek. I have a surprise for you."

I did as he asked and waited for his command. Hoping he would continue with more stories about his adventures.

"Ready? Open your eyes when I count to three," said Sebastian turning me around, "one, two, three, and voila!"

I opened my eyes and saw two painted faces in the mirror. One was supposed to be me and the other Sebastian. I had transformed into a real Queen of Hearts, with hair teased into a frizzy brown cloud, a white powdered face, huge outlined eyes and a tiny heart of a mouth painted in the middle of my powdered lips. A sad clown with a pale face, black lips, and a painted tear on his cheek gazed at me from above.

"Pierrot at your service, Your Highness. How about a snack in the royal kitchen?" Said Sebastian and bowed offering his arm.

"Oh yes, kind Sir, or off with your head!"

Sebastian grabbed his head in a mock horror and ran away from me. I followed him laughing all the way down.

Winai almost dropped the platter when we showed up breathless with laughter in our weird makeup, but smiled like a conspirator as he poured tea.

"This is so much fun, we should play more often. I want to learn how to do the theater makeup. Can we get a book?"

"I feel like a kid again. To the theatre, to the imagination of the innocents," said Sebastian and toasted with his tea as always.

"How would you like to go to a real performance, Your Highness?"

"Yes, please, the Queen would be quite happy indeed."

I have never been to the theatre. Only in my imagination when I read books. Sebastian promised to get tickets to something interesting soon. I did not care. Any performance would be exciting. We had tea and played cards until Sebastian told me to go wash off the makeup and start my homework.

"Wait, I forgot to show you something."

I slid off the chair and went to my new room for two leather bound books I found on grandmother's bookshelf. I went through the books and magazines hoping to find something else about my mother, most books on the shelf were only on plants and horticulture.

The two books I found had titles "The Herb Lore" and "The Craft." Pages of "The Lore" had notes in Cecilia's small script on how to make remedies from medicinal herbs. The second book had no handwriting, only underlined passages about growing herbs. I showed the books to Sebastian and told him about my wish to plant a small herb garden and make remedies the way grandmother instructed.

Sebastian had no objections and only encouraged me, "Spending time with a rewarding hobby will take your mind off sad thoughts about your mother and grandmother. I know you ponder about them, you need to release the darkness. Gardening will help."

My hands itched to begin gardening, to plant, to take care and in return receive magical gifts of herbs and flowers.

Saturday mornings kept me busy with lessons at the library with Professor Dix. After lessons, we always had lunch in Boston, and then visited Tilde on the way home. Sometimes we went on a long walk on the beach if the weather allowed.

One Saturday Sebastian asked me to wear something special.

"In the afternoon we are going to an opera performance. Gaspar and Anna are coming with us."

"Opera, do I know which one?" I wanted to show off my newfound knowledge. After Sebastian's tale about his theatre adventures, I read up on performing arts and he bought records of different types of music for me. 'Famous Opera Arias' became one of my favorites among some jazz and classical baroque music of Handel and Mozart. I did not care for the loud rock or whiny country music.

We drove in Hermes the Rolls Royce. I stepped out as a real lady dressed in a dark blue dress with a lace collar and my hair in a high curled ponytail. Sebastian gave the keys to a young valet in front of the theatre and we walked into the tall white narrow building.

To me, the Boston Opera House resembled a castle fit for a grandest Queen. The crystal chandeliers, sweeping staircase, well dressed people proceeding to the red velvet and gold balconies reminded me of Cinderella's royal ball. I admired the blue painted sky ceiling with angels floating on clouds looking down at us.

We found our seats. Professor Dix and Anna were already there. Gaspar switched with me so I could have a better view of the stage. I sat enthralled by the sights and sounds of a performance just about to begin. Anna commented on the unusual number of young people. She also complained how opera always reminded her of wailing cats as Professor Dix took swig from a flat bottle hidden inside his jacket.

A hush fell over the audience as the lights dimmed. A scarlet curtain flew up and the singer came upon the stage in slow measured steps. His arms were reaching towards the audience, hands hidden in the long sleeves of his tunic. An expression of sadness graced his painted face. The conductor raised his arms. The music affected the whispering and fidgeting audience into a complete stillness. The melody flowed in a gentle wave as the actor began to sing in an angelic soprano. I checked Sebastian's reaction. The singer appeared to be a grand opera master, his voice so clear and beautiful.

"What is this aria? It's so sad."

"*Lacrimosa Requiem*" by Mozart, his last composition, and the actor is singing in *falsetto*."

I had no idea what *falcetto* meant, but wished the beautiful moment held forever. It did, until a loud jolt of a rapid riff from electric guitar shattered the magic.

A second curtain flew up at the back of the stage, and revealed a rock band exposed in the pulsing lights. The band continued its interpretation of Mozart's opera in a wild beat.

The musicians whipped their long hair. Their tattooed arms worked the loud instruments. The opera singer changed his angelic voice to shrieking, moving and gyrating along the stage. He ripped the tunic off to reveal the black leather pants and a torn top. The youth from the audience moved closer to the stage and cheered with raised arms. Some older people just left.

I squeezed Sebastian's arm, "Sebastian, what's happening?"

Sebastian said something, his words drowned in the noise. I noticed Anna's empty seat and poked Professor Dix.

"Where is Anna?"

"Let's hope she doesn't fall in the orchestra pit," he pointed to the jumping crowd.

The wild music seemed to excite them. The fireworks exploded at the end of the show the audience whistled and yelled for more.

At last, the noise subsided, and the crowd spilled down the grand staircase carrying us along. I could hardly hear, as if my head was full of cotton. Disoriented, I clung to Sebastian's arm.

"Are you all right Veronica?" asked Sebastian, his voice came from far away.

"My head feels funny, my ears are plugged."

"It's the loudness. You are not used to it. It should pass soon enough."

"Loved the concert, Seb my man," said Professor Dix and slapped Sebastian on the shoulder.

"It was too loud," I said while Sebastian kept silent.

Anna Varley appeared behind us, her eyes flashed under the smudged makeup, hair wild like Medusa's.

"Max Black is a dream! A Rock Star pretending to sing opera and switch midway. I laughed so hard at the stuffed suits that left. I'm in love. Totally."

"I'm sure *I* would never love anybody who's that loud, and especially a lying Rock Star," I said to blubbering Anna meaning every word.

"Never say never," said Sebastian with a remote expression.

"Oh, touché cliché," said Anna and pulled surprised Professor Dix by the hand, "Let's go, Dixie, I need to make a love potion to snare Max Black."

"See you next week, friends," said Professor Dix and did his favorite thumbs up. Sebastian gave him a weak wave and put his hand on my shoulder.

"I had no idea. I assumed it would be a real opera. I apologize, Veronica."

"Don't worry Sebastian, maybe one day I might learn to like rock music. You will take me to the theater again, right?" I said, touched at his apology. The concern he had in his eyes was worth one thousand opera performances.

In a few weeks, my life became quite busy. Mr. Prendergast and I worked on the lessons assigned by Professor Dix. I also practiced my scales on the piano in the drawing room. Mr. Prendergast would sit and nod with his eyes closed until falling asleep as always.

After lunch Sebastian and I meditated, later I would study my Tarot cards and astrology books from the library, or I was free to work in my garden.

I cleared the flowerbeds from the last year's growth and added compost, pruned shrubs and roses with Winai's help. We swept the stone walkways and prepared the space for our summer lessons in the gazebo. Once the initial preparations were completed, I gave my full attention to grandmother's books. Sebastian was quite interested in them, but I wanted to plant everything without his help and to surprise him with the results.

"True enlightenment begins with the pain in your back and calluses on your hands," he said. The meaning of his words soon became clear as I worked.

I had tackled the first book. "The Lore" had a list of plants to be seeded. I picked up a seed catalogue in Boston and with Mr. Prendergast's help made up the order.

The seeds arrived a few days later in tiny paper envelopes with planting instructions. *Matricaria Chamomilla*, chamomile flowers, liked well-drained top soil and a sunny spot. *Plantago Major*, plantain, preferred sandy soil and wind. *Alchemilla*, lady's mantle, on the other hand, liked to be near the streams and moist rich soil of the pastures. Every plant needed its own conditions for growth. It became quite frustrating to find correct growing spots for the seeds, similar to pleasing a crowd of fussy children. In addition, I had twenty tiny envelopes.

Winai came to the rescue after seeing how I crouched on hands and knees for hours. He showed me how to prepare a raised foundation, make a little groove with a trowel, and seed the plants like putting salt in the pot, rubbing my thumb and index finger together. I showed him the printed instructions. He shook his head, and raised his arms to the sky and sun.

"You mean nature will help me?"

He nodded, the skin around his eyes crinkled as he smiled. I had to water the soil for three days and stop for another three until the first pale green sprouts showed up. Impatient, I checked several times per day if my herbs had grown. Winai pointed his palms to the ground and made a slow pushing gesture. *Calm down, plants will grow when the time is right.* I decided to take his advice and turned my attention to the second book "The Craft".

I did not ask Mr. Prendergast for help and ordered the seeds myself. The envelopes took longer to arrive. I prepared another raised bed not far from "The Lore Garden" and planted "The Craft Garden". Winai made a low fence to separate them and I painted the name plaques with my calligraphy brushes listening to Bach and chuckling about the stupid rock opera concert.

The end of June brought warm and kind weather. The sea behaved as a calm gentle lamb, and the night crept in much later giving us white nights to enjoy. We lounged in the gazebo by the lanterns and read, or Sebastian would tell stories. He was an excellent storyteller. As he talked and I imagined the blue faraway shores of exotic lands washed by the brilliant sea, or patient water buffaloes in the rice fields, the sound of a tolling bell carried by the wind over the Alpine valley. He told stories of the Far East and his discovery of spiritual life, and the desire to share his knowledge with others.

"I met a unique man. His name was Bodidharma, a true Guru. He became my spiritual father, my teacher. The beginning of the path showed me my weaknesses. He taught how to access the inner guru and be self-sufficient. I have never chosen the way of the monk, but tried to live as one. To share the blessings."

"Where is your teacher now?"

"He had passed on to the next level of existence. He was Winai's Guru as well, the same one he is honoring with the seven year silence."

"So what happens next?"

"He will have to return to Thailand and get his power of speech back after a special ritual."

"I wish we could go too."

"And we will. We are not going to sit here and grow roots forever. You need to experience the world, Veronica."

His words instilled hope. They opened doors for fantasies, 'night flights' as I secretly called them. I would lie in bed and let my imagination take me on an exploration of the stars and fantastic magical worlds. In one of them, I hoped to meet my mother. I continued to have a lingering hope she was alive somewhere and waiting for me.

To show my appreciation for Sebastian's storytelling I invited him to my new herb garden.

"Can I invite Professor Dix and Anna? And can you please pick up Tilde, she cannot walk this far now."

Sebastian took my hand and turned it over like a fortuneteller.

"Oh! I see a garden party soon. My wish is your command Your Majesty," he said in a silly mock accent.

"It's the other way around, Sebastian."

"Sorry. Oh, I see Majesty's bedtime approaching."

"I get it. Good night then, Mr. Misfortune Teller." I could stay up and listen to his stories forever.

On the day of the garden party, I dressed in a green taffeta skirt and a black top, my curls left unbound. I paced around the courtyard trying to work off the knot of nervousness, pride, and anticipation. The result of my efforts, my first "grown up" project was about to be open to the world. From the tiny seeds sprinkled in the dark soil, I nurtured a small oasis of amazing plants, each a separate universe.

In the morning, I heard noises coming from the kitchen and guessed Winai was cooking up a fantastic lunch. Dr. Schuele arrived early to make phone calls in the drawing room. Sebastian dressed in white shirt, green vest, and black slacks, waited by the gate running fingers through his long silver hair. No one could appear so cool and composed for our first house party.

With a screech and a cloud of dust, Gaspar Dix arrived in a flamboyant winged bright yellow car on sleek back wheels with a white stripe. It did not surprise me when he jumped out dressed in same bright yellow jacket. It clashed with his red lion mane and torn jeans.

Anna exited the car in her usual black and a scarlet line of the lips. She wore a suit that made her look like a figure eight and very high heels. Sebastian grabbed her by the waist as she lost balance on the uneven paving bricks of our courtyard. I felt a little jealous when I saw his fingers press into her lower back.

They picked up Tilde from the Cider Village. She emerged slowly from the winged yellow car, resembling a wise old turtle. She also wore green to complement Sebastian and me, because I told her about our outfits a day before.

"Ready to party?" said Gaspar Dix looking around.

"You are always ready," Anna jabbed him in the ribs and he doubled up laughing. Sebastian waved for Dr. Schuele to come down and meet everyone. I helped Tilde to climb the stairs.

"Welcome, friends. I have something to entertain your taste buds. Follow me," said Sebastian and showed our guests in.

Winai met us in the hall with a tray of bite size canapés.

"Great pad, Veronica," said Professor Dix and whistled, "I did not know you live in the castle."

"Any ghosts here, secret passages, a dungeon?" said Anna darting her eyes around dramatically. She did not sound crazy now as she did once in the library vault, just curious and excited. I was beginning to know all of them quite well.

"Let your fears rest Ms. Varley," said Dr. Schuele, embracing her by the waist as he showed her inside, "This mansion is not old. It was built by Etienne LaRose in 1935 when he came from France and purchased this seaside property."

Why are they always trying to hold on to her waist? I thought with mild irritation. Sebastian dropped bits of history about our house as we proceeded to the drawing room.

On the center table, he had arranged goblets, Absinthe LaRose, a crystal pitcher of ice water, sugar cubes, and a special spoon shaped like an Eifel Tower.

"*Deos meus*, oh my god, I just died and went to heaven," sighed Gaspar Dix when he spotted the arrangement. Everyone flanked the table, curious to see what would happen next.

Sebastian lined up the goblets and measured a shot of Absinthe LaRose for each. After, he rested the silver spoon with a sugar cube on top of a glass and slowly poured the ice water from the misty pitcher. Absinthe LaRose label described this ritual in steps. The ice water created mysterious milky swirls in the emerald green absinthe, as if some new life developed within and the drink became opalescent.

"*Le Louch*, liberation of the essence and of the mind," said Dr. Schuele and smacked his lips. Sebastian passed goblets to everyone. Even I received one. Tilde began to object, but Sebastian called the drink my birthright. It did not stop him to take the glass away from me after I took the first sip. Professor Dix snatched it from Sebastian and held on to both glasses as if he won something. Anna and I laughed.

"To love, friendship, and happiness," said Sebastian raising his glass.

"Prosit," Gaspar Dix raised his goblet.

"To health," we echoed after him.

The moment had come. All eyes turned to me as I opened the French doors to lead everyone in the garden.

"I found books left by my grandmother Cecilia. She wrote about growing the special kind of plants. They are pretty and healing. I planted them with Winai's help and now I am going to share the results with you."

Everyone clapped and I heard encouraging catcalls from Professor Dix who received another jab in the ribs from Anna. We walked down the garden stairs to our vegetable patch where I had my two rows, *The Lore* and *The Craft*.

"How lovely, they look like graves," said Anna and clasped her hands with delight. I guess they did. They were also pretty with abundant healthy plants.

"And you made a calligraphy note beside each one. In Latin." Professor Dix sounded proud, "Now let's see, *Taraxacum officinale, Matricaria chamomilla, Alchemilla vulgaris*. Enlighten us, Veronica."

I took a deep breath and begun my presentation.

"They are medicinal herbs and they help with different health problems. The ones that Professor Dix named are Dandelion, Chamomile, and Lady's Mantle. There are also..."

"They are also known as weeds, Veronica. Are you saying that you planted the garden of weeds? Most gardeners strive for quite the opposite," said Professor Dix interrupting me.

"Let her continue my friend, she must have a good explanation," said Sebastian and placed a calming hand on Gaspar's shoulder.

"Why do you call them weeds?" I said, "Take dandelion for example. It's great in salads instead of spinach, makes great tea against tummy aches, and can made into wine. Now, how is that bad? And chamomile is good for calming the nerves and for making the hair all nice and shiny." I would go on with my hot defense but Dr. Schuele reached for my hand and shook it with such vigor my shoulder hurt.

"The child is absolutely correct. I use herbal medicine where nothing else works. Cecilia used to be an expert in making remedies."

"Yes, Gaspar. I guess you found something new you never *knew*," said Anna.

"You did everything right Veronica, we are proud of you and your little garden," said Sebastian, "By the way Gaspar, absinthe is made with these very weeds you scorn."

"Mr. LaRose mentioned once that the secret ingredients of his absinthe may be found underfoot and in the garden," said Tilde nodding her head, "and when people asked which ones he would name yew berries as one of them."

"Are they not poisonous?" asked Gaspar.

"Obviously not, we are still standing," said Dr. Schuele and toasted everyone with his goblet.

"How about showing us the other row?" said Sebastian.

We moved to next green row and again, Professor Dix read the names on the plaques. "*Digitalis Purporea, Veratrum album, Sanguinaria Canadensis.*" This time Dr. Schuele interrupted him.

"What? Foxglove, hellebore, bloodroot. I do not believe it Veronica. You planted poisonous, extremely dangerous plants. Why?"

"Because grandmother's book said these herbs made the person who grows them powerful, and they can also help in small amounts. Isn't it good?"

"But just a few drops of Foxglove could kill a grown man, and the blood root you can't even touch! Powerful poisons, that's what they are."

"I touched them, nothing happened to me." I was disappointed, not ready for such a reaction.

"Now, now my flower. No need to get upset, the good Doctor is only concerned about you, love," said Tilde and pulled me into embrace.

"I suggest we destroy these plants before the child hurts herself and everyone around," said Dr. Schuele.

"I understand your concern, Doctor. We will do nothing of the sort. Veronica worked very hard and researched the subject. I am sure we will take all possible precautions. If she was clever enough to grow the garden, she is clever enough to know what to do with it. Good job, Veronica," said Sebastian, "now let's go back and pay appreciation to Winai's efforts with our lunch."

Everyone clapped including Winai and Dr. Schuele who appeared serious and worried. I noticed Anna did not utter a word during our last exchange and was staring at me in a most disturbing way.

As we walked back to the house, she asked me to show her the painted mandalas, and we excused ourselves for a few minutes. The moment we entered the meditation room, Anna closed the doors behind her and pounced on me.

"The herbs in the first row, what were you planning to do with them?"

I tried to take a step back but she dug her scarlet nails in my upper arms.

"Dry them in the sun and grind them into teas. Let go, you are hurting me," I said looking straight into her dark eyes. I could see no irises, like staring into bottomless black holes.

"And the others?"

"Make them into liquids and lock them up in crystal bottles. Now let go," I said louder and shook her hands off.

"When were you planning to do it? Tell me Veronica, please." She did not dare to grab me again.

"When the moon is young of course, and does not pull the energy," I said without giving it a second thought. The reply came out naturally. I researched the subject well.

"I knew it from the moment in the library when you demanded to see those old manuscripts."

"I don't understand, Anna, please explain, you are scaring me."

"Veronica you are a magical person. You have The Gift, very special and a rare one. I tried to be like you once. Your magic is much stronger. You seem to know things naturally. Magic is drawn to you."

"What's going on here? I thought I heard someone yelling," Sebastian pushed the doors wide open.

"Nothing," Anna and I said together.

"Then please join us, our feast is awaiting," said Sebastian scanning our faces.

Winai created a vegetarian lunch suitable for a Maharaja. We showed our appreciation by finishing every dish to the last crumb. Mushroom tofu soup followed by curried rice, spicy vegetables in coconut sauce, bamboo salad, rice flour muffins and black bean ice cream for dessert. Anna and I kept exchanging glances. I could not stop thinking about being magical. I believed her, because deep down inside I knew. Perhaps the lost crystal bead had awakened this knowledge.

Before everyone left, I came to Anna's side and invited her to come over more often. As usual, she did something unexpected by kissing me on both cheeks.

"If I ever have a daughter I wish she will be as special as you, little sister."

The next morning I found Sebastian meditating by the stream in the early sun. The gentle wind carried the cries of seagulls from the beach. I tiptoed down and sat behind him. His shirt was off, a tattoo of a script ran in two rows down his back. I reached and traced the characters with my finger. "What do these letters mean?"

"This is a life mantra in Sanskrit *"Have dreams, life is abundant. Life is abundant, dreams are gone."*

"I don't understand."

"When you have a dream, you have a purpose. Now, imagine you had no dreams. What would you be? Do not try to answer these questions Veronica with your mind. Think with your heart, this is how you understand."

"But why is it on your back? You don't see it."

"It's for the person who is meditating behind me. I would meditate on the mantra written on the person's back in front of me. The order I joined had ninety monks. For ninety days, I would have a different mantra to meditate. The pattern would be repeated again as a way to enlightenment."

"When was it? Why did you leave?"

"It was a mistake to join in the first place. I thought I could make a good monk. Alas, I am too much in love with the world. I hated the solitude of the dark cave I had to endure for nine days every three months. I like light and laughter," he said and tickled me, "besides, I was meant to take care of you, Veronica."

I looked in his eyes for a long moment and shifted my gaze.

"The stream is so beautiful and clear now. It's hard to believe it killed my grandmother and took away my crystal bead."

I looked at Sebastian again, his open honest face with straight features and clear eyes. The sun highlighted the natural blond streaks in his long silver hair. I noticed fine lines around his eyes and a deep one running on his forehead. I loved him for his patience, his friendship, and most of all his ability to listen and understand.

"When I found my crystal bead it told me about my mother. When I fell through the ice I thought she came for me."

"Your mother?" He sounded worried.

"I know things now because I understand the magic. Anna said I have The Gift, and I believe her, the crystal bead told me the same." I moved closer to him and took his hand. "The crystal bead brought you, Sebastian. You came and made my life different and happy. Like a dream came through, now I dream of finding magic."

"You make me happy too. We will go on adventures, I promise. You will continue to learn. There is a magic in you. It is your own imagination. I knew way before Anna said anything."

We heard the bell Winai used to announce lunchtime.

"Ah, lunch. Now I feel like Pavlov's dog. Veronica, let's go and toast our happy life with the fine green tea Winai makes. I'm starving," said Sebastian pulling his shirt on.

He held me around the shoulders as we walked back to the house. I felt protected and loved like never before, and already dreaming of adventures waiting for me ahead.

7. PROSHA, OR FIVE YEARS LATER

Sebastian's faint voice came through the open window.

"Veronica, I need to talk to you, please come up."

I ignored him, preferring to brood about my recent encounter with the locals. I have been sitting on the stone steps in front of the mansion for an hour. They promised to come over, but no one showed up, as I expected.

A few days ago, I took a walk from the Cider Village in the rain, enjoying the rare windless afternoon and the April mist drifting along the road. My sixteenth birthday a month away gave me a lot to think about. I pulled the hood off to absorb the fresh scent of the spring and shook my long curls free. Over the past five years, my hair turned a shade darker than my childhood chestnut and became even more untamed. Soon the rain plastered the curls over my face, and I kept pushing them aside in order to see ahead, enjoying the gentle raindrops.

A car drove by with a big splash and stopped a few feet ahead. As I passed by, a village girl rolled down the window. A familiar looking blonde was at the wheel, two of her friends were visible inside.

"Hi, you are from the mansion, right? Do you want a lift?" asked the girl. The other two just stared.

"This is kind of you, but why are you offering?" I asked, skeptical because the village kids usually avoided me. Always in flocks, they even crossed the street to the other side when I walked by. Only Evan Wood mocked me on occasion, but somewhat out of habit now, because I never reacted to his baiting the way he wanted me to.

"Um, it's like, raining and stuff," said the girl beside the blonde driver, and blushed. The girl on the back seat snickered. I never believed they stopped out of a desire to help, rather saw it as an opportunity to satiate their curiosity about me.

"All right, thank you," I said and opened the back door. The snickering girl moved over as I dumped my soaked bag and coat on the beige seat between us. The car started and slowly navigated towards LaRose Gris. The two girls continued to stare at me in silence until I introduced myself. They followed my example. Nancy the driver, Penny the tomato face, the girl beside me mumbled some name and snickered in her hand again, then more awkward silence. I watched them from under my curtain of hair and thought how different they are in comparison to me. These village girls were so bland and proper, and I bet they knew nothing about death, ancient manuscripts, or the opera.

All of a sudden, the mumbling girl beside me made an odd comment.

"The guy you live with, how old is he? He's dime," her tone of voice implied something inappropriate. The girls in the front seat froze anticipating my answer.

I decided to use her own weapon, "Why don't you come in and ask him yourself? He might like you too."

The reply came out rather rude, so to give them a second chance I said, "I will show you around the mansion."

The girl snickered again, Penny shrugged and asked, "I like your dress, is it your grandmother's?"

I knew she was mocking me, but played along, "As a matter of fact yes. I love wearing my dead grandmother's things. Don't you?"

"Was she a witch?" asked Nancy the driver.

"The most powerful witch. And I'm just like her. You want me to show you?"

The girls at the front sat up a little straighter, the one beside me mumbled, "Told you," to no one in particular and we continued to drive without any further conversation.

When we got to the stone gates of the mansion, I asked again, "So are you coming in? It could be fun."

"Next time, tomorrow maybe," said Nancy.

"All right, see you tomorrow at noon, thank you for the ride," I said and got out.

This stilted ride was the first and most likely the last interaction with the people my age from Cider Village. They never intended to come back. I wished they did, and try my herbal teas that would make them do silly things.

Certain plants have properties to make one see in psychedelic colors, feel like the ground is caving or the fabric falls apart at the touch. Observing reactions to hallucinations are fun. Anna and I had gathered, dried, and prepared dozens of plants that make the dreams vivid and the spirit light. Gaspar Dix volunteered to be our test subject, as long as I recited their names and properties in Latin. Gaspar's teaching made this task easier. I became fluent in Latin by thirteen. This language opened the gates to understanding Spanish, French, and Italian with ease.

Sebastian interrupted my musings again by coming through the doors and joining me on the step.

"Veronica, it's important we discuss this matter. According to your grandmother's will you are coming of age in less than a month."

"I don't care. Leave me alone. I don't want to talk about the money. Do what you want."

Sebastian ignored my moodiness. He became familiar with it when the moods took permanent hold of me when I turned fourteen. Everyone I knew had to stay away during the times when the darkness ruled in my head. I enjoyed melancholy, solitude made me happy. Nobody seemed to understand that, even Sebastian.

"You're right, it's about the money. We need to make important decisions about your legacy, and you are an owner of this estate."

As always, only an eternal patience emanated from Sebastian.

I turned to face him. His long hair became silver over the years.

He wore it in a graceful wave over his shoulders, his eyes clear and cool as always, full of concern, with vectors of wrinkles at the corners. The black shirts he favored emphasized his paleness and slimness. The scent of fresh sandalwood lingered around him like an aura.

We had this conversation before. According to him, our funds were running low. The travelling we did over the years and the estate upkeep drained most of the trust left by my grandparents. Sebastian refused to sell the remaining Absinthe LaRose and rejected to sell some land around the estate. Conversations about money annoyed me. I felt powerless when the time came for the "real life" decisions. If Sebastian asked to do a translation or a Tarot reading, I would do a stellar job.

"Sebastian, leave me alone. I can do more translations. Gaspar will send even more cheater students to buy my Latin essays. And we have a whole list of people who keep sending money for the fresh tinctures and tisanes. And don't *you* have any money?"

He shook his head, "Whatever humble means I have would not be enough, I tried to live as a Buddhist monk before coming here, remember? I had another idea. Instead of selling the land, we can build on it. The Cider Village became quite a vacation spot. Dr. Schuele has offered to put up some funds for the buildings. We will have to pay him back of course."

"Build what?"

"The cottages. To rent them out to the summer crowd."

"Where?"

"This is your decision. Where do you think would be a good place to start?"

Poor Sebastian was trying to involve me. I did not want to be caught on that hook. Cottages meant people, and I did not want anyone around. With a final look at the driveway, I scrambled to my feet and walked towards the door.

"I don't care. Leave me alone," I said again and went to brood upstairs.

"Go and meditate Veronica," Sebastian said to my retreating back, "invite the white light into your thoughts and your being will float on the wings of change."

I shrugged, Sebastian was always right. The change remained the only constant in our lives. If we did not experience change, we would not live. I needed a change. The life at LaRose Gris became too dull, too predictable. I felt stifled, like my face was pressed against a glass ceiling. I needed to get away, alone. To explore the world on my own terms, without a guardian always holding my hand and explaining every step of the way. I dreamt of discovering profound wonders laying in wait for me somewhere. After years of studying, creating a large herb garden, reading, and deciphering compelling ancient manuscripts in Gaspar's hidden vault, I craved more knowledge. I wanted to travel. The sixteenth birthday would give me the freedom I needed to get away.

In my bedroom, I stood in front of the mirror and looked deep and long into my own eyes. *Are you sure? Are you ready?* I asked my pale reflection, pulled a raincoat from the wardrobe, and went out. I needed to clear my head, to think. I had discovered long ago, that solitary walks on the beach, open to all elements, had always put my thoughts in perspective, and calmed me down.

The sand turned dark gray from the recent tide. I walked among the seaweed looking for shells or other odd items like old shoes or rubbish washed back to land. I liked to gather those presents from the sea and arrange them on the dried tree branches scattered on the beach, like strange skeletal 'Christmas trees'. Many decorated the dunes, untouched by the sea and elements. My beach, my dunes, my loneliness plunged me deeper into melancholy. As I walked, different scenarios on how to break the news to Sebastian played in my head. Should I write him a letter, tell him outright or just run away?

Deep in thought, I did not notice the new tide had soaked my boots and the hem of my dress. I decided to turn back and took the path by the garden wall. As I turned the corner of the carriage house I saw Dr. Schuele's car parked in front of the mansion.

"My dear, you look lovely. You're growing like a sapling, taller every time I see you," Dr. Schuele kissed me on both cheeks, European style. I had to bend, being a little taller than he was. Tilde, our old housekeeper, still lamented after all these years about my thinness. I liked the way I looked - tall, thin with wild hair, green eyes, and straight nose peppered with fading freckles.

"Thank you for helping us with the cottages. Sebastian told me about his plans. Are you here to discuss the project?" I said hooking my arm through his.

"In a way. I have something else to discuss with you."

Sebastian asked us to the kitchen for tea. We followed. I poured the water in the kettle while Sebastian turned on the stove.

The kitchen stood bare and cold for a year now. I missed Winai who always created such a lively tempest with pots and pans. He had decided to stay in Thailand after fulfilling his oath of silence. We traveled overseas together for the ceremony. On the day we left his monastery, he put his hands on my shoulders and told me that we outgrew the need for his presence. Sebastian and I would do fine without him.

"I will always be here if you need me, and I will always help if you ask. You are my seedling lotus. If I continued to nurture the seedling, you would not bloom, because the true strength and beauty develops in storms and through self-reliance. I will give you a mantra before we part: *There are no coincidences, but messages from the eternal spirit,*" said Winai and wiped my tears with his gentle hand.

I did not agree with him, with his oath of silence fulfilled, he had to come back with us. I begged and cried, and asked for another year or two, but he agreed to be a schoolmaster at the school of his order without telling me. Sebastian knew about his plans, but did not interfere. Perhaps my moodiness began with Winai's departure. I considered it one of the reasons.

I perched on the counter by the sink with the tea mug in my hands. Sebastian was leaning on the window ledge and Dr. Schuele took a chair by the table. He stirred his tea for a long while.

"I will do everything in my power to help you, but this is not why I am here," he put the teaspoon down, "I am retired, and my arthritis is getting worse, so is Tilde's. As a matter of fact, we have known each other for almost fifty years," his voice drifted. I kept staring into my tea, because I was afraid of what Dr. Schuele was about to say next.

"This damp cold climate is taking its toll on both of us. We talked and decided to move to Baden where I was born. The mineral springs will be a good therapy for our health."

"I knew it. You are leaving me too," I jumped off the counter and threw the mug in the sink.

"Veronica, stop this," murmured Sebastian.

"All right, I understand. Go. Have a nice life."

I wanted to run out but Sebastian stopped me by taking hold of my shoulders, his arms like an unyielding vice.

"I'm sure Dr. Schuele and Tilde do not need our permission. Don't you think they deserve a better life?" said Sebastian and released me.

Dr. Schuele looked at me over his glasses as he always did, and said as if addressing a child, "I want to live out my remaining days in my Motherland. I have been away for too long. Tilde has been my close friend for almost fifty years. We need each other."

He took off his glasses and reached for the handkerchief in his pocket. The sight of his tears made me uncomfortable so I disguised my embarrassment with indignation.

"First Winai left, and then a month ago Gaspar and Anna announced they were leaving. And now you and Tilde."

A spasm in my throat caused me to take a deep breath, then sarcasm and fury poured out with all the force I could muster, "Happy birthday, Veronica, we are leaving. You are all alone now. *Have a nice life*," I mocked them, "Oh sorry, I have Sebastian. When are *you* leaving, Sebastian, tomorrow, in the winter, next year?" I directed my wrath at him, "Well guess what? I am leaving too. I do not need you and I do not want you"

I stormed out, feeling guilty for my outburst, but happy to proclaim my intentions. Everything happens for a purpose.

For weeks, I mulled over the fact that Gaspar was leaving. Anna, a true Bostonian who swore not to ever betray her beloved city, decided to follow, because she loved him more.

"We wouldn't survive a minute without each other," she said without her usual mockery. I understood, and decided not spoil her decision by expressing my own hurt and disappointment.   Their work at the Boston Library had ended. They fully translated and classified all of the ancient manuscripts, which lay bound and waiting for the future scholars.

As I progressed with my studies, the mysteries of the ancient writing became revealed to me over the years. By following their path in history, we discovered that the old manuscripts came with the initial donation of books to the Boston Library from France in the nineteenth century. They were not books of magic, but books about magic. Hundreds accounts of witnesses, gathered and recorded by priests and scholars over the centuries. They did not teach how to use the power of magic. The manuscripts provided a recorded proof of its existence in unexpected places, sometimes even within the hand's reach.

Anna continued to nurture my 'Gift' by introducing me to folklore, and dragging me around to participate in the covens and occult gatherings she joined out of curiosity. We were always on the lookout for the unexplained, unusual, and sometimes horrific. Once she even got in trouble with Sebastian when I bragged to him about witnessing a real demonic ritual with reversed prayers and a possessed priestess who tore off her clothing and screamed prophesies in an unknown tongue.

"How could you be so naive? It is just another cruel and greedy cult. They prey on lambs like you for their energy, money, time. Don't be naïve, Anna," he stared her down as she was about to stage one of her outbursts of contradiction, "If you want divinity, look within yourself. You are divine. Everything starts here," he tapped his chest and his temple, "you create reality with your own thoughts and dreams. Veronica, were our lessons in vain?"

"No, of course not, Sebastian," I said and noted not to mention our escapades to him, even when they were funny.

Over the years, Anna and I became best friends, and in time, I began to regard her as a sister. Now I had no one left, except Sebastian. They were all leaving like the actors at the end of a play. The curtain fell and I remained alone in a silent theatre, with shadows of memories and echoes of applause still sounding in my head.

On my sixteenth birthday, I left early in the morning in Hermes the old Royce. I had no permission to drive yet because of some silly rules about having a driver's license, but Sebastian gave me lessons since I was fourteen. Hermes was my car, I kept the Rolls spotless clean and shiny. My appearance never failed to elicit stares and rude snap shots from the tourists. I guess the combination of my long dark dresses and the huge Rolls Royce Phantom were quite a shock to them.

I drove to the cemetery and had a long conversation with the angel-fairy statue at the LaRose mausoleum where my grandparents rested in an eternal sleep. I knew my mother's tomb stood empty. It made me happier, she might be alive somewhere. My mood lightened up after expressing feelings without anyone contradicting or preaching. The angel smiled at me in the most serene way, its stone eyes focused in the space above. I brushed the dust off its wings and laid a laurel wreath on its head. I would be gone for a long time, and laurels do not wither.

After the cemetery, I went to visit Tilde to assure her of my support about her decision to move to Baden on the edge of the Black Forest and the healing springs. I promised to visit and to write. It was a lie. I intended to do neither. My travels would take me far away. Telling her about my plans would provoke one of her crying scenes, and my own tears were on the verge of spilling.

"I will try to come every day to help you pack, Tilde dear. We have a long time together."

"Have yourself a happy birthday, my flower, so beautiful and grown up now," said Tilde pulling a handkerchief from her sleeve to wipe her eyes. I kissed her and left the little cottage to pick up a cake at the bakery, for a modest celebration with Sebastian.

He did not meet me at the door as I expected. The house stood empty and quiet as I walked through the hallway into the drawing room.

Someone covered my eyes from behind.

"Guess who?" said a familiar throaty voice and a chorus of voices sang "Happy birthday dear Veronica!"

I peeled Anna's hands off, turned around, and smiled for the first time that day because of the fine sight before me.

Sebastian, Anna, dressed in elegant black, Gaspar in a bright green suit, which clashed with his rust colored hair as always. I dropped the bakery box when I saw a huge birthday cake with sixteen candles sitting on the grand piano. A loud pop and a hiss of champagne exploded behind us. Gaspar thrust a goblet in my hands and ordered to drink up. I drained my drink, blew out the candles, and wished for all my dreams would come true. Then I remembered Sebastian's mantra *"Have dreams, life is abundant. Life is abundant, dreams are gone."*
and corrected myself *I wish that my dreams will never be lost.*

Sebastian came over and gently drew me to him. I returned his hug with pleasure for could not stay mad at him, especially when he did not deserve it. Anna kept fidgeting behind me like a little girl.

"Anna, what are you hiding from me?" I asked.

"Ask them," she pointed at Gaspar and Sebastian.

"Ask what?"

"Your birthday present. Don't you want to know what it is?"

"I wasn't sure I would be getting one."

"Silly girl. Come outside and you'll see," Anna whispered in my ear.

"Let's blindfold her first," said Gaspar.

Anna removed her perfumed scarf and tied it around my eyes. I did not object, enjoying the suspense.

Sebastian led me by the hand. I heard the front door thud behind us. On the count of three, Anna untied the blindfold. I had no idea how I missed it, perhaps it appeared by magic. On the driveway sat the cutest little car I have ever seen, just like a toy, black and shiny with round headlights, tiny doors, and fat little wheels with a white trim. Where one would imagine a wind-up key, the little car had a huge silver bow on its roof.

"This is your very own brand new Austin Mini Mayfair," said Sebastian, "Hermes is a little too big and serious. We thought you would like something cute and zoomy. The car is a gift from all of us, Dr. Schuele and Tilde too. But you need to get licensed."

"I tried to convince them to get a hearse, but they wouldn't listen," said Anna.

Everyone laughed. I knew that she was not joking. Anna loved the macabre. I cried and laughed hugging them all, overwhelmed by the best birthday surprise ever.

"Get the keys, let's to go for a drive."

Sebastian gave me a warning look.

"Around the estate," I added.

Anna and I climbed in, and the Mini zoomed forward, flying like my own magic carpet.

"What are you going to name it?" asked Anna as I was checking out the shiny controls.

"Hermie."

"Out of all deities you choose Hermie? How original."

"Makes sense, the large one's Hermes and the little one's Hermie."

Sebastian and Gaspar caught on to Hermie's name right away and the rest of the night turned out just as fantastic. Gaspar drank and joked a lot. Sebastian entertained us with stories. Anna and I put a meal together from whatever we had in the house. Then I played "The Blue Danube" on the piano. Anna and Sebastian danced with a theatrical panache, Gaspar bobbed to the music.

No one mentioned moving away until Anna something said

about reading the house descriptions sent by an agent, and not liking them.

"I need a house with a ghost or a dramatic past. Best protection from the burglars ever."

"Why don't we just get a dog? *Canis vulgaris*," said Gaspar.

"I'm sure they have plenty of haunted houses in New Orleans. And a special ghost waiting specifically for you, Anna," said Sebastian.

"Veronica would like that, would you not? To have your own pet ghost," said Anna looking straight at me, "come live with us, just for a bit. The voodoo shops! Imagine the fun."

"I will some day. I am leaving too, just as soon as you go, or before even. Didn't Sebastian tell you?"

"Veronica, stop that. You are not being serious," said Sebastian.

"I am leaving to find magic. You said yourself once. Remember, Sebastian? The round world has corners where magic still exists."

"That's a great line. I should write it down. *In orbem ubi sunt magicae angulos regit*. Brilliant," said Gaspar applauding.

"Shut up Gaspar. She is serious," Anna shot him a warning look, "sounds like she's determined. You better let her, Sebastian, or she'll run away."

"Yes, this is exactly what I am planning, now that I have my Hermie."

Sebastian stood up, "We'll talk in the morning, when the sun clears the clouds from your reasoning."

"What if it rains?" I shot back.

"Sebastian, you have to trust her. It's not like she's never been anywhere, you have been traveling in the past five years. Let her experience some adventures of her own."

"Anna's right, trust in Veronica's intelligence, and don't forget her language abilities. Just give her a few months" said Gaspar also taking my side.

"She's only sixteen, no arguments." said Sebastian.

"Sebastian, don't be a hypocrite, you ran off when you were

fifteen, with the traveling theater, and became an adventurer. I listened to your stories well, Sebastian. If I will run away, good luck finding me," I said encouraged by the unexpected support from my friends.

"I do wish you came to some sort of agreement, enough of this bickering," said Anna and retreated to get more wine.

We were quiet for a bit until Gaspar demanded more cake. We hastily complied, happy to escape the awkward situation.

Anna and Gaspar's looming departure dampened my mood. Gaspar had to begin his professorship of quantum mechanics in June for the summer term, just to get his feet wet. He bragged how he already got a University of New Orleans tee shirt, with a bow tie to match. We laughed. He always had a knack for diffusing any kind of gloom. I was missing the both of them already.

In the morning, Sebastian tried to pretend as if nothing had happened and headed to our meditation room as always. I went in the opposite direction and made an appointment for the driving test over the phone. Now that I had my Hermie, the promise of freedom was sweeter than ever.

At breakfast, I opened the mail and read a letter from the law firm. It informed of my responsibilities as a legal owner of the LaRose Gris estate, and a scheduled visit to their offices in Boston to review an inventory of the assets. Bored by the prospect, I decided Sebastian should handle the lawyers, threw the letter on the table and left.

I had no legal right to drive, but went anyway. I drove along the coast on the empty winding road, crisp ocean breeze blasting through the open windows. Hermie and I became one as I lost myself in the thrill of speed and even closed my eyes for a bit to feel the momentum. It was pure magic.

Our silent dance around my willpower continued for a few more days. I busied myself in the garden, no plans for planting this year, just cleaned up the debris left by the departed winter. This became a farewell to my garden. I walked around the shrubs touching their fragile new branches, pressing my palms deep into the tree bark so the imprint remained, inhaling the scent of soil and moss infused with the salt of the sea. The garden knew I was saying good-bye, for it stood strangely silent and windless, frozen in time.

Sebastian found me by the stream. The rocks on the bottom fascinated me since I was little. The rocks shined with color in the water, but when I fished them out they became dull and grey, defeated looking, like a wrinkled balloon or a cut flower.

"I was thinking about your intention to travel alone. If for one minute I would agree to let you go, what is your plan, and how do you intend to support your travels? You must have a plan and the means."

He caught me. I did not have a plan. My imagination painted wild adventures, but in reality, my feet could only reach the gate by the end of the driveway. I shrugged and continued to play with the water.

"Fine, Veronica, I would agree to let you go and to support your endeavors. But, there is always a 'but.' You have to show that you are capable of solving difficult situations, you know yourself there will be difficulties. To assure me of your capability, you must pass a test."

I looked up at his face and saw he was serious, with resolution in his cold eyes. Instead of showing relief and joy, I just shrugged again and said, "Whatever."

He asked me to follow and went in the direction of the carriage house, the large garage where we kept Hermes and where Hermie has found his new home. I followed Sebastian to a workshop area at the back.

The sunlight streamed through the small windows, dust specks danced in the rays. The workshop smelled of oil, metal and dried earth, which fell in clumps around a collection of garden tools. A large glass candy jar without a lid sat on a rough worktable in the middle of the workshop. A creature pranced inside the jar, trying to climb the smooth glass, its tiny feet making a faint scratching noise. I stared at the creature and then at Sebastian.

"Why is there a chipmunk in the jar?"

"Think of it not as a chipmunk, think of it as the world. And you have to tame it."

"Is this your test? You must be joking, Sebastian. How am I supposed to tame it? It's a rat in a disguise."

This time Sebastian shrugged. "I don't know, but this is what you have to do. Just a word of caution, it's hungry."

I sighed, resenting Sebastian and his new twist on the issue, carried the jar to the table in my bedroom. Once alone, I took a closer look at the captive chipmunk that represented the world. We stared at each other from either side of the glass. The chipmunk stood on his hind legs and leaned on the glass with its front paws. They were tiny and pink with five fingers and sharp claws. *Cute*, I thought and met his eyes. He watched my every move with his black small eyes, shiny as glass beads outlined with a precision of an artist, his brown nose twitched.

"Nice cheeks, and whiskers," I whispered, "are we going to be friends?"

I went downstairs and got a handful of almonds from the kitchen. The chipmunk lay curled up on the bottom of the jar when I came in. His nose pointed upward as I dropped the almond. The nut was gone in a second. I was not sure if he ate it or hid it inside his round cheeks. So I dropped another one, the almond disappeared again. *No way*, I thought, *he would munch so fast, maybe Sebastian was right about the hungry part.* I reached into the jar and stroked his striped brown back with my finger. He flattened himself onto the bottom. The more I petted him the flatter he became, like a furry pancake. *Strange*, I thought, *but nice and soft.* I could not resist and reached in to scoop him out of the jar. As I was about to cuddle him, he bared his ugly long yellow teeth and plunged them in the fleshy part of my thumb. I did not expect this and squeezed him. He bit me again.

"You ungrateful little rat! You worthless piece of fur, how dare you?" I yelled at the creature.

The blood started to stream down my hand in dark rivulets. The searing pain fueled my anger. I ran to the bathroom, without thinking threw the evil creature in the toilet, and grabbed the handle to flush him.

I never knew the chipmunks had voices. They usually skittered in silence by the tree roots, their cheeks bulging from the pilfered seeds of my precious plants. This chipmunk screeched and scrambled in the toilet water, its snout pointing up and its little feet flailing helplessly, slipping on the smooth porcelain bowl. I have never witnessed such a pitiful sight in my life. Letting go of the flush handle I reached into the toilet and fished him out with my bloodied hands.

"You'll regret if you bite me again," I said and took him back to his jar. He did not move, his sides bulged from the labored breathing, his wet coat matted and stained with my blood.

"Clean up and then we will start again," I said and went back to the bathroom to take care of my wounded hand. The inflicted wounds were deep making red rivers of blood in the sink. The bleeding took a while to stop. I sterilized the gashes with alcohol and applied the golden seal salve to prevent infection and to speed up healing.

When I finally came out, the jar was empty. I stood by the table thinking about the ways he could escape. Perhaps driven by fear he jumped out the moment I disappeared through the door. Now I faced the challenge to find his hiding place. I scanned the room: the windows were too high up, the door to the landing outside stood closed, and the wardrobe stood locked, and under the bed would be too open and accessible. Like a hunting tiger, I got to my hands and knees, put my chin on the floor, and looked around from the chipmunk's point of view. *Of course!* The bookcase stood close enough to the table with the jar, with a narrow space between the wall and the shelving.

I sat on the floor, closed my eyes, and imagined myself in that dark narrow space. I would appreciate the safety of the darkness and the narrowness, but soon I would get hungry, miss the light and the freedom, and then come out. *So sooner than later, he will show up looking for food.* I told myself to be patient and went to the kitchen for more almonds.

Checking for Sebastian, I loaded up a tray with nuts in a jar, snacks for myself, and a large teapot of fragrant linden tea. I had no problems waiting for Chipmunk-the-World to show up. With a good book and something to snack on, I could last days.

Few hours passed as the scratching noise from the vicinity of the bookcase jolted me out of *The Picture of Dorian Gray.* I crawled to the footboard of my giant bed and threw a nut. It landed with a thump just a few inches away from the source of the noise. I froze, trying not to breathe. In a few minutes, the chipmunk skittered out, grabbed the nut, and disappeared. We repeated the same routine a couple of hours later. Our maneuvers lasted for hours, and every time I would throw the nut closer to myself. I was delighted to watch the creature's trust growing. Sebastian's wisdom of symbolic wild and unfriendly world, ready to hurt me at the slightest provocation, finally dawned on me. The entire chipmunk test became clear. I had to learn a lesson of taming the world.

The chipmunk became used to me, coming nearer every time. In the morning he came and took the nut right from my hand and instead of running away ate it in front of me. He trusted me enough to climb onto my lap and sleep curled in the folds of my dress by the end of the week. We were friends now, all past hurts and wounds had healed, the time came to show him to Sebastian.

I found Sebastian in the library doing paperwork and came in without knocking, with the chipmunk sitting on my shoulder. Sebastian raised his eyes, dropped his pen, and smiled.

"You did it, Veronica. You tamed the world. Congratulations, now tell me, what have you learned?"

"I learned that the world is hungry and ready to attack and hurt me at any moment. To achieve harmony with the world one needs to have empathy, patience, and a dream. One needs to be strong, alert, and kind in order to survive. I always knew that, Sebastian. You and Winai taught me well. I will be fine on my own."

"Bravo, Veronica. I could not have said it better myself. Does your new friend have a name?"

"His name is Prosha. Remember the clown at the circus in Moscow? The one who begged people to see their watches only to steal them on the sly. I named my new friend after that clown. My Prosha is an amusing little thief."

Sebastian stretched his arm across the table, Prosha jumped from my shoulder onto his open palm.

"He knows you?"

"I have tamed the world a long time ago, Veronica."

Sebastian released Prosha on the floor. He never ceased to intrigue with his mysticism. Did he speak of taming the chipmunk or the real world?

"Will you support my plans for travel?" I asked.

"Yes, as I have promised. Now, get a notebook. We need to make a list of the arrangements before the new moon."

8. THE FLUTE AND THE BOTTLE

I left in the midst of my going away party, just slipped quietly away while they enjoyed themselves, toasting to my "educational tour" as Dr. Schuele called it. He told us about his own tour when he finished school. A faded European tradition for young people of his time to go on some sort of traveling spree before they embarked on the journey to the rest of their lives.

My own journey lay ahead. Dressed for travel in black jeans, turtleneck sweater, long coat, and high top Doc Martens, I finished stuffing my backpack with necessities.

I glanced at my reflection in the wardrobe mirror, so strange to be wearing pants. They made me appear taller, like a slim boy. I left my long hair intact after a long deliberation in front of the mirror with scissors in my hand, and not enough willpower to cut it. The hair stayed, but rest of me I would change. Gone would be freckles on my nose, and the nose itself would be shorter, my mouth would be made less wide. Anna called me a wild beauty. To Gaspar I always remained a green-eyed pixie since childhood.

My friends celebrated together for the last time and I did not want long tearful goodbyes at the end of the party. Trembling with the anticipation of my journey, I reminded myself to breathe. Amazing how something this desirable would cause such cold feet at the end. So instead of tearful parting, I decided to make a clean cut and run in the night.

I slipped on a lanyard with a black plastic bankcard Sebastian had given me. It would work at any bank all over the world without any questions asked. By Sebastian's modest calculations, the funds on this card could cover one year of travel. His way of ensuring I would be back home within a reasonable time. Then I stuck a passport with a plane ticket to Italy in my inner pocket. They were all planning to take me to the airport in the morning. But Italy was not my true destination, because I decided to go where my feet would take me. To seek the real adventure, not the one planned by Sebastian. I picked up my heavy backpack and left by the back door to say farewell to my garden.

I stood under the trees for a few moments absorbing the nocturnal sweet scent of soil and foliage, remembering how I believed fairies lived in the plants. Perhaps they really did. On a whim, I scooped a handful pebbles and stuffed them in my pocket. I needed a token from my garden to keep me safe.

Sebastian stood waiting for me by the gate at the end of the driveway, leaning against the wall, long hair obscuring his face. At the sound of my steps, he raised his head and said,
"I would do exactly the same as you, Veronica, leave without much ado. But *I* would see *you* before leaving."

"I wanted to, but I was afraid that when the time came to see you for the last time I would change my mind and not go. I did not wish to hurt you by leaving like this, Sebastian." I said, as came closer to face him. We looked at each other for a long moment. Sebastian's face was a palette of shadows and reflections from the light above.

"Send me the postcards from the places you visit, don't call unless it's an emergency. I will be thinking of you every moment you are gone, my energy will protect you."

I felt the sting of tears in my eyes and went forward to embrace him.

"Good bye my Veronica," he whispered against my hair and kissed me on the forehead. Then he released me and disappeared in the direction of our desolate beach. I walked away with a last glance at *LaRose Gris*, hoping that one day I would return and find it as if I never left.

The only bus stop in the Cider Village was located in front of the post office. I checked the schedule. The first bus would be arriving at four in the morning. The bus came, and the driver asked where I needed to go.

"Just the end station," I said.

"South Station it is, Miss," nodded the driver and closed the doors behind me. I walked half way to the back in the dim light and found an empty spot by the window. The backpack went on the seat beside me.

"South Station," boomed the voice above and I opened my eyes. The last one off the bus, I stood on the platform without any plans about my next move. The rush of the morning crowd made me feel out of place. I slung the backpack over my shoulder and headed towards the exit.

"Hey you!"

I heard a voice behind me, but continued walking. Then I heard someone whistle.

"Hey you, in the black coat!"

I turned around and looked in the direction of the rude whistle. Three kids were sitting at far end of the platform. One of them raised his hand and gestured to come over. I had nothing else to do, so I did.

"Come chill, you look like one of us, kind of," said the boy. He had on a long black coat like mine, only studded with large safety pins, high lace up boots on huge platforms. He also had remarkable hair, spiked up and dyed green on one side.

"I'm Marc, this is Adam," he pointed to a chubby boy also dressed in all black with straight dark hair, his eyes outlined in black. "And she's Una." The girl raised her hand in a striped fingerless glove and waved. Her black hair was short in front aside a long braid in bright pink snaking around her chest. Una's outfit intrigued me. A black leather jacket, a pink tutu which matched her braid, and torn up fishnet stockings. She wore Doc Martens, just like me.

"Nice boots," she said when I sat down on the platform beside her.

"Thank you," I said and leaned my back against the wall, "I'm Veronica LaRose."

"Where're you off to Veronica?" Asked Una

"I do not know yet."

"Runaway huh," said Marc.

Adam did not comment. He had his ear to the small handheld radio.

"Yes, I guess," I said.

"I told you she's one of us, I am a psycho," said Marc.

"Psychic, not psycho, you idiot," said Una.

"I know, I am just joking, it takes so little to provoke you, Una," Marc said and mock-punched her in the shoulder. His cultured tone of voice and manner of speech would make my old tutor proud.

"So you are runaways too, why?" I asked. I liked these kids. They seemed honest with something magical about them, maybe because they looked different from everyone else.

"Oh the usual," said Una, "nobody understands us and the school sucks. You?"

"I am on the quest for adventure and magic."

"What sort of magic, bunny-out-of- a-hat or the lamp genie type?" said Mark.

"The lamp genie type, the power-giving magic."

"What's the power for?" asked Una.

"Control the elements, transform things, change fate," I said hoping they would understand. Una looked at me with a new interest.

"Magic? You got some magic shrooms?" said Adam finally, and set his radio down. He missed most of our conversation and I decided to humor him.

"Yes, I have a bit of dried fungi from my garden, for tea that makes good sleep and sweet dreams."

Adam dug inside his jacket and produced a bagful of greenish dried herbs, "Trade?" I took the bag and opened it, releasing a sharp odor. "Cannabis Sativa," I said with a solemn nod, "not the freshest batch, not as potent as it was *two* seasons ago."

"Damn, the bastard said it was fresh. You sure?" demanded Adam, he looked menacing for a moment.

"Yes I am sure, I have been studying herbal lore since I was ten. I know how to distinguish old harvest from new." I said to impress them. "But I will trade you anyway. Just to warn you, use a bit at a time, or instead of happy dreams you might get nightmares. Besides, I could use some cannabis for tea. It's an effective pain reliever."

"What?" said Adam.

"She means that you might have a bad trip with her shrooms, and your weed is good for the cramps, right?" said Una.

"Let's blow a stick now, leave shrooms for later," said Marc, "I have an ace ready."

Reluctant at first as they passed it around, but after a third round I began to relax.

What a sight we were, bunch of misfits sitting on the ground at the bottom of the bus platform enveloped in a cloud of smoke. I laughed, and they followed my example. Adam made his portable radio louder to blaring rock music. They were so different from the prim teens of the Cider Village. It was a nice feeling to realize there are people my age in the world I could call friends. The loud radio noise interrupted my thoughts. Crazy beat and guitar riffs intermittent with gruesome shrieks cut my relaxation to shreds. I asked to turn it down. They gave me an incredulous glare.

"Are you nuts? It's Max Black, his new hit," said Adam.

"Don't you like Maximus Black?" asked Una.

Marc just sat there nodding to the beat with his eyes half closed.

"Oh, I have been to his concert when I was young. He pretended to sing opera then."

"Wow that was a cool era. His first. Lucky you," said Adam with envy.

"I prefer to listen to the real opera," I said.

"Which one do you like best?" Marc broke his silence.

I thought for a second and said, "Rigoletto. Makes me cry every time."

Marc got up on his unsteady knees and sang,
La donna è mobile
La-La
La-La-La.
We all clapped, radio forgotten.

"Go back to your prep school, will you?" said Adam and Una laughed.

"Yes, why won't you? To learn the rest of the words," I teased.

"So where you said you were going?" said Marc in the attempt to shift focus away from him.

I told them about my ticket to Italy, but no wish to go there, besides my plane was already gone. Instead, I wanted to go where my intuition guided me, where the magic was hiding.

"Let's join hands and think where Veronica should go to find magic," offered Una.

"I'm not holding hands with a dude," said Adam, so Una moved over to sit between him and Marc.

Both boys grumbled it was stupid, but joined hands with us anyway. We sat in silence for almost half an hour until I asked them if they had any brilliant ideas, they did not reply. I released our circle, quite dismayed. No ideas about destination came to either.

Then Marc offered to try a different approach, to catch the first interstate bus that leaves the terminal. I agreed it might work, remembering what Winai said two years ago. *There is no such thing as a coincidence.* Una kept asking me about Winai. I think that she liked me, because she stared the boys into silence every time they came up with silly witticisms at my expense. I had fun talking and being with them, but there a nagging thought at the back of my mind reminded need to keep moving. I had to go. Four of us scrambled up, I turned out to be the tallest and Adam the shortest.

"The first bus out of this place, right?" asked Marc as he offered to get the ticket.

"Fine, let's make it a Russian Roulette," I said. After all, I had nothing to lose. It did not matter where I would be going. Magic waited anywhere. He returned in a few minutes holding a long blue ticket.

"The first one out – Albuquerque, New Mexico. It leaves in twenty, arrives in two something days. Sounds like fun."

"Wow, New Mexico, it's a desert country - hot," said Una.

"Travel two thousand miles to see rattle snakes, and cow sculls," said Adam.

"Alright, I get the picture, thank you." I said. The destination surprised me, because it was the last place I would choose. As a child of fog and cool ocean breeze, I would never even think about scorched dry desert.

They walked me to the right platform, and we stood with hands in our pockets. It was awkward to say good-bye. We probably would never meet again. Una reached to the back of her head, unclipped her crazy pink braid, and gave it to me.

"For luck, who knows you might need it. Nice to have met you Veronica, hope you will find what you're looking for."

"Hope you will find your magic lamp, Veronica." Marc opened his arms wide and gave me a bear hug.

Adam dug in his pocket, "She don't need luck, she needs something to eat," and gave me two granola bars, "I always keep them around, for when munchies strike."

I sat on the bus with my nose to the window and waved to them, they waved back. Una kept looking over her shoulder as they headed back to their usual spot at the bottom of the platform.

"Damn punks," said a bald man in a seat in front of me.

Damn you, I thought and bumped the back of his seat with my heavy bag that his head lurched. *They are my friends.*

I never imagined the distance travel by bus would be so hateful. Sebastian and I traveled by plane, car and train. Train travel was popular in Asia; an airline was obvious solution for the intercontinental, and the car for local daytrips in a pleasant countryside. The bus travel proved to be very tiring and tedious. The acrid smell of the diesel engine, the airless cabin and endless swaying plunged me into a melancholic nostalgia. I regretted leaving home. In my mind, I searched for excuses to come back.

I could not read, the ride made me drowsy. The only entertainment I had was to look out the window at the boring flat countryside if mid-states. Most of the dwellings along the country roads were run down and pitiful, so different from Massachusetts. Desolate freeways ran in hypnotic loops. I grew indifferent to the scenery, until the bus broke down somewhere in the New Mexico desert.

The other passengers also felt the angst associated with the bus travel. My grumpy fellow travelers spilled out of the stale bus cabin once the driver announced the emergency stop. I squinted at the bright desert sun and asked the driver of our approximate location. He just shrugged and said that the service truck was on the way, and that we should be arriving at our destination without much of a delay.

I encountered the desert up close for the first time, its strange landscape, and colors. The wild contrast of red sand and an incredible blue cloudless sky mesmerized me. The boulders that resembled toys of some childish giant, and an unfriendly looking flora dotted the landscape. I tore some twigs off the dry plants to smell their scentless core, and eyed the untouchable cactus plants. Their long needles covered the body of the plant with a thick mane. To me, cactuses resembled an alien's fingers that pointed up to the sky in warning. I brought my backpack from the bus and settled by the warm boulder to have a snack. For two days, I had nothing but Adam's granola bars, pop and chips from the vending machines at the quick stops. A sympathetic passenger gave me an apple and a roll of mints when she left at some remote stop in the prairies.

I munched on the apple and watched the scenery. The rest of the passengers had scattered in the area around the bus. The heat made me drowsy. I leaned on the boulder and drifted off. My nap did not last long, one of the passengers roused me and said the service truck has arrived, we should be leaving soon. I considered returning to the bus and hide from an afternoon sun, but decided to do a little exploring instead. I had enough of the bus and craved change. I left my coat folded over my bag and went in the direction of the larger boulders, maybe I would be able climb one and see what lies beyond the desert horizon. Was it as dark and unreachable as the horizon at sea?

Away from our forced layover, the desert enveloped me in mysterious silence. The alien landscape distracted me. The dry air scorched, my boots made a crunching noise when I walked on the coarse red sand. The wind howled a lonely song between the boulders. The desert nature so unlike from the moody Atlantic of my home, it had a different poetic beauty about it.

I needed to find some shelter and rest a bit before heading back. In the distance, I spotted an earthen hut and headed in its direction hoping for some shade and water.

An abandoned adobe in a grove of cacti offered neither. I had no other choice but to head back. The desert did not welcome me, and its spirits were not friendly as fairies of my beloved garden.

The walk exhausted me. Upon reaching my destination, I realized the bus and everyone had left. I sank at the side of the empty road cursing the driver and everyone onboard. *How could they leave me behind?* My backpack and coat sat in the same spot behind the boulder where I left them. The sun began its descent. The air grew cooler. I knew enough geography to expect the temperature to drop in the desert, and the wild creatures like snakes and coyotes to come out. I needed a shelter for the night, and decided to head back to the abandoned adobe hut amid the cacti. I put on my coat, shouldered the bag, and headed towards the meager shelter once again.

The night descended quicker than expected. As I made my way back to the adobe, I saw someone else making use of it. A hunched figure stirred a small bonfire in front of the dark entrance. A barefooted man, dressed in homespun shirt and pants, with rows of wooden amulets on leather strings that clanked around his neck and wrists. His long hair had braids with feathers and herbs woven into them. The reflection of the bonfire painted his face red.

The stranger did not acknowledge or even look at me. I sat down by the fire facing him. He continued to stir the embers and mutter. I wanted him to acknowledge me first. My intuition told me to wait. He made no eye contact, and yet I knew he was watching me. His muttering became louder, he spoke to the fire urging it to build up, and it did. The flames grew higher and higher, licking the night sky with their blue tipped tongues. The heat from the fire burned my face, but I did not move away because the air felt icy behind me.

I remained frozen in space between the heat and the chill, tired, thirsty, and fascinated. At last he quieted down and gazed at me with his strange orange eyes. I asked him if he had any water. He muttered something, felt around the fire with his hand and threw an object at me. I caught it, and saw a wooden flute. *Interesting, I asked for water and he gives me a flute.* The man made a gesture to play. I brought it to my parched lips and blew. A sudden whoosh of a fresh breezy rain swept over and the cacti around us began to glisten with fresh water droplets. I got up ready to take a drink, but the angry looking needles prevented me. I could not reach and gather the water with my hand, nor could I bring my lips to it. I stared frustrated and helpless, at the cool water droplets with fire reflecting in each one of them.

"How am I supposed to take a drink?" I asked.

The man poked around the fire again, and threw another object at me, this time a small bottle with a wide neck. Happy I turned to the cactus to gather some water, but found none. I looked around for a flute to call for more swooshing rain, but could not find it as well.

"Where did the flute go? I need to call for more water," I demanded. The thirst drove me mad.

The man snapped his fingers and I was holding a flute in my hand once again, the water droplets returned to needles. The bottle was gone.

"Why take the bottle away? Are you mocking me?" I said frustrated with the weird man.

"Can't have both now, girl. Choose: the flute or the bottle."

"But I want both!"

"Those are the rules. I am The Rule Maker."

"Can you change them?"

The man said nothing and pointed up to the black desert sky alive with millions of stars. I looked up, and felt myself rising towards their blue cold light, thirst, and anger forgotten.

"I choose the flute then."

"Wise choice, girl. Learn to wait, girl, for the right time, and you'll have it all," said the man as I drifted off to sleep among the stars. He lulled me to sleep with his soft voice "Girl, girl, girl..."

The hot fire scorched my face once again, and I heard another urgent voice calling me.

"Wake up, you stupid girl, or you'll fry to death in this heat."

I opened my eyes with difficulty. The eyelids stuck together and were gritty with sand. The stars were gone, and instead red cruel sun blazed down at me. I looked up and saw a man in a brown uniform and a wide brimmed hat towering above me. He prodded me with his boot and urged me to get up.

"You're not about to die on my watch. Get your ass up and let's go, you stupid girl. What is it with you teenagers, going into the desert at night? Want the rattler to get you? Trying to be brave?"

"Stop kicking me! My bus broke down. I went for a walk and they left me behind."

I tried to get up. The man grabbed my coat collar and hauled me to my feet. He was much taller. I saw my disheveled reflection in his aviators. He sized me up chewing on a toothpick in the corner of his mouth. An absurd memory about some TV show flashed through my mind.

"Yea, it was you then. They noticed you were missing, but too late. Been looking for ya since late last night. What ya been up to?"

"Just fell asleep by the fire that man made," I said and pointed towards the direction of the adobe. The little hut was gone. There were no traces of a bonfire. The officer checked around, shook his head, and transferred his toothpick to the other side of the mouth.

"Gotta to take ya to the doctor, get ya checked out. There is nobody 'round here for miles except for the damn snakes. Come, I'm Officer Joe Matys. My cruiser is parked not far from here. Have a drink first," he said and passed me the canteen. I drunk with abandon, water never tasted so sweet in my life.

"Then it must have been a dream. Just take me to the nearest bus station please," I asked him, ready to agree to anything as long as I could get away from the desert.

As he drove, I kept my eyes on red landscape, but my thoughts were with The Rule Man. I gave this name to the stranger by the bonfire. Dream or no dream, the memory of last night's adventure was quite real to me. The Rule Man sounded wise. Sebastian would say something like this. I closed my eyes and sent Sebastian my love, and wished I could share these events with him.

"So, where're ya headin'?" asked my rescuer.

"My bus headed to Albuquerque. But I did not intend to stay there for long."

"What's in Albuquerque, family or a sweetheart?"

"None. A boy at the station in Boston got me the ticket for the first bus out. It was a gamble."

"Ya look and sound too intelligent to be a runaway junkie. Wanna tell me 'bout it?"

"I am on a quest for magic," I said before thinking, "one thing I know for sure now, the desert is not a place for me," venting my frustration felt good, "It's too dry, too dead, too monotonous, I miss the sea and the rain, the snow storms even. Anything is better than this. I went south and ended up on Mars."

Joe Matys produced a deep good-natured laugh. He calmed down, and I heard a genuine interest in his questions.

"Magic? Like voodoo? Go to New Orleans, they got plenty of stuff like that."

"No, not voodoo, and no New Orleans. If I show my face in that place my friends, they live there now, will never let me go," then after a moment I added, "I want to head back to the sea. Where should I go to the east or west coast?"

Joe laughed again and told me to go east. Miami was his hometown with a large seaport. It sounded like a good plan to me, to travel by a merchant ship like Sebastian. The ship out of Miami was a great idea and it felt right. I would follow Marc's advice again, catch the first ship out.

At the bus station, Joe offered to buy me a meal. We walked to the cafeteria. Joe Matys did not need convincing about my robust health when the waitress brought me two peanut butter sandwiches, hot chocolate, and apple pie. I munched on it all with the bigger gusto than Joe Matys ate his egg sandwich.

"What a character you are, Veronica LaRose," he said as handed me my backpack along with his water canteen, "Traipsing the desert with no water, spending the night with the rattlers, and trusting fate. I wish you luck with your quest. Stay safe."

We shook hands like old friends and he left in his cruiser. The horn blared as he turned the corner.

I purchased a ticket to Miami, and posted a card to Sebastian. On this postcard of a red desert, I wrote *Greetings from Mars.*

"How long to Miami?" I asked the driver as I handed in my ticket.

"About thirty hours, two transfers and no movies on this one. The thing broke." I did not care about the movies. I had a lot to think about. What forces made me travel almost three thousand miles only to spend one night, then come back to the same coast I came from?

On the almost empty bus, I examined the canteen Joe Matys gave me. It had a camouflage canvas shell, a sturdy strap and a cup over a wide neck.

"Where were you bottle last night when I needed water?" I asked aloud turning it around in my hands. Then I reached for the backpack to find my book somewhere near the bottom. My hand closed on something thin and long. *What can it be?* I did not remember packing anything like that. At last, with some twisting and pulling I freed the mysterious object. I stared at it not knowing whether to laugh or cry, it was The Rule Man's water flute. I brought it to my lips once again and blew. A strong spray of rain washed over the bus at once, right on the desert freeway.

It took the bus six hours longer to reach Miami because of the unusual heavy rainfall we had encountered. I sat clutching my flute and a bottle in a tight embrace, mesmerized by the torrents of rain cascading down the bus windows, and thinking about the magic behind my crazy desert journey.

9. DIESEL BRANDY

Perhaps Miami had it all as the brochure in my ticket boasted, the warm sea, the beaches and friendly people. I did not arrive as a tourist, but as an explorer. The lengthy bus ride gave me time to think. In my initial search for magic, I stumbled upon an actual magic flute, but the meaning of this artifact eluded me. My resolve to follow wind took never wavered. It became even stronger.

I disembarked disheveled like a wild-haired hobo, half expecting everyone to recoil from me. With enough sense in my foggy state of mind, I politely asked a taxi driver for a lift to a hotel near the seaport. He even complemented my politeness. I liked his laid-back attitude.

"I know exactly the place, clean and suitable for a nice young lady. Going on a cruise, miss?" he said after settling me in the car.

"Of sorts, tomorrow I will look for a merchant ship that would take me aboard."

"A merchant ship? That's a novel idea for someone your age."

Avery Jones, according to the badge stuck to the taxi sun visor, chatted without expecting a reply. He informed me there is no rushing in the south. Only the "snow birds", the visitors from the north rush. I laughed at his humor and thanked him by his name when we arrived at the hotel.

"Go see Milo Jones at the port. My son might show you around if he's got time. I worked there for thirty years myself," he said and lifted his large callused hands that looked like they had seen too many years of labor.

The hotel appeared as Avery Jones described, family owned and clean. I paid for my room and went upstairs. One look at the bed and I felt my exhaustion. My entire body ached, even the elbows. After a bath, I fell asleep lulled by the quiet hum of the air conditioner.

In the morning, I sat by the diner window checking out the happy-go-lucky Florida crowd.

"Excuse me, miss. Am I getting you right? You want two orders of fruit salad, bran flakes, French toast, and a cheese plate?"

"Yes please, and big pot of tea. And a blueberry muffin," I said ready devour a truckload of food. My fist morning in Miami, I had to fill up and get ready for a new dose of adventure. The food arrived and I did my best to put a large dent in everything. The waitress packed the rest in a 'doggy bag'. She joked about never meeting someone who ate so much and remained as skinny as myself. I did not disclose the fact that I have not seen a decent meal for a week, except for the breakfast supplied by Joe Matys in Albuquerque. My jeans could fit another me inside.

Dressed in a black tee shirt and jeans I walked to the seaport, backpack slung over one shoulder, a halo of curls bouncing around my head. I was overjoyed to see the Atlantic again. The sea appeared kinder here than at home.

The seaport buzzed like a city, or rather an industrious anthill. I admired the majestic cruise ships lined up by the numbered piers, people getting ready to embark or wish a 'bon voyage'. A festive feeling filled the air. Taxis sped by, busy porters carted the luggage pocketing the tips. I headed to the commercial area of the port with tall cranes and serious looking workers in helmets and gloves directing the container traffic. It appeared as if they were playing with huge toy blocks. Some workers eyed me. I looked out of place in this steel city.

A man in a uniform directed me to the one story building lost among the rows of cargo containers. Inside, I requested to see Milo Jones and a receptionist told me to wait in the dusty waiting area, the port superintendent was busy. Fifteen minutes became thirty, and after forty-five minutes of waiting my elation evaporated, replaced by impatience. I sneaked out, headed in the direction of the piers. A burly security guard stopped me. I asked him which merchant ships were heading out. He shrugged and pointed me back to the office.

When Sebastian told me stories of his travels, everything sounded so easy. Now, I felt trapped and frustrated. Someone must have sensed my frustration when I ended up back at the dreadful waiting room. The receptionist informed me that Milo Jones will be able to see me for five minutes only, and waved me into his office.

"What's this all about? I told them a thousand times, no student tours," said Milo Jones. The port superintendent stood almost as tall as a doorframe, and the business suit he wore would look better on anyone else but him. In my mind, he should have been a gladiator, tall, strong, with thick neck, and unwavering gaze. I introduced myself and told him his father sent me.

"Dad sent you? What have you done to impress *him*? What can I do for you? Hurry up."

"I would like to take a voyage on a cargo ship. Do you have any departing today or tomorrow?"

"We got ships arriving and departing every three hours, miss. But not all vessels take the passengers, and on some you got to work for your fare."

I told him that working did not scare me and asked for the introduction letter. The receptionist recorded my information, printed out a list of vessels leaving in the next twelve hours and an introduction letter from the port administration. I paid the fee, glad to leave the dingy office.

"So, Veronica, where's home?"

"Boston, Massachusetts," I said happy that he asked.

"Beautiful place, history, bad weather," said Milo Jones. I laughed at his laconic description. He was right.

This time the burly security guard did not dare to stop me, not with tall Milo Jones at my side. I felt like a little girl walking beside Sebastian years ago.

"One of those two would be your best bet, they take on

civilians," Milo said and pointed at two huge cargo ships flanking the pier 6. One grey the other red, both rusted and banged up, no new shiny cruise ships here. We parted by shaking hands and he wished me luck.

When he left, I stuck my nose in the list and found pier 6. The grey ship, called *Tennessee*, headed to Boston. The red ship, called *Vjeter*, had the destination 'An Island', which one it did not mention.

I wondered how many thousands of islands were scattered in the ocean and my heart gave a familiar lurch. I knew for sure that *Vjeter* had to take me to my next destination. Not the grey *Tennessee*, I just came from Boston, it was too early to return.

I had to pass by another security guard. He opened the gate to the pier 6. The *Vjeter* appeared fully loaded, the crane tracks stood empty.

A scene straight out of nineteenth century greeted me at the end of the pier. A sailor in a striped shirt sat on a low stool by the gangway peeling potatoes whistling a polka tune. Two huge cauldrons stood in front of him and a bucket for peels. Peeled potatoes bobbed in the water like ivory stones. So engrossed in his task he failed to notice my approach.

"Good morning. Is the Captain aboard?"

"Da?" Said the sailor, his bright blue eyes almost popped out when he saw me.

"Privet," I said, my arsenal of Russian had only four words, "I need to see the Captain please."

"Capitan? I Capitan, I no cook. Vladimir Petrovich Galkin. Call me Capitan Vovas," he said, stretched out his hand wiping it with his apron first. We shook, and I gave him Milo's letter. He squinted at it.

"So you want voyage? No can do."

"Why? Mr. Jones told me that you take civilians. I am willing to work."

"You American. We go Cuba. No can do," he repeated and handed the letter back.

I understood why Milo Jones told me to go pier 6. He thought I wanted to go back home to Boston. I also understood why the manifest stated 'an island' without giving it a name. All of a sudden Cuba became my next destination. No way would politics stand between destiny and I.

"Are you stopping anywhere else on the way to Cuba ?" I asked, grasping at straws.

"Nassau. Then Havana. Do svidanja." I knew it meant *good-bye*.

"Wait, can I sail to Nassau on *Vjeter* with you?" I asked. Bahamas could be interesting. I have never been to the Caribbean. From reading adventure novels by Raphael Sabatini, this whole region had a colorful romantic past of battles, tall ships, and pirates. Caribbean must hide some magic still. Captain Vovas took off his beret and scratched his head.

"Davai. Only to Nassau. Then you leave ship."

"Thank you Captain Vovas. How much do I owe you for the voyage?"

"Potatoes can do?" he asked and made a peeling motion with his knife.

"Deal," I said, stretched out my hand and we shook again. His shake was firm and reassuring. Then he asked for the letter again.

"What your name is, French?"

"Veronica LaRose. My grandfather was French."

"Hard name for remember. I call you Vera, means *faith* in Russian."

I laughed and reached for the knife to start earning my keep, but the Captain said that I should settle first and took me up the gangway.

The deck seemed well used, but spotless. The tiny passenger cabin located at the lower level had the waves splashing just a few feet down from the round porthole.

I sat on the cot covered with a grey woolen blanket and checked out my bright green accommodations. They painted everything the same color, the cabin, sparse furniture, even a lamp on the side table. *Just like my own little garden at sea,* I thought and tried to block the memories. They crept up when I least expected. Those memories caused guilt mixed with regret. I had to concentrate on looking ahead, returning home now would cause more regret. Just like *The Last Unicorn*, from the film I loved, I knew regret.

Vjeter had to set sail before midnight. Soon enough, the rest of the crew, including the cook whose job I was doing, started to show up at the gangway. The Captain lounged on a crate beside me puffing on his cigarillo. He told me stories of his mother-Russia where everything was bigger, brighter, and better tasting. It could only mean he missed home just like me. It became apparent when he told a story of how he swore not to go ashore anywhere except for his beloved birth city of Vladivostok. The snow there could reach up to a third story and the Pacific Ocean was anything but calm. I have not told him much. To the returning crew he introduced me as Vera. They just smiled or nodded and went on their way. There were fourteen men, all different ages, and two female cooks. I guess they were all accustomed to the potato-peeling passengers.

I must have peeled a ton of potatoes for the cooks to boil and serve with smoked fish and vegetables pickled in brine, Russian style. The food was familiar to me, and I won the crew's approval when I told them about my visit to Moscow when I was younger. Sergei, the ship mechanic was from St. Petersburg called it a most magical city in the world with baroque architecture, bridges, and a magnificent Winter Palace. I took a note of it. For now, the wind was taking me to the islands.

The mess hall on *Vjeter* fascinated me. Captain Vovas proudly showed off this altar of superstition and Sergei took me around for a small discovery tour. The room had no free space. All kinds of artifacts thought to ward off a bad fortune and a random collection of wonderful weird things crowded shelves, walls and any other surface that could hold stuff. Sooty Byzantine icons with images of thin saints, incredible variety of Buddha statuettes, evil eye charms, carved candles, horseshoes, rabbit's feet, scarabs, portraits of Lenin and Dalai Lama, crosses with Jesus, Leonardo's Mona Lisa on postcards, Chinese jade animals and much more. Anna would adore this place for its eclectic witchery.

"What is this?" I asked and pointed to the interesting rough stone a little bigger than my fist. It sat shoved between a copper Ganesha and a wreath of garlic. Under a coat of dust, this stone caught my eye.

"What? This?", said Sergei, "I don't recall, but it's no good, black stones are not good. Take it if you like. It could be crystal or onyx. No idea how it got here, everyone picks something in ports and drags it here. We Russians have superstitious nature. Sailors doubly so, all sailors are. Trust me." He spoke fluent English. According to Masha the cook, this was his eleventh year at sea.

"Thank you," I said and picked up the black stone, "Masha mentioned you have been sailing for a while. My friend sailed too. He said that he went around the world a dozen times at least." I said referring to Sebastian as friend, feeling awkward to call him my guardian in front of these people.

"Da? What vessel and what his name?" asked Captain Vovas.

"Sebastian Van Stratten, he sailed on *Magdalena* out of Rotterdam. Do you know him?"

Captain thought for a moment and said that he did not but the ship's name sounded familiar.

During the meal, the crew passed around a large metal canister filled with alcohol. Sergei offered me some. I knew to refuse a drink could upset my new friends and accepted. Sergei said it was an 80 proof and I should be careful. LaRose Absinthe was 70 proof. I knew what to expect. I downed the shot and gagged. It had a distinctive flavor of gasoline. They kept the alcohol in the used engine oil container, and it tasted and smelled like diesel.

"You like?" asked some of the crew.

"Very good diesel brandy," I replied with watered eyes, and stuck a pickle in my mouth. Everyone laughed and applauded. I passed the test, Sebastian would be proud. Captain told me that we should be arriving in Nassau in the morning and I have until early afternoon to disembark.

Late at night, I pondered of how not to miss the opportunity to explore Cuba. By the time I fell asleep, rocked like a baby in a giant cradle that was the ship, the plan had hatched.

"Let me help. I want to repay for your hospitality," I said to the Captain Vovas who sat at his usual spot by the gangway peeling potatoes.

"Sure, Vera. Spasibo, you good girl," said the Captain and passed me another paring knife. I stared at the horizon and could not decide where the blue sky ended and the sea begun, *Caribbean the incredible*, I thought. Too bad, I would have no time to explore the Bahamas. The Captain and I chatted another hour, until time came for me to leave and find another destination. He rose and took hold of my hand ready to say good-bye, not farewell, he explained. I told him how the journey on *Vjeter* would always remain a special memory to me, and offered to drink to that, Russian style. I took out a bottle filled with the "Diesel Brandy" pinched from the mess at breakfast, and two glasses. He filled the glasses and downed his. Mine went over the gangway unnoticed. We shook hands for the last time and I walked away.

The telephone booth at the edge of the pier was a good spot to wait and spy on the Captain. He poured another glass from the bottle, lit a cigarillo, and sat for a bit staring at the turquoise sea. Soon, the cigarillo fell from his hand. I noticed the white wave of smoke curling by his stretched legs, sure sign for a safe return. I danced around sedated Captain Vovas who snored peacefully in the breeze, and made my way back up the ship. The containers towered high in the cargo area, I hoped nobody would go there at dinnertime or at night. I intended to leave the ship the moment it touched the pier in Havana. Settling in a corner between the containers, I took out Joe's water canteen, an apple, and silently thanked my herbal tinctures in a black lacquered box at the bottom of the backpack, especially the sleep inducing belladonna extract.

10. AN ISLAND

The narrow streets of Santiago traversed the city like wrinkles on an aged face. I ended up in this city after leaving the bustling Havana, where *Vjeter* docked at sunrise.

I traversed this lush island for a week stopping at impoverished fishing villages for food and shelter and once even sleeping in a deserted cabin on a National Nature Reserve. I tried to blend in with the locals by wearing a large straw hat with a floppy brim and a drab jacket. Cuban staccato dialect sounded quite different from the Spanish I learned. I tried my best to keep silent and communicate by gestures and laconic phrases.

No one had bothered me when I entered the city, or demanded documents. Perhaps because of buses full European tourists, that careened through the dusty streets alongside bikes and burros. Not even a hint of magic could survive in this poverty and neglect.

Peeling wood marred the facades of long ago whitewashed buildings. Rusted iron gates tied by crude chains or rope cordoned the courtyards making it impossible to steal a glance inside. Talismans to repel an evil eye of a passerby hung on walls. Old images of saints stared at me from the cracked terracotta tiles, carved ornate crucifixes, once impressive, hung on the buildings crooked and forgotten. Upside-down window frames, installed that way on purpose a century ago, to confuse the evil spirits. How could those relics repel anything with their rust and curling old paint, defeated by the elements? This entire city reeked of old and silent despair.

By intuition, I walked closer to the road. It felt more comforting to be closer to the slow moving traffic, than to the barred buildings.

Those buildings hid more than poverty. I could sense generations of broken hearts and unfulfilled dreams. Years of waiting for something better, perhaps a sliver of a good fortune brought by the trade winds.

As I explored Santiago, tapping at its desperate life under the blue skies, pitted against the heat and tyrannical rulers, I could not stop thinking of the inhabitants. Generations survived on this island beaten by the elements, mutinies, cruel colonizers, and greedy trade. Somehow, they had found a way to cope. In my idealistic understanding, perhaps some strong magic was an instrument to their spiritual survival.

I had explored old churches. There were a few of them in this city, similar in appearance with sun bleached stone steps, weathered heavy wooden doors, and dark cool interiors. Same story of suffering and redemption unfolded inside. Candles flickered, slowly burning the prayers into oblivion. Yet, the ones who had lit them believed, hoped, and prayed behind the closed doors, believing churches protected them from the elements and evil. Their prayers were never answered, and a melancholy surrender replaced the hope. In this place, the magic was lost or forgotten.

The afternoon heat chased me into one of such churches. I sat at the pew among a small congregation. The priest moved around the altar, his movements mechanical. He stretched out his hands and intoned "Pater noster, qui in coelis. *Thy will be done on earth as it is in heaven. Give us this day our daily bread: and forgive us our trespasses, as we forgive them that trespass against us. And lead us not into temptation,* Sed líbera nos a malo, *deliver us from evil.*" He could be a shaman evoking a spirit by incantation. I remembered the same deadpan stare and mechanical body movements once, when Anna and I witnessed a shamanic weather ritual.

I watched the wretched priest. He never made eye contact, pretending not to see me. I was nothing to him, just another desperate female in black who prayed for peace. He would never guess my true reason for being in his church: a search for magic.

Urgent whispering came from behind. Words eluded me. The whispering interfered with my pondering and began to annoy me. I glanced over my shoulder and met with a gaze of an old woman. She wore a common dark floppy hat and a shawl around her stooped narrow shoulders. Rosary beads snaked in her hands. Yet, something did not seem to be quite right. I looked closer at her rosary of black beads with something dangling at the end, a skull instead of a crucifix.

My annoyance disappeared in an instant. I had stumbled upon something interesting at last. I came around the pew and sat down on the old woman's bench. She looked at me sideways, raised her hand, and pointed her index and small fingers at me, an ancient gesture to ward off an evil eye. I repeated the same back at her, just to see the reaction. She nodded, got up and walked out into the sunshine. I followed in a few moments. Shielding my eyes from the bright sunlight, I spotted her in an instant standing by the dry fountain full of dead leaves and wrinkled newsprint. A dozen of orange, white, black, and calico cats surrounded her. They circled around, rubbing against her long black dress with evident affection, like faithful familiars.

The woman caught sight of me at the entrance and gestured to follow her. She moved down the deserted street in the cloud of cats. I skipped down the church steps to catch up.

"I need to talk to you, por favor."

She nodded and pointed her cane to the dusty small park at the end of the street.

I could feel the heat of uneven cobblestones through the soles of my boots. The park spared very little shade. We sat down on the wrecked bench with missing planks and graffiti all over the remaining wood and stone supports. Cats milled about us, their faces full of curiosity and longing.

"They seem to like you," she said with approval. The rosary dangled around her skinny neck now.

I pointed at the skull, "Why do you wear it?"

She cupped it in her hand and brought it to her lips.

"It's part of a great magic," she said.

"Then show me," I begged.

She smiled. Her teeth were strong and white behind the dark lips.

"I can't, but I know someone who will."

"Sorry, I'm not interested in a woman, who makes Voodoo dolls, or a charlatan, who sells dried grass as herbs. Please do not bother, for I have already spoken to them. They know nothing of what I seek. They told me about you. Find the Cat Lady they said. She is a guardian. I want to learn about your old magic. Please."

She listened to my impassioned speech with a frozen smile. No kindness in her eyes, just a calculating glint, or hunger. I shivered.

"Those you speak of, just prey on the tourists, they are my watchers, they know very little. I like you. You are young, and daring," her silent cackle turned into a deep cough.

"I will send you to someone who can teach you. He is the part of ancient magic on this island. I am merely a guardian."

She patted my cheek, pointed to one of the meandering cats, a pregnant calico with a long black tail.

"She will take you there. It's a long walk up the mountains, but walk you must. Be sure to go alone, and do not even think of telling anyone."

I hesitated for a moment, what she just said sounded completely bizarre. I would have second thoughts, if a year ago someone offered me to follow a cat, climb the mountains, and meet an unknown wizard. Not so now, not after meeting a shaman in New Mexico desert, not after I had committed to follow the wind.

I sprang to my feet, grabbed my backpack, and told her I was ready for a journey, with plenty of water and some dry food.

"Food, yes, we all need food," she said.

I reached in my backpack to share my granola bar. The Cat Lady paid no attention and walked away in the direction of the old church again. The cats followed her, all except one. She sat watching me, her tail twitched.

"What's your real name, Cat Lady?" I called after the old woman.

"My name is not important. Your guide's name is Smeela. Follow her."

"Smeela," I repeated and stroked the cat's head with my fingertips, "good kitty, will you be my friend?"

I picked up my backpack and followed Smeela in the direction of the mountains visible beyond the edge of the heat-exhausted streets.

Smeela and I walked past the buildings and deserted squares with dry fountains. Buildings became smaller and shabbier towards the edge of the city. We climbed the rocky path. Some way up, I glanced back and the sight of the bay stunned me with its natural beauty of shimmering blue water, golden crescent of the beach and green belt of tropical trees. Not all was desperate here. Nature remained as majestic as ever, and its beauty invigorated me.

Smeela's pregnant belly did not deter her. She navigated the rocky trail with grace and agility. The mountain trail became steeper, and at times dropped down again.

Generations of adventure seekers and their burros carved this path into the face of the mountain. How many hopefuls, I wondered, went into the mountains in pursuit of dreams, and how few returned fulfilled?

"Smeela, I wish you would slow down. I only have two legs," I called after the cat.

She stopped, sat down, and groomed herself while I struggled to catch up.

Exhausted and short of breath, I plopped beside her, pulled out my bottle and drunk deeply. I poured some water in a canteen cap and offered it to Smeela. She accepted it, and while she lapped, I took a closer look at my odd guide. She appeared to be quite healthy with shiny coat and large clear green eyes. Her belly gave her a chubby look, when I stroked her there were strong muscles beneath my fingers. She seemed to enjoy the attention, but carried on as if she was doing me a favor by allowing me to pet her.

"I would love to have a familiar just like you, my friend Anna would die from envy," I whispered and she seemed to nod in agreement.

Our moment shattered, when she sprung and started up the path again. I got up as well, gathered my stuff, wiped the dust off my pants, and followed.

The sun had begun its journey down. We needed to hurry before the nightfall. I imagined Smeela leading me to some dwelling up the mountains where I would meet a mysterious benevolent wizard. Suddenly the path turned, and a large boulder blocked our way. It looked like a dead end. I watched Smeela leap and disappear behind it. I tried to do the same, its enormous size stopped me. The only way was to scramble over.

Clutching at the rough side of the boulder, I managed to climb to the top, only to see the disappearing path below. This menacing mountain crumbled under my feet. I stared at the destroyed path and a chasm below. Jagged rocks pointed in all directions like in some abstract painting. *One of Mother Nature's wonders*, I shuddered, as I lay on my stomach to slide down legs first, hoping Smeela waited for me below.

My feet found a narrow edge and I was able to find balance, then made a welcome eye contact with Smeela. She continued down the steep drop. I was not as brave.

"Are you crazy?" I called out, too scared to move. Smeela glanced at me and raised her tail in one beautiful question mark.

"Fine. I trust you, my brave Smeela," I muttered and squatted searching for a spot to rest my foot. Stooping closer to the ground, I noticed a narrow path leading down. As I continued my slow descent, my thoughts returned to the sacrifices one had to make in search of knowledge or dreams.

Dusk approached the mountainside, and the silence became a messenger of the night.

"Is it much further Smeela?" I asked hoping not to spend the night on the rocky path. She did not turn, just flicked the end of her tail as if telling me to calm down.

Stars begun to show up in the infinity above us, and the pale moon appeared behind a thin veil. We walked for a while longer, until Smeela leapt up and settled on top of another large rock at the mouth of a cave. Her pose reminded me of a mysterious Sphinx.

I leaned forward to examine the cave. Smeela leapt up and hissed exposing her fangs. I buckled at this unexpected behavior from so far docile creature, and guessed she did not want me to enter. The cat seemed to read my thoughts and settled back into her Sphinx pose. I followed her example and found a spot to perch beside the rock. I had abandoned my daydream of spending a night at a dwelling of a mountain wizard.

The moon gained strength and bathed the landscape in silvery blue light. This is the world I loved most, no colors. Mystery of the dusk, Sebastian called it. Hades, an ancient god of the underworld would love a daughter like me. The one who reveled in the night and solitude.

We waited in the moonlight, enjoying each other's quiet company and listening to the deep silence of the broken mountainside. A total absence of sound registered in my tired brain. I felt a strong desire to run and glanced at the cat. She calmed me down with a steady gleaming gaze and leaped into my arms to rub her forehead against my cheek. Her scent was that of sweet milk and dust. I took out the canteen and we shared water again.

"Smeela, you are so beautiful, so clever, you have eyes like the brightest stars," I whispered stroking her ears. Smeela purred and smiled. The owl hooted in the dark. At once, the cat left my embrace, stretched and walked towards the dark cave.

I squeezed past the rock and entered the mouth of the mountain cave. In the dark, I heard Smeela's call short distance away and felt around. The walls around me were rough. The floor felt smooth.

Our journey continued for about a hundred of my loud heartbeats. The pitch dark gave me goose bumps, but Smeela's presence provided some confidence. I could not describe my relief when a glow appeared up ahead. It propelled me forward until I came to a large open space.

The room, if one could call it that, appeared wide and dry. A pile if wood lay at the far wall. A small bonfire burned in the middle surrounded by rocks. Wisps of smoke disappeared into a crack in the ceiling high above. The walls danced alive with drawings of magical winged creatures. I stood still, transfixed by their unusual shapes. They gave impression of moving in the orange glow. I walked closer and touched the painting.

A tap on my left shoulder snapped me back to reality. I turned, but nobody was there. Then I heard a giggle, looked the opposite direction over my right shoulder, and recoiled. The creature in front of me stood short, hairless, with rod thin arms and legs sticking from under a filthy poncho. With skin so white, that at first I thought he was wearing a theatrical makeup.

Perhaps the shock on my face elicited another flow of giggles and I noticed dagger sharp teeth behind his bloodless cracked lips. Acting by instinct, I dashed past him and ran back to entrance of the cave. He caught up with me in an instant, giggling again. *All right*, I thought, *you want to chase me. I will show you.* I ducked, caught some pebbles from the cave floor, and threw them at him, like a good Shadow Girl. He shielded his head with bony hands and drew a sharp breath. I took off again, expecting his footsteps behind me. None had followed. I stopped and listened.

At first I heard nothing, just a distant crackling of the fire and my own breathing. Then I heard sobs. I stood there struggling between fear and curiosity. The latter had won.

He sat on the floor, hands clutching at the dusty floor and sobbing with a total abandon, just like a child. I came closer and crouched. His sobbing became even louder. *Childish trickster*, I thought, and waited for him to calm down.

"How about you stop crying, and I will give you these to play with?" I said after a few patient minutes, and showed him the pebbles from my garden. I still carried them in my pocket. He stared at me without any comprehension in his dark eyes. I had to repeat the question in both Spanish and English. He reached with his spidery fingers and touched the pebbles.

"Hungry," he said in English. I did not know how to react. He hung his head and started to sob again.

"What's your name? I know you understand me. Why am I here?"

He wiped his nose with the back of his hand and said "My name Bagus."

"Are you Thai?" I asked.

"I no sure."

I searched almond shaped eyes for clues. They were so similar to Winai's eyes.

"You look like my friend."

"Why you do this, talk to me?" he interrupted, "You should be run away scared I catch you and drink your blood."

I did not know how to react to this eerie admission. Library manuscripts contained descriptions of vampires. Sebastian argued the real vampires drained energy, not blood from their victims. Gaspar insisted on both types and they had nothing to do with bats. Anna thought them romantic and attractive for some reason. I had no interest in them at all, preferring fairies and angels, until now. This creature fascinated me. I hoped there was more to his story than childish pranks. I had to make a decision, hoping it would not be a big mistake.

"All right," I said, paused unsure for a moment, and rolled up my sleeve.

"Drink my blood then, only until I say *stop*. Or I will turn you into a rock, I am a powerful magician."

He stared at my arm, licking his lower lip. Then with a wide gesture, he pushed it away. "No"

Oh good heavens, I thought. *What a brat!*

"Fine, I will tell you what *I* want. *I* want you to tell me about yourself. You see, I came here from very far away to learn magic. I met this old woman in the city below, she told me to go and find a great magician who lives in the mountains. Are you him?"

At the mention of the old woman, he sprang away from me, just as I did when we met.

"What's the matter?" I said. "Oh no, do not start crying again, come on, tell me, please."

He inched closer to me, took my arm, and placed his bony finger just above the wrist. I closed my eyes and nodded. He brought my wrist to his mouth. I saw a swift glimmer of sharp teeth. I felt an innocuous sensation, just like a rough tongue of a cat.

"Stop!" I said, a few minutes later.

He let me pull my arm away. Two dark bloodstains marred the sleeve of my sweater. With hunger satiated somewhat, a little sparkle appeared in his ebony eyes. With a little further prodding, he told me his life story.

Bagus did not know where he was born, or who his parents were. He grew up in a Turkish harem at the Imperial Palace in Constantinople with the other slaves. Boys like him prepared to become eunuchs at the age of twelve, and be in service to the Sultan's wives.

Bagus had a good life, the women in the harem doted on him. Many had their children taken away and sold. Some did not have any babies at all. They schooled him in the art of organizing the feasts, making bath oils, and massage. His mistress dressed him in fine clothing and kept his hair long like a girl.

One day a foolish eunuch fell in love with one of Sultan's concubines and ran away with her. The Sultan flew into a terrible rage. He ordered a flogging of the entire eunuch population. The women of the harem panicked. They did not want their precious Bagus flogged. It was too cruel. They dressed him as a slave girl, smuggled him to a market, and sold him to a foreigner who needed a servant.

Bagus never met the man who bought him. The handlers whisked him to the busy port of Constantinople, and shoved inside of the hold of a large ship. The ship had to be loaded with goods packed in wooden boxes, heading for the West Indies.

To his dismay, Bagus discovered his new owner slept in one of those boxes. He appeared above trembling Bagus and announced the child would be his source of food during the long journey at sea. With no means of escape, a ten-year-old boy dressed as a girl gave in to his terrible fate.

The life onboard turned out very different to the one at the harem. No one bathed on that filthy ship, and he had to use a communal slop bucket. The unwashed lice ridden bodies of the sailors and the use his master had put him to sickened him to the core.

Master's name was Henderson. A British gentleman, lured to the West Indies by the stories of plenty. He slept in his box by day, and came out at night to feed and be bored. To cope with the boredom he taught Bagus some English. Bagus had a quick mind and learned well. Henderson fed on the boy's blood, and called him his little pudding. Bagus lost his appetite and became thinner with every passing day. He grew weak and contracted a shaking sickness. Henderson witnessed the drastic change, felt pity for Bagus, and left him alone to hunt for healthier prey.

Soon, a rumor started aboard about an incubus. It spread like fire. Henderson became terrified and stopped emerging from his box. Bagus had to lure drunken sailors down to the hold and close the trap door leaving the poor soul at Henderson's mercy. After, Bagus had to dispose of the bodies by throwing them overboard. The strain made Bagus even sicker and he begun to feel the need for blood. He would suck on the wounds of Henderson's dead sailors, even tried to ensnare one. He never had the courage to act upon it and resigned to finishing Henderson's bounty and catching rats. Bagus realized he became just like Henderson, and crawled to sleep in the same box with his master because the sun burned his tender skin.

One night, the ship came to a sudden halt. They had arrived early. The port authorities boarded the ship forewarned by the messenger about the missing sailors. The orders came to check every cargo box, and the ones under suspicion be thrown overboard.

The soldiers combed the ship. Henderson panicked again and refused to leave his box. Bagus slipped out and hid in the bolts of sail fabric. From his hiding place he witnessed how they discovered Henderson, bound him with chains, thrown in the box. He watched how the soldiers nailed the box shut and threw it in the sea. Henderson's piercing screams bounced off the terrified faces of the onlookers. They kept crossing themselves in horror, but were too superstitious to put a real end to Henderson's life. It would be more humane to burn him, than to let him linger in the depths of the ocean for eternity. Bagus slipped out and hid in a little dinghy helmed by a slave boy who delivered fruit.

A tavern keeper discovered terrified Bagus. The keeper, Pedro Malia, ordered his wife Marianna to bathe and feed the child. A fresh exotic girl made a good slave. Marianna discovered Bagus' true nature, and devised a plan. Marianna, a religious woman, feared sin and the punishments that would follow. However, her greed for riches and gold proved more powerful than piety. She set up Bagus to pose as a courtesan, and instructed him to murder his "clients". This allowed her and Pedro to steal the victim's gold without dirtying their hands, so they could go to the confession with a clean conscience.

Bagus had a good life again. He was well fed by the blood of the tradesmen and sailors, dressed in fancy clean clothing and living in a comfortable room with Marianna's slaves catering to his needs. In a while, he begun to realize he was a prisoner. He also began to understand that he was the victim. Repulsion and loathing simmered inside his heart until he revolted and refused to murder his victims. By then, Pedro and Marianna lived in the grandest house on the island, with a talk of him becoming a Governor. They knew that without Bagus they had no other means to easy riches. Nevertheless, they taught him a harsh lesson by locking the poor little vampire in the cellar. Bagus spent six months in a complete darkness and no nourishment. When at last the Melias freed him, they had encountered a different Bagus. He had become wild and vicious, insanity had overtaken him, and he murdered the entire family in his rage. When he came to his senses, he stood covered in blood and gore of his captors. Weakened and wishing for death he ran to the ocean. Domenico, the last remaining Melia brother captured Bagus and forced him to a different location.

This time poor Bagus had no sweet life, no slaves, just rough sailors who gave their lives and to be robbed of their hard earned coins. Bagus found his new prison in a dingy shed with an earthen floor and a hole dug in the ground to hide from the sun. He even tried to escape on several occasions, gave up, lost count of time, hope, and finally became catatonic.

A stray cat that came at night to sit with him was his only friend. Dominico, an old man by then, saw no more use for Bagus. He threw him on the donkey cart, took him to the mountains, and left him there for the sun and vultures to finish. An easy job, Bagus became a husk of his previous self over the years. One hundred years passed since his arrival on the island. The cat came with him and stayed as he crawled in search of shade. Badly burned, he stayed alive. She had led him to the cave and sustained him with her milk. Since then, generations of cats descendant from her had kept Bagus company and nourished him with their milk, including Smeela. A woman came to check on him and brought firewood. Her name was Charo Malia, daughter of Dominico, and the last remaining member of the Malia family. Torn by guilt of the evil deeds of her ancestors she tried to make amends. She never married to have a family of her own, dedicating her life to Bagus. Unlike her family, she had no greed, and lived her life by practicing simple magic, and taking care of cats and Bagus. Finally, an old age caught up with her. At ninety, she was not able to make long journeys to the mountain cave anymore, or to gather wood for the small fire. Sometimes, she sent Smeela to deliver basic supplies like matches and even paints with brushes in a small bag strapped to her back. Bagus begged the old woman to put an end to his miserable life, she refused. Old superstitions lay heavy on her mind. She promised to send someone to do what he asked. Bagus believed me to be the one. The chosen one, who would carry out this mission of mercy, which would set him free before the wood runs out and he would remain in the dark forever.

His voice became weak as he leaned against me for support. I stroked his head and he laid it on my shoulder. We sat like this for a while.

"You have to free me, please. I have no will to do it myself, because of fear to die alone."

I understood his quiet despair, but dreaded this request. I had never helped anyone like this before. I almost drowned Prosha the chipmunk. It was just a hotheaded reaction.

"You will be set free."

The words escaped before I had a chance to think, driven by pity above anything else. The fire burned out, just gleaming embers remained. The dawn approached.

Gathering his light shape in my arms was easy, so was carrying him to the entrance of the cave in the early light. I laid him down below the rock, stroked his cheek and he smiled at me. The sunrise came in a sudden wave of pink. I would call it beautiful on any other morning. On that day, it delivered a cruel murder.

Bagus slowly turned to dust before my eyes. He gazed up at the azure sky, holding my hand. In his last moments, I had caught a glimpse of a beautiful child he had once been, not the monster. Now the monster was gone, only a sad memory and ashes remained.

I gathered the ashes into my empty canteen, shook out his poncho and folded it into the backpack, then tried to find my way back to the city. Smeela had vanished. Perhaps she made her way back to Charo Melia, the Cat Lady.

On the long way down the mountain, I thought about the futility and hopelessness of existence. Of injustices and of disappointments one had to face. Happy ends happened only in stories, not in a real life. Burdened by thoughts as heavy as the rocks on the path, I had to sit down and balance my breathing. I meditated on the mountainside until the happier thoughts emerged. The magic lay in realization of love, of kindness, and in sacrifice. This is how the inhabitants of this island survived. There was always the one who carried the torch of love forward, like Charo. Whom did I have? I had nature, memories, and Sebastian waiting for me at home at LaRose Gris. I had my ideals and my search for magic. I also had met someone special and learned a precious lesson to never give in to despair, never to lose hope, fight to the end.

My spirits picked up a bit when I caught sight of the beautiful crescent bay again. A plan formed in my mind. I hurried down the mountain path towards the city to find Charo Melia. It did not take long. She waited for me by the church steps. I eyed her, uncertain what to do next. She approached and hugged me close to her bony frame.

"Muchas gracias, cariña, bless you, I knew you were the one to help us."

I embraced her, and we stood with arms around each other, absorbing the currents of grief running through us.

"He loved you, and he had forgiven your family," I said.

"Now I can die in peace." She said and covered her eyes.

I lowered her hands, and showed her the canteen. She asked

what was inside and took it from me, untwisted the cap and dipped her finger inside to apply a bit of the ash to her forehead.

"I will scatter the rest in my garden back home," I said.

She nodded, wrapped the shawl around her shoulders, and shuffled away without saying another word. The cats followed her. After taking a few steps, she turned.

"Did you share your blood with him?"

"Just a little"

"Then you will never get sick and stay young a very long time, larga vida. Some of his magic is in you now."

She was right. I already felt energy of his magic surging in my veins. I believed it was faith in a better day.

"The priest at the church asked about you. What should I say to him? Maybe he will say a prayer for you to Santa Maria?"

"Tell him that I am on the first merchant ship out, and his prayers are appreciated."

We hugged for the last time.

I ran straight to the port master's office. A tanned man in a blue cap stood on the ladder by the doorway, whitewashing the building.

"Do you have any merchants leaving port today?" I asked.

"Hurry up. *Consuela* is leaving in one hour," he replied pointing to the pier.

I rushed over to the gangway and saw a group of sailors smoking by the berth.
Breathless, I asked for the Captain. A stocky Asian man smiled and tipped his cap.

"Captain Joyo at your service," he said.

After a brief discussion, we made a deal to cross the Atlantic, no potato duty, just cash. *Consuela* headed to Istanbul. I appreciated the coincidence, for little Bagus came from there almost three hundred years ago.

Something touched my leg and I looked down. Smeela's curious and loving face appeared by my feet. I scooped her up and raised my eyes questioning Captain Joyo. He laughed.

"A cat is for luck. No worries, plenty of milk aboard."

Holding Smeela close to my heart, I boarded the ship, excited about the new adventures waiting for me at the border of two continents.

11. ALCHEMY AND FOX

During the six-week journey to Istanbul, I became accustomed to the ship's routine spending most of my time on the deck enjoying the ocean wind. To everyone's surprise, I did not get seasick as the other passengers sometimes did. On the contrary, the sea infused my body and spirit with the energy from its salty winds and the dark waves.

Consuela had a crew of fourteen people, including several female members who took care of the housekeeping and light cooking when the chef took a break. The same chef made sure I never skipped meals. This reminded me of Tilde and her constant lamenting about my weight. The pot-bellied chef, Saikat, did not even mention my slim frame, but his sighs spoke louder than words when he placed yet another delicious looking pastry in front of me.

I liked the mess hall on *Consuela*, a simple open space just like our meditation room at home. mandalas adorned the walls and the incense always burned in front of smiling Buddha. Everyone on board liked to share stories in their spare time just like the Russian sailors. My stories about Winai impressed them. They loved that I had a Venerable Lama for a friend. During this quiet journey, I began to keep a journal about my adventures. Putting the thread of mysterious events on paper made it easier than constant sorting and thinking.

Smeela had two beautiful calico kittens. When the kittens were able to roam on their own, they became the darlings of the crew, eliciting bursts laughter with their antics. I fashioned a bed for Smeela with the old poncho left by our tragic Bagus and she showed her appreciation with scratchy kisses and loud purring.

One early morning, the loud sound of a dropping anchor announced we reached Istanbul. I flew up to bridge marveling at the view of this majestic city in the distance. The morning sun chased the mist away, and the city stood eternally beautiful against a backdrop of an azure sky. I stopped a crewmember and asked why we were not approaching the port. He explained the port is huge, and hundreds of vessels arrived daily from all over the globe. Everyone took a place in the queue and entered the port guided by the tugboat. True enough, dozens of vessels of all sizes waited their turn to enter the port of Istanbul. I watched the tiny tug guide *Consuela* and imagined Constantinople where little Bagus lived all those years ago. The tall ships running the waves with their sails spread over ancient blue-gray waters of the Sea of Marmora.

Smeela came and asked for a cuddle. I kissed her between the ears and wondered how we will travel together with the kittens, then heard quiet footsteps behind me. Saikat the chef had a package in his hands. Smeela jumped down from my embrace to greet him.

"Miss Veronica, last year we were anchored in Boston and I was given this by a friend. Can you deliver it to someone in Istanbul? I don't have time. Too much to do before the next sailing."

"I will try, do you have an address?"

"Yes, it's right here on the top. I appreciate it very much, Miss Veronica."

I took the package wrapped in old-fashioned brown parcel paper bound with twine, and checked out the address written in sloppy cursive. The handwriting looked somewhat familiar. I could not shake this impression on the way to my stateroom. In a moment, tripping over Smeela, I turned around and ran back to the chef.

"Chef Saikat, who gave you this?"

"Oh, that's easy. Professor Gaspar Dix. It's for his friend, Professor Ira Silverman. He did not wish to post it, said that from hand to hand is safer. I trust you, Miss Veronica."

"How do you know Gaspar? He taught me Latin."

"His mother is the greatest pastry chef. She was *my* teacher."

This twist of fate stunned, and Winai's words swirled in my head. *No such thing as a coincidence.* A familiar excitement of a new adventure about to begin surged through me.

A knock on the door interrupted my packing. Captain Joyo stood outside my cabin cradling a kitten.

"We make a small party for you before you leave, Miss Veronica, come join us."

"Thank you Captain, you didn't have to," I said, sensing there was more to it.

"One question, I want to ask, as a friend. Why you travel, go to Istanbul, alone?"

I hesitated but decided to tell him the truth, "I'm searching for magic."

His face showed incomprehension.

"My purpose is to discover something new, wondrous, and beautiful. To learn about the unusual, and then share with those I love."

Captain Joyo smiled.

"You no need to go far, just look out, you'll see real magic. Ocean is magic, as you say wondrous and beautiful, makes me happy, sharing with everyone."

He was right. I knew the sea was wondrous. But how could I explain angel voices, secret creatures with eternal life, or rainmaking flutes?

"Miss Veronica," said the Captain when we came up to the common room, "we loved having you aboard, and you are welcome on *Consuela* at any time. So are your beautiful Smeela, and her kittens."

The crew cheered him on.

"We would like the cats to stay here with us," said one of the female crewmembers, "how are you planning to take care of them on your travels?"

This came as a surprise. Still, I became somewhat relieved by this announcement. The crew was right. What would I do with three cats on my quest? It was unfair to drag them into the unknown, perhaps even dangerous adventures.

"All right, I understand your concern, and I thank you," I said, "but you have to promise me, when I get home and you dock in Boston, I get them back."

"You have a word of a Captain," said Captain Joyo and placed a hand over his heart.

I knew parting with Smeela would be the hardest thing in my life. Harder even than saying good-bye to Sebastian, because she depended on me. I pressed her to my chest, kissed the black nose, and looked into luminous green eyes.

"You have my word that I will come back for you, my brave Smeela, I swear by our poor Bagus from the cave."

Once again, backpack thrown over the shoulder, I came ashore. If the port of Miami resembled a busy anthill, the port of Istanbul proved to be a thousand times busier. Full of noise and rush it stunned, especially after spending six weeks at sea of semi-solitude.

At the port office, a clerk shrugged at my request for a city map. She gave me a booklet with a warning that in a city as old as Istanbul not all streets would be marked. I had to begin somewhere and decided to deliver Gaspar's package, in hopes Professor Silverman would help me with advice on where to stay. The clerk looked at the address I had copied on the piece of paper and said it was located in the Grand Bazaar area. Anyone would be happy, she explained, to provide better directions once I reached the Bazaar.

Istanbul begged for exploration. This fascinating city knew the rule of Roman emperors as Constantinople, and endured since the ancient cradle of culture known as Byzantium. The museums brimming with antiquities, magnificent Hagia Sophia, and ancient hills of Anatolia beckoned with magic awaiting discovery.

According to the map, the way to the Grand Bazaar appeared easy. I could walk, but did not trust my weakened sea legs to carry me far in the congested city, plus the heat. Instead, I hopped on a tram filled with tourists speaking in dozens of different languages. I listened to their conversations, marveling at my miraculous ability to comprehend French, Spanish, and even some Dutch. No, not miraculous, thanks to those boring long lessons of Latin at the Boston Library where Professor Dix yelled out the difficult verbs trying to drill them into my head. His teaching proved right, "*Unum tantum*, you need only one language to understand all."

The Grand Bazaar looked like a city within a city with thirteen entrances, enveloped by the web of narrow streets buzzing with shoppers, vendors, and tourists. Stores by the entrance where I ended up spilled their wares direct on the sidewalk.

A slim young man in a white shirt holding a sign advertising a guided tour offered to show me around. I gave him an address, which was not an address in its traditional sense, but some location landmark at the Grand Bazaar where no addresses exist. Happy to get my own personal guide, I gave the man a few dollars. He whisked me on the craziest walk of my entire life.

The Bazaar overwhelmed like an unexpected storm, with the smells of roasting food, the stunning abundance of exotic and flamboyant things.

"You won't find a better carpet in all Istanbul I guarantee, beautiful lady," said the carpet vendors as they shook their rugs in front of me.

"This is a caftan that will transform you into a princess, with shoes to match," yelled the caftan vendors.

Hundreds of sparkling crystal chandeliers displayed in rows dazzled. Their beauty echoed of my long lost magical crystal bead.

"Come to my store, choose any bauble, best price," promised sweet-voiced men by the jewelry stores the moment they caught my eye. The guide kept propelling along without letting me stop.

"You never escape them until you spent all your money," he explained.

I have never seen such staggering amounts of jewelry, pearls, and precious stones drowning the gold alley.

"Cigarette, tea?" offered the salesmen with neat mustaches resplendent in pristine white shirts, "come inside, free just for looking."

They praised, yelled, smiled and called out endearing nicknames, "my beauty," "darling," "my friend," anything to attract me to their wares. I loved this exciting sensory barrage. Everywhere I looked the collision of east and west burst into unimaginable. Swiss watches and French perfume sold alongside harem slippers and belly dancer hip belts, modern dresses from Europe and cotton caftans, exotic gold jewelry, and Coca Cola six-packs. The contrasts impressed me, and probably thousands of other visitors who came to explore the Grand Bazaar on that day.

My rapid-talking guide talked about the spice market and the silk market, warned about the pickpockets and unscrupulous store vendors who would cheat me in a blink of an eye. I had no chance to ask questions, he bombarded me with information without a pause.

At last, we stopped in front of a small shop with a faded striped awning and old English gold leaf lettering on the window, *Librorum ex Argenteas*, Books of Silver. The guide stuck a card with his name and location in my hand before taking off in search of a new client. It would be quite impossible to find him again, for I had no idea where I was.

I pushed the weathered door and entered an antique bookshop. The scent of the old books welcomed me to a different world of muted sounds and subdued colors. Rows of books pushed at the ceiling, wood ladders on tracks flanked the cramped shelves. I drew a breath of relief, happy end up in the world I loved and knew best.

"Hello, is anyone here?" I called into the silence, looked around, and waited for an answer.

The shop appeared empty, only the dancing dust specs swirled in the sunshine from the small window. Enjoying the silence, I traced the book spines with my finger, scanning the titles.   To   my delight, most were in Latin. I pulled one out and began to read about the life of an 11th century Syrian gemologist until someone coughed in an obvious attempt to distract me.

"Oh, sorry, I was looking for Professor Ira Silverman."

"But why, may I ask?" asked the tall thin gentleman with unmistakable British accent. He stuck a pince-nez on his hooked nose reminding me of Sherlock Holmes.

"Is this a real pince-nez?" I gestured to his spectacles, "very nice."

"Indeed, thank you Miss... I did not catch your name," he said, looking pleased.

"Are you Professor Silverman?"

"In this life I am," said the gentleman, and chuckled at his own joke.

"My name is Veronica LaRose. I have a package for you from Gaspar Dix, my teacher." My turn came to smile because his pince-nez fell off to dangle on a gold chain from the lapel of his shabby green jacket.

"But why? Was he waiting for you to grow up before you could deliver it?" He stuck the glasses back on. "I requested those translations over two years ago."

"The package traveled on a merchant vessel with someone he knows. I just got to deliver it by a pure coincidence."

"I do not choose to believe in coincidences, Miss LaRose, everything happens for a reason," he said.

This statement proved I ended up in a perfect place.

I pulled the package from my backpack and he cut the binding twine with a small pocketknife. We unwrapped the notebooks one by one. He examined each text, smacking his lips with pleasure, and then passed them on to me. The notebooks contained translations of the manuscripts from the library.

"Look," I said pointing to the top of the page, "*Translated by V. LaRose*. That's me Professor, isn't it amazing, to travel half the world and find something I did years ago?"

"We never know what we put in motion when we begin something. Are you familiar with the butterfly effect theory?"

Not waiting for a reply, he picked up the notebooks and walked away. I guessed the question was just rhetorical. He called my name and I followed, squeezing between the bookshelves into a small laboratory.

An array of bottles, beakers, burners, mortars, and a strange steaming apparatus reminded me of old apothecaries described in books. Professor Silverman motioned to a stool in the corner and asked to tell him the story of how I came into possession of the package and of my relationship with Professor Dix. I complied, omitting a few details to make him think I was on my "educational tour" as Dr. Schuele had called it.

"What is this laboratory? Why in a book shop?"

The beakers bubbled with a blue liquid. Opaque glass bottles with yellowed labels lined the counter. Something glimmered in the mysterious apparatus emitting a bittersweet smell of a wet tree bark.

"It is my lifelong project, Miss LaRose. With it, I plan to change the perception of the world as we know it."

"With this bubbling blue water?"

"This is not water, and I am conducting a precise alchemical process," said Professor Silverman and plunged into a lecture about something I knew little about, alchemy.

"You think alchemy belongs to the ancients and it's a non-science as stated by today's so called scholars? Then you are wrong, my young friend. Alchemy is a science that embraces possible and impossible. Alchemy destroys boundaries between physical and metaphysical, it teaches the alchemist about miracles in the mundane. With alchemy I am achieving the so-called impossible, for I am not afraid to destroy in order to create, to go beyond alpha and omega, transmute *prima materia* to *tempus, salve coagula...*"

The longer he talked, the more confusing it became. Several times, I tried to insert an inquiry of my own with no success. At last, I raised my arm and waved, this caught his attention.

"Yes, you have a question?" he asked as if addressing a student.

"It's very fascinating, and I would like to learn from you very much, Professor Silverman. But can you help me find a place to stay first, please?"

"Oh, my apologies, how selfish of me. Here, go to this little inn, it's not far from here."   He scribbled something on the edge of a newspaper, tore it off. I had a feeling he was not too pleased to be interrupted by the 'mundane'.

"Where is *here*? It took my guide more than an hour to reach this shop."

Professor Silverman glanced at me with surprise.

"We are right by the entrance. He must have led you in circles to earn his pay. I hope you did not pay him much, they are a sly lot."

He took a piece of notepaper and with a few quick movements drew a diagram with a fountain pen he pulled from his front pocket, which according to my observation contained a whole arsenal of tools.

"This is the Grand Bazaar. These are the entrances, and we are right here," he drew an X. "The whole bloody place seems like a rabbit warren at first. Use the Gold Street as a main landmark and it becomes clear in an instant."

I examined his crude map.

"So where is this Ural Inn? Is it named after the mountains?"

"No, the owner's name is Ural. And it's right here," he said, and drew another X at an intersecting street. I thanked him again for his dinner invitation as soon as I am settled at the inn.

The noise and the bustle assaulted my senses the minute I closed the door of the tranquil bookshop behind me. A young man, by his looks a bit older than I, perched on an overturned basket across the narrow street. He slowly rose and approached with a lazy gait as I tried to figure out the direction on the hand drawn map.

"Hello there, so you are the Prof's new student," he said, hands in his pockets, and smile wider than the Cheshire cat's.

"No. Are you his old student?" I said, and lowered my bag. He laughed and shook his dark neat head. I noticed the amazing contrast of his vivid blue eyes and a tanned face.

"I used to be. Need directions?"

"How much are you charging?" I remembered the Professor's warning about the 'sly lot'.

"Nothing if you have dinner with me."

I shook my head at this sudden invitation and started to walk away. He followed a few steps behind whistling a tune. In about five minutes, I lost my way. He stopped as well, trying to charm me with his dimpled grin.

"All right, show me to Ural Inn," I said, exasperated.

"And I'll introduce you to this maze. Don't be afraid, I'm not a Minotaur," he said and offered his hand, "I'm Jason Fox. My parents and I are British expats, artists. I'm studying archeology at the U."

I told him my name. He carried my bag slung over his shoulder. We walked side by side on the narrow sidewalk. He asked when I arrived and from where. As we passed the street vendor, he bought a bag full of Turkish delight. I never tried it before, and loved the soft texture of this sweet tasty dessert.

"We're here," said Jason, and pointed to a doorway painted bright blue, *Ural Inn* in bright yellow letters above it. "But before you go in, wipe the sugar powder off your face."

I laughed and thanked him.

"See you around," he said and left me alone by the entrance.

Mr. Ural gave me a room on the top floor of the three-story building. I performed a ritual with the Tingsha to cleanse the energy just as Winai taught me, and went on a little balcony above the courtyard.

The scene below glowed with life, so unlike Santiago. A pergola wound with the grape vines, bright splashes of potted red geraniums and black chickens with shiny feathers pecking at the pavement. Rhythmic sounds of eastern music came from the inn's cafe. Appealing scent of coffee and cinnamon came from a faint warm breeze.

My floor housed two more rooms and a large shared bathroom with a huge bath, Turkish style. Blue and white checkered wallpaper adorned the walls of my room. A bistro table and two chairs stood on small balcony.

I eyed the white wicker bed and wondered if falling asleep would be as easy as on a rocking ship. Then decided to try it, and slept until the warm rays of sunset touched my eyelids through the thin gauze of the curtains.

In the hallway, on the way from the bathroom, I bumped into my neighbors, a British couple in their twenties on their honeymoon. Both tall blond and tanned, they carried on as if they knew me forever. *People are sure friendly here* I thought on my way down to Professor's shop for dinner.

I found the way taking my time, afraid to get lost, and all the while had a feeling of someone following. Several times, I stopped and looked back, but noticed no one except for the shoppers milling about.

The Professor showed the last customer out while I browsed the store's impressive collection of antique books. First printed editions of astronomy tomes had scorch marks. These books survived the book burnings made by the opposing church. History lessons given by Gaspar helped to recognize and understand the precious material in my hands. I found shelves of books on alchemy and astrology. To my delight, the shop had books on herbal lore written in the past centuries. Some dated back to the 14th century, which made me wonder whether their author or owner was immolated for possessing this knowledge. If I lived then, would that be my fate as well? It certainly would be Anna's lot. She always said that, as a joke, of course. I realized how much I missed Anna, and how much fun we would have exploring the Bazaar. We had to come here together one day.

The books cheered me up. I hoped Professor Silverman had a few tomes about magic tucked away in his collection.

"Do you know the herbs are an integral part of an alchemical process?" asked the Professor, when he looked over my shoulder at the book I held.

"I have been studying herbal lore and growing plants since I was a little girl," I said unwilling to part with the book based on the writings of Hermes Trismegistus.

"Then I shall select several tomes for you, in my gratitude for your translations," said the Professor and put up his hands at my avid objections. I saw the lofty book prices in the catalogue. Nevertheless, he insisted and I could not refuse such precious gift. Finally, we went out to have dinner in one of the neighboring restaurants.

Lounging on the wine-colored carpet cushions, we drank amber tea from the gold-plated green glasses. The flavor of the tea reminded of my favorite Earl Grey with lots of hot milk. We snacked on dried apricots while they prepared the main course. The brass lights flickered with a red glow to the tune of the eastern cymbal tune playing in the background. Were it not for my afternoon nap, I would have fallen asleep right there. Our pilaf came along with roasted vegetables and a delicious stuffed eggplant dish called dolma. I could refuse the Turkish delight and halvah for dessert with more tea.

"I met your student, Jason Fox," I said to keep the conversation going and to steer away from questions why I traveled alone and where was my family.

"He's no student of mine, stay away from him, Miss LaRose," said Professor very animated all of a sudden, "He is a fox, that's certain, a thieving fox."

"I think he wants to be friends. His parents are artists and he is a student of archaeology, and he escorted me to the Ural Inn." I did not mention Jason's charming dimples.

"Con artists rather, and he is an antiquities smuggler, a very smooth operator."

"Did he steal something from you?"

"I hired him to help at the store, to free more time for my alchemy project. That little rat robbed me blind. Stole the parchment tomes from Uzbekistan, blamed it on the shoplifters. The rare writings, the legacy of the entire nation secured for the Tashkent Museum. I traded some of my best Confucius translations for them.

Priceless! He probably sold them to some shark in the East." Professor Silverman became quite bitter and upset until I assured him to stay away from Mr. Fox. I did not intend to do so. My curiosity raised its head like an awakened cat.

"Why did you set up your shop in Istanbul and not London, Professor Silverman?" I said to change the subject.

"It's a long story. But please, call me Ira."

"Then stop calling me Miss LaRose, it makes me sound like someone's aunt. Share this long story please, Ira."

"Fine, I will make it short. Gaspar's father and I were partners and friends once. Had an antiquities shop in Vienna, but we closed it down and moved as far apart from each other as possible, but we correspond, to my chagrin," said Ira and took a ferocious bite from the halvah.

"So what happened?"

"Gaspar's mother happened. She thought his father was a better match and married him. I keep in contact with the boy, brilliant mind. End of the conversation. Better tell why your last name is so familiar to me."

"I am not famous, perhaps you are thinking about my grandfather Etienne LaRose. He made Absinthe LaRose, when it was illegal in the United States," I said trying not to sound too proud.

"Yes, a drink from the Muse born of Alchemy. For years, I tried to get my hands on a bottle from a chap named Van Stratten, Gaspar's friend, offered a hefty sum, but no luck. I wonder why, still."

"I will make sure to send you a bottle when I return home. Sebastian Van Stratten used to be my legal guardian."

"Small world, who would have ever thought of such coincidence, I would immensely happy."

Ira Silverman insisted to accompany me to Ural Inn. According to a local custom, a woman should have an escort after dark. As we left the cozy restaurant, I noticed a familiar slim figure turning the corner. The mysterious Mr. Fox followed us trying to stay as far behind as possible on the deserted street. I chose not to point it out to Ira and asked to describe his alchemy project instead.

"Come to the shop tomorrow and I will enlighten you," said Ira once we reached the Ural Inn.

"Fine, thank you, until tomorrow then," I said in a loud voice and did my best not to laugh as Jason Fox, who still tailed us, ducked behind the empty street stall.

Mr. Fox was on a hunt, and I looked forward to finding the reason behind it.

12. TREASURE DUST

A scent of strong Turkish coffee tickled my nose and woke me up. The sun bathed my room with its golden glory. I stretched and remembered a day of exploring ahead and called down for breakfast. On the way to the bathroom, I bumped into a veiled woman in the hall. She must have been an occupant of the third room on my floor. She passed by with her head lowered and without any acknowledgement. Women in traditional Muslim garb were everywhere, but I did not expect to see her alone, they always had a male escort.

To my surprise, my own male escort presented himself in the hotel lobby and caught me on the way out to explore the city. Mr. Fox waited decked out in bright blue dress shirt that matched his eyes, with not a hair out of place, and perfumed like a notions salesman.

"I was just passing by and wanted to see how you were," said Jason and checked me over. I did not look nice, dressed in my scuffed black jeans and a wrinkled shirt. Cringing under his appraising eyes, I wished for my elegant long dresses.

"I see Mr. Fox decided not to lurk behind today."

"I'm not lurking, I know Silverman can't stand me. Where are you headed, need a cheap guide?"

"I am on my way to get something nice to wear." I lied, and had no idea why.

"Then let's go, I will take you to the best silk merchants and we will bargain."

"I don't bargain, and I have an appointment later on. Thank you anyway," I said, and walked around him.

"They expect you to bargain, it's part of a deal. And the Prof will still be there even if you are late."

Jason smiled with those adorable dimples. He was right about Professor Silverman, and shopping for silk clothing enticed me.

As we walked, Jason described the history of this four hundred year old market. Some of the storefronts belonged to same family for generations. Silk merchants and the silversmiths were the most respected.

Jason guided me through the silk street and every store appeared the same to me with the abundance of materials, colors, and adornments. I kept wondering about making a right choice in this kaleidoscope of color.

Jason ignored most of the yelling vendors and nodded to some until he opened a door to a shop with a large brass bell hanging by the entrance. A man dressed in a traditional spotless white shirt greeted us smiling from behind a luxuriant black mustache.

"Natasha! You come to the right store. Sit down, we show you our best. Tea?" he said and gallantly led me to the armchair in the middle of the showroom. Another clerk brought a gilded glass of steaming tea on a silver tray.

"I am not Natasha," I told the salesman, "why can't I look around by myself?"

"They call every young girl that, because to them it's beautiful. This is not a cheap stall, you show them respect by sitting down. They won't hold you back if you decide to leave. Relax, Natasha," said Jason, and gave me an assuring smile.

He exchanged a few words with the clerks in Turkish. The man disappeared in the back room and in a few minutes came back with a four-way mirror. The assistant arranged the mirrors into a dressing room and asked me to get behind them, after taking my measurements. Once I entered this mirror box, he proceeded to hand over the dresses for trying on. Enclosed by the mirrors I saw how the clothing looked on me at every angle. I did not expect it to be so much fun.

"Now bring me the black with grey, or the purple but longer. The sleeves on this one are too narrow. I do not like the gold trim. Do you have shoes to go with this one?"

My every wish came through within seconds. The beautiful garments kept passing back and forth until I made a choice. I chose a black silk caftan style dress over the sky blue tunic, a pair of soft leather slippers and a black silk scarf.

Upon seeing the total cost for this finery, I headed towards the door. My modest budget could not support this outfit. Jason said something and the man retorted. The rapid exchange continued until the salesman asked a much lesser price. I grabbed my new outfit with joy and went to change.

"Give me a kiss, Natasha, and it's free," said the salesman and tapped his clean shaven cheek. Jason smacked him on the back and they both laughed. I did not know the source of their amusement, and just ignored them. All my travel clothing and Doc Martins went in my backpack.

The silk fabric of the new outfit clung to my skin with cool softness. Jason whistled.

"Now you look like a native. It suits you Veronica. You are a pretty girl. Now, how about some lunch?"

"Thank you Mr. Fox, but it's time for me to go. Maybe tomorrow," I said surprised at my promise to meet him again.

He walked me to the intersection and pointed in the direction of Professor's bookshop. I became accustomed to the Bazaar area and had no fear of getting lost again. When we parted, his friendly pat on my shoulder left me wishing for something a little more.

"The shop is closed, please come on another day," said Ira Silverman when I walked in.

"It's me Ira, sorry for being late."

"But why, Veronica, you look lovely. What happened to the lanky curly youngster from yesterday? Now you need an escort for sure, or you will be followed around by scores of adoring Turks."

"Thank you Ira, it's still me under all this. I just wanted to feel like a girl again," I said touched by his complement.

"No matter, you are a lady in anything you wear. Never forget that. Now, how would you like to go on a small excursion with me?"

I had fun shopping, and loved to do more exploring. Museums and searching for magic seemed like a far off idea at that moment.

Back on the street, I wished for the heat and crowds to disappear. Professor Silverman must have heard my thoughts and we turned into a narrow lane unfit for cars. We walked the old chipped walkway, between the leaning old buildings with arched windows. Not a plant in site, the only plants I saw in Istanbul so far were in clay pots, and very few pitiful trees. I missed the greenery. My eyes have not rested on it for almost two months since I left Cuba. This was not a city of gardens.

Professor stopped in front of a brass door and made enough noise to wake an army with a ram's head knocker. The door opened in a few moments and we walked into a small oasis.

A playful three-jet fountain stood in the middle of the tiled courtyard, and a pergola adorned with grapevines behind it. Pale yellow grape clusters cascaded down the vines in abundance from a house of Bacchus. The sun shone through the golden grapes turning them into jewels. The man by the open door wore a traditional Turkish caftan with a tussled dark red fez on his head. His face hid under the grey beard, but his dark eyes were friendly and the smile welcoming.

"Welcome my friends. Silverman, I have not had the pleasure for weeks. What were you up to?"

"But why, has it been that long old chap? This young lady is Miss Veronica LaRose. Veronica this is Kazim, my old friend."

"Aero, please come and meet our guests," said Kazim as he bowed over my hand. An older woman dressed in a same manner as Kazim appeared through the doorway and smiled. She had long braided hair and kind eyes.

"My wife will show you around, and then we will feast," said

Kazim, hooked Silverman through the arm and they disappeared through another door, which shut behind them.

"Let the men discuss their business, don't worry, we'll know it soon enough. How would you like to freshen up after a walk on a dusty street, and help me to set up for the meal?"

Aero and I chatted while she hovered around the kitchen adding this or that to the steaming pots and giving soft instructions to the cook. She complemented my outfit and the quality of the fabric. I thanked Jason in my mind.

While the cook made the final touches to our dinner, Aero gave me a tablecloth to lay on the low mahogany table in the courtyard by the fountain. A rich thick rug covered the stones, and we were to sit on the large cushions, Turkish style. Scents of nutmeg and saffron drifted from the kitchen. I could not resist and plucked a few elongated grapes from the vine, they were sweet and warm, like biting into a small sun.

"Ah, *Lady Finger* grapes, sweet as a lady should be." I heard someone say behind me.   Professor and Kazim appeared in the doorway. Kazim carried a chest of polished mahogany. I smiled, because they looked like a number ten to me, Professor Silverman tall and slim, Kazim short and round.

"Veronica, we need you to look at something and settle our argument at once," said Professor. Kazim nodded in agreement, the tassel on his fez bounced. They came over to and flipped the chest lid. Rows of folded envelopes lay inside. Kazim extracted three envelopes and placed them on the low table. Professor unfolded them and asked me to take a closer look. I could not take my eyes off from the uncovered objects. Three blue stones, each the size of the grape sparkled in front of us.

"These stones are precious sapphires, the highest quality, from Burma. They have a brightest hue, almost no inclusions, exceptional clarity. Silverman here insists they have a green tone, I say blue. What do you say?" said Kazim and passed me the loupe.

I stared at the stones. They were magical and I felt their natural

147

power. I read so much about these stones in the books Sebastian once gave me. Described as the throat chakra stones, they promoted spiritual growth. I carefully examined each of them. They were all blue but each had a different beautiful hue.

"This one is the purest blue," I said choosing the perfect stone radiating magic.

"Ha, we put it here for comparison, a red herring, not even a sapphire, this is a tourmaline. Choose from the other two, which one is the purest blue," said Professor.

"Wait, the girl is right about the purity of the tourmaline, and it's very old. I have a written characteristic," said Kazim and pulled out a yellowed parchment. "I can't understand much, it's in Latin."

"But why, give it to the expert, not to me, old chap," said Silverman and gestured at me.

"You won't say. You know the language?" Kazim's round face radiated surprise and admiration.

I read the parchment and translated the poem.

The blue as sky and depth of ocean will lead your spirit to eternity.

"Eternity you say? Kazim, I will take this stone, and the script too if you do not mind. Name your price."

"Aero is ready to serve our meal, we'll discuss after," said Kazim and the precious stones disappeared back in their envelopes.

We made our way back to the shop at dusk after Professor asked me if I wished to learn about his project or leave it until the next time. The stones impressed me and made me curious, especially after watching Professor tap his inner pocket with satisfaction.

To my dismay, I also noticed Mr. Fox in one of the shop's windows we passed, but he did not raise his eyes from the magazine in his hands. I knew that he was watching me again, and did not have any idea why. Feeling a little better inside the secure walls of the bookshop, I settled on my stool in the little lab to listen to Professor's presentation. Instead of talking, he passed me a thick binder. Inside I found stories. Professor asked me to read one aloud.

"Look them through and choose any one you like, Veronica.

Don't question for now," he said and settled in his armchair in the opposite side of the room.

I opened the binder, looked through the index, turned to the appropriate page, and began to read aloud.

Story of the Swan Maiden

Once upon a time, there lived an old man in a village by the lake at the edge of the dark forest. His wife had died long time ago and left him with a little son to take care of. He earned his modest living by constructing wood toys. His most special toy was a swan with the wings that could move by pulling the attached string.

People of the village were hardworking and honest. Everyone helped each other and the boy grew up happy and strong. One day, the King's men came to the village and announced that the war was about and the King needs more money for his army. They took all the villager's possessions as duty, including the set of tools that the boy's father used to make the toys.

The villagers were bitter, but powerless in the face of the king's collectors. Poverty settled over the village. People became fearful and stayed indoors. Only the boy went out into the woods to walk and talk to the trees, because he was a dreamer and saw beauty in everything. He would come back from his walks with stories of a swan that could turn into a beautiful maiden and swim in the lake. Nobody believed him and called him a silly dreamer.

"She is just like the swans you used to make, father. Just as beautiful."

"You are a good boy. Do not think of these fancies, they will bring you nothing but heartache."

The determent boy decided to prove his father wrong and one day came back to the village with a swan in his arms. Its wings were tied. He put the helpless swan in front of the surprised father and the swan had begged in a human voice to let her go, she would give them any riches they desired.

"Alright," said the boy, "we will let you go, but I know you have the magic to make our village whole and happy again." He untied the swan and she disappeared with a flash of blue.

In the evening, the entire village assembled by the lake. Everyone saw a blue lightning and a beautiful maiden in a white flowing dress appeared on the clearing. She had a crown on her head. The villagers heard music and the maiden danced for them. As she danced, a blue dust escaped from her sleeves. When it came from her right sleeve, the tables appeared laden with a feast fit for a king. When she waved her left sleeve, the rich gifts appeared at people's feet. With joy, everyone joined her in a dance.

After the feast, the boy approached the maiden and begged to take him with her. She agreed and gave him a handful of blue dust to release on the lake at her command. The boy said good-bye to his father and promised to return. He held hands with the maiden, and in a flash of blue, they disappeared.

He kept his promise and came to visit every year. His father always watched for a blue flash that preceded his son's arrival. The boy, a young man now, told stories of wondrous places, and said that he became a traveler and the maiden was his lady. The old man believed him and wished him happiness until the end of time.

The End.

"Ira, I enjoyed this fairy tale very much. But what does it have to do with your project?"

"Take a look at the other stories. Not all are fairy tales. Some are eyewitness accounts from centuries ago, just like the ones you delivered from Gaspar Dix. Some are recent. There are examples of folklore from diverse nations and geographical locations."

I leafed though the binder for accounts of angels appearing from the blue light, people disappearing into the blue light. The binder offered countless tales of a blue lightning delivering change, either good or bad.

"Ira, do you think it's magic? I found a crystal bead once. I thought it was magical because it had a blue sparkle, and made me think of angel voices. I lost it a long time ago."

"You may call it magic, but it's a natural phenomena methinks," said Professor and plucked the pince-nez off his nose, "to be harnessed by the power of alchemy, no other. Sorry about your crystal."

"I think it's magic," I said looking at the beakers filled with an electric blue liquid, trying to grasp their meaning.

"Just think, Veronica, it may be the way to access time parallel to ours, to see other worlds beyond our imagination."

"Legends throughout the existence of our civilization and even beyond, like Atlantis, tell of strange visitations, time travel, aliens, disappearances, and other similar phenomena. There is a common denominator. In most of the stories, some sort of light preceded the occurrence. Most of the time, it was a surging blue light, or a lightning. For example, it is in the Indian epos of Ramayana, or a blue aura radiating around the angels who addressed some bewildered traveler. Concluding that, I have begun the search for something containing this type of energy. Something, that might exist in any dimension," Professor continued to pace the floor waving his pince-nez around.

"And did you find it?" I asked from my perch.

"Not only found it, isolated and used it," exclaimed Professor stubbing air with his poor pince-nez.
I almost fell off the stool. This was the best I could hope for, inter-dimensional travel. One could not grasp at the magical resources of that.

"Can you tell me how?"

"The very precious stones you saw today and hundreds like them," said Professor with triumph. "I selected the truest blue stones, and then using alchemy dissolved them, isolated their essence which later crystallized into a fine light blue dust of an immeasurable power. Power strong enough to tear the fabric between the parallel worlds."

These theories were hard for me to grasp and understand. I had many questions, and needed time to think them over.

"How long did it take you to conclude this experiment? And can we try it now?"

"Way too long, my dear, years. And no, we cannot try it. It's in testing, and could be dangerous."

"But you told me that you already tried."

"The small excursions I took left me depleted, as if I my skin had turned inside out. I could show you a part of an alchemic process if you like. Only tomorrow, it's getting late."

We found the inn locked up for the night and had to knock hard to wake Ural. He grumbled something about waking up at two in the morning, but wished me good night nevertheless. When I reached my room, I noticed that the door across the hall occupied by a veiled woman stood slightly opened. The moment I entered my room, it closed.

I was in the middle of a dream with someone building a house. The hammering would not stop. Suddenly I realized that someone was banging on my door and it was daylight. Groggy from the dream, wrapped in a robe I opened the door. A beaming face of Jason Fox hovered over a tray covered with a white towel.

"Lunch, remember you promised to have one with me today?" he said and meandered into my room with no ceremony whatsoever, looking dapper and handsome as always.

"Lunch? What time is it? And why are you following me around?"

"One hour past noon, Sleeping Beauty, and because I like you."

"Alright, give me time to wash up and I will be right back. Let's eat on the balcony."

I gathered my bathroom things, clothing, and shoes. After a short struggle with my gravity defying hair, I came back flushed and ready to take on Mr. Fox.

"What gives you a right to barge into my room and bring me food I did not ask for?"

"Why don't we go sightseeing today?" said Jason lounging on my unmade bed.

I glanced at the tray on the balcony table laden with pita bread and small bowls filled with dips and a steaming Turkish coffee in a brass pot.

"It's for two, dig in, Veronica," said Jason and joined me at the little table. He kept smiling at me with those irresistible dimples. His blue eyes reminded me of the precious stones form yesterday.

The food tasted delicious, coffee invigorated me. I began to relax in Jason's company. The wind came from nowhere and swept over the balcony, scattering paper napkins around us, a few even fluttered over the railing like giant butterflies. Jason tried to catch the rest. I went inside the room and rummaged in my backpack.

"Hey, Jason, take this and place it on top of the napkins, the weight will keep them down," I said and gave him the black rock a sailor gave me on *Vjeter*. He took the rock, twirled it in his hand, and tossed it in the air.

"Why do you carry coal around?"

"Just a souvenir. See, it came handy."

He continued to play with the rock, until I playfully grabbed it from his hands and placed it on the flyaway serviettes where it belonged.

"So how's our friend Silverman, you seem to spend a lot of time at that shop of his? Does he at least take you anywhere?"

"You saw us yesterday, and do not pretend. What are you up to, Jason? Ira said not to trust you."

"Yes, so if I did. Do you know whom you went to see?"

"Old friend of Professor's and his wife."

"Do you also know that he is a diamond and precious stones dealer? Did the old Prof buy anything?"

"I would not know, his wife kept me company." I became cautious. His questions carried more than just curiosity.

"Come on, I know he buys diamonds on regular bases," he said and touched my cheek.

"No, sapphires, maybe", I blushed. His toying touch unnerved me. The many questions became annoying. The time was getting on. I could not wait to find out more about Professors discoveries.

"Sorry Jason, I have to go, you may stay here and clean up. Thanks for lunch," I said, picked up the stone, stuck it in the backpack, and left Mr. Fox alone in my messy room.

"Say, old girl, is that smooth chap Fox bothering you? He is always nosing about. And his smile has too many teeth for my liking," said Jeff, my British neighbor. He and his bride Jenna were in the small lobby reading and having coffee at the small tilled table.

"Do not hesitate to ask us for help, love," said Jenna agreeing with her husband.

"Thank you guys, I can handle it for now. And I can see through his toothy smile well enough." Their concern touched me.

A 'Closed' sign hang on the bookshop door, but I found it unlocked. Professor met me with open arms as I appeared. A large pile of books lay assembled at his feet.

"I wanted to select some books for you, Veronica, but got carried away. There is so much knowledge I want to impart."

"I can see that, Ira, you don't need to do it. Those books are priceless, your business needs them."

"Take them, Veronica, and remember that the magic is in the reading," he said fitting the yellowed volumes into a scuffed suitcase. I was happy and bewildered at the same time. *How would I carry this weight on my adventures?* However, did not voice this question, not to offend the kind Professor.

"Now, on with our project," said Professor rubbing his hands together and looking very pleased with himself.

A bright flood lamp illuminated the lab and the apparatus puffed on the table. Professor gave me the precious stones including the one he got yesterday and told me to lower them in the steaming container inside the apparatus. I put on the rubber gloves, and with the long pincers lowered them into a jar of dry ice. The stones became even bluer. In a few moments, the apparatus began to expel a clear liquid which Silverman gathered into a beaker and asked me to use different pincers to extract the frozen stones and place them in the liquid. After I had done that, he positioned the beaker over a flame element and set it to low.

"I will be ready in thirty minutes, and then we begin the crystallization process."

"Why are we doing that?" I asked ready to learn.

"We are creating the energy conductor which is able to rip through the space time continuum using the...."

He stopped speaking midsentence interrupted by the laughter from the direction of the darkened shop. Jason Fox appeared at the lab door. With disbelief, I stared at the cold eye of a gun that he pointed at us.

"Stop your gibberish, old fool, give it up," said Jason, his charm gone.

"Jason, you are crazy," I tried to intervene.

"Shut up, here," he said and threw a canvas bag at me. "Put the diamonds in here, or I will shoot."

"Jason, you're mistaken. These are not diamonds, I swear. But we'll give them to you," I tried to convince him to lower the gun.

"Come on, give me one diamond," he just waved the gun again.

I saw no use of arguing with him, and his idea that Silverman and I had diamonds in the lab. I understood why he followed me. He planned to rob Professor Silverman.

"Alright, they are in the back. Hold on, I will get them for you," said Silverman and rushed to the back of the lab.

The following things happened very fast. To me, they appeared in slow motion. A veiled woman from Ural Inn suddenly sprung up behind Jason and hit him over the head with something heavy. Jason fell backwards. The gun went off and smashed the light. The power went out. A flash of brightest blue pierced the darkness of the shop, and Professor disappeared with it.

I stood frozen in the dim lab for a few moments until I realized the need to run. I felt the wall for a light switch. Jason lay sprawled on the floor unconscious, with a thick book beside him. The mysterious veiled woman disappeared as well. I feared Jason might be coming around soon. I had to deter him before he could attack me again. I did not wish to hurt him, just to hinder for enough time to escape. I grabbed my trusted backpack and located Una's pink braid.

"Sorry, Una," I said, tying Jason's hands behind his back with the braid in a marine knot.

Back in the shop, I grabbed the suitcase with Professor's books. Leaving them behind would torment me. Then ran to the Ural Inn with all the might I could muster.

At the inn, I bumped into Jeff and Jenna who parked their dusty old Fiat in front. I ran up to ask for help, briefly telling them about Jason, and that I need help to get out of town.

"We were planning to leave tomorrow. I see no problem with hitting the road today. Come with us," said Jenna, "we'll be ready in five, will you?"

"I just need to get my stuff, five is plenty."

I gave Jeff the suitcase with books and rushed upstairs for my things. The door in the room across the hall stood ajar, the maid worked inside.

"Where is the lady that stayed here?" I asked her.

"No lady here, Miss. It was rented to a foreign gentleman," she said, wiping her hands on a towel.

I threw my things in the backpack, tucked some tip money under the lamp and run down the stairs thinking about the mysterious veiled woman. Too bad, I had no time to investigate further.

First one in the Fiat, I crouched down on the back seat in case Jason freed himself and came in search of me. Jeff and Jenna appeared with their luggage, in a few minutes we took off. I watched Istanbul from the back seat and regretted not having a better opportunity to explore the city.

"Where are we going?" I asked Jenna.

"Where would you like to go?"

"As far away from Jason Fox as possible," I said.

"You know all roads lead to Rome," said Jeff, glancing at me in the rear view mirror.

"To Rome then."

"Swell. Darling, we are off to Bella Roma," said Jeff, and kissed his bride.

13. POETS IN ROME

My British friends left after spending a few days in Rome. I remained alone in a small hostel near the Coliseum. Restless and brooding over the Istanbul fiasco I wandered the streets. The trip from Istanbul should have taken us a day, but we took our time to enjoy the drive. Once we crossed from Turkey to Greece, the road continued along the coast of the Ionian Sea, past some sleepy fishing villages swaddled in nets and grape vines. We had boozy dinners at the local taverns absorbing the local flavor, wine, and companionship. I enjoyed long walks along the beach thinking over my ordeal in Istanbul while Jeff and Jenna slept off the previous nights' reveling. Nagging thoughts of Professor Silverman and his safety, the mysterious veiled woman, and Jason Fox could not leave me alone. Especially Jason Fox. I almost fell for him, and his charm. How could I be so naive, why did I not listen to Professor and stayed away? I had a feeling the truth escaped me, and I became trapped in events beyond any understanding. Meditation helped to place everything in perspective. It calmed me down. I decided not to push, and simply wait for the truth to reveal itself.

Ancient city of Rome greeted me with its acrid smell of diesel, garbage on the streets, and scents of cooking drifting from every doorway. Yet, her beauty awed me, and power radiated from the ancient walls. Each piazza held a delightful surprise, and the doors to every church became gateways to the world of art and architecture. I could not wait to explore Vatican's vast museums and gardens. From Vatican, I had posted a card to Sebastian. A fragment from the Sistine Chapel, *Miss You* I wrote right on the front where the hands of God and Adam were about to touch.

The crowds of tourists thinned out, and the October rains chased the buses away. Cleansed by thunderstorms, Rome stood ready for the end of another year in its twelve centuries of existence. I have been away from LaRose Gris, my home, for over four months. It felt like centuries. Futile thoughts of magic saddened me. I failed chasing a dream. Sebastian would forgive me for running away. Perhaps time came to head back home.

To get away from the busy city for a day I took the morning train to Ostia, a historical port an hour away from Rome. The hostel manager described it as nice coastal town with empty post-season beaches.

I walked the deserted beach and watched the dark grey sand turn black at the water's edge, just like on my beach at home. A sudden thunderstorm soaked me through. On the train, I felt feverish. Freezing cold crept down inside my bones heavy as mercury.

Like an old creaky woman, I found my way to the hostel and crawled under the blankets. Dampness and cold permeated every inch of my room. With no heat, the tiled floors added to the dampness, and the hot water ran only for the few hours in the mornings and evenings.

For the first time since leaving home, I wished my old nanny Tilde. I craved a hot cup of tea, and had no one to bring it, making me feel even more miserable. Only my herbal tinctures from home were able to get me some comfort, reduce the fever, and halt the ache in my bones. In a few days of misery, I thanked Bagus. My immune system would not be able to cope with the sickness without his bite. Pulling at the shreds of energy, I shuffled to the corner shop for some food. The woman at the counter stuffed my pockets with oranges and boiled eggs. The store did not stock much food, plenty of cigarettes and bottles of cheap wine. I had no interest in either.

Back in my room, I thought about my situation. Rome is a cradle of magic, but I felt none. The fire of adventure had burned out. I eyed the suitcase full of books, but did not wish to evoke the memories of Istanbul. Time had to heal me first.

Someone knocked on my door and I replied from my bed. I hated to leave the warmth of the blanket.

"Veronica, che fa? What's the matter? I leave for a few days and you get sick," said Marisa, the hostel manager as she came in, concern on her rosy face.

"I will get better. Grazie tante. Do you think I could get some heat in the room?"

Marisa came back with coin fed electric heater and more blankets. Everything was coin fed in Rome, elevators, public washrooms, lights. I learned to carry a bagful of change for every occasion. My heater needed a coin every two hours. Blankets helped at night when the heater was off. She also brought an electric kettle, and I asked if it had to be coin fed as well. Marisa laughed relieved I could joke in my sorry condition.

That small kettle became my savior. I could get packaged soups and noodles from the store and eat something hot aside from bread, hard cheese, oranges, and eggs. In a few days, my health improved, except for a dry nagging cough that kept me awake at night. The storekeeper noticed the cough and suggested I find a cypress garden, for the air infused with the essence of those trees would help it.

Rome has many historical gardens. I agreed, the fresh air would do me good. Wearing my warmest clothing, I set out on a garden tour. Somehow, I did not notice how the late fall arrived. I captured its presence in the Roman air and thought of Sebastian back home, the leaves fluttering outside our rain-splattered windows. Roman autumn seemed much kinder. Despite the inconvenience of my coin fed heater, I enjoyed the clear mornings and the warmth of the afternoon sun.

One such sunny afternoon I ended up in a small cemetery, enclosed by the tall wall. On a whim, I pushed an ornate gate, because I noticed the tops of cypress trees peeking over its spikes. Behind the fence and the trees, the cemetery reminded me of a lush garden. English ivy cascaded from the old headstones, their lettering weathered away or blackened with lichen. I walked in solitude among the graves. One white headstone caught my eye, with visible writing and no name. A small bouquet of dried field flowers placed on the grave fluttered in a gentle breeze. I read the epitaph.

This grave contains all that was mortal, of a YOUNG ENGLISH POET, Who on his Death Bed, in the Bitterness of his Heart, at the Malicious Power of his Enemies, Desired these Words to be engraven on his Tomb Stone: Here lies One Whose Name was writ in Water.

"I wonder who that young English poet was," I said aloud and stroked the headstone. Soft footsteps sounded behind me. A young man with longish hair wearing a short black jacket stood under the cypress trees. He came closer and spoke,

"O SOLITUDE! If I must with thee dwell,
Let it not be among the jumbled heap
Of murky buildings; climb with me the steep,
Nature's observatory - whence the dell,
Its flowery slopes, its river's crystal swell.
John Keats."

"Hello. The young poet buried here is John Keats?" I said, and felt a lump in my throat. The emotion rolled over me like a heavy wave of happiness cemented in grief. I remembered Sebastian reading poetry to me by the glow of the fire, his voice caressing the poignant beauty of the simple words. The stranger came closer from the shadow of the trees and the sunlight fell on his face revealing gentle brown eyes and a shadow of a youthful mustache that accentuated his smile.

"Yes, and over there is where Percy Bysshe Shelley rests, beside his son William. My name is Emmanuel; my studio is in the villa next door."

"I'm Veronica. Are you a poet?"

"In a way, I am an artist."

"I stumbled on this place. It's very peaceful here..." I said.

160

The stranger kept his eyes on me. His gaze radiated peace.

"Are you planning to be here tomorrow? I will show you my paintings. Meet me on the bench in the courtyard of the Villa D'Argento?" asked Emmanuel, his gentle voice appealing and kind.

"I will try, maybe around three?" I said trying not to appear eager to meet first thing in the morning or at night like a date. He nodded in agreement, and walked away. Just before he disappeared behind the gates, he turned with a parting wave. I waved back, my hand as feeble as my knees. I had to pinch myself. The pain jerked me back to reality. I was in Rome, at an English cemetery making plans with a complete stranger. Not able to shake off the dreamy state, I sat down by John Keats' grave and tried to remember more of his poetry.

With my eyes closed, the memories came flooding back. For the first time in months, they did not cause pain. I felt much better, complete, as if I found new magic. My pensive mood had brightened. The fate brought me there to meet this young man for a good reason. I had to discover why. Winai, Sebastian, and Ira Silverman were right, there were no such things as coincidences.

My nerves played tricks on me. I tried to calm down, with no success. A few cups of lemon balm tea, a quick stroll around the block, nothing helped. I even washed my hair to calm down. Nothing seemed to work to get rid of the jitters before my meeting with Emmanuel. My selection of outfits proved negligible. The only passable option remained a black turtleneck sweater and a silver scarf from Istanbul. My hair still damp, I added a touch of red to my pale lips, donned a parka and took off an hour earlier than planned.

He waited for me when I arrived at the Villa D'Argento, sitting on the stone bench with folded arms. He rose and offered me a seat. Still nervous, I suggested we go for a stroll.

Emmanuel showed me a small gate from the courtyard to the cemetery, and the hiding place for the key in a crevice between the bricks. We did not talk much, he kept glancing at me with interest and I kept glancing away to hide mine.

"Would you to see my studio now?"

"Yes, you are right, it's getting cooler by the minute," I said, shivering.

Emmanuel pointed to the doors with the wrought iron grille, visible from the bench where we first met. Moss covered stone path took us right to them.

Emmanuel lit the candles on the candelabra in the niche just inside the entrance to illuminate the dim foyer. We climbed the narrow winding stairway and came to the round room at the top of the turret. Arched windows let in the colors of the sunset, which made the white drop cloth over the paintings seem orange. One by one, Emmanuel removed the covers and revealed the rich and warm colors of his art. His still-life paintings were alive with flowers, wine goblets, and candlelight. The familiar cemetery looked even better on his paintings. The green palette pulled and refreshed right off the canvas. I noticed he skipped the last painting and asked why. He did not reply to my query and continued to tell me about himself.

"My mother was English and she wanted me to be a musician, a violinist like the great Rossini. My father, a Venetian, wanted me to be an artist like the great Leonardo. I just wanted to play bocce with my friends."

"So your father won then?" I said, smiling at his joke.

"No one won, they died when I was ten. My grandmother brought me up. I became an artist and a violin player to honor their memory."

"I was brought up by my grandmother too. She died when I was eleven."

"Oh, Veronica, don't look so sad. Sit down, I will play for you."

He opened the curved case and took out a dark brown violin. When he began to play, my heart stopped as I became lost in the music. His long fingers ran on the surface of the instrument and it sang and cried like a living being. He played for one piece after another, until the studio became dark and cold after the sunset. In his abandon, he seemed not to notice and played on. The clock on the cemetery cenotaph struck, he lowered the bow, and silence enveloped his figure barely outlined in the twilight.

"I must go," I said, and stood up. He did not move, just stood holding the silent violin.

"Come tomorrow?"

"At three on the bench?"

"I will be waiting for you starting with this moment," he said and showed me out.

Walking home, I did not wish the dream to end. Emmanuel was a dream, so gentle and humorous, he looked like a painting himself. No one I ever knew was this beautiful, Sebastian perhaps, but in a different way.

I could not wait until three o'clock and anxiety gripped me with the familiar jitters. Walking in circles around my room, I picked up a brush to tame my curls, and then dropped it to make a cup of tea. Nothing worked again. I threw on my yesterday's outfit, grabbed the backpack, and took off in the direction of the English Cemetery. Only Emmanuel could bring me peace.

The Cemetery appeared deserted again. The trees stood undisturbed by the wind and the dried bouquet still lay on the Keats' grave. I enjoyed the crispy late fall day, Roman winters were supposed to be dry and sunny. I settled to wait for the clock strike three. The welcome calm descended on me and I relaxed in the pale sun. It was strange to be in the city of millions of people, and yet, to be alone like this. My light head reminded me I had nothing to eat since last afternoon. I did not eat dinner the night before, missed breakfast, and now decided to have a small picnic of granola bar and an orange with Keats and others for company. *Much better*, I thought, *to have dead poets for company than someone who pretends to like you, like Jason Fox.*

Just before three, I got up and found the gate concealed by the trees, opened it with the hidden key, and entered the courtyard of Emmanuel's villa. To my dismay, the bench stood empty. I sat and waited, eying the turret with the studio. The clock chimed three, and in a few moments, he appeared, walking on the path towards me.

"Veronica, you are beautiful today. Shall we go for a walk; I want to ask you something,"

I could not take my eyes off him. He had such a noble profile, high forehead, his oval face framed in waves of soft caramel colored hair. Even his clothing of dark velvet jacket, white ruffled shirt bespoke of an artist, a creator. I barely knew him, and yet he mesmerized and drew me. I silently called myself shallow, how could it be possible for a smart person like me to fall for a guy second time in two months? I could not help it. His mystery drew me.

"I want to ask you to sit for me, for the portrait. You are the most beautiful woman, Veronica. Can you do it for me?"

It meant that I would see him every day, be with him.

"Yes, Emmanuel. I will be your model."

"Then we meet at the same place and time every day?"

"Yes," I said, wishing it would be earlier than three.

We went back to his turret, and he brought a plush armchair on curved legs. I asked if we could light a fireplace, he shook his head and gave me a blue heavy silk shawl by wrapping it gently around my shoulders.

I watched as he prepared the canvas and started to sketch with a charcoal glancing at me every so often. Every time he looked, I felt a wave of warmth. At six o'clock, he came around the easel and saw me out. He barely touched my shoulder and I wished for his kiss.

From that day onward, I came to his studio every day. In the evening, I would go home, fall asleep. In the morning, I idled around waiting for two o'clock, so I could start my daily trek to the Villa d'Argento and my beloved.

Our meetings fell into a comfortable routine of strolling, then he would play the violin, and after I would sit for a portrait. He never showed me the progress of his work, always making sure to cover it with a drop cloth at the end of the session. I would sit there in the rays of the setting sun and watch him as he painted. I imagined what it would feel like if he came over and kissed me, to feel his soft lips on mine, his arms around me. At times, I had to ask myself if it would be proper to come up to him, run my fingers through his hair and cup his face in my hands in a long lingering kiss. To my disappointment, he never even tried to hold my hand or to touch me in any way. Was he cold, or was I unattractive to him? I could not think of anything else. My ambitions to find magic were forgotten, the time was forgotten. Only he and I remained in the universe.

One afternoon, a bearded stranger watched us as we strolled the cemetery grounds. I decided it was just a caretaker and focused my attention back on Emmanuel. In a few days, the caretaker came again, and I felt he wanted to say something to us, but did not. We walked past him. He ignored Emmanuel as he made a small greeting gesture staring only at me. I thought it rude and pretended not to notice. To my dismay, I saw him sitting on our bench in a few days. I knew he was waiting for me and decided to confront him before Emmanuel came down. His arm stretched over the back of the bench, in the other he held a long pipe. I stopped in front of him and glared at his ruddy face enclosed in a round beard with no mustache. He reminded me of the olden day sailor, right out of Melville's novel.

"You are trespassing. This is a private villa," I said, trying to sound older. He removed his arm from the bench and motioned for me to sit.

"You are the one who is trespassing, and being trespassed upon," he said with a Scottish brogue.

"My friend lives here, you know that. I saw you following us in the cemetery."

"He does not love you, it's not you he's after, but you seem to be paying for it, lass," said the caretaker, and puffed on his pipe. It was as surreal as meeting a smoking caterpillar, how did he know about my feelings for Emmanuel?

"Please leave, he is coming down soon, I do not want to make a scene," I said, checking around, afraid that my gentle Emmanuel would have to deal with this nutty Scotsman.

"Look at you, thin as a reed, stained frock. When did ye bathe last? Ye hair's limp. I see a lass teetering' on the edge between the light and a shadow. He'll draw you into the shadow, jus' like he did with the others," declared the caretaker, puffing away.

I lowered myself on the opposite end of the bench. The trees and the villa seemed to be leaning away from me, the sky became a colorless void. His comments did not shock me. I knew he was right about my state. Only the two words out of his enigmatic speech affected me, *the others.*

"What others?" I whispered, my mouth dry, hollow feeling in the heart.

"Come, I better show you," said the caretaker and stood up.

"I can't leave. Emmanuel will be disappointed if he does not meet me on time."

"Don't worry. He comes only when you are here alone. Come, lassie." His voice gentle all of a sudden as if he spoke to a child or a wounded animal.

I followed him through the gate. Then like an obedient child down the winding path among the gravestones until we reached the far wall. He approached the wall and moved the ivy aside revealing two graves side-by-side, headstones blackened by time. Motioning for me to come closer, he used his sleeve to wipe the inscriptions. I traced the names with my finger.

Emmanuel D'Argento, 1827 – 1847. Maria D'Argento 1829-1847.

I stood there immersed in grief, trying to comprehend the reality. I could not wake from this nightmare.

The caretaker pulled me away from the graves, and told a story as I stared into nothingness, struggling to wake up with no success.

Villa D'Argento burned down in 1847. The entire family perished with it, including the young bride of artist and musician Emmanuel D'Argento. He died as a result of trauma and wounds inflicted by the fire while he searched for his young bride in the burning rubble. A distant family member restored the villa and converted it to an art gallery. It had closed when the benefactor passed away a few years later. It stood empty for over a hundred years. No one walked there except for the ghost of Emmanuel searching for Maria inside and outside its walls.

Strange things happened at the villa. Young girls died in the turret. To this day, no one knows if death was of natural causes or they committed suicide by starvation. Dark curls and green eyes were their similarities, and they were all vagrants. The police had no success in solving the mystery of their deaths. People talk, and memories hidden in this cemetery are long. Some believe, the ghost of Emmanuel every so often spots a girl just like his bride Maria and seduces her, draining her energy, feeding on her love until she loses her strength to live and dies.

The last incident happened in 1970, long before the present caretaker's time. He heard stories, and decided to warn me of a possible predicament. The caretaker never met anyone in the deserted villa, it stood empty, and no artist or musician lived there.

I had no wish to believe any of it. To me, Emmanuel was real, his music and his art were real.

"I would rather die than believe you," I said, hating the caretaker and his vile lies.

"I knew ye'd say that, but ye look like an intelligent lass. Here, read these," he said, and pulled out a scrapbook from his coat pocket. He stuck it in my limp hands and I had no choice but to look. I leafed through the news fragments glued to the pages and read accounts about deaths of the girls around my age. Each article rekindled an old ghost story. I dropped the book, cradled my head in my arms, and wept. I heard my own sobs echoing through the cemetery grounds. Nothing stirred, the cemetery was used to grief, and the walls absorbed it.

With tears comes epiphany, I looked at the caretaker busy with his pipe, and tried to deal with my emotions.

"How do I escape it? I love him. I cannot live without him. He is like magic to me. I won't leave here, ever."

"Don't go over the extreme, lass, ye jus' met him, 'tis the spirit magic in your head, no less, especially no true love. The real magic is the bravery, the will to go on, not to give up on you. There is a way. And you must follow it through, no matter how difficult," said the caretaker. I looked at him through tears and nodded.

"You got to make him finish the painting. After, he should find the final rest and leave the cemetery shadows for the better place."

That afternoon I did not go to meet Emmanuel. Walking back to my place took forever. Deep in thought, I picked at the orange, throwing small peel bits on the road. When I tried to eat, the fruit tasted bitter. I tossed it in the ditch and walked on. The further I walked away from the Villa D'Argento, the more stretched I felt. As if some invisible ties ripped inside, and the real Veronica floated like a balloon above my body. I sat down on the steps of some church to compose myself, and looked up at the sky. The angel faces carved into the church facade stared at me, their eye sockets dead, empty. Higher up the gargoyles watched me too, like carrion birds ready to devour my remains. I got up, climbed the stairs to the holy water font, and splashed some on my face. Green slime covered inside of the font, its rotten smell made me gag. I shuffled home, dragging my backpack, with straps flailing like spilled intestines.

When he played, I caressed him with my eyes. How could he be not real? He was so beautiful, so warm, and so human. Wrapped in the blue silk shawl, I watched him put the instrument down, and pick up his palette with a brush.

The shawl slipped off my shoulders as I stood up and approached. He stopped for a second and looked at me, then started to paint again. I stood a step away from him, tried to inhale his scent, and perceived none. Not even the scent of the oil paints. I walked around to look at the canvas he created for the past few weeks. I would not dare before. Looking over his shoulder, I could not see a thing. The canvas remained white as a sheet, not a drop of paint. Yet, my beautiful Emmanuel moved the brush in the precise short strokes, his eyes focused on the spot where I sat and the blue shawl trailed off the chair.

"You are beautiful, Veronica, you are tired, my love, we will continue tomorrow," said Emmanuel and lowered the paintbrush.

I moved to the shrouded painting in the corner. He never

showed it me. The unfinished portrait appeared scorched by the long ago fire, but still I gasped at the likeness of a dark haired girl with green eyes and an easy smile on her rosy face. Much like the happy me, when I lived at LaRose Gris with Sebastian. I picked up the portrait and took it to Emmanuel who watched my movements with sadness in his eyes.

"We need to finish this painting, Emmanuel. I am not tired, my love," I said, and placed the painting on the easel instead of the blank canvas.

Back in my chair, wrapped in a shawl, I wept. The pain in my heart intensified every time he rested his eyes on me. I felt like a murderer every time I asked him to finish the painting. The clock chimed midnight, then two in the morning.

"We must finish the painting, my love. Please, Emmanuel."

The angel of slumber descended upon me and put honey on my eyelids gluing them together. I fell asleep assuring Emmanuel of my love.

I must have slept for hours. The cold woke me up together with the sunshine. The room stood empty, except for the shawl around my shoulders and a finished portrait of Maria D'Argento against the wall. Emmanuel was gone.

No traces of grief remained in my heart. I savored a forgotten sensation of hunger. Just like a healthy hunger after a long struggle with sickness, and on the way to recovery. I craved pizza and red wine, pastries, boiled potatoes, tea, eggs, anything.

First, I had to find the caretaker and thank him for saving my life. With joy, I could not wait to meet the world outside the villa D'Argento walls.

"Where are you, Emmanuel?" I asked aloud and listened to silence. "What should I do now?"

Go home, you will find the answers there. The whisper came from the direction of the painting.

"Just like that? How about finding magic?"

Living in Rome for the past weeks, I found nothing but loss. I sat on the floor and listened for the voice, contemplating if it was part of a dream. After a while, I tucked Maria's portrait under my arm and headed towards the stairs, only to stop as I heard the voice again.

You already did, the magic is in you.

14. MAGIC NUMBERS

At last, the plane landed New York. I was almost home. Even the fact I arrived penniless failed to dampen my joy. Bleary eyed I left the plane, stood in line with the other jet lagged passenger,s thinking of a simple way to turn happy individuals into zombies without any magic, just put them on a ten-hour flight.

It hurt how much I missed home. Only now, the stories I read about nostalgia and homesickness made sense. One last leg of the trip remained. I had to take a train to Boston and place a surprise call to Sebastian to pick me up from the station.

Given my financial situation, I could only walk home. The last of my funds went towards the plane ticket and for bribing the Italian customs officer to take my books out of Italy. He accused me of smuggling antiques when he saw them and Maria's portrait rolled up in the suitcase. However, pocketed the money rather quickly and waved me on, eagle eyes on another cash-clutching victim.

I had some change in the pocket, a backpack filled with the essentials, magical mementoes from my adventures, and a suitcase full of books. Old musty books, in forgotten languages, filled with magical knowledge. I could not wait to get home and start reading. I remembered what Professor Silverman said, *magic is in the reading*. I knew the means to get home would come, felt it in my bones somehow.

"You wanna lift?" I heard a hoarse voice behind me.

It belonged to a complaining fellow passenger from the plane. She whined the entire flight about needing a smoke. True enough, the minute we were in her Volvo a joint appeared in her mouth. She inhaled like a thirsty man in the desert. This was my first glimpse of New York, through the cloud of marijuana smoke.

She dropped me off in the Central Park. I hobbled to the park bench with my possessions. Stuck the suitcase under it, and fell asleep with my head on the backpack, defeated by the jet lag and the second-hand cannabis fumes.

Emmanuel spoke to me. His hand lay heavy on my shoulder, while the cold rain pecked at my forehead.

He said, "Missy, missy wake up."

Through the haze of sleep, I realized it was just a dream. Someone shook my shoulder in the rain. I rubbed my eyes. A hobo stared back at me.

"Alright, alright you can let go of me now," I mumbled sitting up and trying to remember how I ended up in the park. He perched on the bench across mine.

"Thought you would need this" he held out a broken umbrella with spidery spindles.

"No thanks. I got a parka, somewhere in my backpack, if it's not stolen yet."

"I'd not steal from you, damn demon," said the vagrant, and snorted.

I had no strength to reply, and rummaged for the parka hoping to find some crumb to pacify my rumbling stomach. It seemed to be very early in the morning. I did not own a watch. Sebastian said I did not need to keep time to be happy.

A granola bar from the backpack made me feel a little better. I took a closer look at my new acquaintance. It was hard to put an age to his droopy face. He wore a hat with floppy ears like a basset hound. It gave him a look of humanoid from the *Island of the Dr. Moreau*.

Now who is the demon? I chuckled, but held my tongue.

"So you like to read?" he said pointing to my suitcase.

Lovely, he went through my things, like a true hound. The thought made me shiver.

"Nothing good is going to come out of them books, whatever they are. You need something more to keep you warm and dry."

"What do you mean warm and dry, they are not for fuel. If you touch them again, you will regret it, Mr. Hound!"

"No, no, don't get all flustered, I liked my literature too, once. I mean you need them newspapers."

"I am not interested in news, thank you. It's always bad anyway."

"Not for reading, you silly chicken, for sleeping. Nothing keeps one of us warm and cozy than a bunch of newspapers. Nobody want to steal them, that the best part. They might use them books for fire like you said, though."

"I am not one of you. And my books are a source of dark magic," I said, trying to scare him away.

"Sure, missy. I understand, we all forget to take our meds. But take these anyway," and he pulled a bunch of folded newspapers from his soiled coat.

"Now lie down as you did before, the rain has stopped, no worries."

For some bizarre reason I obeyed him. Mr. Hound unfolded the newspapers and covered me from head to toe. I felt warmth spreading through my limbs and fell asleep again.

When I woke up, the sun came out spreading its early spring warmth. The light caressed my face through the rips in the newspapers. The bench I occupied was far from the road, and allowed a relative privacy. Mr. Hound's bench stood empty, he was gone. My suitcase still sat where I stuck it. I found some loose change in my pocket, enough to get much needed hot tea. After spreading the newspapers over the suitcase to hide it somehow, I went to the park concession nearby.

A buxom woman at the kiosk appeared busy cleaning the spotless counter. She had no other customers. I approached and asked for tea, Earl Grey with milk, just the way I like it. While she prepared my order, I noticed her nametag.

"You have a pretty name, Sadiyah."

"Oh goodness, thank you! I always forget about the damn name tag"

"You know it means *lucky* in Arabic?"

"It may mean *lucky*, honey, but I surely ain't," she said smiling.

"You know, it's easy to fix, your luck I mean. Just use your lucky numbers," I said, happy to speak to someone friendly.

"And what might those be?" she said placing a steaming cup of tea in front of me.

"Write down your birth date, and add all the numbers until only one digit remains, then this is your lucky number! It's that easy, it's called numerology. Try, it might bring you luck."

"Alright, I will. How are you so smart?"

"I just read a lot."

Friendly banter with Sadiyah and the hot tea gave me much needed energy. I basked in the sun, watching New Yorkers pass by, and weighing my options to get out of this city. I thought of the books under the bench and tapped the suitcase with my heel to reassure myself they were still there. Then I remembered Mr. Hound's newspapers.

I picked them up and started leafing through the pages skipping the front page with useless headlines, and sports, past the torn comics' page, until I reached the classifieds. These are always a good way to find about real life in any city. Perhaps I could stumble upon something that would help me get home.

I scanned the columns, nothing useful in jobs, for rent, and pets. Next, I stopped at personals and it shocked me how many lonely hearts were desperate enough to place ads for love. Some read like blatant lies but some, I felt, were genuine. Thoughts carried me away to Emmanuel, until my eyes found a services column. Cleaning, nannies, delivery, magical services, I focused on the last one.

Magical Services required for completing an impossible task, room and board provided. Serious replies only, no jokers or you will be cursed. Apply in person at 63C Sterling Place, Prospect Heights.'

I had to find Prospect Heights. My intuition told me, it never proved me wrong. Getting there would prove difficult, for I had neither the idea of its location, nor money. I considered asking Maria's portrait for advice, but decided against unpacking it in a public place. Then thought of someone I could ask.

Sadiyah had no customers when I came up again to talk to her.

"I have been doing my lucky numbers, they are..." She announced.

"Stop right there, do not tell me. Do not tell anyone. Telling will jinx your luck."

"Oh, I see. Just like my age, tell it to a good lookin' fella and all my luck's gone."

We both laughed and I asked her about the Prospect Heights. Turned out the place was in Brooklyn, on the other side of the river.

"Real old place turned nice by the rich wannabees, doing restorations and selling at sky high," said Sadiyah, "You can fetch a taxi, or go by subway."

"All I have is change left from the tea, I will have to walk," I said.

"Silly girl, you should not be walking that distance. Let me lend you a tenner till better times."

"Thank you, I am used to walking. I have walked half the world and been to many places. I will be fine. It's my books, Sadiyah. I cannot carry the suitcase all that way. Can you keep it for a bit, until I come back?"

She checked around her little stand for a second and agreed to keep them safe. I brought the suitcase over and we stowed it under the counter.

Armed with her hand-drawn map of an approximate location, and a torn out classified ad, I embarked on yet another of my walking adventures.

Whoever called New York a jungle was wrong. Jungles are fragrant, lush, brimming with life. I would call it an eyesore, with giant concrete scabs. Skyscrapers everywhere I looked, no horizon, no clean wind, just a foul dust-chasing draft. A bit of precious nature of the Central Park disappeared behind its sentinel buildings, as if it never existed.

I stopped at the taxi pool and found a driver who appeared amicable enough to give me better directions to Prospect Park in Brooklyn. A cabby introduced himself as Frank. He gave me a small map and a whole bunch of advice on how to take care of myself in The Big Apple. I listened without interruption until excusing myself and headed towards the Brooklyn Bridge. It could take few hours he warned, as he handed me grease stained bag with a half of his cheese panzerotto, which made my stomach very happy.

I have never witnessed such a rush in my entire life. Places I traveled resembled a memory in slow motion compared to the beehive of Manhattan with its thousands of cars, smog, and a torrent of people. They never halted or paid attention to anything. I watched people munching on bagged food, reading, swearing at the erratic traffic. Everyone avoided eye contact. People bumped into me from every direction, some stepped on my feet or pushed me aside without a word of apology. I kept biting my lips not to curse. It was not their fault. Life in a big city made them that way.

The human tide swept me into the Fourth Street where it became thinner, then diminished at the last turn before the mighty Brooklyn Bridge.

Such a pleasure to cross the famous landmark, the wooden planks under my feet felt like a welcome mat. The breathtaking vista from the both sides of the Hudson captivated me to the point that I had to sit down to absorb it all. Enjoying the river breeze, I identified with the New Yorkers, with love and pride of their city. I had the same feelings for the LaRose Gris, my home. Enjoying the fresh wind in my face and hair, I unfolded my arms and yelled off the bridge, "Help me to get home, oh mighty New York!"

Brooklyn had a different soul from Manhattan, down to earth, friendlier. People rushed about and erratic traffic again. An eclectic array of cultures caught my eye as interesting.

Hasidim in their black hats and coats walked with many children in tow. Chubby Italian women carried large bags of groceries. Latino youth danced to the music of their loud radios. Black kids chased balls on the parking lots. However, the city loomed around, swallowing them. They were flowers that could not grow to their full potential, because of the lack of nurturing only the Mother Nature can provide.

I enjoyed my walk, just like a tourist on a stroll. Brooklyn proved easy to navigate without getting lost. That is, until I came to the area marked Prospect Park. To my delight, I discovered a real park zone with a botanical garden. The streets lined with linden trees reminded me of Central European towns Sebastian and I visited many years ago.

Three story walk-ups huddled along, in various conditions. Some appeared neglected, but some were shiny and new. I remembered Sadiyah's remark about the restoration of this old area and consulted the ad again to check the numbers for Sterling Place, the little lane off the major street lined with similar walk-ups. Each had an endearing little patch of green by the front steps enclosed by wrought iron fencing like a sorry attempt to feel closer to nature. One could access the main entrance only by passing through the low gates and climb the stone steps up to the second floor. Most buildings had apartments marked with numbers or letters.

I searched for the 63C that could be on the third floor, for the letter C. I came to the end of the street without even finding the number 63. Then I crossed the narrow street and scanned the numbers again. Intrigued, I found houses from 61 to 70. A nanny with a blond child in a stroller passed me by. I asked her where the number 63 might be. She just raised her hands, in *who knows* gesture.

"Try knocking on the doors, maybe you be lucky and find correct numbers that way, señorita."

With no desire to disturb the neighborhood by knocking on doors, I closed my eyes, and concentrated for a few seconds. Just like Sebastian taught me. The answer came in a few moments, and I went straight to the number 61.

I guessed this number to be the clue. Its two digits added up to a lucky number seven. The sum of 6 and 3 added up to an ultimate lucky number nine. Both lucky numbers must had represented the same building, 61 was 69 as well.

The building did not appear to be a part of the restoration project, just a shabby townhouse with a rusted ornate fence in front. On the tiny patch of green in front, grew a gnarled rose bush stifled by weeds years ago. The little gate squeaked as I pushed it. The air seemed to change once I entered the inside perimeter of the fence. Street sounds muted, thick syrupy stillness enveloped me with warmth and quiet. I had a sudden yearning to stretch out on the scuffed steps, and fall asleep. Trying to ignore my sudden lethargy, I climbed up the steps to a pitted wood door with a grimy stained glass insert and tarnished brass handle. I pressed on it, and entered the hallway with two doors on the opposite sides with a curved staircase between them. *Choose the right - find riches, choose the left - find love* a line from the old fairy tale floated in my mind. I tried both doors and found them locked. Rusty handles squeaked as if they stayed unused for at least a century. Then I noticed the tiles on the floor. Small white and black tiles set in the shape of a dove. Some tiles fell out, and the dove appeared perforated. Someone painted the doors and the staircase light blue, but I could see they were yellow before, in places where the blue paint peeled off. The sunshine reached through the grimy glass of the door insert. I made out flowers and a garden in the stained glass picture, my heart lurched. Was it my garden, or was it just my imagination because I missed it so much?

I started up the stairs, past the walls covered by faded wallpaper with yellow and purple pansies and green hummingbirds. The scent of this silent place became stronger as I climbed higher up. I smelled the confectionery shop from my childhood. The waffle cones, vanilla and candy apples brought on a sudden wave of hunger. My stomach started to complain. I massaged my middle and continued up enjoying every whiff of the sweet air. A door on the third floor had a bell in the middle, the kind that needs turning to produce the chime. It stuck and did not want to ring, so I reached for the handle and the door swung open.

A small foyer still in the same garden wallpaper led into a parlor with two tall windows. The high ceilings combined with carved crown moldings gave the room elegance. *Such a beautiful nostalgic room, but so neglected and dusty*, I thought noticing the herring bone parquet under the thick layer of dust.

A tarnished crystal vase with a bouquet of dried roses stood on oval Queen Anne table in the middle of the room. Tufted bow legged armchairs scattered around the table and a moth eaten faded settee hid in the corner. To my delight, a gramophone stood by the window, with a collection of discs in yellowed envelopes piled high. This place was right out of a story, which someone left off in the middle, and never came back to it.

I plumped down on the settee making a small dust cloud. Then caught my reflection in the dim mirror and pulled the elastic band off my hair to shake the curls free. Feeling like a fool, I concluded that an ad must have been a practical joke, and the delicious candy store smells must have drifted from the outside.

About to take my leave, I glanced through the dirty window and saw two ladies pushing a rather large pram up the stairs below the front doors. It intrigued me and I considered my options. I could hide somewhere and sneak out later, or wait for them to discover me. I decided on the third option, to meet them head on and ask for an explanation of the mysterious advert. The worst they could do was to show me out.

On the way down, I heard the ladies talking, but not in English. Their chatter stopped at once when I came down. They froze staring with astonishment at my entirely black outfit and huge curly hair.

"Oy vey!" they said in unison after a long silent moment.

"Oy gevalt!"

"Did you call the chimney sweep, Feige?"

"Kitty, you probably called an undertaker?"

"No we did not," they said in unison again.

I gaped, certain that my eyes played tricks on me. The ladies were identical. Both had neat white hair gathered with the tortoise shell barrettes. Black pointy shoes peeked from under the hems of their long Wedgewood blue dresses with round white lace collars and cuffs. Both had an amused expressions on their fine featured faces, their soft blue eyes twinkled with mirth. I had an impression of two little girls making fun of me.

"My name is Veronica LaRose. I came because of the ad in the paper," I said waving the torn wrinkled piece of paper.

"Are we still running that mechugene ad, Feige?"

"You know we do, Kitty."

"She found us."

"And, she figured out the house number."

"So she must be Der Nes Macher, The Miracle Maker," they said in unison again.

By then, I realized the twins always spoke in this peculiar way.

"Please help us up the stairs."

"This pram is heavy, no?"

"Come, we will have a nosh upstairs!"

We picked up the old-fashioned bulky pram with the huge white wheels and carried it up the stairs. The baby kept quiet, probably asleep. We entered the room with the tall windows.

"How can you bring a baby to a dusty old place like this?" I asked them.

"This is how," said the one called Feige.

"We will show you," said Kitty.

"Geeb-a-keek!" They both exclaimed and clapped their hands three times.

Suddenly, a bright sunlight streamed from the spotless tall windows, no more grime, no more dust, and cobwebs. I stood in a changed room.

The white organza curtains fluttered in the breeze, the parquet floor shined with polish. The furniture in the room became velvety and inviting. A bouquet of fresh white roses bloomed in a beautiful Bohemian crystal vase. Small bowls filled with chocolates stood in a row on the mahogany table, Black Forest cake joined them on a platter along with wafers, cookies, honey covered almonds, and a frosty pitcher of pink juice or punch. The scent of a candy shop floated up my nose again. I came over to the table and picked up a cookie. It tasted delicious, just like my grandmother's baking. I felt like a little girl again.

"Why do you need a magician? I need to learn from *you*," I blurted with my mouth full.

"All in good time, liebe."

"First we have to eat."

"We are all tired, hungry."

"Sit down, libling, darling," Faige patted the settee.

"You want a piece of cake. Yes?" Kitty pinched my cheek.

"Thank you, what about the baby?"

I could not stop eating. I loved the adorable twins. I loved their magical home, loved everything. In addition, I could not shake feeling odd as well, because the real Veronica was never this happy.

"Moishele will eat when he wants."

"You can come out now Moishele, undzer sheyn boychik, our beautiful boy," called Feige.

The pram shook. The blue cover flew open and the baby jumped out. I jumped too, from the surprise, dropping the plate with pastries on the floor.

In front of me, grinning, with pudgy arms open wide like an actor entering the stage, stood a tiny faun. His pink skin glowed and the hair shined with the color of pure gold framing a friendly face with endearing ringlets. A golden fleece covered his chubby legs, ended with the tiny golden hooves instead of feet. The sisters dressed him in a tiny sailor outfit of white shirt and navy shorts, like a real boy. An aura of pure happiness radiated from him. I loved little Moishele at the first sight. When I moved to hug him on an impulse, I sensed the candy shop again and realized the delicious sweetness came from the faun.

"Ah, you love our Moishele," said Feige joining in on our hug.

"What a cutie, just look at this face," Kitty cupped his chin with obvious affection.

"Our child, our life and joy."

I could not believe my teary eyes. I caressed his golden head and found two small golden horns, a real faun. Overcome with emotion, I realized the magic had found me when I least expected.

15. STORIES AND CAKES

Mommies, please, stop all this mushy stuff. Our guest is bursting with curiosity," said Moishele the faun, and beamed another endearing smile. His soft speech resembled the sound of a happy stream bubbling over the rocks in my garden. Sisters let go of him, and began to pile up his plate with cake.

"Oh, snack time, oh, cake time," sang the faun, "Let's make it a drink time."

He reached into the pram and pulled out a robust wine bottle. Feige and Kitty hurried with the crystal goblets, and we raised them in cheer.

"To our meeting," I said.

"To us," cheered the sisters

"To going back together," said Moishele.

Intrigued by Moishele's strange toast, I tasted the sweet red wine. The faun squeezed between the sisters on the settee, I sat facing them in one of the bucket armchairs.

"We have stories to tell," said the faun.

"You first, Veronica," suggested Kitty.

"Our tale comes later," Faige completed Kitty's sentence.

Moishele refilled my empty goblet as I told them about growing up at LaRose Gris. My story began with the magical crystal bead. How it made me believe in magic, and how my grandmother's life came to the tragic end. About Sebastian who came into my life because of it. I told them about my grandmother, they nodded with compassion, as I described the cause of her death, and my torment of guilt and sadness. I told them about Gaspar's language lessons, how Anna tried to develop my magical talents. They heard about my rebellion when I left my childhood home to look magical knowledge. I did not delve into my adventures much. I broke down admitting how much I missed my home. My tale ended with the account of coming to New York without any money, because I spent all my remaining funds to get books on the plane.

"So what kind of magical knowledge did you find? What do you know?" asked Moishele.

I felt quite uplifted with the possibility to share, and presented a torrent of my exploits.

"Well, everyone I met on my journey shared their own take on magic. I met a vampire child whom I trusted, and his bite made my body stronger. Then I met a ghost of an artist, and he taught me about sacrifice. The desert spirit gave me the flute that makes rain, and an Alchemist introduced me to the possibility of travelling to the parallel worlds. I know how to access an answer to any question by meditating. What about you? You can do magic I only dream of. Where did Moishele come from?"

Enraptured, I listened as Feige and Kitty told me their story with their habit of finishing each other's sentences, and having little arguments about the chain of events, with some giggles and tears along the way. I felt that Moishele heard this story many times before, but he still participated by kissing them on their soft cheeks, patting their hands and laughing at their expressions.

The sisters were born in Lithuania in a small shtetl, a village by the Polish border. The times were harsh. The Russian civil war tore apart a quiet life of the small Jewish settlement, one of the many around that part of Eastern Europe. Bands of unruly bandits roamed the countryside disregarding the borders.

Feige and Kitty were children of a Cantor Yossi Galkin and his wife Minna. They had an older brother Moishe who was five years their senior. Yossi made a modest living by singing at special occasions. Minna was a real talent in the family. Her fame as a lace maker reached as far as Warsaw and Vienna.

The sisters did not remember much of their early life. Their memories revolved around the sunny patch where they played and how their father sang funny songs to make them laugh.

The last memory of their home was a great fire. The dreaded bandits attacked in the night. The fear became a reality. It happened quickly. The bandits torched the entire village. The sisters remembered the urgent shouting, running shadows and then darkness.

For days, they hid in the cellar with their brother Moishe while the fires raged burning down their home, their parents, and their sweet life into nothing. When it became quiet, the children lifted the trapdoor of the cellar. They called and searched for their Mama and Papa amid the stinking smoking rubble. Moishe was the oldest, twelve - almost a man, decided to take them to the city. There was great Rabbi in Warsaw, he told them and hoped he would help.

The children walked for hours on a deserted and dusty road. At sunset, some peasants picked them up. They traveled to the market with their harvest of turnips, parsnips, and beets in a cart pulled by a pair of brown oxen. The Polish peasants had fed them those vegetables for the entire three-day journey through the bleak countryside. Since then, Feige and Kitty refused to eat anything that even resembled a turnip. The peasants delivered the kids directly to the Rabbi's gate in Warsaw and left them there. Feige developed a fever on the way and Moishe had to carry her. Kitty remembered how she followed them, by holding on to his belt.

When they entered the courtyard, they saw dozens of people, families, young and old. All sitting around on the suitcases or clumps of belongings, tied in burlap. Raya Bronstein, Rabbi's wife, spotted the grimy starved children at the gate. She gave them a bath, supper, and tried to spoon feed Feige.

They were not the first victims of pogroms who found their way to this safe house. The Rabbi's home was open for everyone. The Rabbi, with the help of the other community members negotiated passages out of Eastern Europe to England, and then to America where the orphans and the displaced would find a new life. Raya and Rabbi Philip Bronstein were also leaving. They sold their home, and most of their belongings waited packed in the courtyard. After the brief meeting, the Bronsteins offered to take Moishe and his sisters with them. They were sure some family would be willing to adopt three beautiful orphans.

Moishe, the big brother, became the hero to Feige and Kitty. Somehow in their minds he and their father merged into one and they began to regard him as a father figure. Young Moishe took his responsibility to care for them with uncommon maturity. He played with them and made sure they were fed and happy.

Sometime in the early fall, they boarded a train for a long journey to France, and after a sailboat to England.

The memories of the journey were of the Rabbi, who was trying to teach them some simple English phrases from a textbook. Moishe and the sisters had caught on well, but Raya's pronunciation sounded so completely off and she made such funny faces, the children laughed until their own faces hurt and the eyes were blurry with tears. Later they guessed she did it on purpose to infuse some fun into the tedious trip, and to take their minds off the horrors they had experienced.

The same horror seemed to follow them like a hungry animal. On the way from French port of Le Havre to Manchester, the sisters became seasick and Raya suggested that Moishe should take them out on the deck for some fresh air. How could she know that a sudden Atlantic storm would hit the small vessel with all its windy might? The waves came high and furious. They attacked within minutes. Moishe grabbed the sisters and tried to carry them to the stairwell. When he ran burdened by their weight a huge wave swept him off his feet, he had only a moment to push the sisters into a crevice below the deck, as the wave took him away. It had swept him out to the violent sea never to be seen again.

"The ocean filled with our tears, bitter and salty," sighed Feige wiping corners of her eyes with a napkin.

Death of their brother devastated Feige and Kitty. Raya and Philip Bronstein prayed for God's forgiveness, because they felt it was Raya's fault for sending them above. After a long prayer, Rabbi announced they were adopting the girls. When the time came to disembark in England, they declared the family as Rabbi and Mrs. Bronstein and their two daughters Feige and Kitty.

"It was like waking up to the sunny morning after a terrible storm," said Kitty.

The Bronsteins fared better than most. The sisters did not experience hardships usually associated with the plight of immigrants.

They had a vague memory of the Statue of Liberty on Ellis Island and no memory at all of their adapting to New York City. The only story they could tell of those early days was that Rabbi and his wife were always mistaken as their grandparents. And it was easy to forgive those who asked, because by that time Rabbi Phil and his wife Raya were in their late sixties. They had purchased the brownstone walk up, the sisters were sharing now in a predominantly immigrant neighborhood. Feige and Kitty, the blue-eyed twins, became the center of the attention of the entire block. They learned English at school, but at home and around the neighborhood, they still spoke Yiddish, the language of their childhood.

Rabbi Phil was the first to pass away.

"The heart, it simply gave out," said Feige touching her chest.

"So his heart of gold, just stopped, he died in his sleep," said Kitty.

Moishele reached and held her hand.

Raya lost her spark, her chutzpah, after Philip was gone. She sat for hours by one of the tall windows looking into nothing. The girls tried to cheer her up. It was their turn to see that Raya had her meals. Feige played the piano and Kitty sang Raya's favorite Russian romances.

"She died of the broken heart," said Feige.

"But the coroner said it was a sudden aneurysm, what did he know," said Kitty.

The sisters were just teenagers at the time of their adopting parents' death. They had to quit school to start earning a living by performing at the community events. Both had inherited their father's talent for music. Kitty learned to crochet and received a modest income for her handiwork. Unfortunately, the popularity of crochet items faded and the craft became old fashioned. The new modern era emerged, and an ugly monster raised its head in Germany in 1936. The sisters were sixteen.

Their neighborhood was quite diverse. A large Jewish family from Ukraine occupied a house across the street. An old Irish widow lived in the house to the right. The house on the left had a rapid turnaround of eclectic tenants. Plenty of old friends of Rabbi and Raya came to visit, hauling large bags, and pots of food enough to feed an army. Kitty took the items to the house across the street, where the large family accepted it with gratitude.

Feige and Kitty stayed at home most of the time. Their only social outings were to the parties where they had to play and sing. Their work and taking care of their house kept them too busy to think about boys. However, they had a secret hobby. They liked to play dress up and pretend to be grand ladies of the past.

"Oh, how we loved the hats with feathers, and elbow length gloves. So romantic," said Faige.

"And the long shawls, shoes with high heels. So ladylike," shared Kitty.

"We collected such a beautiful wardrobe."

They set up a small patio on the roof of the brownstone. Curtains and potted palms adorned it in the warm months. They had also bought a mirror to model their outfits. In their free time, they would scour the flea markets for the vintage clothing, and repaired it to perfection. They would model it to each other in front of the large mirror on the roof.

"It was such fun."

"It took our minds off from bad news coming from Europe."

"We were so happy to be in America."

For two years, they led a quiet life. Until one day it all changed. The news from Europe became graver, and the stories of mass murders were unbearable. The girls packed up their dresses in boxes and left them in the attic. They took down the curtains, sold the potted palms, and wrapped up the mirror, leaving it where it was until the happier times. Then they immersed in a volunteer work to help the tortured souls who arrived from Europe in the new wave of immigration.

One wet April night, they came home quite tired from their volunteer round, and had a modest dinner before retiring. The rain drummed on the windows, its streaks reflecting the yellow streetlights. The storm increased with the booms of thunder. The lightning appeared so often, the night disappeared in the flashes of blue. The sisters rushed around the house to shut the windows. This was when they heard the tiny cry. At first, they thought it was the wind, but heard it again, coming from the roof patio.

"We looked at each other, very scared."

"But decided to be brave and check it out."

"We thought that it was a piglet at first."

"But it was me," Moishele sprung to life excited to be an active part in the tale.

The sisters found what appeared to be a piglet on the roof by the attic door.

Moishele made a face. He did not like this part of the story.

"Why did they think that I was a pig, I still don't get it," he said.

They brought the creature down to take a better look. It was an instant motherhood for the both of them. The odd baby became a center of their life. He was so sweet, so golden, and so clever.

"But I do not think the story ended then, how did you learn to do the magic?" I asked.

"It just happened."

"Maybe we can explain."

Again, with exclamations, protestations and more wine the story continued.

In the beginning, the sisters had a hard time caring for the baby. They named him Moishele after their heroic brother. Moishele did not seem to thrive. He did not want to eat the traditional baby food and became thin and sickly. Feige and Kitty borrowed books from the library to read up on the baby care. They decided that taking Moishele to the doctor would be dangerous and the strange looking baby would be taken away from them for the medical experiments. They lived in fear and confusion. Until one day, old Raya's friend came over and brought a chocolate cake. By then, they rearranged their home and moved the living quarters to the second floor away from the prying eyes, leaving the first floor for visitors only. That afternoon, they were sitting with Raya's friend reminiscing, both of them taking turns to go upstairs and check on the baby. The chocolate cake was so delicious that Feige fetched a plate with her to nibble on the way up. The minute she entered Moishele's room he reached, grabbed the cake and devoured it, then in a clear voice said, "More please!" Feige flew down the stairs, and pleaded a sudden migraine to their visitor. The minute they were alone, Feige grabbed the rest of the cake to run upstairs with speechless Kitty in tow.

Since then Moishele thrived. At last, they discovered how to nourish him and make him happy. Cookies, cakes, cream filled pastries, jellies, ice cream, any kind of dessert made him healthier, stronger, and smarter. Their entire household smelled of sugar, together with the wonderful delicacies from the bakeries and confectioneries all over Brooklyn.

"So this is all you eat?" I asked amazed, "and you don't grow fat and get sick from eating too many sweets?"

"Nonsense," said Moishele, "old wives' tales. People don't get sick from eating sweets. Just look at my dear mommies. See how young and healthy they are, even way over sixty."

At this point, the sisters' faces lit up with love. And tears of affection glistened in their eyes. I felt like my heart would melt. Although I was not sure, was it from the sentiment or from too much wine.

"But tell me the rest of the story. About the transformation and making things invisible."

"Oh, it was terrible," said Faige.

"I still have shivers," Kitty pulled on her shawl tighter.

"We killed her."

"Killed who?" I said, worried by their expressions.

"The evil eyed widow Dullahan, she had evil eye for our Moishele."

The sisters worked very hard to conceal the new addition to their family and kept Moishele on the top floor of the brownstone. They took turns to run errands. On the nights when they had to sing at the parties, they had to return home as soon as the performance ended. Feige and Kitty had eyes only for one boy, and they were not the only ones. Their neighbor, old widow Dullahan, had spied Moishele's little clothes drying on the rooftop. A vicious gossip spread through the neighborhood. Everyone whispered how one of the sisters had gone the wrong way and had an illegitimate baby.

With Brooklyn's ethnic population, and their rusty way of thinking, this was a worst reputation a young woman could have. The community snubbed them, and even their parents' friends stopped visiting. This affected their income, the invitations to sing at the parties had ceased.

The sisters suspected who was the gossipmonger. Finally, when they spotted the widow lurking around the roof, they confronted her. The terrible row had arisen, the widow Dullahan accused them of being whores, shaking her fists and yelling how their saintly parents would turn in their graves if they knew of their sinful ways. She even shrieked it would be her duty to grab the "brat" and drown it in the Hudson. That did it. Feige drew her breath and yelled,

"You are a terrible meddling woman, Mrs. Dullahan. My greatest wish is to see you go lame so you can stop following us."

Kitty as angry as her sister, completed her curse,

"And I want you to look back at us with one eye."

At that point, something unexpected happened - the woman collapsed. Feige ran out to call for help, and when the widow left by the ambulance the sisters looked at each other in dismay. They were quite relieved to see the old gossip gone. An even bigger surprise came when someone from the hospital, a social worker, came to gather the widow's belongings. He informed them that Mrs. Dullahan would not be returning because she had a stroke that left her in a wheelchair and blind in one eye.

Feige and Kitty understood right away something unexplained happened. They began to experiment with their wishes. First, simple wishes like to have a bird sing on their rooftop at night, or for the white roses to bloom in front of the house. To their wonder, everything came through, and experimented some more. Until realizing, they could have anything. They knew Moishele was the source of this magic and asked him to explain. He did not provide any answers. He just laughed and hugged them. The house next door remained empty for a long time, and the sisters decided to purchase the two adjoining properties in order to retain their privacy and raise Moishele in peace.

"Wait a minute, just one minute," I interrupted their story, "how could you purchase anything, let alone two houses in Brooklyn without having a source of income? Didn't you say that with your reputation nobody wanted you to sing at the festivities anymore?"

As I said it Moishele stretched, "I am tired of sitting, let's dance."

"The stories can wait."

"There is always tomorrow."

"You are staying with us Veronica, please."

"Yes I am. I have nowhere else to go. You sort of adopted me, and I want to hear the rest of the story," I said, feeling bashful all of a sudden.

Moishele pushed the furniture to the walls to make space. The sisters took the dishes and empty glasses to the kitchen. I meandered to the ancient gramophone. Moishele appeared by my side, the crackling sound of the record filled the air. After the first notes, I recognized Grieg's *King of the mountain cave* and we began to dance.

We danced in a circle holding hands. Our blue shadows danced on the walls around us. Just like in Matisse painting. Faster and faster, we twirled, finally collapsing on the chairs and laughing. I never felt this happy, this sweet encompassing kind of happy. I swam in a chocolate fudge of happiness. When at last I pleaded an imminent collapse, the sisters took me downstairs to the guest bedroom. Kitty gave me a long nightgown trimmed with ivory lace. I splashed some water on my face looking at my drunken flushed reflection in the bathroom mirror.

"There is always tomorrow, Veronica. This has been a very long day. Yes? No?" I mimicked the sweet twins. I could not stop smiling as I crawled under the soft quilt and fell asleep.

16. THE MIRROR

I dreamt of a candy shop, the smell of a fresh waffle cone tickled my nose, and the Crème Brule in the display case appeared irresistible. About to reach and dip my finger in its crusty middle, I woke up in the bedroom on the first floor of the 63 Sterling Place. Moishele the faun slept at the foot of my bed curled up like a kitten. His little golden hooves peeked from under his blue pajamas. I watched a golden wisp of hair moving above his face with his breathing. He slept with his pudgy hands folded under his cheek. I had a sudden need to cradle his small body in my arms and kiss his sweet face. Perhaps this is how his mothers felt when they took care of their baby. But this was no baby. This creature looked like an adorable toddler, and by my modest calculations, Moishele was around fifty years old. According to the sisters' tale, they found him in1937. Under the spell of his sweetness, I cradled him in my arms and took a closer look at his small adorable face. I examined his perfect pink cheeks, small heart shaped mouth, tiny chin, round funny nose with a tiny cleft and golden curling eyelash. His plump pink hands had pretty dimples, except the fingernails were golden just like his hair, tiny horns, and hooves. He smelled like chocolate and cream, so sweet and delicious.

Moishele's eyes opened and when he saw me, his face lit up with a sweet smile.

"Moishele, my dear faun, I found you sleeping in my bed."

"Good morning, Veronica. I came down last night to wish you good night but you were sound asleep. My mothers allowed me to stay with you, just in case. And a good thing I did. You kept talking in your sleep about books and a boy called Emmanuel. What's up with that?"

I put him back on the bed and sat down.

"Oh, Moishele, never mind me, it is you I would like to understand. I was just thinking when you were asleep that you are pretty old by our standards, your youth and beauty must be out of this world."

He patted my hand and kissed me on the cheek the same way he showed affection to Feige and Kitty.

"But this is the only world I have known." His large brown eyes had golden specks and oval pupils, not round like human.

"I have been suspecting for a long time that I must have come from somewhere else. Everything around me ages, including my precious mommies. I do not change. It took almost half a century for me to look like a human toddler. "

"Tell me what Feige and Kitty think of it? They never mentioned anything yesterday."

"Yeah, they do like to tell tall stories", he smiled again, "but I know they are scared of the time when they won't be around anymore and I would be left all alone."

"You can always come and live with me," I said realizing it was an absolute truth. I would love that so much.

"I love my mommies so much, they are my world. If they go, I must go as well."

I began to understand the motive behind the mysterious ad, and the meaning behind the intriguing toast yesterday.

"They are trying to find where you came from and send you back. Is this what the sisters are hoping to do?"

"Sweetie, you are correct." Feige's radiant happy face appeared in the door.

"I told you she is the true one." Kitty followed her.

They were wearing identical white robes, pink fuzzy slippers, their white hair hidden under the lacy nightcaps. *Just like cute little old girls,* I thought.

"Breakfast first. Come on, Moishele, let's dress you up for the day, boychik. You too, Veronica, there are some very pretty dresses in the wardrobe. Help yourself to anything you like. And then we eat."

After they left, I went to the wardrobe and opened its carved doors. The scent of cedar and lavender drew me in. The doors had mirrors, hats rested on the top shelf and shoes on the bottom. The middle had a cupboard filled with scarves, gloves, and costume jewelry. I examined the accessories and moved to the dresses. This is what the sisters described yesterday. The vintage dresses made of fine fabrics. They reminded me of my Grandmother's dresses. She favored dark shades of brown and burgundy, but these were ranging from cream to turquoise to black. I kept piling them on the bed, unable to decide which one. They were all so beautiful. I selected a green velvet dress of medium length with a silver thread stitched around the collar and tiny mother of pearl buttons running down to the waist. I put it on and noticed how it complemented my pale complexion, auburn hair, even my eyes looked greener. I twirled around to check how it fit in the wardrobe mirrors. It accentuated my small waist and gave me a look of a girl from a romantic Irish ballad.

I found a pair of black silk stockings, which I tied with ribbons, the old-fashioned way, and black shoes with curved little heels. What a change from my black jeans, turtleneck sweater, and a sensible parka, not to mention the Doc Martens.

As I examined myself in the mirror, I thought that it was a right time to go home and to become a girl again. *No, not a girl, a woman.* I laughed at that, it was a fist time ever I thought of myself as a woman. The clothes did it, they were magical, for sure.

I came upstairs for breakfast all dressed up and my wild curls bushed. A loud round of applause greeted me at the door.

"Such a beautiful girl."

"She is a princess."

"Our lovely and clever princess. Now eat."

We had cherry cheesecake New York style, stewed pears with

cream and cappuccino.

"Do you only eat cake?" I inquired.

"What should we eat? Parsnips and herring?"

"Or broccoli", added Moishele with a grimace.

"Eat quickly. We are going out," said Feige.

"We 'exshplore an' 'ave 'un.' Every day," Moishele tried to explain with his mouth full.

"We like to take walks before lunch," said Kitty.

"Lunch, already?" I raised my eyebrows, forkful of cherry cheesecake halfway to my mouth.

Moishele threw his arms in the air, "Why not?"

We carried the pram downstairs and Moishele climbed in. By the front door, the sisters faced each other, clapped hands three times, and said "Geeb-a-Kook."

The house changed from beautiful sunny to the neglected dusty in a flash. The world seemed grayer and the air harsher outside the small rusty gate.

We spent part of our afternoon in the botanical garden. A blues band played in the center gazebo. People sat around at the picnic tables or on the blankets. In the distance someone tossed a Frisbee. I could hear a happy squealing from the playground somewhere beyond the trees. It was an idyllic family outing. Something I had never experienced before. Sitting in the shade and listening to the music my memories carried me back to the beach walks with Sebastian. They were part of our outings for many years, a ritual of sorts. That was different. Sebastian and I were alone. I loved the empty spaces devoid of humanity. Now, I loved the spaces full of humanity. *What was happening to me?*

Feige and Kitty gathered little sprigs of flowers and plants from the flowerbeds and took them to Moishele. I, on the other hand, amused him by naming and describing the plant's medicinal properties. They listened to me with awe.

"Tell us more, Veronica. This little chamomile flower would really make us sleep better?"

"Is it true if we rinse our white hair in sage tea it would darken?"

Their questions were so open, the curiosity so innocent. Happy to share my knowledge, I could not stop laughing and talking.

We were back at home by lunchtime as intended. Lunch consisted of tropical fruit and ice cream topped with glazed nuts and hot chocolate sauce. Despite the huge breakfast, I dug in, only to pause for a second to devour the fantastic presentation with my eyes.

"Where do you get all these delicacies?" I asked.

"Oh, everything is delivered to our house next door and left in the cold box in the hall," said Faige.

"We have contracts with over fifty bakeries around New York," said Kitty.

"Meals are left there three times per day. No questions asked."

"And we pay for it handsomely."

At this point I wondered if they paid handsomely for the food, or for 'no questions asked', but decided not voice it. I remembered the abrupt way our conversation had ended last night when I mentioned money and their ability to purchase the buildings. Sebastian taught me not to force anything. The information would appear by itself as a reward for my patience. They would tell me the rest of their story soon enough.

After a while, I came to realize the rest the story was not coming any time soon. Day after day, we feasted on lavish meals. Explored museums and galleries, attended ballet and opera matinees, or took strolls in the park. Moishele always stayed hidden in the pram. In the evening, we drunk wine, danced, and ate more delicacies until I collapsed in my bed and had carefree dreams of flying.

One day we went to the Central Park to pick up my case of books. My friends were delighted to meet Sadiyah. But we had to rush off, pleading lateness, because she kept on insisting to see our 'baby'. I had an odd feeling of being watched, and glanced up. Mr. Hound scurried in the opposite direction, he was watching me, but I could not care less.

I had lost the count of days. My life belonged to beautiful

Moishele, he became the 'light of my eyes and the meaning of my life', just like the sisters said it. I also noticed my cheeks becoming plumper and pinker, and had an unfamiliar heaviness to my breasts, middle, and backside. The true revelation came one day, when I tried to pull my jeans on. *Oy vey* I thought, *I am turning into a butterball, this has to stop.* Then with horror, I remembered my childhood nemesis Pigele. I flew upstairs on an instant to break the news to the sisters and Moishele.

"Why do you call yourself a fatty, you are beautiful."

"This is the way a beautiful girl should look, darling."

"Really beautiful and healthy girl."

"Veronica, you shine with beauty and happiness," Moishele reached his hand out to me, "when we met, you looked like a waif."

"But I came here for a reason, why don't we continue with your initial quest? I am here to help. Eating and entertainment will not open any secrets for us. Let's do it!"

They were surprised. The same look of dismay darkened Sebastian's face when I demanded freedom.

"She is red in the face. Is she angry?"

"She wants to help us."

"Mommies, she is right."

"So let's do it. Let's continue with our quest," said Faige, "but dinner's first."

I fell on the settee laughing, told them how much I adored them, and apologized for my outburst.

After dinner, I asked the sisters to tell me the story of discovering Moishele from the beginning. I already knew about the storm and the thunder, but I wanted details. I wanted to see the exact location.

The night fell by the time we finished dinner and went to the roof. The amber light from the neighboring buildings, and a lonely bulb above the door illuminated the small area.

"Where did you find him? Show me the spot."

Feige took my hand and led me over.

"Now, let's sit down here and close our eyes. The three of you listen to my voice and follow my instructions."

They complied and we sat on the tar-coated roof in a circle, holding hands. I hoped to try Sebastian's meditation method with them.

"Take a deep breath and exhale. Try to remember the rain, the thunder. Remember your feelings as you continue with your slow breathing. What did you think when you first heard the tiny sound coming from the roof? Keep breathing. Now you are on the roof. Feel the rain on your faces. What do you see? Keep breathing deeper. What else do you remember when you found him? Keep breathing deeper and deeper. Now, with your mind's eye, look around and tell me what you see at that precise moment. Take time to concentrate on your deep breathing and on your feelings."

We sat motionless. I could hear their breathing, the faces barely visible in the semi-darkness.

Moishele's voice rang out breaking the stillness,

"I just saw a lake and felt a soft grass. But it disappeared in a storm and a burst of lightning."

"Moishele, boychik, are you sure?"

"You were just a baby."

"I am sure. It was as vivid to me as this morning's strawberry tart."

Astounded at this memory I demanded more of what he had seen or felt. He could not remember anything else.

"I feared that whatever was crying would drown in the rain," said Feige.

"And I can't shake the terror from the flapping wrappings of the mirror, the wind had unwound them and it looked like a huge winged monster," whispered Kitty.

"Anything else?" I said, with hope.

Feige and Kitty could not say. They became small and frightened. I could not bear it and urged them to go back down for tea.

We made our way down. Deep in thought, I carried Moishele in my arms. The sisters were not exchanging their usual funny commentaries behind me. In the parlor, we made tea and snacked on a strudel. The mental exercise made everyone hungry. We did not dance that night. I retired early, and could not fall asleep for a long time. The sleep was the last thing on my mind as I lay in the darkness recalling their story and dwelling on its details.

Bright light streaming through the window woke me up. I had forgotten to draw the shade the night before. The porcelain clock on the dresser counted last minutes before eleven o'clock. After a quick shower, frowning at my new curvy form in a foggy bathroom mirror, I went over to the wardrobe to select a dress. The wardrobe contained enough dresses for every day of the month. I chose a dove grey with high bodice and black velvet bows at the collar, waist, and back. I stood and looked in the mirror for a long time. Only I did not look at my reflection. Something else was bothering me, a nagging idea at the back of my mind. I could not put my finger on it, and it distracted me. As usual, I made my way to the sisters' and Moishele's quarters upstairs. A strong scent of cinnamon rolls and coffee made me forget my elusive idea for a moment. Halfway up the stairs, I caught my reflection in the mirrors of the wardrobe, which I forgot to close. With all my might, I rushed up taking two steps at a time and burst into the parlor.

"Where is the mirror you had for modeling the fashions when you were young girls?" I demanded of the astonished group.

Feige was about to pour coffee for Kitty and froze in mid-action. Moishele stopped chewing on his marzipan bunny, his cheeks bulging, and eyes wide. Feige bumped the carafe on the table and pointed to the roof. I took off in that direction. They followed in a small stampede.

"You know something?"

"You will tell us?"

"Come on, Veronica. Enough already. Speak up, please!"

A large object wrapped in burlap leaned against the wall at the far end of a small patio. Like a demon, I removed the wrappings. The mirror's surface shone with clear light, just like new.

"Now show me where you found Moishele."

The look on my face extinguished any arguments, and together they pointed at the spot right in front of the ornate brass frame.

I gently touched the mirror's surface. My fingertips failed to leave any prints. I brought my face close to the glass and breathed on it. My breath did not even leave a mark. Our reflections were beautiful in the mirror. We all had fresh faces. I marveled at the texture of our flawless skin and hair shiny as silk. We did not look like this in real life or in any other mirror. Except for Moishele, he was beautiful on any day. His reflection in this mirror was an epitome of perfection, like an angel.

To break the spell, I began to wrap the mirror up back to its original state. The sisters helped and I noticed their unusual silence. We made our way down to the abandoned breakfast. Feige, Kitty, and Moishele watched me with quiet anticipation.

"I had this nagging idea, but I could not put my finger on it." I said. "Tell me where did you get this mirror?"

"Do you remember, Kitty dear?" said Feige.

"We also got a gorgeous blue hat with an ostrich feather that day," added Kitty.

"It was so hard to schlep that mirror from the flea market, it weighed a ton."

"It took us two days to haul it upstairs."

"But it was worth it. The mirror made us look so beautiful."

"So you bought it at the flea market. Do you remember from whom?"

"There was a lot of junk in that place."

"We had to really dig to find the good stuff."

"They sold off things abandoned by the immigrants at the customs. The proceeds from the sales went to help the community."

"And you do not know where the mirror came from?"

The sisters shook their heads.

"No matter where it came from, I think that the mirror is a portal," I said with conviction.

"What's a portal?" Three pairs of eyes stared at me with childlike curiosity.

I smiled. They smiled back and everything became normal again. The sisters asked me to wait with my story and busied themselves with the tea and a new batch of cakes. Moishele climbed onto my knees to brush my hair. I let him, although it did hurt. My curls were not easy to tame.

After everyone had a slice of cranberry cake with a cup of fresh tea, I conveyed the rest of my idea. The storm described by the sisters must have created a vortex of energy around the house. That energy had concentrated in the mirror, which perhaps was one of the ancient portals I had read about in the Boston Library vault. With a burst of thunder, the portal had opened up between Moishele's world and ours. The force of wind must have swept the baby faun into our world. Any magical portal, according to the accounts described in Professor Silverman's books, needs to have a corresponding similar portal. One was on our side, which was the mirror and one on the other side, which probably was the lake.

"The lake I saw during our meditation?" asked Moishele.

"Yes, the lake should have been smooth as a mirror before the storm."

"What does it all mean then?" asked Faige.

"I think I can guess. You found a way back for Moishele. But how?" said Kitty.

"Remember I told you about Professor Silverman in Istanbul. He told me about the worlds that are parallel to each other. Perhaps there are millions of them, all different. Our world is different from the world where Moishele comes from."

"But if the worlds are parallel, how come nobody even knows about them?"

"Should we not be aware of a different world within our reach?"

"There could be people like me?" said wide eyed Moishele.

"No, the worlds do not touch. Paths exist between the different realities. They are portals. Some people in our world can travel from reality to reality without leaving their seat, by meditation. Or like Professor Silverman, using treasure dust he made from the precious blue stones with alchemy."

Explaining this I remembered about how much I missed Ira and his eccentric ways.

"Our father the Rabbi taught us that if we have a strong belief, everything will come through."

"We did not think much about his lessons. They were just a part of our life."

"The life we abandoned, the moment sweet Moishele came to us."

"But do you understand what I mean?"

"Yes, but we always wanted to be Operetta actresses. Not philosophers."

"Oh yes, my mommies dance and sing beautifully. You can take it up again when I leave."

As Moishele said it, the look of horror appeared on sisters' faces. Moishele began to cry and the sisters followed his example.

"But he does not need to leave alone," I tried to console them, "you will follow him, he still needs his mothers. It does not matter where you live, here or somewhere else."

My words calmed them down. They begged for reassurance and professed they would not live for a second without Moishele.

"Then why run an ad for a magician, to send him back?"

"We did not think it would happen so fast. To us it was an impossible task. It could take years. Remember?"

"Right, we have to come up with a plan on how to send all three of you to Moishele's world where he can grow up at last."

"Sounds like a great plan," said Moishele, "but..."

"Let's eat first," I completed his thought, and gave him a chocolate kiss followed by a real one.

17. MOISHELE'S GOLD

e ate in silence and quickly. Anticipation hung in the air. I liked to
be in control, but felt a little guilty for disrupting the sisters' and
WMoishele's lives. I thought my actions would nudge them out of
the crazy-lazy routine. The reason for our fateful meeting had to have
some purpose.

Once again, we settled in our chairs with three pairs of eyes
glued on me. I began my speech by asking them not to place a
complete trust in me, because I acted on part intuition and part logic.
In return, Feige and Kitty called me the smartest and the most
brilliant girl in the world. *I just wish my grandma had same opinion when she
was alive,* I thought with a slight bitterness. The theory surfaced as I
continued to expand on Sebastian's teachings of cool logical
approach, and my belief in magic.

I spun a theory of how the storm brought the energy vortex
down to their house and opened the portal between our worlds.
Same energy swept Moishele into our world. The sisters heard his
wailing, and came up to the roof too anxious to pay attention to the
opened portal. Once Moishele was safe, the life had changed for
Faige and Kitty. They were so busy with the baby it did not occur to
them to investigate his true origins. Perhaps they made a crucial
mistake, the portal stayed open for a while, and they had a chance
cross over and return Moishele to his world.

We had to devise a plan how to make the portal in the mirror
open up again. For this we had need to wait for a storm with enough
energy to create another vortex.

"She called it a mistake," said Faige, quite distraught.

"It was a divine gift," Kitty clasped her hands by her heart.

"It brought us happiness. Not a mistake," they said, clearly worried by my words.

"Alright, I am just trying to use logic, forgive me," I fell silent, afraid to offend them.

"Veronica is right. If this happened before it can happen again," said Moishele taking my side.

"And who knows how many times it did open afterwards - the mirror is still here," I said, encouraged by Moishele's support.

"And it did," said Feige.

"Tell them, Feige dear," Kitty prompted.

"Tell us what?" I said, expecting some news.

"Better yet, we will show you."

Moishele and I exchanged looks.

The sisters came back with an object wrapped in one of the Kitty's crochet tablecloths. They gave it to Moishele to unwrap. He did it just like any child with eager impatience. We gasped. He held up small shiny golden harp. Flowery carving adorned its sides entwined with nymph-like figures. I reached and stroked the gilded frame with my finger. It was warm and smooth like butter. Moishele snatched it and examined the carved figures with undivided interest.

"Where and when did you get this little golden harp?" I asked.

"About thirty years ago."

"We found it on the roof."

"Now we understand that the mirror must have opened up again."

"May I?" I reached over to Moishele to take the harp.

"It's quite heavy, and looks shiny and new," I ran my fingers on the strings once or twice, "and it does not make any sound when I pull the strings. I wonder why?"

"I think the sound is heard in my world. You pull the strings here, and it sounds there. Mommies, why not show it to me before?"

Both sisters fidgeted, and I guessed why.

"Oh, Moishele, they did not want you to get upset and lose your appetite."

I saved them from embarrassment. They were uncomfortable with those erotic nymphs on the harp.

At last, we made a decision to watch the weather and wait for the storm. I inquired if they had a radio or we could arrange a paper delivery. As it turned out, there was an old TV set in one of the locked rooms downstairs. It had an antenna and a VCR to watch the movies.

"We watch it only in the winter," said Moishele

"And only the movies," added Faige

"We love Barbara, the Funny Girl," said Kitty.

"And it's nothing else but Barbara, no cartoons, no nothing" grumbled Moishele.

I carried the TV upstairs to keep a closer eye on the weather forecast. We needed time to plan the big escape before the early autumn thunderstorms begun.

Despite the preparations, our life had taken its usual course of sumptuous meals, cultural excursions, and walks in the park. The sisters disappeared alone from time to time, and came back happy and flushed. A flood of affection towards Moishele and me came after each excursion. I had no complaints. I just loved to be loved.

One morning, I came upstairs and felt an air of urgency in the room. A box filled with trinkets sat on the floor. Feige and Kitty were busy separating its contents into several piles.

"Ah, what are you doing?"

"We are packing."

"Deciding on what's important."

"Stuff to take with us."

I helped them sort, and found old photographs of their parents, some old fashion magazines, books of Moishele's fairy tales, crochet hooks, and many other little knick-knacks.

"We are packing light," said Faige.

"Just memories and sentimental stuff," explained Kitty.

"Why bring old stuff to new life?"

"Sit down, Veronica, we have something for you," said Faige.

I went to the settee, and examined the ransacked room. A breakfast of stack of crepes in black cherry sauce sat on the table along with the teacups. The beautiful rose bouquet in a crystal vase dominated with its beauty. All of a sudden, it felt like farewells.

Moishele climbed onto my lap. The sisters left the room only to return with a large wooden chest on wheels. It had a brass lock in front, painted red and gold cabbage roses on the black lid. Faige produced a small key on the chain around her neck and unlocked it.

"It's for you Veronica," said Kitty, her voice soft and gentle.

I opened the lid and disbelieved my eyes. Small gold bars filled the chest to the top. At first, I had a mad notion they were chocolate bars wrapped in gold foil. I picked one up, and realized it was real gold. The sisters and Moishele chuckled. The look on my face was probably worth the entire collection of these gold bars. The chest held probably a hundred of them at least.

"You are giving them to me? Why? There must be at least a hundred here."

"Ten thousand."

"Nine more chests filled with bars are in our bedroom closet."

"And yes, they are all yours."

"We will not need them where we are going."

"But how would you know that? Thank you so much, but I cannot accept such a gift. You are too generous."

"Thank Moishele, it's his hair."

"What, Moishele's hair?" I touched his soft curls, "I definitely need to hear about this. Will you tell me?"

From their story, I was able to understand that Moishele-the-Golden-Faun-Child was so precious to Feige and Kitty they collected all his hair and nail trimmings. They thought it would be a sacrilege to discard them. One day, Feige scooped honey for her tea and a drop fell on Moishele's hair clippings that lay on the table. His hair grew so quickly that he needed a trim every week. The instant the honey touched the hair, both solidified into a gold nugget. At first, the sisters were skeptical and took it to the old friend of Bronstein's, a diamond dealer in the city. He in turn, showed the small piece of gold to someone else. In a few days when sisters came to see the friend again, he gave them a wad of money for the nugget.

"And from only one drop of honey."

"We had heaps of hair and buckets of honey."

"Since then we were set to make the gold."

"Meaning you made gold for the last fifty years or so?" I asked not believing them.

"Well, we had to live on something."

"Remember, we were ostracized by everyone, and had no means."

"It takes two bars per year to live on."

Then I learned that instead of random sprinkling the hair with honey, they would put it in the special molding dishes purchased from the jeweler. Finally, their amassed fortune of gold bars was enough to last a lifetime, even several lifetimes.

"And all because of me," said Moishele with air of importance.

I reached to tickle him, "You are our biggest gold bar, sweet Moishele."

The sisters assured me that Moishele's gold would be the last thing they would want to take with them to his world. To them, he was the ultimate treasure. I was touched beyond tears by their empathy, until they produced another surprise. Moishele opened a cabinet drawer and pulled out a file of important looking documents.

"What is this?" I asked when he offered them to me.

"The deeds to the houses."

"What houses?"

"The one we live in, silly, the two on the either sides and the three across from us."

I was speechless. They were giving me six houses. My mind reeled. How could I go from penniless urchin to such riches?

"You wanted to know how we lived and purchased property without income."

"Now you know, and we give it all to you, Veronica LaRose."

"Because we love you, Moishele loves you. You have made our boychik happy."

The heavy folio, bound in black leather with silver embossed Chancery lettering: *Shachmundes, Freeman and Pen, Barristers and Solicitors.*

So this is an answer to your mysterious afternoon disappearances," I said, shaken and touched beyond words.

I hugged and kissed each of them. Excused myself and found a way downstairs in a mental haze. I needed time to come to terms with the latest events. In addition, oppressing migraine, perhaps from the roller coaster of my emotions, gripped my head in a vice. They were kind enough to understand, and Moishele followed holding my hand.

I piled my pillows high and lay down on my back with a wet cold cloth over my forehead. Moishele curled up beside me.

"Try to understand, Veronica. They are getting ready to begin a new life. Let them tie up the ends. The last time it happened was so unhappy for them, the loss of their home, parents, and their older brother. This transition will be much happier. I know it."

"I understand, Moishele, let me close my eyes for a bit," I said trying to fight the migraine.

I was dreaming again. This time the dream was about standing in the middle of a war movie. The cannons blasted and the ground shook with explosions. Then I shook, someone was shaking me. Moishele was shaking me.

"Wake up Veronica. The storm, the storm is coming."
I arose, picked him up, and went upstairs. The sisters sat on the settee holding hands.

"Do you think it's time? There was nothing on the television. The television was wrong. What do we do now?" The barrage of questions continued.

"Mamas, stop panicking. Just take our things and let's go to the mirror. Right Veronica?"

"Right." I said without hesitation, but with no conviction.

The storm became stronger, the wind howled and shook the house, and the electricity played tricks with the light bulbs. The entire situation became surreal with frightened sisters, shouting Moishele and flickering lights. I gestured up and waved them to follow me. They each took Moishele by the hand as we climbed the stairs to the roof. The windblasts were so strong, I unwrapped the mirror in no time.

We positioned ourselves in front of it and waited huddled in the relentless rain for what seemed like an eternity. When the lightning flash pierced the darkness, we could see the reflected bolt in the glass. I touched the surface of the mirror to check for changes. The lightning bolt appeared again accompanied by ferocious thunder, the mirror shook, and we jumped. I touched the surface again. Nothing. The rain has begun to subside soon after the last rumble. We stood there soaked to the bones, pitiful and disappointed. The wind decreased and the clouds appeared torn like some tired rags. I spied the moon behind their tattered remains. Moishele looked up at me, crushed hope reflecting in his eyes. The storm had ended.

I told them to wait on the roof and rushed down to my bedroom. In the closet on the bottom of my trusty backpack was hidden the rain flute. I planned to use it as my last resort, but had no time to test. I ran back to the roof and showed the flute to my astonished family. Before they could barrage me with questions, I blew the flute and another storm descended with a sudden swooshes, just as I had experienced so long ago in the desert.

The rain fell in buckets. The lightning was brighter than the sun. Suddenly, the sun shone in the mirror, a blue sky appeared, and a lake with the green meadow around it.

This could not be an illusion, the contrast between the stormy night and idyllic vista in the mirror jerked us into action. Moishele tore away from the sisters and jumped over the mirror frame, he yelled something at us, but we heard no sound. I urged the sisters to go ahead. They stumbled. I helped by whispering encouragements as they joined Moishele.

Expression of wonder came over their lovely faces. Moishele kept on beckoning to come over and join them. I just stood on the wet roof, glued to one spot. I could not make myself do it. It was not a right time for me, not my life path, as Sebastian would say.

I yearned to follow them. To pick up Moishele for the last hug and kiss, to embrace the old girls. The fear of not be able to come back prevented me.

In a few moments, their faces started to grow smaller as if I was raising high above them, until they became three small dots by the diminishing lake far below. The mirror dimmed and a dark gray fog begun to cloud the scenery.

I felt hot tears running down my face, as everything on the other side became invisible. The mirror turned solid again. I stared at my own disheveled soaked reflection and felt nothing but the icy cold gripping at my heart.

The loss was unbearable with my little family gone. I ended up with my usual friend - the solitude.

18. MY GOTHIC GARDEN

They are gone, time to move on. The sad thoughts played in my head in one continuous loop as I wandered around the empty brownstone.

I had no reason to maintain our old routine, because they will never burst in again with Moishele in tow telling me about their day with their dear bickering. I missed holding Moishele's small body in my arms, and the way he liked to eat with such gusto. The food continued to arrive from the bakeries every day. The rooms were crammed with stale cakes and other sweets. I went back to my usual diet of tea, granola bars, and fruit. Even looking at those cakes and pastries turned my stomach with grief. It was time for me to go home.

I tidied up already clean house, left the note and a few hefty checks to discontinue the deliveries, and packed my trusted backpack. With a flutter in my heart, I wrapped the flute, dusty rock from *Vjeter*, Bagus's ashes, Maria's portrait, and the golden harp. The chest, full of gold bars, with the deeds to the property and the books from Ira Silverman were packed and waiting downstairs. Beautiful and mysterious spoils of my journey confused me about their purpose. My search for magic led me to more questions and none of the answers I was hoping to find in the beginning of my journey. I had a strong suspicion Moishele left the harp with me on purpose, and touched the strings hoping he would hear me in his world.

I wrangled with the choices on how to get home. With my new riches, I could hire a jet. My wish was to arrive silently and unexpected, the same way I left. I planned to surprise Sebastian. I sent him a few postcards from New York, assuring him I was all right.

Early fall had arrived. Hard to believe that one whole year had passed since I fell in love with Emmanuel. A little more than a year since I found Professor Silverman, lost little Bagus and left Smeela on the cargo ship. Almost two years had passed since I left my home and Sebastian.

I went to Prospect Park and walked the path watching the kids play, lovers kiss, and old ladies stroll. On my last day in New York, I went for a walk before the taxi came to take me to the train station. The park looked transformed with cheery festival banners. Hot air balloon wagons stood everywhere drawing small crowds. Multicolored clouds made of silk, ready to fly away into the blue abyss took up the entire green space. I wished one could take me away too. My dark mood lightened up a bit as I walked around the balloons stretched on the grass, and the excited people milling around.

I approached the most unusual balloon at the festival, with a grinning Jolly Roger on the red background. It suited my mood to perfection. The captain stood by the gondola fending questions from the group of teens.

I joined in and listened, then asked a question myself, "So is death laughing at us or with us?"
The captain grinned at me wider than Roger on the balloon did. At the closer look, he appeared to be in his thirties, tanned and energetic, with a black paisley bandana wrapped around his head.

"It's here to remind us to live the life, before it collects."

"This is how you enjoy your life? Ballooning?"

"It's the freedom, go wherever the wind takes me."

"Can it take you to north of Boston?"

"I don't see why not. Is this where you heading?"

"In the matter of fact I am. Can you give me a ride? I am willing to pay, just name your price."

At this point in our conversation, he realized I was serious and gave me a long look.

"Long flight, anything can happen. You not scared?" His grey deep-set eyes bore into mine.

"No, I am not. How can I be scared of freedom?"

A crowd swelled around us. I heard excited whispers and the kids were pointing at me, some called their parents over. Everyone was in our conversation, until a bespectacled blonde-haired woman came over and poked my balloonist in the chest with a pencil.

"You know the regulations, Hunter Ash, no passengers, or you will be disqualified from the race."

"Screw the rules and regulations. I got a freedom loving soul to deliver to where she needs to be. An' that's good enough for me. Consider me disqualified," said Hunter Ash and pointed at me, "we leave before noon."

"Would not miss it for the world. I am Veronica LaRose by the way," we shook hands like the old friends.

The blonde race coordinator squinted at me and asked if I was not afraid to be alone with this guy. Before I could come up with a suitable reply, Hunter dismissed the implication.

"She'll be safe enough with me, I'm not into ladies, if you know what I mean."

The girl looked offended and I blushed, because the male advances were the last thing on my mind, despite his rugged good looks. Amused, I remembered how Anna used to lament that all handsome men were either gay or married. Hunter blew a mocking kiss at the blonde and she walked off, straight as a ruler.

"If her eyes were daggers, I would be in shreds by now," announced Hunter and the crowd cheered.

The taxi came to haul my weighty luggage to the park. The other gold-filled chests remained hidden in the bedroom closet under the shoe and hatboxes. Nobody would even think to look there, especially after the closing spell. I stood in the same room where I first met my darling family all those months ago. So many happy memories caused sadness. I brought my hands together as Faige and

Kitty taught me, clapped three times, and said "Geeb-a-kook!"

The cozy interior changed in an instant into an old, dusty neglected house. I turned around and left, my eyes were dry but by throat tight with emotion. *Good bye, brownstone, I will come back one day.*

I clutched the edge of gondola under the puffing burner and watched the houses shrink into matchboxes and the people into toy soldiers. The horizon called us beyond the skyline of New York. We floated over the neighborhoods towards the shore and once the Atlantic opened up for us we headed north to New England.

Hunter Ash proved himself a master balloonist. He operated the balloon with an agility and strength of a spider monkey right from the take off. He did the job of four men alone, inflated the balloon and prepared the gondola, loaded the ballast and my belongings. I watched him navigate, until the cold wind cut my skin. He noticed my shivers, threw an old serape blanket over my shoulders, and told me to sit down. I did not comply and stood transfixed by the vista of freedom surrounding us until he came up behind me and put his arm around my shoulders.

"Beautiful, free, and never dull," said Hunter swigging from a whiskey bottle, "I feel alive up here and I will die up here."

"I understand, Hunter. I would do the same, it's magic," I took his proffered bottle and swallowed some of the burning liquid.

The whiskey warmed me up and when the heat reached my toes I thought that everything is going to be alright. I pretended the balloon did not exist and imagined myself in a free flight, and the occasional noise of the burner was the sound of my giant wings. The higher my wings took me, the farther away my adventures seemed to be. I was leaving them behind. *LaRose Gris, your child is coming back.*

I read the seashore map north of Boston and showed Hunter the location of my beach. He said it would be no problem for him to land there. I watched the sun sink into the sea, lulled by the gondola's gentle movement. Hunter was up smoking and watching the fiery horizon with his back to me. I drifted in a dream state feeling safe and secure above the world and under the stars.

"Sleep now, Veronica. I will wake you in time for the greatest show on Earth, the sunrise," said Hunter turning around, only the red point of his cigarette and the Milky Way visible in the descending night.

Hunter was right about calling the sunrise the greatest show on Earth. It was not the same as witnessing it from the ground, the sea, or even the mountaintop. I felt like Aurora riding in her chariot, cold winds forgotten, only golden Apollo the Sun beckoning me with his divine beauty.

"Hold on tight or sit down, we are about to descend," said Hunter and manipulated the balloon's controls. The descent came fast and silent. I watched as we pierced the carpet of clouds below us, like a knife through the soft butter and ended up in the world familiar to me from the childhood. The grey cold misty New England seashore I called home.

The gondola touched the sand, the balloon jerked up like a tethered stallion. I saw a familiar beach surrounded by boulders, the grey perimeter wall of LaRose Gris, hiding behind the veil of early morning fog. Nervous and excited I lowered myself onto the sand with Hunter's help. Without speaking, I gave him a hug and stuck a gold bar in his hand. At first, he could not understand what it was, and then he whistled and gave me another hug.

"Any time you are out for another adventure or want to get away in silence, call me," he said and wrote a number on a label of the empty whisky bottle, "Only three people know this number now. My mom, the person I care about, and now you, Veronica."

"Thank you Hunter, you might hear from me one day."

"I take it as a promise, alright? I gotta fly now, the storm's abrewing and I want to ride it."

He was back in the gondola and within moments, the balloon ascended into the sky. A part of me departed with it.

I left all my things on the beach excited to run home and surprise Sebastian by bursting into the house yelling *I'm back!*

I circled the wall, went through the gate, around the carriage house up to the side entrance, found the key in the planter, and unlocked the door. A draft of damp cold air and darkness touched my flushed face. I switched the lights on, and saw the furniture covered with sheets. I called Sebastian's name, it echoed through the upper floors and I realized I was alone. The parlor, library, music room, meditation room met me with dark emptiness. The kitchen looked sterile with a shut off fridge. I run upstairs. My room was neat and clean, like a student's away at school. Sebastian's quarters did not change, modest and basic. The same stacks of books on the floor and a mandala on the wall.

"Sebastian, where are you?" I called into silence and all I heard was the rain drumming its fingers on the roof, same way when I was little. I sat on the top step and thought what to do next, whom to call and what to say.

I had to retrieve my things from the beach. I remembered a dolly in the carriage house, got the key from the kitchen. Hermes sat under the protective tarp, and so did my Hermie. I threw the cover off and noticed that despite the protection it had a thick layer of dust, as if no one touched the cars since I left.

The fog covered the grounds with its tattered remains, and I could see no one cleared the autumn leaves and other debris from the driveway and the front steps for months. My garden became overgrown and neglected. The English ivy, that covered the grey mansion all the way to the roof, remained the only thriving plant. I hauled my things from the beach and brought wood for the fireplace in my chilly bedroom. The fire warmed up the room a little and cheered it up a lot. I climbed under the damp sea scented sheets and watched the little fire dance until falling asleep.

My dreams were uneasy. I remembered looking for something, not finding it and riding with Hunter into the storm. However, it was not Hunter. It was Sebastian. I kept clutching at his hand, but the wind tore him away from me and pulled him into a vortex. The sound of the storm woke me up, the shutters rattled outside my window, the house moaned and I felt a damp draft blowing from under the door, like some monster's breath. It scared me, as I was not scared before, even when Jason Fox pointed his gun at me or when Bagus confessed his hunger baring the sharp teeth. I was alone and scared in a huge dark empty mansion. Maybe Anna was right about the ghosts. But, why should I be afraid of ghosts? *Fall in love with them is what I do best.* This thought about Emmanuel made me chuckle and chase the silly fears away. Instead of cowering under the covers, I decided to find something to eat. Life with Moishele and the Bronstein sisters taught me well. Unfortunately, I found nothing in the pantry except some of Winai's spices. Finding nothing in the kitchen, I moved to the dining room and found an unopened Absinthe LaRose bottle surrounded by dusty goblets. This was not a good snack for someone who had whiskey for dinner and no breakfast. Discouraged, I went back to bed and slept again until in my dream state I remembered our vegetable garden.

The storm had passed and the sun's timid rays reached through the ivy covered window. I grabbed a bowl from the kitchen cupboard and went out through the French doors in the dining room. My poor beautiful garden needed attention. I strolled to the gazebo, greeting my trees and yellow chrysanthemums. The stream had overgrown with reeds. I would have to take care of it in the spring. My herb beds ran amok, everything I have ever planted grew into a tangled mass. The vegetable garden failed to disappoint me. It was afire with the cherry tomatoes. Abundant heavy clusters filled my large bowl within minutes, and I ate my fill of their sweet tangy goodness. Then I found a squash hiding among the yellowed leaves. My late lunch and dinner became complete with a bunch of the string beans. A few trips back and forth, pinching the mums and pulling a weed here and there, managed to lift up my spirits.

Then I heard a doorbell. I flew to the front doors thinking it must be Sebastian returning from his mysterious absence.

The surprise turned nasty as I came face to face with Evan Wood, my old childhood tormentor. He was not a kid anymore. He stood mean-faced on my doorstep sporting a buzz cut and a police uniform. Instead of a proper greeting, he smirked and walked in without an invitation, rudely brushing against my shoulder.

"So, the little witch is back, what foul wind carried you in? I thought the old place was abandoned by your kind for good."

"Evan, get out, you are not welcome in my house," I said flushed with sudden anger. Memories of his snide remarks and mockery came back in an instant.

"Not so quick. This place was empty for almost two years. The tall weirdo is gone, now you show up all 'hoity toity'. Something's fishy here," he said, looked around and headed to the kitchen.

"I am also tall, and you always called me a weirdo. Nothing changed here, Evan. And, you are still a pompous fool. It's none of your business what's going on in my house." I trailed behind him guessing he is just scouting the territory for information to use at the Cider Village for gossip.

It would be silly for me to threaten to call the police, because Evan looked like a rookie policeman. He walked with his chest forward, like a turkey. I did not acknowledge his new status and felt it irritated him. I bet he wanted to look like a powerful authority.

"Seen everything? Now leave," I said pointing to the door.

He walked around the kitchen, stopped by my bowl of tomatoes, and grabbed a handful without permission.

"You better get no more weird things here, you hear. I'll be keeping my eye on you. Giving our town a bad name, this place," he said and headed back to the entrance brushing against me again. I cringed with disgust, he smelled like an old potato sack and aftershave.

"It's none of your business, Evan, nobody's business. Stay away from me, no matter who you are now," I said with contempt and shut the door in his meaty face.

I have been through a lot in the past year, but Evan's appearance and remarks unnerved me. Especially his remark that LaRose Gris stood empty for the entire time I was away. That meant that Sebastian was gone as long as I was. The mystery deepened. I had some phone calls to make hoping our old rotary phone worked. I stirred my bubbling stew, turned the stove off, and thought of whom to call first.

It took a while to get the New Orleans operator, who told me they had no listing for Gaspar Dix in the area. Then I remembered the way Anna took care of everything and asked the operator to locate Anna Varley. My guess was correct. The operator dictated the number and disconnected. I dialed and held the receiver for a long time, no one picked up.

The evening approached and my dinner waited on the stove. My stew turned out delicious. To my delight, my old herbs and Winai's spices retained their robust flavors. I made a lot, the stew would last me for another day, before I would venture outside for groceries. I thought of the neglected grounds, the fallen leaves. The steps to the house and the courtyard covered with the carpet of yellow. It would take a day of work to rake it all into several big piles.

Next morning, I rolled up my sleeves, donned rubber boots and went to work. The leaves danced around me. The scratching sound of the rake suddenly reminded me of my grandmother's rasping voice, her monotonous harangue directed at Tilde, anyone in vicinity, or me. So much had changed since then. I grew up, and the twirling leaves were nothing but the postcards from the past.

Once I thought of this, the rake fell out of my gloved hands. I run to the garage, quickly wiped Hermie from dust and cobwebs, turned the coughing engine on, and braved the drive to the village post office.

The Cider village did not change, with the tourists gone for the season it appeared the same, only some locals milled around. They stared without hiding their disdain and no one welcomed me back. I left Hermie parked at the curb. The post office clerk did not even ask what I wanted. She just went to the back and returned with a box full of mail grumbling it was about time someone had picked it up. I zoomed back home and dumped the contents of the box on the dining room table. The small mountain of mail included my postcards to Sebastian.

It meant he never received them, all of them. I gathered the post cards and relived each every one: New Mexico, Miami, Istanbul, Rome and a few from New York. The last ones brought the tears, I missed being happy.

The magazines and other Sebastian's subscriptions I swept aside to use as a kindle the fireplace. Statements, receipts and other dull information, I would forward to our lawyers. Among all that junk I found a creased envelope with a Turkish stamp. My heart raced, right away I thought of Jason Fox tracking me down. I tore the letter open and looked at the signature. The waves of fear subsided. The letter was from Professor Silverman, mailed to me almost a year ago.

December 1, 1987.

Dear Veronica,

I am back, and you deserve my apology. I did not mean to leave you in a bind with that rascal Fox. It happened so suddenly, I threw the treasure dust and tumbled down a kaleidoscope of amazing experiences, which I am currently analyzing. I will send my journals to you once I am finished. Better yet, come down to see you with Gaspar. I will be writing to him next. My research appears to be only in the early stage. It's just plain luck I ended up back to our world. No worries about our wily Mr. Fox, nobody had seen him since the 'robbery'. I do not understand why he demanded diamonds. Those overrated pieces of coal do not possess the alchemic qualities. Kazim sends his regards. All the best to you and remember what I said before: the magic is in the reading.

Sincerely yours,

Ira

I smiled at Professor's letter, written with a fountain pen in dire need of a fill. He had introduced me to the exciting concepts of alchemy and dimensional travel. I will never look at the fairy tales as simple stories ever again. The knowledge he was all right lifted some burden off my heart. I made a mental note to send him a bottle of Absinthe LaRose.

The letter also gave me confidence and I dialed Gaspar's number again. It rang and at last I heard a familiar throaty voice which begun to squeal with delight when Anna recognized me and I told her about being back at LaRose Gris.

"Veronica, dearest! When did you, guys, get back? I was beginning to worry. No news from you for weeks. How are you? I miss you so much. There is so much to tell you," Anna could not stop talking. I heard Gaspar's excited voice in the background, shooting off questions.

"Anna, I miss you guys too. Wait, what did you mean by 'you guys'? I am all alone here. Do you by any chance know where Sebastian is? The house is empty, my garden neglected, the police came to snoop."

"Sebastian? I thought he was with you the entire time since you left. He took off like a madman, told us to close up the house."

"What? I was traveling alone the *entire time*," I said with a sinking heart.

"Veronica, darling, he called us from all those faraway places and told us not to worry. Last time was from New York, before it was Italy. He even called from some Russian ship once. Wait, here is Gaspar, he wants to talk to you."

I was not ready for it. My mind reeled from Anna's revelation. I could not concentrate on Gaspar's questions about Professor Silverman. He kept asking me about his laboratory and I replied with some vague answers. Gaspar also carried on as if Sebastian was in the thick of things in Istanbul with me. All I could think of was Sebastian, and how he followed me. My head begun to spin and I interrupted Gaspar, trying to hide anxiety in my voice.

"What was the first place you heard from Sebastian after I had left?"

"Let's see, I don't quite remember. Here is Anna. You should come down to New Orleans. I miss my best pupil."

I asked Anna the same question.

"I think it was Arizona. No, New Mexico, in a week or so after you left," she said after a short pause.

"Anna, I was alone the whole time. I am not joking. I thought Sebastian stayed back home to wait for me."

"I don't know, Veronica, all I'm saying now I missed you. He called us regularly to say you're alright. Maybe he just followed you around and you didn't even notice. I know you, always living in your own world."

"Maybe. Anna, can you come to stay with me?" I said trying to stifle a sudden sob.

"Honey! I would love to. We would raise hell in that snob village of yours, but I can't now. Gaspar's working on a new thesis and needs my constant assistance, not to mention the fact that he would forget to eat or to put his pants on if I wasn't here to remind him."

"What kind of thesis? And where would I look for Sebastian, did he leave you any information?"

"Didn't you hear him on the phone? Quantum physics theory of the dimensions. Don't worry about Sebastian, he can take of himself. We'll find him when he wants to be found."

My head hurt from all that. I excused myself promising to call soon, and even to come for a visit. I looked at the silent receiver and had a sudden urge to smack myself on the head with it for not calling Anna from my journey. She would have warned me about Sebastian, and I would be on the lookout. Perhaps I could even spot him. How would my adventures unfold then? I felt manipulated. The entire picture started to come together in my mind.

I thought about the desert in New Mexico, and the cop who rescued me. Joe Matys, aka Sebastian Van Stratten's brilliant piece of acting. Then the treachery of Captain Vovas, who said he never met Sebastian, but the name seemed familiar. All the while Sebastian sat behind me impersonating a crewmember.

I sketched a diagram to follow my reflections and by midnight, the whole puzzle came together. I blamed only my own stupidity for not recognizing someone helping me along the way. For keeping me safe and for warding off trouble I constantly got myself in. How was I unable to see Sebastian in the priest at the Santiago church where I met Charo Melia? I guessed the identity of a veiled 'woman', who appeared just in time to disable Jason Fox by thrashing him with a book. And, of course the pièce de résistance, his impersonation of a Scottish caretaker, who saved me from being seduced to death by Emmanuel's ghost. Mr. Hound from New York could be him for sure. What a brilliant an actor he was. If he were here now, I would confront him about his devious ways. Unfortunately, he was gone. He never even followed me to LaRose Gris. I wondered why.

The best way to keep the blues away is to work. I immersed myself in the garden. Every corner needed my attention. Every shrub, tree, or stone cried for my loving hands. I raked, cleaned, weeded, and trimmed with no rest. My muscles hurt so much, the pain eclipsed the ache in my heart. The drizzle and the relentless Atlantic wind never ceased. Bundled up, I toiled, trying to put my garden to sleep before the first snowfall. It would not be far off at the end of October. It was always a hard time for me, full of memories and darkness. With Sebastian gone, it doubled. My soul drowned in melancholy, as if my adventures never happened.

Standing on the top of the steps, I surveyed the results of my labor. Suddenly, and to my dismay I saw a police cruiser creeping down the driveway. Wondering what Evan would want from me again I steeled myself, and went to meet him head on. It was not Evan. Another officer approached, and we stared at each other for a second.

"May I help you?" I asked, wishing he would go away.

"I am Officer Brown, and I would like to ask you a few questions about the Officer Wood's visit here the other day."

"I never called him, he just showed up and nosed around my house without an invitation," I said not even trying to be polite.

The lanky pale cop stared at me as if I did something wrong.

"Yes, it was indicated in the station log that no one called for assistance, but he came here anyway. Do you mind telling me why?"

"I don't know why, Evan always hated me and my house. Called me weird and told me we are not welcome in the Cider village. Anything else? And why are you asking me, ask him."

"It may sound strange, but Evan Wood had died shortly after visiting you. I am conducting an investigation."

"Died? How? He seemed well enough to me. Are you accusing me of something?"

The news shocked me. I did hate Evan, but not to the point of wishing him dead. Although, he did cause me grief every time we met, year after year.

"The doctors think he had a severe allergic reaction or had been poisoned. Do you mind showing me where he went on his last visit here?"

"Sure, follow me," I said.

He came in and looked around the hallway with a great care, as if he was expecting something to pounce on him. We went through the rooms and into the kitchen.

"This is it. He did not go anywhere else, I threw him out," I said and guided the officer back to the entrance doors.

"Did you offer him any substances perhaps? Or some exotic food, I hear you just arrived from overseas," said Officer Brown measuring me up and down with his small prickly eyes.

"If New York City is considered overseas, then be it. I didn't give him anything. I had no food even for myself. Except for some vegetables I found in my garden."

"Alright, I will note that. For your own good, try not to leave town. In case there are further developments," said Officer Brown and headed back to his car.

His last remark angered me. So what if Evan Wood died, why blame me? They did not scare me, I did nothing wrong. Or did I?

Back in the kitchen, perched on my favorite spot on top of the counter, I thought back to the scene when Evan pestered me on my first day at home. The way he walked around like a pompous turkey, his sweaty paw in my bowl of tomatoes. I felt a cold current down my back and jumped off the counter to look for the bowl, there must be some cherry tomatoes left in it. Could they cause the allergic reaction?   I pushed the small tomatoes around the bowl, and noticed something else on the bottom. Red berries a little smaller than the tomatoes. It appeared familiar. I must have picked it along with the cherry tomatoes. The plants became very tangled in my garden, the vegetables, the healing herbs, and the deadly ones. The deadly ones. Then I knew exactly what I held in my hand: the fruit of a beautiful and poisonous Moonseed plant. I grew it to make herbal tinctures. In minute amounts, it helped stomach upsets, but sure would cause a bad reaction or worse, in undiluted form.

Back in the garden, I located the twisting vines. Tomato and Moonseed entwined and were easy to mistake for one another. I ran to the house, my first thought was to call Anna and ask her what to do. Then decided against it, I detested long explanations. My other trusted adviser was still on the bottom of the suitcase, rolled up.

I had not touched Maria's portrait since I left Italy. Now, I unraveled it carefully on the grand piano. Then I tried to meditate for answers and to use Maria's image as I would use a mandala. She did not fail me, and helped to reach into the depths of my soul.

Maria, what is happening? Did I cause death? What should I do?

She looked at me with her merry green eyes, a dimpled smile on her face. Perhaps she laughed at my worldly problems.

I heard a faint whisper in my head, like a gentle wind. *The garden did it. It wants you to stay. It protects you.*

I believed her, it was not the first time death appeared at LaRose Gris because of me. My grandfather wanted to send me away when I was born, and he died from the heart attack in the garden. Then grandmother wanted to send me away when I was eleven, and she died saving me from the icy water of the garden stream. Now Evan threatened me and died from the garden berries. No such things as coincidences, said Sebastian, Winai and Professor Silverman. Perhaps it was a good thing that Sebastian followed me.

Should he stayed, something bad would happen to him as well.

Later, I went for a stroll to clear my head. I whispered to the old garden professing my love, and questioning it at the same time. I sank to my knees by the stream and thought of my fate of living alone in the empty mansion with no friends or loved ones. Surrounded only by the magical force of my garden, unable to chase away the dark thoughts, I gave in to the melancholy.

19. FRIEND FOR LIFE

Acrushing feeling of loss weighed on me as I tried to keep myself occupied. Days flowed by like a half-frozen stream in the garden, slow and murky. I rarely left the estate, dreading to go to the Cider village for the supplies, especially after the incident when some shrill girl accused me of killing Evan. I just backed away from the store to avoid the confrontation and left in a dignified silence. The animosity in the Cider Village became so palatable that I chose to drive miles away to the town up north or to Boston for necessities, winds tossing my Hermie around like a toy, on slippery roads.

For weeks, I waited to hear from Sebastian. Telephone conversations with Anna brought only pangs of regret. I knew she was trying to cheer me up, but it was not working. Hoping to recapture a happier frame of mind, I had begun to sort out my travel journals. Every time I plunged into a new revision the sense of duplicity pulled me down, *why did he leave after following me over the continents?*

I had found some magic, but had no grasp of it. Just like holding on to the handful of air. My magical artifacts sat on the table. I spent hours trying to understand the reasons behind them. I never forgot to play the silent golden harp for my beloved Moishele to let him know I missed him and the sisters very much. Maria kept me company with her easy smile. Bagus's ashes waited to bring sustenance for my favorite plants, come springtime. The true enigma lay in the rain flute. I decided to follow my old rule and to wait until the answer and an opportunity presents itself. The chest full of gold sat under the table. I had no idea what to do with all those gold bars. One could not simply walk in the store and buy groceries with them. I had to use the petty cash Sebastian kept in a tin on top of the bookshelf. This stash melted away with every trip.

I found some consolation in ancient books Professor Silverman gave me. Written in Latin, old English, French, and Hebrew they provided a way to keep my mind from wandering into the dim realms of self-analysis and falling off the cliff of dejection.

On Thanksgiving Day, I called Tilde and Dr. Schuele. The guilt of neglecting them for such a long time had twisted my soul in knots. To my relief they were happy, asked me to come to Baden for a visit, and sent their warmest regards to my guardian. They did not know he was missing and I did not tell them. Then I had a bright idea and called Mr. Shachmundes. His name came with the folio from Kitty and Feige's estate. I dialed, and then realized the offices were closed for the holidays. I fumbled for the right words to leave on the machine, embarrassed by my own mumbling.

On the following day, the doorbell chimed. I mistook the sound for ringing in my ears being so used to silence. I opened the protesting icy door, expecting to find someone unpleasant as always. A pair of warm brown eyes and a friendly face behind a wispy red beard met me.

"Miss LaRose? Boruch Shachmundes. You left a message yesterday. I drove from New York City. May I come in?" Said the man and pushed a glossy business card in my hand.

"Aren't you closed for the holidays?" I said feeling awkward in a nightgown and a robe way past noon.

He came in lugging a large briefcase. I glanced outside before shutting the door. His salt splattered car sat on a mound of drifting snow. With an apology, I excused myself to go change while he waited in the parlor.

When I came down dressed properly, I found him in front of Maria's portrait.

"Beautiful painting, I thought it was a photograph at first.

Interesting style, looks like you. Antique, right?"

"I'm not that antique," I joked without offering any explanations, but flattered by his comment, "thanks for coming down on such a short notice, it was not that important."

"You are important, Miss LaRose. Explicit instructions from the Bronstein sisters. We are at your service at any time, regardless."

The farsightedness of the sisters impressed me again, and their genuine care for me. I felt uncomfortable about bringing up a topic of gold bars. The lawyer sensed my shyness and asked first.

"Is it about the gold bullion you called? I have everything here. What will it be, one or two units?"

He opened the briefcase. Bundles of cash neatly filled its ample interior. I continued to stare, not sure what to say. Mr. Shachmudes sighed and took out a document from a folio on the table. It outlined the weight and the cost of one gold bar. The amount was staggering.

"Are you sure it's this much? The bars are so small."

"Yes, this much for the purest gold we had ever witnessed. I am sure, fifth generation goldsmith, and the first lawyer in my family," he said and patted his chest.

"There are also houses," I said unable to overcome my shock. Gold bars were like souvenirs to me, but money had a completely different meaning. I could stop being frugal first time in my life.

"No worries, all taken care of. The upkeep, maintenance, insurance, etcetera. How are your aunts anyway, enjoying their new home in Hawaii?"

"Oh yes, Hawaii is great," I said, smiling at the white lie.

I offered him a cup of tea and apologized for not having much else. Mr. Shachmundes complemented LaRose Gris and kept the conversation light. At his departure he inquired if I had any wishes.

"Can you locate a missing person?"

"Someone you know?" Boruch Shachmundes raised his red bristly eyebrow.

"Yes, my guardian seems to be missing. We traveled together in Europe, got separated and I arrived home first. But he did not come back and nobody knows where he is. I am worried."

"Alright. Send me the information about his last location, his description, passport number, list of friends and relatives, etc. And I'll see what we can do. I'm sure we can locate your uncle. He's not a needle and the world is not a haystack."

"Not uncle, guardian. And he can become a needle in a haystack if he wants to, believe me. I can give you the number of our Boston lawyers, they might have some information."

Mr. Shachmundes took the number and warned me I would need to sign some legal documents before they contact the Boston lawyers. I agreed with everything he said, willing to find Sebastian at any cost.

Despite the warning not to leave town, the police never bothered me after Evan's unfortunate death. The story of his untimely demise made the front page of the local paper. I did not have other feelings except relief. The world would not suffer with one less bully in it. Evan was the third person in my life who died. When I found out about grandma's death, the fear and guilt tormented me for months, until the redemption came with Sebastian's teachings. Bagus's death taught me compassion, but Evan's brought only relief. I knew it was shameful, but deep inside I also knew that Evan's bullying of me would one day turn into violence. Now the course of fate was altered, thanks to my garden.

I was all alone for too long. In time, I began to feel it, despite my love for the solitude. Left only with Maria's portrait and myself to talk to made me yearn for a companionship. The snowfall was so heavy at times that I could not see beyond a few feet past my window and the lights went out all the time. One time I had no power for a few days and was quite startled when the mansion came alive with lights in the middle of the night. Reading by the candlelight and sleeping in front of the fireplace to keep warm was the only alternative on those cold days and nights. I loved it. My ancient books seemed even more magical in the amber glow of the candle. Sitting on the rug by the cheerful fire, surrounded by dictionaries and translation manuals I immersed myself in the world of wizards and philosophers.

Professor Silverman was right when he said that magic was in the reading. My most favorite tome was a grimoire of old alchemist and wizard Erasmus who lived in medieval France, *Vox Erasmus, Voice of Erasmus*. He lived sometime around the eleventh century. His writings were in Old French and Latin. The grimoire was difficult to translate and even more difficult to comprehend. Erasmus wrote about the concepts of transformation of the physical into different forms. His experiences with the astral projections read more like Jules Verne's adventure novels. They were full of wondrous encounters and creatures. This seven-inch thick book found a permanent place on the library rug. It had browned at the edges, printed with tiny letters with narrow page margins that crawled with illegible notes left by readers over the centuries. An illuminated letter crowned each new chapter. I could spend hours laying on the floor studying the intricate graphic artwork depicting fantastic flora and fauna. These pictographs unlocked a flood of happy childhood memories of studying at Boston library vault with Anna and Gaspar Dix.

This book became even more amazing when a thin vial of shimmering blue dust tumbled out when I was leafing through. The vial lay hidden in its thick spine. Right away, I recognized Ira's magic dust. His reminders 'magic was in the reading' took a complete new meaning in an instant. I chuckled, because it was so much like him not to place all the eggs in the same basket. By slipping his precious magic dust in the book, he made sure of a "back up" in case something happened to his laboratory. I hid the vial inside my black lacquered keepsake box with the intention to question Professor at the first opportunity.

A strange chapter called *A Friend For Life* intrigued and captured my imagination, making me forget everything. *The Voice of Erasmus* spoke to me over the centuries. It described a process of animating a dead body and transforming it into a faithful friend.

At first, I had an academic question: what kind of body did he imply, animal or human? Then I wondered why not try it myself and put an end to my loneliness. Create someone who would never leave me, someone I could trust. Maria watched me with approval from above the mantel. The steps were described in a logical fashion with some faded notations from others, scribbled on the pages. So it must have been done before. Without much hesitation, I found a composition book and begun to write down an action plan, based on Erasmus's instructions.

Ignoring the wind howling in the chimneys of the cold fireplaces in the rooms upstairs, my empty stomach and cold feet, my imagination raced ahead of my thoughts. First, I had to brew a potion with the ingredients listed in the book. The herbs were easy because I had most of them. Also I needed to find some sulfur, mercury salts, magnesium and other alchemic elements for blending. The potion had to be brewed with pure water for three days and three nights over the fire. Once completed, I would be ready for the step two, to find a newly interred body. I decided it had to be human. In my mind, Erasmus would not suggest getting a dead deer or a cat. The notations never suggested an option. The book always referred to it as 'a body'.

This part of the plan proved to be more difficult. I was not sure if they held burials in the winter. The logistics of stealing the body could be beyond my physical ability. This is why I decided it had to be someone young, not too heavy to lift. And the idea of reanimating an old body repulsed me. I needed someone young for sure. The third and final step was to place the body in the potion to keep it warm and see what happens after a few days. The ideal result would be a reanimation. My friend would be complete and I would never be lonely again.

With a renewed energy, I gathered the herbs, made a trip to Boston one bright winter morning to purchase the ingredients from a science store. I also picked up a large cauldron from the camping supplies, and dropped by the library to find better translation books. I rushed home with a new friend on my mind, thinking of a name, of all the books and music we would share.

The snow from my garden filled the cauldron to make pure water. I ground up herbs with a pestle and mortar and added them to the simmering liquid. Next, I diluted minerals and dripped the solution slowly into the cauldron from a beaker. The liquid bubbled brown at first. It smelled of pine needles. After I added the minerals, it turned bright red, hissed, and erupted in a pungent heavy scent reminiscent of Gaspar's cigars. Erasmus also instructed to chant verses as I blended the ingredients. Standing in the kitchen over the cauldron stirring the hot red liquid with a long wooden spoon I chanted, reading from a notebook in my other hand.

From dust of stars
From frost of Earth
From heat of embers
Come angel who remembers

The potion simmered, I had no sense of hunger, or fatigue. Only excitement and anticipation surged through my veins.

The time came to find a young body. Another trip to the Boston library and I was able to find information in the newspaper's obituary notices. My luck held as I located a notice for the funeral of a young student in a town just a few hours away.

On the morning of the funeral, I drove to the small town's cemetery to scout the location. The gaping grave breathed with a fresh scent of turned earth left by the diggers. I spotted a lone caretaker securing the snowy burial site, now marred by dirt and footprints. His dog followed nosing around. I got out of the car and approached them.

He must have mistaken me for a mourner because of my usual black attire. I cringed inside, the last caretaker I spoke to was Sebastian dressed as an old Scott. This one was not Sebastian, just an old drunk in a furry hat and a soiled jacket torn at the shoulder.

"A bit early for the occasion, Miss," the mist came out of his mouth as he spoke, a powerful smell of alcohol came with it, "the party won't be arriving till three."

"I know, just paying my respects beforehand," I said, sniffled and wiped my face with a sleeve to appear sincere.

"Want to get it out alone, keep appearances later. I know, I know. Seen it all in my day," said the caretaker and sighed, "I'm over at that hut by the gates, in case some of your friends want to leave a little token of appreciation, if you know what I mean."

I pretended to be grateful for his understanding and asked if he preferred beer, or whiskey. Once he confirmed his drink of choice, I was off to get ready for my clandestine evening adventure.

I returned to the cemetery at night after the funeral. The full moon illuminated my way through the gates and beyond. The snow shimmered blue under the sparse silvery clouds. I wished, the moon would hide. On this night, I did not need beauty, only secrecy.

I left Hermie by the gravesite and walked back to the caretaker's hut. The dog greeted me like an old friend and I gave him a fresh bone from the butchers along with a good rub behind the ears. We were instant friends, and he did not mind at all when I placed the whiskey bottle by the door, knocked, and took off. From behind a gravestone, I watched the caretaker come out, ask the dog who was out there, and bend down to pick up the bottle. When his silhouette disappeared behind the door, I knew it was the last I have seen of him.

Now I was faced with a backbreaking labor of digging. My feverish mindset did not allow me to feel the pain of the straining muscles or a backache. All I felt was the sweat streaming down my back and the silk shirt clinging to my skin with its icy fingers. I tried very hard not to dwell on the nightmare of unearthing the grave, and tried to convince myself it was just another 'flower bed' to dig up. I jumped on top of the casket, freed some space around it, and climbed down. The mud smeared casket was locked, thanks for the notation in the Erasmus's book, I had a dagger ready inside my boot. A few flicks of the sharp blade and the lock clicked open.

I lifted the wooden lid with reverence and gazed at my pale faced friend. The satin upholstery of the casket shimmered in the moonlight, her serene mask of death and silence of the cemetery made it poignant. Pain and fatigue forgotten, I tied a rope around the body and climbed out of the pit, pulled with all my might and after the third try she came up. I dragged the body to Hermie and strapped it in the back seat. Then back to work again, I had to cover up the grave.

This time I worked faster, as if Mercury the god of speed aided me. With the fresh mound of earth back in place and the wreaths around the grave, we were finally ready to leave.

Then I noticed a small plaque pinned on top of the wooden cross, *E. D. Lee*. Her name was E. D. Lee. I would call her Eddie. A wave of euphoria washed over me as I rushed to the car to whisk my Eddie away from her brief resting place.

Back at the mansion, I half-carried half-dragged Eddie to the guest bathroom on the main floor and arranged her body in a claw foot tub. One thing I did not foresee was the weight of the cauldron with the potion. The night's exhaustive labors left me moving on nervous energy alone. I ladled the liquid into a smaller soup pot and carried it to the bathtub where I poured it over Eddie trying not to spill. After few trips back and forth, a trail of red droplets followed me from the kitchen to the bathroom. Eddie had dark long hair and slim body, shorter than I. I wondered about the color of her eyes, and hoped to find out soon enough when she came alive.

The tub finally filled with the potion and additional melted snow. As per instructions, I placed a low gas burner under the tub to keep the liquid warm and collapsed by the bathroom wall exhausted and happy about my completed task.

I could not believe I did it. I created pure magic. All of a sudden, I felt like running and dancing with joy, I felt like telling someone about it. To make them be proud of me. But there was no one, my exuberance cooled down. I went upstairs, took a shower, made a makeshift bed by Eddie's tub, and sank into the deep sleep just as my head touched the pillow.

Back in the kitchen, stirring the potion in a cauldron with a wooden spoon in one hand and Erasmus's instructions copied into my notebook in another. The tenth day of brewing more potion, and the tenth day of pouring it over Eddie. Still, nothing happened. Except the red liquid turned blackish in the bathtub, and Eddie sank below it. Her skin acquired a strange slimy sheen and turned green.

I examined her sunken eyes. They gave no indication of opening up. I wondered why the magic refused to work. I had followed every instruction to the dot, and went over the steps countless of times, measured every ingredient, made no substitutions. Still, I could not find an answer in the book or in the handwritten notations. Who could help me? Maybe I had to call Anna. She might know what to do. I reached for the phone and suddenly noticed my stained pale hand with dirty broken fingernails, then caught my reflection in the mirror on the dining room wall. A hag with limp hair, stained dress and hollow face stared back at me. I dropped the receiver and touched my tangled hair, then noticed the smell for the first time. The stink of rotting flesh and nauseating sulfur permeated my clothing and the mansion. *Is this what I had become? Is this what magic is doing to me?*

In the bathroom Eddie disappeared completely under the dark steaming liquid. I pulled her body up and heard the rib cage collapse with a sharp snap. Black slime oozed from her slack mouth, nose, and ears. I dropped the rotting body back in the tub and threw up in the sink, not able to bear the revolting sweetish stink. Then found my way back to the chaotic kitchen to consult the book again. Clutching my throbbing head, I began to read the instructions for the hundredth time all the way down to the last sentence. I took this part for granted, until now.

Keep warming the body of your friend with nourishing potion and heat, wait, and see what happens.

It finally dawned on me, that the great Erasmus himself did not even know what to expect, what should happen, or what kind of transformation would take place.

I felt lost and betrayed. For the first time in my life, I understood magic was not glorious and mysterious, but cruel and final. It scared me. Steeling myself, I went back to the bathroom and fished Eddie out by hair. The clump of it detached from the scalp with a quiet tearing sound and remained in my hand. I examined the body closer. The dark veins twisted under the translucent green skin like black seaweed. Most of the flesh rotted away, and the protruding bones seemed brittle as if the potion dissolved the body into some absurd stinky jelly. On the thin neck, I noticed tiny green spots and picked at them with my fingernail. They resembled scabs, but after examination with a magnifying glass, they appeared more like scales. Tiny green amphibian scales. Was Eddie turning into a lizard, a beautiful magical green lizard friend? Now I understood the Erasmus's philosophy of transformation even further. One lifeform becomes another. *Solve et coagula*, something must be broken down before it can be reborn in a new form.

I left Eddie in the tub, added the remaining potion, and went to bed. Like Scarlet O'Hara, I decided to think about it in the morning. I was too exhausted.

The clock chimed noon when I woke up from my dreamless slumber, still in my stained dress, and feeling grimy. After a long hot shower, first in many days, and in a clean change of clothing I came down to make a cup of tea before braving a new visit to Eddie's bathroom.

I noticed a slight change in the stink emanating from behind the door, not of a rotting flesh anymore, but of something primal, something familiar, but could not remember what. Once the bathroom ceiling lights were on, they exposed the entire grotesque scene.

Usually I used the wall sconces and candles to create a calming atmosphere. Now I wanted to see the result of my experiment in its stark reality. The bright fluorescent lights exposed every crack on the green walls, cobwebs in the corners, rusted claw feet of the tub, black and red stains splattered on the white floor tiles. An enamel tub filled to the brim with dark liquid resembled an ugly oil spill. A long thin object like a bone stuck out from the spot where Eddie's head used to rest.

A part of me was happy Sebastian did not have to witness this fiasco. With a deep breath of resignation, I went down to my knees, and with sleeves rolled up felt for the remains of the body under the warm liquid. The gas burner worked under the tub and the heat helped to dissolve most of what remained of Eddie, leaving just a few of her thin bones on the bottom. Finally, I decided to examine the dreaded long object.

To my amazement, I recognized a young tree, a sapling yew by the looks of it. A thin trunk with tiny budding branches covered in evergreen 'scales'. I made a wrong assumption. Eddie did not turn into a lizard. She became a tree instead.

I breathed a sigh of relief, there was nothing more known and loved by me than plants and trees. The new scent in the bathroom was that of a rich soil. I knew exactly what to do next.

I ground up the bones to use as a fertilizer for Eddie's new planting pot, which I found in the workshop at the back of the carriage house. Large Chinese porcelain planter with dragon designs was a perfect place for the tree to spend the winter until we found a permanent planting spot in my garden. I used the rest of the potion to water the soil and the little tree flourished. The branches grew and became greener. It showed its joy as a new life form. The bone meal gave the tree strength to grow in the meager winter sunlight peeking through the windows. I cleaned up the mess created over the past weeks, organized my house, and concentrated my attention on Eddie.

We sat together for hours listening to my favorite opera records. I read Keats and Tennyson, Hans Christian Andresen and Stevenson aloud to my friend. I talked about my adventures and read from the journals. In return, I felt the little tree's soul reaching up to mine, the love and understanding coming in waves from its green scented branches. On a whim, I added some of Bagus's ashes to the soil wishing that Eddie would always be healthy and thriving.

We were never apart, except for the brief periods when I had to get supplies on those scarce pale days when it did not snow or the wind was not as biting. Somewhere in the background I heard the telephone ringing, but chose to ignore it. The Christmas holidays came and went. I enjoyed my peaceful life and did not want to burst the mysterious magical bubble yet.

I never forgot to play the silent harp, or meditate as Maria watched from her place above the mantle with a new respect in her eyes. Her smile appeared as encouraging as ever. She was urging me to move forward and to conquer new magical frontiers.

I carried Eddie all over the house with me. It kept me company in the kitchen when I cooked, in the bathroom while I took afternoon baths, in the library when I studied, and even at night beside my bed.

One morning, noticed a crop of red dots on my arm just below the shoulder as I brushed my hair by grandmother's ornate mirror. I looked closer, and to my dismay realized they were piercing marks right on the arm closest to Eddie, whom I kept by my bed at night. Wondering how the gentle soft branches could pierce me, I placed the planter on the opposite side of the bed to experiment. And in the morning similar marks appeared on the other arm.

"Are you piercing my arm at night?" I asked examining the little tree. Upon a closer examination, I saw Eddie's branches became lush and the trunk had thickened. It happened exactly a week after I added Bagus's ashes to the soil.

"Are you turning into a little vampire?" I asked the tree again, wondering if a new, even more exciting transformation was taking place.

This must not continue. If Eddie kept taking my blood, I would become anemic and die. No one would take care of my dear friend, my garden, or wait for Sebastian. At the same time, it seemed, Eddie needed the blood to thrive. I had to think of an alternative food source for it.

"Eddie, you have to be careful, take just a little, or I will die," I said stroking the green branches. The tree seemed to understand, I sensed its regret. A tiny whisper of sorrow blew in my ear. It was a symphony to me, a sound of pure magic. If I could understand Eddie's emotions, it meant that perhaps I could communicate with other trees. I thanked Eddie and promised, that soon we would find other sources of blood.

Learning became a priority. I wanted to increase the knowledge of magic. My feet just barely touched the threshold I tried to cross for my whole life. I could not wait to glimpse an exciting world beyond. Only if I knew where on Earth Sebastian was hiding from me, so I could show him the kind of magus I had become.

The wind changed direction at the end of March. It ushered in an early spring, scattering the winter clouds and inviting shy rays of the sun. Anna and Gaspar called nonstop with demands to explain my silence over so many weeks. Professor Silverman's letters kept piling up on my desk full of news about his transdimensional research. Each letter bordered on a wild sci-fi novel and a lecture on alchemy. Took me hours to read them, and even longer to understand, if ever. I wished to see him in person and Gaspar Dix too, what a discussion we might have.

A thick envelope with papers arrived in the mail. I found a request to the lawyers in Boston to release old documents, information about two cottages on the property as summer rentals, but nothing about Sebastian. I read and signed everything Mr. Shachmundes sent.

He came midweek to collect it in person. In his tailored coat, he sipped tea in the parlor and told me about his firm's attempts to locate Sebastian Van Stratten. My guardian proved to be a needle in the haystack to his dismay and to my grim amusement. Eddie sat between us with branches by the lawyer's resting hand. We sipped calming chamomile tea and Eddie sipped the relaxed lawyer's blood. I pushed the planter aside after a while, despite Mr. Shachmudes's protest. He loved the plant and declared it fitting for the best botanical garden in the world. I thought, it was a ripe time to get Eddie a more stable source of nourishment and not a sporadic one from my scarce visitors.

One rainy afternoon kept me busy with taking stock of the herb seeds and preparing the orders for garden supplies. The telephone rang like a shrill banshee in the mellow silence of the day. At first, I did not understand what the female voice on the other end said.

"What quarantine? Excuse me, can you repeat it again," I said, quite confused.

"Your animal just completed one month quarantine. You may come to the facility and pick it up. Or it's going back," repeated the impatient voice, but I did not understand.

"You must have a wrong number," I said ready to put down the receiver.

"Are you Veronica LaRose?"

"Yes, who are you?"

"I am calling from The Port Authority. We have been trying to reach you for a few weeks now, at the request of Captain Joyo. Do you want your cat or not?"

My heart lurched and stopped. *Smeela!*

In a heartbeat, I found myself speeding down the road to Boston to pick up Smeela from the port quarantine.

At last, I located a low depressing building in the shipyards and flew down a dingy bleach scented corridor. Two green eyes stared at me from the crate, I tore open the little door and she leapt into my arms purring, licking my face rubbing her nose against my cheek and I against hers. She smelled of dust and milk. I held her close, buried my face in her neck, and stood still for a long happy moment.

The woman coughed to get my attention and gave me a pen to sign the release form. Overcome with emotion and unable to speak I waved to her and with Smeela clutched to my chest went home.

"Oh, Smeela, I have so much to tell you. I missed you so much," I stroked her back and trying to steer Hermie from wavering on the road. She appeared well fed, her coat shiny and the eyes green and attentive as ever. "Where are the kittens? Well, I guess they are not kittens anymore, so much time had passed."

At LaRose Gris, I opened the front door and let her in. I had read somewhere that by letting a cat in first ensures a good luck. Smeela walked inside, looked around the grand foyer with the round table in the middle, then entered the drawing room and begun her exploration by leaping from one piece of the furniture to another, onto the table, then the grand piano. I followed, watching her graceful form, hoping she would love her new home. It would be her first. She lived her life on the parched streets of Santiago, in a cave with a child vampire, and then on a merchant ship. My Smeela sure had a few interesting lives.

She did not miss a room in the entire mansion. In Sebastian's bedroom, she sat on the bed and gave me a questioning glance.

"Yes, he is gone. But he will be back," I said.

Smeela nodded and continued to my bedroom, she made it hers at once. In the parlor, she came to meet Eddie by the French doors. She took her time to examine the little tree, then jumped in the planter and curled up at the roots.

"Yes, Smeela. Eddie has a part of our little Bagus in it, and also needs blood to thrive."

I made dinner, boiled eggs with some cheese, carrots and bread. Now with someone else dependent on me I had to get supplies more often. We retired together in my big bed. Smeela curled on the pillow beside me.

For a while, I lay awake listening to the wind in the chimney and Smeela's purring. The sound awoke an elusive feeling in my heart. After a while, at the brink of asleep I understood it was contentment.

The garden thawed, the frost showed up less often in the mornings and the time came to find a permanent planting place for Eddie. I hauled the planter in a wheelbarrow and the three of us made rounds in the garden, the driveway, and even beyond the garden wall to find a perfect spot. It had to have plenty of sunshine, a bit of a shade, good drainage and an access to someone who could give Eddie blood from time to time. The three of us made quite a procession with Smeela leading the way, then me carting Eddie.

Everywhere we stopped seemed to be wrong. Smeela or Eddie rejected the places and urged me to keep on looking. I did not want to end up frustrated and sick. We needed to find a planting spot fast, because Eddie wanted my blood more often. It was understandable, because the robust plant growth always happened in the spring. One sunny morning I worked on my flowerbeds, digging and separating the daylily shoots. Smeela sat a few steps away guarding me like a centurion. Eddie basked in the gentle sunny patch nearby. All of a sudden, Smeela was up and skipped towards the end of the driveway. I followed her and came upon a young couple. They stood by the wrought iron gates trying to take pictures of LaRose Gris in the distance.

"May I help you?" I asked incredulous at their trespassing. They were unfamiliar, dressed as city folks, not the locals.

"Do you mind if we take some pictures of the mansion? We do not wish to trespass, but it looks so beautiful in the sun," said the young man with the camera. His companion gave me a winning smile, although I sensed a great deal of discomfort behind it. I understood her dismay. Anyone would be nervous to meet someone with long wild hair, dressed in a vintage black dress, burlap gardening apron with sharp tools sticking out, and a ferocious looking large cat in tow.

"Sure. You are not locals, right?"

"We're here just for the weekend, rented one of those cottages down the lane," said the young man, the girl continued to smile trying to entice Smeela to come closer. The cat kept ignoring her.

"Oh, those are my cottages. They are part of the estate. It stretches all the way to the beach. You can walk there if you like," I said, trying to sound hospitable and to diffuse the impact made by my appearance. They both smiled and thanked me. I noticed the speed of their departure, as if they were happy to put some distance between us.

I turned around to go back and continue with the digging, but Smeela did not budge. She sat on the spot by the gates, staring at me, trying to convey something. I guessed her intention.

In the garden, I picked up Eddie and carted the wheelbarrow to the sitting Smeela.

"How would you like to be planted here?" I asked Eddie, pointing at a clearing between the stone gate posts and the lane. Smeela jumped up the wheelbarrow and rubbed against the tree. Eddie seemed to be happy with its new home. I had spread a thick layer of fragrant red mulch around the roots and dragged over an old garden bench for the passersby. The sunny location visible from the steps of mansion, and occasional unsuspecting visitor as a source of nourishment were an ideal solution for Eddies planting spot.

True enough, in a few days I spotted some matron sitting on the bench with two children. Renters again, having a picnic right beside Eddie. The kids were nibbling on cookies, Eddie gently nibbled on their soft necks as the matron snoozed in the warm breeze. It was the most idyllic sight.

I basked in my newfound contentment, celebrated every moment of spring and Smeela. Until an unexpected misery knocked on my heart's door yet again.

20. MISERY

"Anna, you know I miss you, but it's impossible to get away now," I interrupted Anna's endless tirade.

"We will have so much fun, Gaspar is drowned in research, and it would be good for him if you come. He would take time off."

"Anna, why don't you come and visit me? Help with the garden. I have so much to tell you. And I know you miss Boston."

As always Anna promised to find time, which I knew would not happen. Eventually, I would have to go to New Orleans with Smeela.

We were talking often now, especially after my lonesome winter when I did not answer her calls for weeks while being immersed in my magical experiment. Her calls raised my spirits and I looked forward to them. In addition, I had the weekly reports from Mr. Shachmundes about locating Sebastian, but nothing new yet. Deep in my heart, I knew he would turn up when the time comes.

My life became a comfortable routine of gardening chores, taking care of Smeela and watching Eddie flourish. Studying books of magic continued to be my main reason for staying up nights, and at last, I had renewed my correspondence with Professor Ira Silverman. He urged me to hide the vial with magic dust and not touch it until I became more enlightened under his guidance. The prospect of going back to Istanbul sounded exciting, and no sweet talker like Jason Fox would intimidate me ever again. Although Ira continued to warn me that Mr. Fox would crawl out of hiding one day, and even might show up at my doorstep. He might try. Sneaks and cowards did not scare me anymore. To show appreciation for Professor's concern, I had sent him a bottle of Absinthe LaRose as I had promised.

I still avoided the Cider Village, not wishing for the unpleasant confrontations. The locals would never come to terms with me, living in a grand mansion on more land, than their entire village, and being different from them. I did not care. Walking on the beach with Smeela, working in the garden, growing herbs, and learning became my life. If I needed anything, Boston was just an hour away. The contentment I found on that first night when Smeela reappeared still lingered in my heart.

One day my quiet life shattered to pieces when I first heard his voice. A record arrived in the mail, another offering of Anna's. She kept sending esoteric books, fashion magazines, and even makeup in order to pull me out of the Gothic mindset, as she referred to my self-imposed solitude. I slipped the record out of the sleeve and holding it by the edges placed it on the turntable.

The music sounded so unlike my favorite Chopin or Vivaldi, its darkness grabbed my attention like a thorn. Then he began to sing. At first, I just stopped and listened. This was not an attractive voice, but mesmerizing, tortured, it caused heartache with its hoarseness. I sat on the floor with my back to the sofa and froze, mesmerized by the music. I heard the entire record without moving a limb. He sang of love and betrayal, futility and disillusionment. The music continued in a heavy beat, with moans of electric guitars and infusion of organ music.

I knew the name on the cover. Last I heard of him was with the kids at the bus terminal in Boston at the beginning of my quest two years ago. Maximus Black. Long before that, Sebastian took me to his debut performance when I was twelve. I remembered how his music hurt my ears and gave me a headache then.

I examined the album art, and traced his features with my fingers. Long pale face over the upturned collar, hypnotic eyes outlined in black, smeared red mouth, slender and leather clad, on huge platforms. Riff raff demons flanked him from behind - his band members. Loving the unusual aesthetic, I reached over and put the record on again.

The next day, I drove to Boston and bought his entire collection of music. At night, with books of magic moved aside, I listened to Max Black. Each of his albums told a story, one more ravishing than another. He reinvented his style in each album, creating different concepts of demons or deities, shrouded in the enigma of a rock star. The music and poetry fired up my imagination, it was a new form of magic for me.

To my surprise, I recognized a kindred spirit, a seeker of magic, hidden behind the veil of time. Just before my eighteenth birthday, I came to regard him as my soul mate and spilled my feelings to Anna. She laughed and called me a 'crazy fan'. Assuring me that my infatuation would pass, I would move on to a different rock star, or movie star or even a writer. I tried to move on, and could not. Nobody even came close to his talent and magnetism. Posters of Max Black adorned my bedroom, along with the rest of the mansion and even the kitchen where I still experimented with healing herbs. Maria understood. She knew what love was. Mr. Shachmundes did not. He called Maximus Black 'a horrible noise' after he spent almost half an hour ringing and banging on the front door, while I ironed my herbarium collection to the loud music.

The lawyer's expression appeared grave when he tried to make a small talk about the weather, while I cleared the plants and the albums away. At last, I sat in front of him. He looked at me for a few moments. I had never seen him grasping for words.

"You have news for me about Sebastian," I said, sensing the reason of his visit.

"In a way. You are turning eighteen in a few weeks."

"Yes, what does it have to do with finding Sebastian? Or, do you want to throw a party? The guest list will be very short. You, me, and the cat."

"Veronica, the law firm which was taking care of your grandmother's affairs transferred the file pertaining to LaRose family and estate. A few facts came up. I think you need to know them, against the previous lawyer's advice. You are a fierce spirit, you can handle it," said Mr. Shachmundes.

He placed a binder on the table and pushed it towards me with his fingertips.

"Take your time. I will wait in the drawing room while you familiarize yourself with the contents."

When he left, I slowly opened it, and begun to read 'The last Will and Testament of Cecilia LaRose', last wishes of my grandmother. At first it was just a list of assets that would pass to me on my sixteenth birthday in the event of her death, bequests to different charities and Tilde, my grandfather's covenants about the land, and the *La Rose Gris,* my home. I was familiar with most of it from Sebastian's words. Until I came to the last paragraphs and read my name again. The chill shot through my body like an electric current as I read.

In an event of my untimely demise regardless of the cause, and if such event finds my granddaughter Veronica LaRose under the age of sixteen, I designate as her legal guardian one Sebastian Van Stratten of Holland and Thailand.

Sebastian Van Stratten is to remain my granddaughter's guardian until she turns sixteen. And after, it is at his sole discretion to continue to act as her father as he truly is according to the attached letter written by my late daughter Lydia Gordon nee LaRose.

So like my stern wise grandma. In a few short minutes, my entire world turned upside down. At last, it made sense to me. It was so simple. I did not even notice it before my very eyes during all those years. The way we shared similar tall and slender physique, even our hands looked similar with narrow palms and long fingers, and the high sharp cheekbones. *He knew, but never said anything at all! How could he, why was he silent all these years? Was he a liar or a coward?*

I grabbed Smeela and tore out of the house past the bewildered lawyer, my face wet with tears. I ran through my garden and took the path to the beach, then continued at the water's edge. Smeela sat quiet in my arms, she understood. When I ran out of breath, I stopped and realized the futility of running away from myself. I collapsed on the wet sand and wept. All my built up frustration of the past few months spilled out. I wept for the loss of my New York friends, the lonely winter, horrors of my experiments with Eddie and above all an absence of Sebastian, my father. I returned shivering and blurry eyed, grateful that Mr. Shachmundes still waited for me.

"Do you want to talk about?" he asked, guiding me to the sofa.

"You know, Sebastian Van Stratten saved me from a miserable childhood. He made my life full and wonderful. He was there for me always, and even supported my wild ideas. Like when I demanded to leave on a quest around the world. He followed and protected me. I did not even suspect, until my friend Anna told me. Now, you bring me those documents, and I am lost. He is my father, and he left without a trace when I headed home. Why?"

"Maybe he thinks you need time by yourself, to grow up on your own terms?"

"You mean he can show up at any time?"

"I don't know. Do you still want us to search for him? Looks to me, he just doesn't want to be found, you were right from the start."

I stood up and paced the room, thinking about my approaching birthday. Maybe the lawyer was right. Perhaps Sebastian decided to let me experience life without his safety net. I was doing well on my own. Still, the news made me feel sad and betrayed.

Mr. Shachmundes asked me to think about his advice and left giving my hand a final squeeze. To console myself I put Max Black back on and cranked up the volume.

I wait for eternity
Brief as a spark
To see you in the end

Curled up in the corner of the sofa I immersed myself in music. When the record ended, I felt as if he was in the same room, consoling me and making things better.

The tears came again, for the loss of Sebastian and for not being able to attain Max. At last, I realised that I lost my nerve and became a sniveling little girl. As an antidote, I called Anna and choking on tears told her about the will. Her reply was unexpected and encouraging.

"Sit tight," she said, "I am flying over."

I looked around at the domestic disarray, remembering the empty fridge and the garden paths in need of sweeping.

"Smeela, the dear guest is coming. Everything is going to be alright," I said, picked up the cat and we were off to shop for groceries and get ready to welcome Anna back to LaRose Gris.

The sound of an approaching taxi brought me to the front door in an instant. I threw it open and saw Anna in her usual black attire, hair pulled back in a sleek ponytail, bright red mouth, but instead of her guitar-like figure, I saw a round belly sticking out between the folds of her raincoat.

"A baby," I enthused as we hugged and kissed, "why on earth didn't you tell me? I would come down instead."

"Right, Veronica, after months of begging you to come, you change your mind. Typical Gemini, but you can't help it. Now, who is this little beauty, your familiar?" Anna scooped Smeela in her arms.

The cat became limp like a rag doll, her usual feistiness gone. She seemed to love Anna, and I loved them both so much.

"Same old LaRose Gris, nothing has changed since our going away party two years ago. I guess no ghosts yet."

"Only the phantoms in my soul," I said hauling Anna's luggage to the room next to mine.

"Sounds like we're in for a ton of fun," said Anna with her usual throaty chuckle and kissed Smeela between the ears.

In the days that followed, we got blessed with good weather by New England standards. Anna lounged in the garden with Smeela purring beside her round belly, and listened to my stories as I planted vegetables, weed herbs, and trained Wisteria vines over the gazebo.

"Stop thinking about Sebastian, he will show up one day. Just remember that he loves you, it was clear from the first day we met.

And, the fact that he hid his true identity, I guess he had good reasons. Maybe it goes deeper than you think. Just do not create a magic spell to bring him back."

Anna's simple wisdom worked after I poured my feelings out. I still could not believe how Sebastian followed me like, a ghostly babysitter, as I traipsed around the world oblivious to everything.

"Magic? No way, it could backfire and bring back something other than Sebastian, like a Frankenstein monster. An experience with Eddie had taught me enough. You are so right, Anna."

I told Anna about my attempts to create a new life and the unexpected ending. Eddie grew taller than the garden wall, thriving on the blood of my unsuspecting cottage tenants and accidental visitors. Anna did not hesitate to give it a hug, but shied away when the branches moved in her direction.

"I would feed you, my love, but the little sucker here needs it more," she said, patting her round middle.

"Well, at least it provides security from uninvited curiosity seekers, and from the dwellers of Cider Village," I chuckled at my own black humor.

"Right, beware of a recluse, who grows herbs for magic potions, talks to her cat and has a vampire tree at the gates to her mansion. Boo," teased Anna.

Anna asked to see the dreaded will. A subject of my mother's letter came up next. The letter sat unopened on the bookshelf since reading of the will. The turmoil it created was enough. I avoided that corner of the library like a snake pit.

"You read it to me, I haven't touched it yet. They are too intimidating, the secrets from the past. I was fine without knowing, the knowledge brought only misery."

Anna took the letter and began reading it in silence, and then she laughed.

"It's so short and to the point, reminds me of you so much. Listen to this, and you will know what I mean."

Anna began to read aloud with a more serious expression on her pale face.

"Mother, I left Robert. I know you are disappointed. But he was more of your choice than mine. I hate being an army wife. I am coming back home, and I am with child. Not Robert's. Someone I met in Thailand, someone I love. His name is Sebastian and he will be coming for me once he completes his spiritual retreat. Just try to be happy for me once in your life. See you and dad soon. Lydia."

Anna put the letter down and laughed again, but a touch of sadness misted her eyes.

"My mother was married before. Tilde told me when I was little."

"Veronica, don't you see it? You are a love child. This is very special. Never mind the old secrets."

"But looks like he never loved my mother, why didn't he come here when I was born?"

"I think your grandmother had something to do with it. But she did a right thing at the end. And you can't jump to conclusions and spread the blame without speaking to him first."

She was right, better to put it to rest for now. I remembered the way voices from the past intrigued me. I was not a little girl anymore and putting my life in order became more important. As I said, old secrets only made me feel miserable. Opposite of magic, they drained me of life, not filled with it.

It was fun, having Anna with me, although we did not do any of the things I planned. She was tired and had amusing cravings all the time, especially when I told stories about Moishele's appetite and the sweet-tooth diet of my dear Kitty and Feige. She sent me out to get a load full of pies, cream cakes, and chocolate dipped strawberries. We celebrated my eighteenth birthday, drinking lemonade and munching on sweets. A few telephone calls from Mr. Shachmundes, Gaspar and even one from Professor Silverman full of background static noise completed my day. I hoped for one more call, and it never came.

"So, no more magic. What about love? You need to meet

someone. You can't be alone forever, sitting here and waiting for Sebastian to show up."

"I don't need anyone, and I am in love. With Max Black."

Her refusal to believe in my feelings for the rock star of my dreams irritated me.

"You are infatuated like any girl your age, I was too when I was nineteen. Remember?"

"He is my soul mate," I said stubbornly, ready to defend my choice.

"Just do yourself a favor, sign up for a class at the college, and meet someone real."

I just could not see myself going to school only to get a boyfriend. I was not Anna. I did not possess an ease of feelings. I had to go through suffering to earn joy.

Anna's visit breezed by like a fresh summer morning. I drove her to the airport in Hermes, in style. Cars moved away at our approach, the huge black Rolls Royce proved to be an intimidating force. I slipped in the parking spot right by the airline gate. With her usual lightness of spirit, she kissed me goodbye as if she was leaving only for a few hours and disappeared in the arms of the revolving doors, luggage carted away by a dutiful attendant.

With her departure, I felt the sunshine she brought into my life was dissipating like a sand castle. Brooding on the way back home, driving slower than anyone else, I contemplated my life. When I came up the dark elm lined driveway of LaRose Gris, my new plan seemed simple. Concentrate on my garden, make herbal extracts, and take care of Eddie and Smeela. Maybe even sign up for a history of occult class at the U.

I had a concrete proof that magic existed, but somehow was reluctant to continue with the experiments. I wished for Sebastian's wise guidance. I wanted Max to appear on my doorstep and to kiss me.

I continued to search for the magazine articles about him. With interest, I traced his tour dates across Europe and Asia, reading about the antics of his fans and unbelievable escapades of his band. First time in my life jealousy burned in my veins when I read about his relationships with women. About the paramours who left him, how he suffered, and created beautiful ballads as a result. I wanted to be his muse. Leafing through my ancient texts, I found a few interesting but excruciating love spells. Some scared me with the gory dark imagery of bloodletting and sacrifice. Even the illustrations did not mesmerize me as before. A small taste of dark magic from resurrecting Eddie spoiled my appetite for a long time. I had to find a different way to meet Max and make him fall in love with me. My heart burned with love, and the thoughts of him pursued me through every waking moment, until I fell asleep and drowned in dreams of us being together. I knew it was an obsession, and made sure not to mention it to Anna again. Until one morning, while on the phone, she told me I seemed sad.

"I want him so much," The reply flew off my lips before I could stop.

"Are you pining after your ageing rock star still? Then why don't you just go and meet him? He must hold court at some punk club in LA, I'm sure. You certainly look the part, my little black-clad witchy-pooh. It will help you to get it out of your system, when you see the real him, not the imagined him."

"Oh Anna, twenty seven is not old, and maybe I will, and he is for real."

I took Anna's off-hand remark as a good advice and began my preparations to fly to California to meet Max Black and make him fall in love with me without any use of magic.

First, I spent hours meditating with Maria and planning the perfect outfit in which I would meander into the nightclub and entice Max with my looks, then with my witty conversation. Those romantic dreams drew tears as I imagined him inviting me to dance in the smoky shadowy club, the music melding our hearts together, his arms holding me tight as we moved across the floor.

Then I remembered that Smeela would be alone for more than a day. Not wishing to abandon her, I had less than forty-eight hours to fly to California, find Max at the nightclub, or at his home, make him fall in love with me and take him back to the LaRose Gris where we could live happily ever after. Absinthe LaRose, I kept sipping straight from the bottle for the past few days, ignited my dreams even more.

At last, I took a window seat on the plane to LA in my best black taffeta dress, feeling lightheaded, nervous, and very excited. When the magic vapors of my grandfather's absinthe began to evaporate, excitement turned into a doubt and anxiety. My jitters increased after the plane touched down and the pilot welcomed everyone to LA with 90 degrees outside. I had lace-up boots on, and a long raincoat suitable for the cool rainy New England afternoon of the late month of June.

At the airport, I found my way down the escalator following the directional signs easy enough to read for a child, and ended up on the taxi platform. My biggest problem was I had no destination address. Instead, I had something that would get me to any destination, a thick wad of a hundred dollar bills.

A taxi stopped in front of me and the ferrety driver got out to collect the luggage I did not have. I jumped in the front seat of the cab and in Spanish told him that I wanted to go to the residence of Maximus Black.

The driver gave me an astonished look and said, "I need address, Señorita. How do I know where this person lives? I'm sure it's not in the phone book."

"This is how," I said, and pulled out a wad of money.

As Sebastian always said, nothing moves things forward better than the green piece of paper, and a smile. The driver took one look at my wad and reached for his radio.

"Enrique? I need take customer to Max Black, the crazy music guy, you know where it is?"

Enrique must have told him to call someone else by the name of Paolo who in turn gave him a name of another driver. My wad created quite a chain reaction just like magic. People became so docile and compliant at the sight of money.

At last, Enrique confirmed he had a possible address and I gave the wad to the driver. To my surprise, he peeled off only five bills and gave the rest back to me.

I witnessed nothing as fake than Los Angeles in my entire life. Everything seemed bright and loud, total opposite to my emerald green world of rolling hills and the blue Atlantic. We passed neighborhood after neighborhood where everything appeared the same from the artificial green lawns to the garish faux mansions they surrounded. The seedy side of town looked much worse with the metal bars over the windows and people with vacant faces sitting on hot tenements. The disparity appalled me.

"Where are we heading?" I asked after almost an hour drive.

"The hills," said Enrique, and gave me a meaningful look.

I guessed it was the "good" neighborhood. Air conditioning in the car masked the heat emanating from the road, but I could see the mirage rain puddles hovering over the pavement. I remembered another heat-drenched city where I met Charo Melia and Smeela for the first time. Santiago had an old soul hidden behind the cracked walls of its buildings, Los Angeles had none left. How could Max live here and create his music? It bothered me that his hometown was so faceless and fake.

At last, the taxi came to a halt at the narrow lane close to the top of some hill.

"Can't go up, too narrow, you have to walk, Señorita. It supposed to be a last house on the right."

"Thank you very much. Are you sure it's a right place?"

"I dunno, the other guy said it's OK. You know what, go check, and let me know. I wait here in case you want to go back," said the driver in broken English as he switched off the engine, lowered the windows, and pulled out a cigarillo.

"How will I know it's a right place or not?"

"You knock on the door and ask," said the driver and knocked on his head, his way of saying I sounded dumb.

Perhaps I did appear slow. Something heavy settled in my stomach and began to grow towards my throat. The nervousness made me stumble as I left the taxi.

I made my way up the narrow unused lane. A coarse grass grew in dusty tufts between the tire tracks. The cool air was more breathable up in the hills and the trees gave a nice shade. However, the dead air had no scent, no verdant fresh plants here. I walked up to the iron fence in front of a three level house with a flat roof stuck to the side of the hill at the end of the uneven driveway.

Vertigo engulfed me and I clutched the rusted bars resting my forehead on them to gain balance. The place emanated neglect. Somehow, I knew it was the right one. A broken electric guitar without a neck and dangling strings hang on the front door. The trees around this abode suffered from dryness or some disease and the layer of brown crinkled leaves littered the driveway, front steps and the roof. I was surprised to spot a dirty porcelain sink on a patchy lawn in a pile of cement chips. Like someone tore it from the wall and threw it out the window. A happy person could not live in a place like this. I had to go to him, give him my love, and make him happy. With resolve, I started up the path, leaves crunching underneath my feet. At the front door I raised my hand to knock, and froze in fear and anticipation. Then felt something wet flowing down my chin and wiped it with a back of my hand. It smelled of metal and was sticky, at first I thought something was dripping from the roof and then I saw red. It was blood.

Terrified, I ran back to the fence and sat on the ground at the edge of the lane. A trickle down my chin became a small river of blood. My nose was bleeding. I was exasperated, to come all this way only to be stopped by a mere nosebleed. First one since I was a child.

For a few minutes, I tried to calm down and plugged my nose with a tissue, contemplating the tragic comedy of this situation. Then my intuition kicked in, and I recognized it as a warning. Something was trying to stop me from meeting Max today. It gave me a red flag, as red as my blood. I cleaned up in haste, grateful the blood did not show on my black clothing, and made my way back to the waiting taxi.

From the distance, I indicated it was not a right place, and then collapsed in the back seat telling him to go back to the airport. The driver complied and took be back to the terminal, probably expecting more bills from my wad. In silence, I stuck a few more bills in his tanned hand and took off.

I had no memory of the flight back, just a vague recollection of looking for Hermie inside ten-storey parking lot and zooming on an empty road to LaRose Gris. Smeela met me at the front doors. I grabbed her and collapsed on my bed, still fully clothed, into a dreamless chasm of sleep.

The morning brought more misery when realization hit me I was at the dead end. Work and long walks always helped to concentrate and come up with the alternatives. The exhaustion from the fiasco in LA prevented all possibility of moving. Maria gave me a scornful look from above the fireplace. I had to admit, there was no other alternative for me to meet Max, but to use magic by dipping into Erasmus's well of knowledge one more time. I needed strength before any attempt to conduct a spell. Food and sleep would remedy that, and in a few days I would be ready to begin.

The ritual seemed to be the least intimidating of its kind in the grimoir. Most of the love spells involved some type of self-mutilation or a gruesome sacrifice. That did not attract me. This particular spell seemed interesting to perform. It even had a name, a *Misery Remover*. As I understood, the misery created by separation of lovers transformed into a tool to unite them. I had enough separation misery. I needed to unite us without bloodletting.

The preparation for the ritual began by mowing the patch of meadow at the far corner of my garden closest to the beach. Then a few trips from the shore with a wheelbarrow full of seaweed, which I dried in the sun for three days. While the seaweed dried, a visit to the hardware store for supplies came next. The required herbs steeped for the reduction to drink after one day of fasting before the spell casting. My thoughts stayed with Max, I had no idea of the outcome of my efforts, but my intuition told me to go on, regardless the doubts.

Smeela followed my every step, helping me with preparations, always murmuring and weaving around my legs with a soft touch of her coat. She was doing what any familiar should do - observe, and keep secrets.

By using a copper wire, I laid a pattern of a circled pentacle on the ground. Large enough for me to lie in the middle of five points enclosed in a symbol of unity. Then, I wrapped the seaweed around the wire to ignite and release elements into the air. When the physical requirements of the ritual were completed, I had to wait until the new moon to mark a new beginning.

The new moon phase appeared right at the end of June. Time flew by like two seconds. I made all phone calls prior to the important day so no one would bother me, and begun my fast. I placed a crystal goblet full of an herbal reduction made of cloves, yarrow, bleeding heart root, and ginseng root in the middle of the pentacle. Wrapped in a white cape facing the new moon I chanted sincerely, feeling every word, hoping it would reach Max somehow.

Go forth my misery
Pierce his heart to pieces
Only I can heal
With love
Go forth my misery
Unite my beloved and me
Make my pain his pain.

I drunk the molasses-thick reduction and chanted again, repeating the incantation until my throat felt scratchy and insides burned from the bitter brew.

The sea wind gained its strength. I watched the black clouds move above me in a starless sky. I was alone in the world. I was the world, and the universe welcomed me. Sinking to my knees, I ignited the seaweed and lay in the middle of the pentacle, urging my misery to grab Max and think of nothing else but me. The smoke from the burning pentacle grew thicker. It stung my eyes to tears as I passed out.

21. BEHIND THE CURTAIN OF RAIN

Smeela's rough tongue brushed over my eyelids. She made sure I was awake and jumped off my chest. I sat up and scanned the surroundings.

The garden stood shrouded in a familiar early morning fog, and traces of blackened pentacle twisted on the ground around me. A chill settled in my bones from spending the entire night on the damp earth. Like an unsteady drunk, I picked up the now empty goblet, and made my way to the house. Faithful Smeela beside me with her tail up and ears perked, acting like a true familiar.

Somewhat rejuvenated by a hot bath, I had a cup of valerian tea and fell asleep again. The hope my ritual would bring results burned in my heart. I saw no other way. The spell had to work. All I had to do was sleep, gather up my strength, and wait until the next step.

I dreamed of Max again. Wild hair obscured his pale face leaving only passionate eyes. In my dream state I realized that I had never seen him smile. His printed images bore a plethora of expressions - sadness, passion, anger, incredulity, and even mystery. No publications ever showed a hint of mirth, and I wondered why.

For the next few days, I scoured the news of him and his band. The magazines irritated me. They pursued not his talent and creativity, but his wild behavior and clothing. I ignored the vile gossip and concentrated on finding essential information. I found it.

To my amazement the spell casting worked, this could not be just a simple coincidence. Instead of New York City, his concert moved to Boston, and he would be arriving in ten days. I allowed myself a minute of the excitement by laughing aloud and doing a little dance with Smeela in my arms.

Soon after, I started making plans and preparations on how to get to Max before the show. It would be difficult; him being always surrounded by bodyguards, roadies, groupies and the band. Media always described him as eccentric. Odd interesting objects were his weakness, and I had to place my bet on that. With just over a week remaining, I dropped everything. Weeding could wait, and fretting about Sebastian would not bring him back.

I decided to start with my looks, because I looked horrible. In the mirror, I saw a reflection of tangled long hair and a starved frame, just like in my 'shadow girl' time years ago. I wanted so much to be pretty.

After examining myself even closer, I decided my eyebrows were too thick. I was happy to notice the freckles that used to sprinkle my nose when I was younger had faded, making it the only part I liked about my appearance.

The thought, that after all my magical efforts, Max would take one look at me and decide I was ugly, was excruciating. My long nose remained unfixable, and so was my paleness because I hated the sun.
I really wanted to have Anna's hourglass figure, her shiny straight hair and bright eyes. I wanted to be like a heroine of the old movies, beautiful and mysterious.

After grilling Anna for the beauty tips during our continuous calls, she gave up and told me to go seek professional help. Someone to do my hair, trim my brows and teach me how to apply make-up. These beauty procedures sounded scarier than Erasmus's rituals, because they promised much more pain and discomfort.

"Beauty requires sacrifice. You are beautiful, Veronica, but you need help to become gorgeous. Go see a professional at the salon, and get a new sexy outfit. He is a Rock Star. Remember, he's used to girls who look their best. Entice with your beauty, conquer with your intellect," said Anna, and I believed her.

Only I did not go to the salon. I went to the library and checked out books on fashion and beauty. I leafed through them and imagined myself in various dress styles, then experimented with hairdos. At last, I concluded that my taste was hopelessly old fashioned, or vintage, as some called it. It explained my love for grandmother's outfits, and refusal to wear anything else aside the long romantic dresses, including those I took from Feige's and Kitty's wardrobe. Except for the times, when I was travelling, the comfort came first over style.

I plucked my eyebrows until they bled, learned to outline my eyes with black kohl without making them look like bat wings. Then I altered my grandmother's old Dior suit by letting out the hem and sleeves for a better fit. In Boston, I purchased a few pairs of gloves in red leather and black lace. As an afterthought, I picked up a hat with an ironic brim. At last, I had put everything on and examined myself in the full-length mirror.

I liked the tall elegant girl in the mirror with long chestnut curls cascading down her shoulders. My eyes seemed greener outlined in black. A hat added a touch of mystique. My figure became like an hourglass in a tailored black suit. The red gloves added a hint of passion. My favorite Victorian lace up boots completed the ensemble. This look should seduce Max Black.

"Veronica, you are beautiful," I told my reflection, and gave it an encouraging wink. Two days remained until our meeting.

Satisfied with my new appearance, I concentrated on the interior of my house and moved the furniture around to create a more elegant decor. The grand piano went to the middle of the parlor right in front of the French doors. Now, I could see my garden and a promise of the ocean beyond, when sitting at the keyboard. Thick pillar candles grouped in the corners created romantic shadows. I placed crystal balls and figurines on the various tables for the candlelight to reflect and twinkle on their smooth surfaces. It was like creating a stage setting for a play. Only it was my life, and a new beginning.

The doorbell interrupted my mellow mood. *Why am I disturbed at my finest moment?* I thought irritated by the unexpected visitor. Through the window, I saw the village mail carrier scurrying down the stairs back to his hunched delivery van.

After investigating, I retrieved an envelope tucked under the door. I always went to the village to pick up my mail. Strangely, he delivered it to the mansion. Then I saw a mark 'guaranteed delivery' on the wrinkled envelope. It came from afar. Several stamps glued to the top appeared Asian. I tore it open and took out a letter written on thin paper in large round print.

Dear Child,

It has been many months since we spoke, yet I think of you daily and send you white light for luck, health, and prosperity.

You should forgive me for not writing right away about our beloved Sebastian. And I hope he will forgive me for giving his secret away. When he arrived here last year, he needed council. I told him to go seek it in Wat Tan in the mountains of Koh. He was in a confused spirit.

Once at the Wat, the Venerable Lama placed him in a solitude cave for thirty days meditation. The cave opened only once in two days for food and amenities. My child, you may find it hard to read next, but my light will guide you.

A few months ago, an attending monk opened the cave and found no one. Sebastian had disappeared. The mystery is how he disappeared, as the door could not open from inside, and the boulders block the cave on the other side. Venerable Lama ordered an investigation. The entire monastery stayed in deep meditation for days and they concluded that evil spirits took Sebastian to the Asura world. I am begging you, my Shining Flower, in case he ever finds his way back to you, and I am sure he will, please let your humble friend know he is alright.

With love and affection, Winai.

The clash of the worlds blinded me for a moment. After all these months of waiting and searching, I found out that Sebastian went to Thailand to seek enlightenment. I felt cheated and angry with him for keeping me in the dark. I was angry with Sebastian for not trusting me, angry with Winai for sending me back to the uncertainty and misery.

I stormed back to the parlor, touching the candles and crystal figurines to ground myself, and stopped in front of Maria's portrait.

"What should I do? Drop everything and go search for Sebastian in Thailand, or continue with my efforts to meet Max?" I asked her.

Walk in the garden, said Maria's voice in my head.

I did not expect that, it sounded asinine. I shrugged and went to the library to check out Sebastian's books on Buddhism and meditation. I pulled one off the shelf. The scent of my childhood sprang up from the pages. I told myself not to cry and leafed through, trying to block the memories of Sebastian.

At last, I found the chapter about Asura, the third state of existence. The one believed to be populated by spirits who did not quite make it to heaven, but were not bad enough to become animals, or end up in hell. Those spirits were jealous of people in Nirvana. Sometimes, they would snatch souls from Nirvana and keep them imprisoned in their shadowy world until the gods granted them allowance to heaven.

It all sounded too farfetched, but who was I to argue? I had a vampire yew tree and a talking portrait in my house. Nevertheless, whatever mysterious circumstances Sebastian got himself into, I still had to make my dream to meet Max Black come true. With this resolution, I stuck the book back on the shelf. Then I followed Maria's advice and went for a walk in the garden.

Fresh air cleared my mind, the verdant scent of the meadow and sea breeze sent me back into my usual thoughtful melancholy. I sat by the stream where Sebastian used to meditate in the early hours, and wished for a sign everything would be all right. *Please, please send me an omen,* I begged with eyes closed in my own meditation. After a while, I got up ready to call Anna to share Winai's letter.

This is when I noticed it, a tiny spark in the reeds just inches away from the stream's edge. I reached and grabbed at the spot. On my palm, surrounded by grey sand, lay the most perfect thing I had ever seen, a crystal bead the size of my knuckle with a blue sparkle within.

The thunder of my heart deafened me, and I forgot to breathe. For eternity, I stared at the bead. I lost it in a tragic accident as a little girl. I used to imagine it spoke to me with my mother's voice. Later, for me, the bead became the messenger of change. Finding it years ago triggered a chain of events that brought me where I was now.

Did it come to me again as a conclusion of the full circle, or a messenger of a new beginning? It appeared untouched by time and the elements, magical and clear, as if I just took it out of my pocket. I looked through it and saw the way the dragonfly would see. I also saw my grandmother with her serious eyes and a thin smile, Tilde wiping her eyes with a corner of her apron, Doctor Schuele stooping down and patting my head, Winai teaching me to cook, and Sebastian, holding my hand on the grand staircase of the Boston Library.

Suddenly I felt happy, reassured, and optimistic. All my plans had to come through, eventually. I had to trust in myself, and in magic.

I hang the bead on a leather string. As an afterthought, I tied it around Smeela's neck. Both were so precious to me.

This was the day. I could not believe it finally came. I had everything prepared. In a few hours, my plan would commence. Dressed in my traveling outfit of black sweater, jeans, and Doc Martens, the familiar weight of a backpack over my shoulder, I stood on the steps of my mansion ready to leave for Boston.

The gentle New England sun painted my garden golden green. White poplar fluff floated over from somewhere. I caught one, made a wish, and blew it toward the sky. In a minute, I was speeding off to Boston in my black little Mini Cooper, Hermie.

The crowds were already gathering at the concert site. Hundreds of youth dressed in flamboyant and eclectic outfits with painted faces reminiscent of Maximus Black musical eras. Some strutted in huge platform shoes, many with impossible hair, and all of them had lots of attitude shining on their excited faces.

The human wave carried me past the ticket stands, reeking

concessions, small groups of teens shrouded in a pungent weed smoke. I asked the security man for the location of the band trailer, he eyed me and laughed, suggesting I take a hike.

I found the band's trailer anyway. My intuition and love guided me. A very big security guard with long hair and shaved temples was pushing a girl away from the trailer doors. She whined and demanded to see the band, calling herself 'entertainment'. The guard towered, she swayed barely able to stand in her high-heeled silver sandals.

"Excuse me, please stop pushing her. I will take her away when I leave," I tapped the guard's shoulder.

"Then do it now, this chick's like a demented annoying fly, the band got enough o'them inside," growled the guard and turned. Delight and surprise appeared on his face.

"Veronica! What th'hell you doin' here?"

He grabbed me and was about to toss me in the air, but I hugged him instead. The sullen kid from the Boston bus terminal certainly had grown, really grown.

"Adam, I did not expect you here either. How have you been, how is everyone? Una and Marc? You have gotten so much bigger since I saw you at the bus station."

"Thanks Veronica, been workin' out, gettin' my act together, gettin' a job, helpin' my old man, ya know responsible like. Work at the arena now, security," he said and flexed his arm showing off the bulging muscle. I poked it, and nodded with appreciation. This was another proof of magic that the burly guard would be Adam, a runaway boy who put me on the bus to New Mexico two years ago. The girl in the silver sandals sat on the ground, watching us with dazed eyes. He ignored her and gave me his old sweet smile.

"Marc's back at some preppy school, Una's in the Amazon rain forest savin' trees, and I'm still into good ol' Rock'nRoll. So have you found magic? Ya looking mighty good, grown up like."

"Adam, I need your help," I said squeezing his rock-hard bicep.

"Shoot."

"I have a present for Max Black. Can you please take it to him for me?"

Adam whistled, "Don't tell me you became a groupie, no way!"

"No, it's something entirely different, believe me. Here, I was going to bribe a guard anyway, but to you I will give it with pleasure."

I took out a wad of money from my backpack. Adam eyed the wad and sighed.

"Good convincing tool you got there, fire away, what d'ya want me to pass on to him. He's impossible, a pissy bastard. But I'll try, not for money tho, cos we're friends."

"Just this," I said and pulled out my present.

"A message in a bottle?"

"Yes. Make sure he gets it soon."

"Okay, after the concert."

"Fine, thank you Adam, it was very nice seeing you again," I said and stuck the wad in his shirt pocket.

Then I grabbed the dazed girl by the hand and led her away to the paramedic station, smug with the knowledge there would be no concert.

The show was about to begin, last of the crowd was swallowed by the stadium, its doors about to close. I went back to Hermie, stood alone in the parking lot among the sea of cars, took out my flute and blew three times.

The thunder rumbled in the darkened sky, an angry wind roused a dust cloud and ripped the flag off the pole at the entrance. The lightning strikes appeared, accompanied by a deafening cannonade of the storm. The lights went out with the power. The arena stood immersed in darkness, a wail of sirens approached as I drove home in the rain to prepare for the arrival of my beloved.

Hermie zoomed past the stone gates of the mansion. For a moment, I glimpsed Eddie waving branches to the orchestra of the thunder and lightning like a mad green conductor. The elms along the driveway stood like giant sentinels in mantles of mist. I glanced in the rear view mirror and saw nothing but the curtain of rain behind me. LaRose Gris was cut off from the world. Everything was going exactly according to the plan, so far.

The rooms looked perfect, filled with an amber glow of the candlelight. The shadows and twinkling in the crystal figurines calmed my nerves. I stood in front of the mirror ready and counting minutes before his arrival. As planned, I donned my suit, hat and gloves, boots, sprayed a generous amount of Chanel perfume.

Something still bothered me, it did not feel right. Of course, why would I meet him wearing a hat and gloves at home? Silly me. I tore the hat off dislodging my coiffure. The red gloves went in the hat. I rushed upstairs to change from the formal stiff suit.

In haste, I threw on a black velvet dress with narrow sleeves. My hands shook as I buttoned the row of tiny buttons that ran from the neck down to the waist. The boots went back in the closet. I dove under the bed to get my harem slippers from Istanbul. While I searched for them, my hair flew all over the place. Veronica's tangled mane came back. I blew the locks off my flushed face, and tried to smooth the rest.

Downstairs, the candle wax dripped on the floor, building upon the pillars. The glow became jittery from the wicks growing too long. I got the scissors and begun to trim them, then I heard the doorbell.

The time stopped at that moment, and so did my heart. Smeela jumped off the piano and rubbed against my knees encouraging me. Dismayed, scissors still in hand I went to the door.

No car engine, and no gritty sound of wheels on the wet gravel warned me of his arrival. He was leaning on the doorframe with one hand, and clutching the empty absinthe bottle I left for him earlier in another. His leather coat glistened with rain, soaked hair stuck to his face, which had a fresh bloody gash on the pale cheek. He did not look very happy to see me.

"Is your mom home?" he did not sound happy either.

The question and the irritation in his voice unnerved me. It was not the query I expected, this was not how I dreamed of our first meeting. I pushed the door open all the way and proffered my hand.

"Veronica LaRose," I said, still clutching the scissors.

He backed away. Quickly withholding my hand and hiding the scissors behind my back, I felt a hot wave of embarrassment. Thankful for the semi-darkness I blurted out,

"Oh, I am the mom. I mean there is no mom, she's dead. I mean forget I said that. Why don't you come in," my voice grew weaker with every word.

Our first meeting was awful. The first impression I made turned to be terrible, and I could not rewind time.

Max eyed me and slowly walked in after taking a quick glance over his shoulder. I looked in the same direction and saw the rain had intensified and the driveway had flooded beyond the gates. The water from his coat dripped on the marble floor, creating puddles. He glanced around taking in the grand staircase and a foyer adorned with beveled mirrors and paintings, the Doric columns, that flanked the entrance to the parlor.

"Nice house you got here. Any ghosts?"

"Welcome to the LaRose Gris. Everybody asks me this question, but the house is not that old. It was built in the late 30's by my grandfather Etienne LaRose, so no ghosts," now I sounded like a docent. I wanted to kick myself. It was not going the direction I planned.

"Etienne LaRose of LaRose absinthe? Was it you who left this bottle with a note?"

I just nodded, choosing silence over the dumb comments, which seemed to come out of my mouth on their own.

Smeela appeared from the shadows and meandered over. He stooped to touch her head, but she jumped into his arms and let out a loud excited meow. I petted her, my fingertips brushing over his sleeve. The scent of leather, tobacco, and aftershave overwhelmed me. This was how I imagined he would smell. I walked over to the mantle and at last deposited the scissors where they belonged.

"I will rekindle the fire, please make yourself at home. Help yourself to some wine."

He walked over to the French doors leading out to the garden and paused. While tending to the fireplace I watched him from the corner of my eye. He wiped his boots on the mat by the doors and took off his coat, hung it on the top of the door leading to the library, just as Sebastian used to do. Without his bulky long coat, he appeared even taller in a black turtleneck sweater, jeans with a wide silver studded belt around his narrow hips.

To my surprise, he did not pour wine in the goblet, but chugged from the bottle like a thirsty desert wanderer. Then without a word, he sunk on the sofa and yawned. His breathing became quieter and slower as I stood listening, stupidly holding a fire poker in my hands. I tiptoed closer, and stopped above at his sprawled form. He appeared to be fast asleep on his back, one arm behind his head and the other hanging over the edge of the sofa still clutching the wine bottle. I carefully took the bottle away, my eyes glued to his still face. All my plans dashed, no romantic rendezvous was happening here.

I extinguished the candles, dropped some towels on the wet floor, and went upstairs to my bedroom with Smeela in my arms. Exhausted and disappointed I stayed in bed until dawn. Did I expect him to smother me with kisses and declare his undying love right away? No. Truthfully, I did not know what to expect. My plans did not go beyond luring him to LaRose Gris. I felt stupid and helpless, and thought about calling Anna, but what would she say?

Sad and disappointed, I crept to my lonely beach wrapped in a shawl and a raincoat, hoping for a glimpse of a sunrise behind swollen lead colored clouds and trying to think about my next move while Max Black slept in my parlor.

Veronica LaRose

22. JUNGLE CATS

I found him asleep on the sofa in the parlor. He must have woken from cold at night, and put on his coat. Another bottle of wine stood half-empty on the sideboard. I covered him with a quilt and tiptoed out.

I was happy he did not leave and puzzled over what to do next. I had to call Anna. In the kitchen, I covered my head with a shawl and whispered into the receiver.

"Stop hissing, speak up," said Anna.

"Why are you so irritable?"

"If you looked like you swallowed a watermelon which swallowed a bus which swallowed a whale, you would be irritable too."

"He's here! In the parlor, sleeping. I don't know what to do."

Anna squealed, "It worked? Your plan worked. Never mind if he's there, it worked. Now, make a love potion and feed it to him."

"I thought about it, but it does not feel right. I want him to fall in love with me without forcing it."

"You're right, but I can't help you. Just be yourself, tell him stories, make him food, men like food."

I heard footsteps, and whispered, "Got to go now, bye," into the phone and hang up.

A chilly draft came from of the wide-open French doors. Max stood on the balustrade smoking. I came over to stand by him. Tall as I was, my head only reached his shoulder. He was staring in the direction of the ocean, but not as if he admired the scenery, his gaze was turned inward. The rain's silver threads still shimmered among the elms and my birch tree showed yellow highlights in its green mane.

I expected him to say something, but he remained silent. I decided to follow Anna's suggestion.

"Would you like some breakfast?"

He ignored me, went back to the sofa, dove under the quilt, and fell asleep again. I stood over him like a nurse, worried. Was he sick or just tired?

While he slept, I cooked. Out came the old vegetarian cookbooks. The stew bubbled on the stove, carrot muffins sat on the counter beside the pot of earl grey tea and a percolator full of coffee. In the late afternoon, I went to check up on him again.

He was trying to start a fire in the fireplace.

He saw me and gestured to the wall above:

"Beautiful portrait. It's not you, though the resemblance is remarkable."

"This is Maria, she was married to the man I fell in love with," I said regretting it at once.

"And she did not mind? I'd love to hear that story."

"No she did not, they were both dead."

"You were in love with a dead man?"

"No. I mean yes. Can we talk about it later?"

It was frustrating to talk to him, he went right to the core of me, I wanted to tell him everything, but it came out awkward and stupid.

He laughed, pushed a long hair strand away from his face with a careless gesture, and dropped into a wing armchair in front of the fire place, stretching his long legs. I chuckled too, feeling relieved and happy he was here, in the same room, where I first heard his voice singing of love and suffering from the vinyl record, not too many months ago.

Smeela jumped on his lap and purred. He caressed her and touched a sparkle at her throat.

"Diamonds on the cat, how original. It becomes her, she's beautiful. Right kitty? What's her name?"

"Smeela. We met in Cuba, two years ago. Got separated for a while, and now she is back for good. And the crystal bead is magical, it brings change."

"Everything here is kind of magical. Tell me more, I'm so tired, the concert was cancelled. Did you have anything to do with it?"

I came closer and touched his cheek, "The gash, how did you get it?"

He did look drawn, dark circles under his eyes.

"You would not believe me if I told you. But again, maybe you will."

"Try me," I said and sat on a footstool by his armchair.

"Thanks for the offer, I'll think about it. But seriously, I think the tree by the gate attacked me. It was surreal, I was trying to park my bike by the bench up front, because the driveway to the house was flooded. I swear, it reached out and tried to grab me. I am not into random embraces, so I escaped, with a gash. A tree love bite."

"You came by a motorcycle not a limo? No wonder you were exhausted, riding in the storm," I said putting a mental note to have a good talk with Eddie. Probably the tree was jealous of Max. Eddie knew all my plans.

"Don't worry about Eddie, it was not attacking you, just being a little territorial."

"You name your trees? What are you, some sort of Earth witch?"

I smiled at his teasing, and the word 'witch'. This is what they called me in Cider Village. However, he said it with marvel, not with malice like the others.

"Eddie is my friend for life, I made it. But it's a long story."

"Tell it to me, I got time. No way am I riding back in this rain." He stood up to refill his glass.

"By the way, I am bunking here for the night again, hope you don't mind. Do you mind, kitty?" He scooped Smeela up and made himself comfortable in the wing chair again.

"How about dinner? My friend Anna said you would love food."

"Is this what I smell? I am not into food much, got more wine?"

"You have to eat, no wine until you have breakfast."

In a moment, I presented him with a bowl of stew, a plate full of muffins and a mug of coffee.

"Smells skunky," he said wrinkling his nose over the mug and reached for the wine.

While he picked at his food, I suddenly remembered Mr. Fox and our breakfast in Istanbul. His love of coffee and food. I pushed the memory back, ashamed to compare wily Jason to my beautiful Max.

I sat on the chair next to him, and told the story of Eddie Lee, my loneliness and the horror in the green tiled bathroom.

He never interrupted, just kept taking sips of wine. The bottle was long empty by the end of the story, dishes with unfinished meal piled up on the table. The candlelight had drowned in the melted wax. The only light in the room came from the glowing embers in the fireplace. He reached for my hand and we sat in the darkness watching the dying fire holding hands until Max fell asleep.

I got up and quietly kissed the top of his head. He was mine. I would never let him go. I fell asleep happy and content in a chair next to his. In my dream that night, Max placed his hands on my shoulders and looked down at me as I stood facing him. His face outlined by long black hair, smiling generous mouth. My heart did the somersaults of love, his smile was the sweetest and kindest, I have ever seen, with a touch of a charming sarcasm.

In the morning, he greeted me with his usual sardonic self, and even tried to be civil.

The fall came, my favorite time of the year. Sad and inspiring, it was a gateway for my spirit to soar before the descending darkness. The treasure beads of our first days together remained tied by the silver rain forever in my memory.

"The tale you told last night made me dream up music. Veronica, nobody knows this. I had a crisis, nothing worked for me. I was totally blocked. Now, I feel the block has lifted. You became my muse. I have to go back, and work on my new inspiration."

I felt the floor move. My entire being reeled against him leaving, I wanted to scream *No!* Instead, I gently took his hand and leaned my head against his shoulder.

"Listen to the storm, Max, it's dangerous to go. Just wait another day, go tomorrow. I will tell you another story tonight."

"Temptress," he said and jokingly pinched my nose, "Alright, I need to get my bike. Do you have any place to store it for a day? Come with me, I don't trust your Eddie tree, more so after your tale."

The rain never stopped in the first two days we spent together, just changed intensity, the fog shrouded the LaRose Gris. The driveway and the part of the garden remained flooded. Sometimes the rain drummed so loud it obscured the ever-present sound of roaring Atlantic surf beyond my garden wall.

Max spent hours in the library, leafing through books Sebastian and I collected over the years. Occasionally, he would bring the book to me and ask to read a passage aloud. Latin, Italian, Spanish rolled off my tongue with all the mastery I could invest in it. The poems and passages he selected were always about love, tragedy, and redemption, his favorite subjects.

We had the same taste in literature. Then there was music. Max was stunned when I sat at the piano and played Mozart's Lacrimosa. He came over to the instrument and begun to sing in falsetto. It was terrible, after knowing the seduction of his natural voice.

"You know, I was at that concert in Boston, the Requiem show. Sebastian got the tickets, thinking it was real opera."

"From your tone I think you hated it. My falsest falsetto, since then I opted out of opera."

"Your other eras are the ones I love. 'The Dark Kingdom', 'Sins of Lady Winter'. 'Masquerade' was my favorite. I have them all here."

"You are inspiring my next era, Veronica. The best one yet. The story you told me about the crystal bead moved me. This is a concept I covet the most. Love and hope rising out of tragedy like a Phoenix. Which story are you going to tell me tonight, my lovely young

Scheherazade?" His words inspired and fired up my imagination.

Two nights of stories became three and more. Finally, the time seized to exist for us. I heard the telephone ring from time to time, but ignored everything: the wind howling in the cold chimneys, the flailing non-pruned roses in my forlorn garden, antique magic books carelessly scattered on the floor, and the near absence of food in the kitchen.

Like two jungle cats, we circled each other, inhaling each other's scent, learning to trust, nuzzling in a playful and careful way, springing apart and coming together again to rub heads. Then when we gained the trust, we entered the jungle, running softly to be lost in its wilderness forever.

Fuelled by Absinthe LaRose, he would play wild music and sing while I sat on top of the baby grand wrapped in a sheet hungering for his embraces, glimpsing mirror reflections of my face radiant with love just as Maria's when she posed for Emmanuel.

"Tell me more, Veronica, my muse, the daughter of an elusive philosopher and magical fairy tales. Tell me a tale of falling in love with a ghost. The jealousy I feel is delicious, murderous, sweet. Like you."

I never tired to listen to his feverish songs. They elated and sometimes scared me with intensity and passion. At the same time, he surprised me by his nonchalant way of receiving my stories of magic. In all honesty, I had expected him to express some feelings of unbelief or accuse me of fantasizing, argue the facts could not happen, and nothing I said was real. He accepted everything as truth, without questioning. At last, I confronted him with my thoughts.

"But I believe you, Veronica, all your stories of magic. Since I was a little kid I knew about the existence of magic, even experienced it myself."

"This is how you became a Rock Star? All your poetry and music came from the belief in magic?"

"Don't be that idealistic, my love. In the very beginning I did it for the money."

"For the money? But I read in your biography that your mother was a rich French aristocrat married to a Cherokee Chief."

Max laughed so hard that he fell off the bed and pulled all the blankets with him. Smeela hissed and ran out of the bedroom scared by the ruckus.

"Veronica, I don't believe you fell for those tall tales, publicity stunts. What other clichés should I mention? In reality, my mother was a poor hippie, living in a commune in Northern California. I'm not sure she even knew who my father was. Ever heard of free love? And how could I have a Cherokee for a father when I am as pale as the moon?"

I looked on in disbelief clutching a pillow. He climbed back to bed, pulled me close, and threw a blanket over our shoulders. Then he told me his story.

Max Black was born as Maxim Blanc to a French Canadian mother and one of the members of the commune where they led a sheltered life. He never went outside the commune and knew only the people he grew up with. The commune had a Guru, who taught him to play the pan flute and Max would go into the hills and play it, listening to the echo of the pure sounds it made. He loved it the most.

His childhood ended when he was eleven and his mother died. She was ill for a while, but the Guru did not allow any conventional doctors to take care of her. Authorities raided the commune when another woman also died. In the end, the commune disbanded. Max and the other children went to the foster care families around the country. Max ended up with a family on a horse farm in Tennessee.

The reality of his situation hit Max hard when the kids at his new school made fun of his clothing and his name. He grew up to be an angry teenager and hated everything, including his name, his new home, himself.

At fourteen, Max liked to venture out to the hills to be alone, play the pan flute and to daydream. One day he climbed all the way to the top of the green mountain and saw the beautiful valley of pastures and farms below. He also saw a cloud of mist, just a few feet away forming on the mountainside.

The fog twirled and Max decided to investigate. He imagined, sitting in the cloud would it feel like being in heaven.

Once in the cloud, the sounds of the mountainside muted. Gone were the whistling of the wind, the cries of the distant starlings, the dry whispering of the grass, growing waist high.

The cloud enveloped the boy with wispy fog fingers. The center of the fog cloud became denser, and to Max, it seemed very large because he walked for a while until realizing he was lost. The fog wisps began to crawl up his sleeves and down his collar, he felt them prickle him and it hurt.

He started to run and cry for help, the fog tied up his legs and he fell. Something cold and evil kept pushing him down and Max felt the cold prickly fingers touch his eyes and enter his ears. When he was about to lose consciousness from struggle and fear he heard loud breathing above, and something grabbed him and shook the cold fingers away.

His rescuer stood enveloped in the same fog, the terrified boy could only see the outline of a giant figure, and feet that looked like hooves. Then the creature grabbed the boy by the hand and made him run. The hand holding the boy was so warm Max felt its heat spreading through his own body, giving him strength. At last, he saw the sun ahead of him piercing the strange fog.

Once they reached the sunny spot, he could see his rescuer, a tall being with long golden hair, magnificent manly physique, and legs like a stallion down to the golden hooves. Max thought it was a dream. That he fell asleep on the mountainside, drunk of whiskey, he brought with him in a flask stolen from his foster dad. The tall creature smiled at young Max showing large perfect teeth and pointed in the direction of the sun. Then he embraced him for a moment.

The other memory Max retained of his rescuer was a scent of chocolate. The cloud disappeared. Max sat in the grass and composed his first song, the song which made him popular at school and a local star. This incident he always called his magical moment which turned him into a musical enigma, known to the world as Maximus Black."

"I believe in magic, the spirits and the creatures exist, but we can't see them. The incident made a mark on my life, a starting point just like your crystal bead. The terror I experienced, the equally scary creature that saved me, the unknown that became the bottomless well for my creativity. Now you see, my magical Veronica, we are kindred spirits, the soul mates, and the children of magic."

I cried. Those were not the tears of joy and wonder, as Max had thought. It was my Moishele Max described. This is how I imagined my baby faun all grown up. For a long time I tried to block the yearning to hold him in my arms again, to kiss his golden curls and tickle his chubby tummy, to hear the tinkling laugh. I told Max many stories, but about Moishele, the old girls, my small New York family, I had not. One day I would, meeting the golden fauns at different stages of our lives was not a simple coincidence.

Veronica LaRose

23. GUILT AND PLEASURE

For weeks, we never left the LaRose Gris, even after the rain stopped. We roamed the garden and the beach scarcely dressed and deliriously happy on the golden Indian summer afternoons. I did not care about my tangled hair, or the only item clothing I wore was a thin nightgown. His love made me feel wild and beautiful like I never felt before.

"Forget about the past Veronica, look ahead. We will do wonders together. You inspired me to write the greatest music ever, everything I wrote before is nothing in comparison. The universe will belong to us."

These words were his oath. He kept repeating them to me. I believed him with all my being. Nevertheless, something cold started to creep up my heart, just like the fog fingers from Max's childhood story. At first, I tried to ignore it. Self-analysis was not for me anymore. Not so, one early morning at four o'clock, I realized what it was gnawing at me. It was guilt. No amount of love and fevered abandon would make me forget Sebastian. I possessed the tools and knowledge that would help me find him. They were waiting for me, and I kept putting them aside for Max.

I looked at his sleeping form beside me on the huge LaRose bed. The paleness of his skin blended with the white sheets in the grey light of the autumn morning. Only the tattoos on his arms stood out, and the wild hair spread on the pillow. I traced on the outlines of the serpents encircling his arms and entwining on his chest like codicil, their tattooed eyes watching, questioning me. He pulled me in his arms and made me forget again.

I woke up late, stretched like a lioness, and reached for Max. My hand touched the cold sheets instead. I thought he must have gone downstairs, and rose to find him. He was not there. I called out his name, only Smeela answered with an inquisitive meow.

"Where is Max, Smeela? Take me to him," I said hoping she would comply.

She jumped off the table and I followed her. Perhaps he was in the garden by the stream, where Sebastian used to meditate, or on the beach. We did not find him, and his motorcycle was gone. I did not find a note anywhere. He left without saying a word.

At first, I cried, full of self-pity and worry, but not for long. My mushiness turned to anger. Anger turned to resolve, the old Veronica was back. So he left me, there must be a reason, which I would find out soon enough. Life taught me not to jump to conclusions, and he would show up eventually. Everything happens for a reason. I wiped tears off my face, dressed warmly for the first time in days and began to take stock of my neglected surroundings.

The mansion appeared like a victim of an indoor tornado. Paper and composition notes littered every surface, books strewn haphazardly over the floor, dust and coagulated candle wax splattered on the piano, chairs, and floor. Eclectic array of discarded clothing, and dozens upon dozens of empty wine bottles scattered all over the area. *We sure had some party*, I thought, trying to come up with a plan on how to clean up this mess.

In the kitchen, I found piles of dirty dishes, bags of garbage left there for later, and no food. Then I remembered that we have not eaten much for days, we lived on wine and love.

I felt sudden hunger, for anything. The cupboards were empty, save for the sugar cubes and tea bags. Well, tea it was.

Out came the large bags, a broom, and scouring powder. I began to gather the results of our wild love and stepped on something soft and squishy. A dozen dead mice piled into a neat little hill lay on the floor by the fireplace. Smeela brushed against my leg. She appeared happy to share. The guilt descended on me again. I neglected not only Sebastian's life, but Smeela's welfare as well. Ashamed, I reached for the phone and called Anna, first time in weeks.

After some long minutes of ringing, Gaspar Dix mumbled into the receiver, "It's the middle of the night, and it better be good."

"Gaspar, it's Veronica. And, it's a late afternoon even in New Orleans. What's happening?"

"Veronica! It's a girl and I have not slept in days."

"Gaspar, I don't understand. Speak up please, where is Anna, what girl?"

"It's a girl, we had a girl, and we live by her schedule. Did I say we had a girl?"

I felt a cascade of icy guilt ripple down my back, then a cascade of searing heat of excitement. Anna had a baby girl, someone called, and I did not pick up in my delirious state of a jungle love.

"I love you guys, go back to sleep, Gaspar. I will call you later." I hung up weak with relief and wonder. Anna had a daughter. I wondered what they named her.

Nothing is as therapeutic as cleaning. My grandmother was right about disorderly house causing bad thoughts. As the mansion became its previous pristine self through my labors, a plan formed in my mind yet again.

I have not heard anything from Max, and tried not to dwell on it. I was scared of falling into a chasm of depression, which would take me back to Erasmus and his book of magic spells. First time in my life, I did not think magic would help. Maria certainly did not help. She just glared at me from her perch over the mantel. *How could you be so self-centered?*

At last, after days of trying to reach her, I spoke to Anna. Her voice hoarser than usual and tired, high notes of happiness infused her usual exuberance.

"You should see the little critter, she is dainty. As big as Gaspar's paw, and a redhead, imagine that, I just adore the little parasite, she needs to grow up fast so we could talk about her past life, how do we preserve that memory, anything in those magic books of yours, I am so exhausted, want to come and babysit," Anna's excited tirade never stopped.

I tried to intervene with questions about her health and sanity, she just went on and on about the baby. Unnamed still, and referred to as a 'critter' or 'beautiful parasite'. I sighed with resignation, Anna was just being herself, and I loved them.

I decided to send a present and thought that the gift of health would be best. I gathered a parcel with my herbal tinctures and teas to help with sleeping, moodiness and general well being, an ivory antique quilt from my grandmother's collection, a bottle of Absinthe LaRose for Gaspar and drove to the post office.

With surprise, I noticed cars by our rental cottages on the way to the Cider Village, and gave myself a mental note to thank Boruch Shachmundes, my lawyer and friend from New York.

Indeed, the Cider Village became quite a tourist hub. I guess the quaint place and a collection of seafood restaurants attracted the city crowd. A familiar face flashed briefly as I passed Tilde's old cottage. I shook my head. No way would Jason Fox even be there. I pinched myself to snap out of delusional paranoia.

The crowds of tourists diluted the vile locals, and I found it refreshing. The relative anonymity allowed me to post the parcel and get a few supplies without much hassle.

Oh my, what we have here, I thought upon seeing the dusty bike of my errant beloved carelessly left in the courtyard. I wanted to pinch myself again, but it was real enough.

"Here you are, my darling," said Max as I appeared in the door, my hands laden with groceries. I was livid at his nonchalant manner, as he just came from a stroll on the beach. I pulled out a baguette, threw it at his head, and did not miss.

"Veronica, you have all the right to be mad, I can explain. Come sit, have some wine."

"No need to explain anything, Max. But, a note would be nice, or a phone call. And no wine, thank you. It leads to disordered house, and bad thoughts."

"What bad thoughts? Oh, never mind. I had to get away, had to share the music we made together. I know you don't like my crowd."

"I thought I was your crowd, Max. What now? Are you going to take off every time you need to 'share'?"

I hauled the rest of the packages to the kitchen, living him alone with his wine in the drawing room. In a few moments, he appeared in the kitchen, undisturbed by my icy response.

"You are my muse. I need you, and don't want to share you with anyone."

"Max, I love you, but I cannot sit here alone and wait for you until you need another fix of inspiration. What about my life, the people I love. What about Sebastian?"

His looked stricken with his arms hopelessly by his sides. He was regretting it, for sure. I assumed a gentler manner.

"Alright. We are at the dead end. Let's sleep on it and make decisions in the morning. I missed you so much," I said and succumbed to his embrace, drowning with pleasure in his scent of tobacco and leather.

The sound of a doorbell pulled us apart. Unsure of whom it was I went to open it, and came face to face with a set of charming dimples and sky blue eyes of none other than wily Jason Fox. It was not a hallucination in the Cider Village after all.

"You! How did you...Get out!" I swung the door shut in his face.

He stuck his foot forward to stop it, and howled from pain when a heavy oak hit it with a loud thud. Max appeared and scowled at Jason writhing on the floor.

"Oh, I know this guy. Hey Rob, what's up. I see you met my girl."

"You know each other? Why are you calling him Rob? Call the police. This is Jason Fox who tried to kill me in Istanbul."

Jason sat up, rubbing his injured foot. I took a closer look at him. He appeared as boyish and handsome as before, but his tan was gone, he had long hair now, and he was thinner.

"Leave at once," I repeated and pointed to the driveway.

Max hauled him to his feet and placed a friendly hand on his shoulder.

"Come on Veronica, this is the guy who supplies me with antique instruments, you know I have a collection. Rob or Jason, I don't care. He never cheated me."

"You mean he is here for you, not me?"

Jason finally spoke up. He found a seat on a lower step with his back to the wall.

"Veronica, you are an icing on the cake. I never expected to find you here, honestly. Nice place, impressive, you never said you had a castle. I did not want to kill you, or anyone else. The old gun went off accidentally. What do expect from a hundred-year-old piece of junk? I really wanted to save those jewels from the grinder at the hands of our mad Professor. And who was that crazy woman who hit me from behind?"

Although he appeared sincere, I still saw him for the sly thief he really was. I asked Max to take him away. As it turned out, he actually rented Tilde's old cottage.

"Okay, I'll leave. You got to remember what fun we had in Istanbul. I'll be back when you calm down a bit, and see the benefit of this situation. Come on Max, help me up."

"Yes Max, please help him out, and take him to meet our lovely friend Eddie."

I plumped on the stair Jason just vacated and listened to the fading motorcycle roar. Jason Fox did not do anything for nothing, and there is no such thing as a coincidence.

I was quite overwhelmed with the morning events. Best remedy was work. I grabbed a rake and went to work making piles of leaves. They rustled like my grandmother's voice, and the wind chased them in the tangy air of the sea and autumn. Smeela sat nearby like a beautiful sphinx. I worked and kept thinking, making plans, searching for answers.

The sound of the returning bike snapped me out of

contemplation. Max came over, took me in his arms, and kissed me. I felt the delicious pleasure spread through my body and succumbed to his embraces. One fiery moment, and I forgot about Jason and our conflict.

Later, in the darkness of night a solution came to me at last. I had a job to do.

Quickly, before I crumbled and changed my mind, I packed my backpack with the usual travelling gear, magical flute, golden harp and the keys from the Prospect Park townhouse. Maria watched me with encouragement. *You are doing the right thing, Veronica.* Smeela followed my every move with a quiet excitement.

Dressed in jeans, long coat, and Doc Martens I stood over the bed and watched Max sleep. I did not feel saddened about leaving him. It was my turn now. Things change. Change is the only constant in life. I slipped a parting note on the pillow beside him and left the mansion. He was welcome to stay as long as he liked and enjoy the solitude of my gothic garden.

Smeela's bright green eyes questioned me.

"Come on Smeela, hop in the car. We are going on a quest. It's time to find Sebastian."

Veronica LaRose

The Quest Beyond

Valerie Rachel Martin

Veronica's adventures continue in the second book.
Enjoy the beginning of the first chapter.
Remember, the magic is in the reading.

Veronica LaRose

1. ONE DOOR CLOSES

I ran out of options, giving up was not one of them. Soaked to the bone, angry and stubborn, I sat in front of that damn mirror for days trying to open the portal into Moishele's world.

I had no other choice. Reading Winai's letter about Sebastian disappearance from the mediation cave, and a suggestion, that he ended up in some other facet of the universe spurred me in one direction. I knew about another world, hiding behind the grey reflection of the mirror on the rooftop of the Bronstein sister's townhouse in Brooklyn. They gave the townhouse to me, and left with Moishele through the mirror portal.

This is where I spent the last week after leaving LaRose Gris, my home on the seashore of the grey Atlantic, and my beloved rock star Max Black.

In my previous adventure to find magic around the world, I came upon a rainmaking flute. I used it to summon the thunderstorm which opened the mirror portal almost two years ago.

There I was, trying to open it again. My plan was to cross the threshold, locate Moishele, Faige, and Kitty and enlist their help in finding Sebastian, either in ours or Moishele's world. I reasoned if there was one parallel world, there must be another with Sebastian in it.

The flute worked, the thunder boomed, the rain soaked me a dozen times at least. New Yorkers were cursing the unusual winter thunderstorms of '89. The portal did not open. And to my distress, Moishele's golden harp, the one that he gave to me as a parting gift, began to produce a melody. This did not happen before, because whenever I touched the strings the melody sounded in the world behind the mirror. Now, I heard the dulcimer tones of the harp and it meant the connection had vanished.

Only faithful Smeela, my cat and familiar, understood my frustration. She never left my side. I had a good mind to call a bakery that used to deliver our delicacies when my little family was still here. Smeela and I did not go hungry. On the contrary, they delivered too much.

I made a few painful calls to Max, who remained at LaRose Gris, immersed in his new music. He spoke to me, woolgathering between the replies. I understood he was in the thralls of creation.

There must be another way. It did not take me long to come up with a new idea. Only the item I needed to succeed was still at home. This was a perfect opportunity to lure Max to New York and convince him to join me on my quest.

The magic was in the reading. Professor Silverman gave me this clue. In a while, I understood what he meant when a vial, filled with blue shimmering powder, fell from binding of the ancient tome written by Erasmus, a magician from 11th century. According to Professor, this substance was powerful enough to open a portal to another dimension. I wanted to experiment with it, and to use it on the mirror.

Although it was a middle of the night, I did not hesitate and dialed a number at home. It kept ringing forever. He must have passed out again from too much wine. At last, I heard his voice, faraway and muffled with sleep.

"Veronica, I missed you. Are you finally coming back?"

"Max, I need you to help me, please. Now. No questions. You know the big magic book, The Erasmus. I need you to bring it to me in New York."

"Okay, fine, the book sounds really important now," he could not hide the sarcasm.

"I will explain everything, just come."

"Yes, love, I will drop everything, the music, the tour planning, and leave at once," said Max and hang up.

I sat there listening to the dial tone and wondered if he meant to help me, or was I on my own again to roam the world.

Had I only known about the morning surprise.

ABOUT THE AUTHOR

VR Martin is an author and artist from Niagara Region in Ontario, Canada. Just like the novel's protagonists, this author revels in beauty of nature and miracle of imagination. '*There is plenty of magic still left in the corners of our round world*' echoes throughout her universe. Readers and art students follow her on this fascinating quest.

Today, dear magic seeker, you are welcome to join as well.